AN UNINTENDED VOYAGE

THE DISPLACED DAUGHTERS

BOOK ONE

MARSHALL RYAN MARESCA

ARTEMISIA

"It's a story about morality, about sacrifice, about what people want from life. It's a fun story–there's quips, swordfights, chases through the streets. It's a compelling, convincing work of fantasy, and a worthy addition to the rich tapestry that is the works of Maradaine."

— SCI-FI AND FANTASY REVIEWS

"Highly recommend this series to anyone who loves high fantasy, political intrigue, magic, fantastic world building, and characters who you can root for."

— GIZMO'S REVIEWS

"Veranix is Batman, if Batman were a teenager and magically talented.... Action, adventure, and magic in a school setting will appeal to those who love *Harry Potter* and Patrick Rothfuss' *The Name of the Wind*."

— *LIBRARY JOURNAL* (STARRED)

"*The Thorn of Dentonhill* was a fast-paced read with action from start to finish. I loved every minute of it."

— SHORT AND SWEET REVIEWS

"Maresca brings the whole package, complete and well-constructed. If you're looking for something fun and adventurous for your next fantasy read, look no further than *The Thorn of Dentonhill*, an incredible start to a new series, from an author who is clearly on his way to great things."

— BIBLIOSANCTUM

ALSO BY
MARSHALL RYAN MARESCA

MARADAINE SAGA PHASE ONE

The Thorn of Dentonhill   A Murder of Mages
The Alchemy of Chaos   An Import of Intrigue
The Imposters of Aventil   A Parliament of Bodies

The Holver Alley Crew   Way of the Shield
Lady Henterman's Wardrobe   Shield of the People
The Fenmere Job   People of the City

THE DISPLACED DAUGHTERS
An Unintended Voyage

MARADAINE SAGA PHASE TWO

The Assassins of Consequence   An Unkindness of Uncircled Mages*
The New King of Rose Street*   A Pride of Partners*

The Quarrygate Gambit   City of the Truth*
The Andrendon Plan*   Truth of the Crown*

MARADAINE SAGA SHORTS
The Mystical Murders of Yin Mara
Hultichia
The Withered Boy
The Royal First Irregulars*
A Proper Lady of Society*

THE ZIAPARR CYCLE
The Velocity of Revolution

*- Forthcoming

Second Edition, February 2024

1 2 3 4 5 6 7 8 9

THE MARADAINE SAGA

AN UNINTENDED VOYAGE

BOOK ONE OF
THE DISPLACED DAUGHTERS

MARSHALL RYAN MARESCA

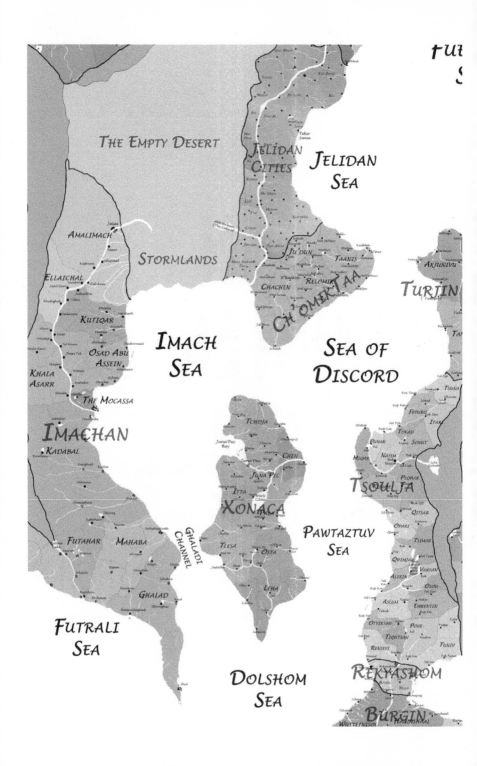

THE SEVEN BOROUGHS OF THE MOCASSA

ALEANDIAL

OREIFFAL

TEAMACCEA

JACHAILLASA

RASENDI

MAHACOSSA

HUSSUA

PRELUDE

THE CAPTIVE SHIP

CHAPTER ONE

GARTEN HAD DIED IN THE night, the ninth so far. Corrie Welling had kept count, added every death to the tally of sins that she would visit upon these bastards.

And those sins were plentiful.

She had been in the fetid, rotting hold of this ship for twenty-seven days, shackled to the wall with just enough freedom of movement to get her hands to her mouth when her captors gave her a cup of water or a bite of moldy biscuit. Water and food was twice a day, and even in this darkened hold, she could tell when the sun was out, filtering through the seams of the hatch above them.

Plus the heat of the daytime had turned ungodly.

The heat, the stench of them all sitting in their own filth, the creep of salty bilge water that was sometimes several inches deep—all of it was too damn much to bear.

The animals who had done this to her and the kids locked in the hold with her, they would pay dearly. Corrie would make sure.

The rest were all kids, and they all had been looking to her. Most of them were around eleven or twelve, some as old as fifteen. Corrie was by far the oldest. By her reckoning, her twentieth birthday passed the same day the ship had made an abrupt swing in direction.

"Southeast to northeast," Garten had said that day. "We went around the Ihali Cape."

Garten had been a good kid. Twelve years old, went to the public prepatory in Dentonhill. He had clearly been a good student, since he knew geography and had a good sense of direction this whole time they'd been in the hold.

He had known when the ship made anchorage in Yoleanne, taken on water and supplies, and then presumed they had kept going south along the Acserian coast, naming cities they might have reached the next time supplies were brought on. Agenza, Corren, Torphia, Hamandaghad.

That one he had been certain about, especially when Corrie had told the rest what she could hear when supplies were loaded. Their captors had shouted out to the supply boats in something other than Trade. They were now off the coast of Imachan.

"Imachan is actually a bunch of countries," Garten had said weakly.

He had gotten sick the day before, unable to keep even water down. Corrie couldn't get close to him, but Eana, shackled next to him, said he was hot with fever. Fever and vomiting had been how it had started for Relia. And Washle. And Nicelle, Samon, and Tirl. For each of them, once it started, death came fast and hard and cruel. Garten had been no different. Corrie had tried to keep him talking, asked him to tell her more about Imachan, tell her more about the stories he read in school, tell them all about his home and his mother and his family, anything.

But he had died in the night.

One more crime, one more sin, that she would hold these rutting bastards to account for.

"He was your fault, stick," Penler said. Penler was one of the older ones, a real rutting pisser with too damn smart of a mouth for his own good. "He hadn't been right since Morger knocked him to punish you."

"That wasn't her fault!" Eana said. "None of that is her fault."

"None of what these bastards do to us is my fault," Corrie said. "But I am sorry they hurt you to punish me. It's because they know I can take it if they knock me."

"So stop pushing them, stick!" Penler said.

"Stop yelling at her," Eana said. "That'll make them come again, and they'll blame her, and they'll hit one of us."

"How do we know she's not in it with them?" Penler said. "It was sticks who grabbed me in the first place. Same for Washle."

"Same for me," Corrie said. Of all the parts that hurt the most of this rutting sewage was the fact that she had been betrayed by fellow officers.

She was a sergeant in the Maradaine Constabulary. The Wellings had served for eight generations. Her many-times-great grandfather had helped found the Constabulary and the City Loyalty. Her father had died with his red and green on.

She was still wearing hers. Maybe the bastards who took her wanted to taunt her that much, put her in this hold with her uniform on, so these kids would know she was an officer in the Constabulary. Crush any sense of hope they might have. Show them that no one could save them.

"Listen," she said quietly. "In a few minutes, Morger will be down here with our rations. None of us are going to give him any blasted trouble this time, give him any reason to stay down here more than he needs to. Not right now."

"What about Garten?" Treskie asked. He was on Garten's other side.

"Don't draw attention to him," Corrie said. The others all groaned and whined. "Listen to me. Listen!" She knew they didn't want to hear this. They were as scared as anything, and she couldn't rutting blame them. They were exhausted, they were sick, they knew they were being shipped to some horrific fate in some place only the saints and sinners knew. The next port might be where they were unloaded, and from there, who even knew what damned atrocity awaited them.

She was a damned officer in the Constabulary, and like her father, like her grandparents, like all three of her brothers and half her cousins, she had taken a damned oath to serve, to stand for the safety and protection of the citizens of Maradaine. The kids in this hold with her, no matter where they were in the world, were still citizens of Maradaine, and she still had her red and green on.

She would fulfill that oath or die trying.

"Listen," she said calmly. "I know it's horrible to be there next to him, to have to smell his rotting corpse—"

"No worse than any other smell down here," Iastanne said.

"But we don't want it to be Morger taking him out. It's got to be Hockly, tonight. So hold on."

She didn't have the sharp mind of her brother Minox—or his magic, that would rutting come in handy—but she had paid attention, noting everything about the hold they were in. She had figured out everything that could be used as a weapon, memorized where it was. She could find it all in the dark if she had to. She learned the patterns of the ship's crew. Morger brought them water and food in the mornings, Hockly in the evenings. Hockly, with bad knee and weak shoulder.

"Tonight?" Eana asked. Her raised eyebrow showed she understood what Corrie was driving at. She, more than any of the other kids, had been sharp and clever enough to see what Corrie had been doing all this time, and kept her mouth shut about it. Eana had a whip of a mind, Corrie saw that. Eana knew what the score was, and she clearly trusted Corrie to get it done.

It had taken twenty-seven days, slow and patient work, but Corrie had cracked the wood holding her manacles to the wall. She knew one good yank was all it would take to be free.

But she had to do that at the precise, ripe moment. She had to be ready to take the ship, free these kids, and make all the bastards on the ship pay for their crimes.

That moment was going to be tonight.

Corrie was a damned constable, even here and now, and she was ready to get to work.

CHAPTER TWO

MORGER HAD COME AND GONE with the morning rations, not even noticing that Garten was dead. That was what Corrie had suspected. The man was fundamentally cruel, but lazy. Like most of the rotten crew on this evil ship, he had little interest in dealing with the prisoners in the hold any longer than he had to. Corrie didn't know exactly what each of the crew did with their day, but she knew Morger wanted to get his work done quick and get back to it.

Rutting pig, he was.

The ship was full of them.

Corrie had used her ears for the past twenty-seven days, listening to the chatter of the crew as they wandered about on the deck above them. She kept track of voices, of names. She made sure she had them all.

There were twelve of them on the crew, all of them men. She was actually honestly shocked none of them had tried to roll her, or one of the other girls. Not that she was remotely interested in that, and if one of them tried she'd have bit their pisswhistle off. But it hadn't come to that. Of those twelve, Morger and Hockly were the main ones to come down and deal with the prisoners. On rare occasions, there were the ones she called Knocknose and Badeye. She didn't get their real names. Up on top, there was the Captain and the Chief, and then six more men she just called One, Two, Three, Four, Five, and Six. No need for more than that.

Focus your mental energies on the important details. That's what Minox would tell her. Coming up with names for the other ones, faceless voices, was a waste of time and thought. No need to do that.

She knew she had little to go on about the eight she had never seen. The Captain was old, moved slow. The Chief had an accent, one she couldn't place at all. He had a deep voice, that made her think he was tall and beefy.

Didn't matter. Once she was free, had something in her hand she could fight with, she could whip any one of them. She was certain of that.

As long as she didn't have to take them all at once.

The hold didn't have the baking heat it usually had today. She wasn't sure why, until she heard them talking up above her. Two and Six.

"Storm is coming fast."

"We can get ahead of it."

"Don't think so."

Storm.

Blazes, yes. That was rutting perfect.

Within an hour—still before the evening rations—the ship was pitching hard, and thunder rolled in the distance. One wave hit the ship, sending everyone in the hold careening toward the bulkhead, filthy bodies crashing on top of each other. Corrie's stomach would have rebelled at that, had there been much of anything in there.

"Corrie!" Eana shouted. Because Corrie was lying in her lap. That knock had sent them flying, including tearing her manacles from the housing on the wall.

"Blazes," Corrie muttered. She had wanted to come free when Hockly was down here, take him by surprise when he was dealing with Garner's body. Now she was off the wall, and they'd see that as soon as they started down the hatch.

"Get 'em provisioned and batten that down!" the Chief shouted.

The hatch. Hockly was about to come down, and if she was spotted off the wall, he'd surely call for everyone to come down, beat her senseless again. Like when those two rutting traitors took her by surprise on the northside docks.

She still wondered what else happened that night. After they took her, shoved her on the ship, did they get Tricky? Was she dead? Somewhere else on this ship? Something worse?

Minox would be shattered. So would Mama. The whole family. They knew—they all knew—any ride out could be the last one, but it was one thing to know that as an idea, and another to face it.

Saints and sinners, they would surely blame Tricky. The lady didn't deserve the hate the family would give her for that. And they would, saints knew. Not Minox, of course. But most of them already hated Tricky, even if she had saved Nyla, and this would lock that down.

Provided Tricky was still alive.

But if she was, all the more reason to fight her rutting way out of here and get back home.

She hadn't ridden her last ride, and, by every saint, she wasn't about to yet.

The hatch was opening.

Despite the rocking of the hold—the ship was really getting battered by storm and wind—she scrambled to her place on the wall, got her arms up. Hopefully Hockly—that sweaty dog—wouldn't notice before it was too late.

"Chows up, cats!" he shouted as he came down the ladder.

"Don't you—" Penler muttered.

"Hush your face," Corrie hissed back.

"What's the whisper here?" Hockly asked as he reached the ground.

Before anyone else could speak, Corrie said, "Garten died, that's what."

"Who's Garten?" Hockly asked. "Blazes, I only remember your name, stick, since you keep it on your chest. Ha!" Not that Corrie had a choice about that—she couldn't reach her brass name badge to get it off. She was pretty sure they only left it on her uniform coat—left her the entire uniform, for that matter—as a taunt. Such a funny jape they had a stick sergeant locked up down here with these kids.

"Him," Eana said, knocking Garten's dead form with her knee.

"Ugh, he's looking ripe as a rutter," Hockly said. "What got him?"

"The same fever that's been running through all of us, idiot," Corrie said.

"Hey, girl!" he snapped, "You give more of that mouth, I'll crack someone's jaw open."

Corrie glowered. Let him think he had tamed her.

He turned to Garten's body, taking the keys off his belt.

"Hurry it up, Hockly!" Four shouted from up top, his words punctuated with a crack of thunder.

"I gotta get this dead one out!"

"Rutting leave it!"

Corrie froze for a moment. She couldn't see Four, couldn't tell what he was seeing from up there, how close he was looking.

This might be the only moment she'd have, and if Four raised an alarm before she was ready, it'd all go to sewage.

But this was the moment. Hockly was bent over, back to her, hands occupied.

Saints watch over me, she whispered to herself. *You too, Pop.*

She darted from the wall, in one fell motion, leapt up and planted her boot hard on Hockly's bad knee.

He would have cried out, but Eana—bless the wits on that girl—grabbed Garten's arm and shoved it into his mouth, muzzling him. Corrie walloped him over the head with the chain of her manacles, and then again. He had a handstick and his belt that he tried to go for, but Corrie snapped at it, drawing it out and pulling it up under his weak shoulder. She slammed her foot onto that knee again while she drove him down, pushing his face into Garten's body.

"You consider yourself bound, pissrutter," she hissed in his ear. "Your charges will be named, including abduction and assault of children." She pulled up the handstick and cracked it against his pig skull.

He collapsed, and as quick as anything, she grabbed his wrists and shackled him in place where Garten had been. She took his keys and unlocked Eana's manacles. Giving the girl the keys, she whispered. "Free the others."

"Come on!" Four shouted from up top.

Treskie called out, doing Hockly's piggy voice. "Give me a hand, man, kid's heavy."

"Saints above, Hock, you can't manage to do—" Four started as he came down. Older fellow, gray hair. Whatever complaint he was going to make about Hockly, he didn't finish, as Corrie landed a blow in the small of his back, and then pulled him to the floor of the hold. One knee on his chest, the other on his neck, Corrie pressed the butt of the hand-stick against his nose.

"Call out and you'll have no teeth before anyone comes."

"You're mad, you'll—"

She pressed harder. "Where are we?"

"About a day off from Mahabassiana."

"Is that where you were taking us?"

"Yeah."

"Why?"

"Best slave market on the eastern coast."

Rutting bastard.

"Why is this hatch open?" someone shouted from the top deck as lightning flashed through the hatch. "We got to—"

"The stick is free!" Four shouted. At the same moment, a crash of thunder rolled across the ship.

Corrie kept her promise about his teeth.

Eana was off the wall, and came to Corrie with the key. Four was in a daze, and Eana got one of the dangling shackles off Corrie's wrist.

"The blazes is the matter with the two of you?" the same voice— Two? Hard to tell—called down. Corrie and Eana dragged Four to the wall and shackled him in Eana's place as the crewman from up top stuck his head in the hold.

"Hey, sheeprutter!" Iastanne shouted. "You run out of sheep to roll?"

He looked to Iastanne, who was on the other side of the hold from Corrie.

"You're gonna get it, slan. You'll see what rolling I can do." He dropped into the hold just as a wash of hard rain crashed through.

Corrie jumped on his back and locked the handstick around his neck. This bastard was almost ready for her, and strong as a rutting ox. If she were in her prime, she'd have a time, but she was hardly in her best fighting shape right now. He threw back elbows, knocking her in the sides. Blazes, that rutting hurt.

She couldn't risk letting go. Push through the pain. This was the only chance. Use the storm. Use the anger. Keep fighting even as his clawing hand came up and grabbed her head.

Thank the saints that machie slan had chopped her hair off in that riot a few months back. Otherwise he'd have been able to grab a real long handful of her hair and yank her off. As it was, he tried to pull her head, but couldn't get a solid grip on her, while she locked her legs around his waist. He knocked her head with a meaty fist, almost dazing her, almost forcing her to lose her grip on him.

She pulled tighter on the stick, and slipped her head to the side of his, clamping her teeth on his ear.

He didn't deserve anything less than full savagery.

He screamed out, and as he did, more hands grabbed hold of him. Eana, Treskie, whoever else, they all came at him, dragging him to the floor. One of them shoved a soiled set of skivs into his mouth. He made some muffled cry of anger and horror, but that was all he could do as they hauled him over to the wall and latched him into another set of manacles.

Corrie had barely noticed that it was coming down in torrents now. The disgusting floor of the hold—already a festering layer of their filth and sewage—now had at least an inch of water, and the ship was being tossed back and forth. She could barely keep her feet, and most of these kids were failing to.

"That's three of them," she said, though she could barely hear herself over the rain and the scream of the wind overhead.

"And then what?" Penler asked, nearly screaming to be heard. "Even you get them all, can you sail?"

"I'll figure it out!" Corrie said. Though she honestly had no rutting idea. First step was just get free, take these bastards down. Once they had the ship, they'd worry about it.

Lightning cracked overhead, lighting up the hold as bright as day, with a crash of thunder that almost knocked her off her feet.

"We're gonna drown in here if you don't close that hatch!" Four shouted. "Hey! Hey!"

There was too much wind and storm for him to be heard up top, if anyone was even nearby it.

"Let them drown," Corrie said. As near as she could see, all the kids were unchained, and she was as armed as she could be, though she wondered if her crossbow was on the ship somewhere. She'd love to have that right now. They had taken her weapons, but left her in her uniform, even if it was a filthshow right now. She still even had her whistle in her pocket, for all the good that would do.

She tossed a handstick to Treskie. "Grab what you can, let's get up top. You see one of those bastards, you just rutting swarm them."

"But what—" Penler started.

"We take the ship!" she shouted. The storm was roaring, like nothing she had ever heard. The water in the hold was up to her ankles. "Then we figure it out."

She climbed up out of the hold, the wind and rain pummeling her body. She couldn't see more than a few feet, no sense of who or what might be up here.

"This is crazy!" Treskie said, right next to her. "We need—"

"Hold on to me!" she said. "Tell everyone, we move together!"

"But—"

She had to push on. The only choice now.

Waves crashed over the deck, and the ship rocked so hard Corrie fell over and slid to the railing. Her body collided into something else before she reached it—someone else—but she couldn't see who or what in the mess of the storm. It was one of the rutting bastard crew, though, so she kicked at him as the careened into the rail. Before either could react, the ship pitched hard the other way, and they both went rolling across the deck together. Even through the rain and wind and wet, she could hear the bastard muttering something of disbelief. They crashed into the far rail together, cracking through it. He tumbled off the side of the ship, and she almost went with him. She had to drop the handstick and grab hold of one pin of the railing.

She had faced drunken brawlers, arrows flying at her, and that machie lady who had messed up her eye, but never before had she been so convinced she was looking down at the gaping maw of death, as she did dangling off the edge of the ship.

"Dear Saint Veran," she whispered as she scrambled to pull herself back up on the deck. "Please help me here. I'll pay whatever cost, just let me rutting prevail."

She got one leg back up on the deck, and with what strength she had left, got the rest of her body on there. The ship was wildly lurching in the wind and storm, and in the next flash of lightning she saw the sail whipping about madly. Then another flash of lightning, and Morger was on her.

"The blazes are you—" he said, lifting her up off her feet by the front of her coat. She punched his chin as hard as she could, but she had nothing left in her arm. He didn't even budge. "You'll pay for that."

She spat in his face, which was pointless beyond the gesture in the whipping rain . "I'll make sure the sinners all come for you."

"Just you—"

Before he finished that thought, lightning crashed again, striking the ship in the main mast. The rack of thunder, so loud it blew out Corrie's ears, knocked them both down.

Then the mast groaned and creaked and cracked. Another wave of salt water slammed across the deck, and as it did, the mast broke free and crashed through the deck.

In a tumble, Corrie was in the salt and wet and dark. She couldn't see or hear or breathe, no sense of which way was what. She was sure to drown, she had never swum before. No way she could rutting survive.

She refused to accept that. As long as her heart pounded in her chest, she was going to fight.

In a final attempt to win, to survive, for anything, she lashed out and tried to grab hold of whatever she could find.

She grabbed someone's hand.

She came up, out into the air—whipping storm and wind and rain but *air to breathe.* Corrie desperately, hungrily, gasped as someone pulled her up onto the wood. Still half in the water, but breathing. Alive.

A rope was being wound around her arm and body. Were they tying her up? Did those bastards get her? She could barely even open her eyes, but she reached out to push them away.

"Hey, hey, stop." Soft voice in her ear. Not one of the bastards. "It's Eana."

"What . . ." was all Corrie could say. She had nothing left.

"I got you," Eana said. "I got you."

If Eana said anything else, Corrie didn't hear it, as she slipped off into the dark.

CHAPTER THREE

CORRIE WOKE TO BRIGHT BLUE skies, blinding sunlight, and open water to the horizon.

She was floating in the ocean, lashed to the broken mast.

Memories of the night, the storm, came flooding back. "Eana!"

"I'm here," the young girl said, her voice hoarse and weak. "You all right?" She was in a shoreboat, tied to the floating mast, with the remnants of the sail rigged up into a rough tent.

"What happened?"

"I think the storm tore the ship apart," Eana said. "I went over when the mast came down, and managed to grab one of the ropes and pull myself up. And . . . by some miracle, grabbed your hand in the ocean when you went in."

Corrie glanced about. Other than a few bits of wreckage, there was nothing to see in any direction. "No one else? Treskie, or—" Her voice cracked, either with emotion or thirst.

"Not that I saw. Not that I really could see anything until the dawn broke. Then I saw the boat tangled in the ropes, pulled it over. I wanted to get you in it, but I didn't have any strength to move you."

"I might rutting not, either," Corrie said. All her muscles rebelled as she carefully crawled over to the boat and tumbled in. Thank every saint for it, being out of the water, being under the canvas. Out of the baking sunlight. Corrie could see that her hands were red, almost glowing. The sun was brutal, as was the heat. She took off her wet, salt-laden clothes, thrilled to let her skin—all pain and sores— breathe for the first time since she had been taken. She had noticed that Eana had already stripped to her skivs as well.

"Now what?" Eana asked.

"I don't suppose there's water or food in this boat?"

"There's a bottle of wine, and another thing that smells stronger. One of the sailors must have hid it on the shoreboat."

"Give me the wine," Corrie said. It would do, better than nothing. She took a swig.

"Like I asked, now what? You had the plan."

"My plan largely involved still having a ship," Corrie said. "But we're free right now."

"Free to die," Eana said.

"We're breathing right now, and no one has us shackled."

Eana took a moment, and it struck Corrie how young she was. Thirteen or fourteen. And she had been so rutting strong in this. Blazes, Corrie was supposed to save her, be the constable, protect these kids. Most of them had gone under with the ship and the bastards, except Eana had been the one to save her.

"We're gonna figure this out," Corrie said. "You and me. All right?"

Eana nodded. "We should say a prayer or something. For all the others."

Corrie hadn't been much of one for praying, outside of . . .

Outside of last night, she made her prayer to Saint Veran—Mama's chosen saint—and he had come through for her. She promised to pay any price for that. So a prayer for the poor kids who went down with the ship was the least she could do.

"That's a good idea," she said. "Who do you pray to, mostly?"

"Saint Deshar, or sometimes Marguerine," Eana said. "Marguerine was my mother's name, so, I . . . I like to think . . ."

"Yeah," Corrie said. She closed her eyes, not really knowing the right words. In their household, they would occasionally go to services on Terrentin—she had been in that damnable ship for Terrentin—and Aunt Zura was constantly making Acserian prayers. But no one in the household had made a point of teaching proper prayers. But she knew Marguerine was a saint of guiding the lost. That seemed very appropriate. "I don't know what to say. Can you?"

"Saint Marguerine," Eana said. "Please gather the souls of all the children who were not as fortunate as we were in this . . . atrocity we all had to endure. I didn't learn all their names, but I trust you will find them, and know them, and guide them away from damnation. Watch over them in passing, as they were—they were—no one watched over them in life."

Eana started to cry, the wailing tears of a shattered heart.

"Hey, hey," Corrie said, coming in close to take her into her arms. "They're . . . they're going to have something better than what awaited them if we had gotten to Mahabas-wherever. We are too."

"What makes you think that?"

"We're hopefully still in a shipping route," Corrie said. "Let me tell you—we worked this case—"

"Because you're a constable, right?"

"Right," Corrie said. "Whole messy case in the Little East. Involved feeks, and tyzos and machies, the whole lot."

"I never went there," Eana said. "I just lived by the Trelan Docks with my pop and uncle."

"That's why you could swim, hmm?" Corrie asked. "Which is how you saved me."

"And now this case you did will save us?"

"Maybe," Corrie said. "All sorts of sewage in that case, but my brother—smart as a rutting whip he is—he figured out that the whole deal tied to the shipping from this part of the world, back to Druthal. You see? There's feek and tyzo ships coming through here going back home. We just got to get lucky. Blazes, the tyzos were trying to do a whole thing where they patrolled these waters."

"So we'll get home?"

"Damned right we will."

Eana giggled. "You swear an awful lot."

"Yeah, well—" Corrie settled down in the boat under the tarp. Every muscle and joint screamed at her as she found a position where she could rest with the least discomfort. "When I was a rutting cadet, they

razzed and hazed me like no one's business. Wasn't much older than you
—how old are you?"

"Fourteen."

"Yeah. Same. About as young as you can be as a cadet. And I tore
through my training, which made everyone else in my cohort mad as all
get out. That made the hazing ten times worse."

"And so you started swearing?"

"My pop, he—he was a great rutting stick, he—"

"Your whole family are constables?"

"A lot. I got an uncle and cousin in the brigade, and another cousin
in River Patrol, another who's a Yellowshield, but . . . yeah, we serve the
loyalty in my family."

"Those are good jobs."

"They—they're not just jobs to us, see. They're callings. Like for
the priests and cloistresses in the church. It's part of who we are. That's
why I was out by the docks the night they took me. I wasn't on shift, but
there was something going down, my brother's partner needed help, so I
rode out. It's what we Wellings do."

"That's the neighborhood where my aunt lives. Welling."

"Wanna know a secret?" Corrie asked. "That neighborhood is named
after my ancestor. He helped found the Constabulary back in the day."

"No way."

"Yeah," Corrie said. "Look, girl, you may be stuck in this awful
mess, but you're in it with the right person. We're gonna get out of this."

"All right," Eana said.

There had been no ships in sight the whole day. Fortunately, before
nightfall, there was another rainfall—a cool, gentle rain that washed the
salt and blood and filth off their bodies. Corrie dumped the whiskey or
whatever it was into the ocean and filled the bottle with fresh water.
Then the night turned cold, and Corrie had to put her uniform back on—
giving Eana her coat—and they wrapped themselves up under the
canvas to stay warm.

The second day, there had been no ships either. And no rain.

Three, four days they kept drifting, no sign of anything in any direction besides ocean and empty horizon.

Eana grew weaker and weaker, and Corrie made sure she got more water, but even then, the poor girl could barely stay awake. They were both so blazing hungry.

Corrie, on the other hand, couldn't sleep. She watched the stars through the fifth night as they faded in the light of the sunrise. And, by every saint, that sunrise on the open ocean was the most glorious thing Corrie had ever seen.

"If this is it," she whispered to Saint Veran, "I understand, and thank you for giving me these days, that I could see this. But, I beg of you, for the sake of this girl here, Saint Veran—let me keep my pledge to her. Give me a chance to get her home. Whatever trick you have up your sleeve, whatever price I have to pay, I will pay it. But let me get her home."

As the sun rose up over the eastern horizon, in the distance she saw it.

Gray sails.

She got to her feet, reaching into her pocket. She still had one thing on her, one tool every constable used when they needed help.

She put the whistle in her mouth and blew like blazes.

PART ONE:

PRAYERS ANSWERED AND PAYMENTS DUE

CHAPTER FOUR

THEIR RESCUERS WERE A TYZO ship of some sort, but Corrie didn't know which kind of tyzo these folk were. Blazes, she didn't even know all the kinds of tyzos there could be. These folks were like the gray-skinned, shaven-headed woman who tried to kill her and Tricky a few months back, but they were a bit darker and didn't keep their heads fully shaved. She didn't know what the blazes that meant they were.

Mostly because not one of them spoke a damned word of Trade.

Despite that, they were kind and hospitable as all blazes. Corrie had no idea what kind of ship this was, but once she and Eana were on it, they were treated like rutting queens.

They were given water and food right away—food that Corrie didn't recognize in the slightest, but it involved fish and pickled vegetables and things she couldn't even identify. It smelled horrible, but at this point it was the most delicious thing she had ever tasted. They were brought to baths of hot water, and tyzo women helped peel them out of their clothing and scrub them clean. Ointments and bandages were applied to the sores that covered their bodies, and they were given quarters with delicious beds. Sheets like Corrie had never felt in her life.

They mostly slept for days, eating when food was brought, having their wounds cared for. They spend a fair amount of time wearing robes of the same glorious fabric the sheets were made of, which Corrie real-ized had to be Turjin silk. At least, that was her guess—she had heard of that, but she had never seen it before.

"You think it's a Turjin ship?" Eana asked as she lay in the bed. "Aren't they, like, really violent people who worship a death god?"

"I don't rutting know," Corrie said, eating another of the delightful fruits they had brought her. Sharply sweet, and she wished she knew what they were called. Delicious is what they were. Once she had gotten a grasp on what these people ate—a lot of fish, often in soups, mixed with grains and just enough spice to keep her tongue interested—she relished every meal they brought. They also were exceedingly generous in how much they brought. "They do know how to treat people in a decent, civilized manner, that's for sure. So I don't rutting care where they're from. But when we get back to Maradaine—"

"Which is when?"

"I don't know. Have you understood a blazing word out of their mouths?"

"I think *kjei* is 'yes.' Or maybe 'please.'"

"Maybe, who rutting knows."

"They do?"

Corrie burst out laughing. "Yeah, I bet on that."

"Corrie?" Eana said, getting up from the bed. "I think I'm getting my blood."

"Oh, blazes," Corrie said, coming over to her. She definitely was. "Is this your first one?"

"No," Eana said. "But it never happened on the other ship."

"All right," Corrie said. "We'll handle this." She went to the door, opening it to find someone waiting right outside. There usually was. "Hey, hey! Snap to it, huh. We need some—damn it."

The woman watching the door looked utterly perplexed—of course, she didn't understand a word Corrie was saying, just like Corrie didn't understand her. Still, Corrie waved her inside. The tyzo woman came in, looked at Eana, the stain on the bed, and her eyes went wide for a moment. She gave Eana a knowing smile and slipped off.

"What do you think she's getting?"

"Hopefully something like blood pants," Corrie said. "I mean, even these tyzo ladies get theirs, you know?"

"Yeah," Eana said. "Cor, you know we're not heading to Maradaine. Not on this ship."

"We're heading north," Corrie said.

"But we'd have to go south first, and west around Ihali, like Garten said, and then north to get back to Maradaine."

"I ain't never learned maps, really," Corrie said. "Of course, yeah, that makes sense. I mean, this ship was already on its way, of course it was. We get to the next port, thank them for their hospitality, and from there, we . . . we figure it out."

Eana took Corrie's hand and squeezed. "Yeah, all right. We just need to stick together."

"Got us this far."

The servant came back with a few other women, who quickly stripped Eana's bed and replaced the linens with black ones. They gave Eana a pair of black pants and a set of wooden sticks wrapped in cloth. After a few moments of confusion, they were able to convey with hand gestures what they expected Eana to do with them. With approving smiles, they took the soiled sheets and all left again.

"That seemed like a lot," Eana said. "Everything they do seems like a lot."

"Maybe that's their way," Corrie said. "I'm not complaining."

"Me either," Eana said. "It's just . . ." Hot tears came to her eyes. "No one has ever been this kind or generous to me before."

"Hey, hey," Corrie said, accepting the sudden embrace she found herself in. "You get back into bed. We deserve to rest until we get wherever we're going."

"Where do you think we are going?"

"Beats the piss out of me," Corrie said, guiding her to the bed. "If you hadn't noticed, I was not exactly a good student when it comes to places in the world."

"I never learned much about that either," Eana said as she lay down. "I went to a prepatory in Trelan, but . . . they didn't exactly teach us like they expected us to go to university when we were done." She sighed. "At least, not the girls."

"Ours in Keller Cove was the same." Corrie sat on the edge of the bed. "But I was already doing page work—saints, I think at eight?—and not even going half the time."

"You didn't take it seriously?" Eana asked.

"I knew where I was going. Took my cadet training seriously. I mean, I can read a blazing map. You had to know the street map of your neighborhood like your heart, especially to ride in the dark."

"Ride in the dark?"

"I was horsepatrol for night shift," Corrie said. "Which is a sewage job, but you got to earn your stripes someplace."

"You were on the south side, though, right?"

"Inemar was my stationhouse, yeah."

"But you were up in Trelan when you were taken?"

Corrie chuckled. "Yeah, well, when I was made sergeant, it was with the Grand Inspection Unit."

"That sounds fancy."

"You can rutting say that. But it really meant I got to work with my brother. Well, one of them."

"How many brothers do you have?"

"Three," Corrie said. "Minox—"

"That's a Racquin-sounding name." The girl's brain moved like a rutting hummingbird sometimes.

"Well, we're Racquin. My mother is, at least. Though we really never knew any of the rest of that family. Anyway, Minox, he's the inspector. Then Oren, he's a bit of a tosser, but he's a lieutenant in Keller Cove. Jace just made patrol regular in Aventil. And then my sister Alma, she's your age. Still doing prepatory. Mother wants her to go to uni."

"Big family."

Corrie laughed. "You don't know the rutting half of it. I told you we're one of the deep loyalty families, right?"

"Been in the Constabulary since it started, right?"

"Which means we're in one of those big, old houses in Keller Cove, on one of the loyalty rows. So almost nobody moves out. In that house we've got my gramma Jillian, my pop's sisters and one of his brothers, and their families. Whole lot of cousins."

"What happened to the other brother?"

"Hmm?"

"You said one of your dad's brothers lives in the big house. So what happened to the other brother?"

"He . . . he and his girls live over in East Maradaine. I actually saw Sherri and Jilly the day before I was taken, so . . . that was nice. Even if I was a jerk to Sherri." Corrie sighed. "Uncle Terrent, his wife got real sick, and the doctors couldn't do anything. She was in so much pain. I still remember those weeks, you could hear her crying through the night."

"Sweet saints," Eana whispered.

Corrie felt her own tears coming—and for once she didn't bother holding them back. She and Eana had already been through so rutting much together, there was no sense in hiding her heart. No need to prove how tough she was here; Eana already knew. "All she wanted to do was die in peace, and . . . my aunts Beliah and Emma helped her do that. Terrent was so angry, he moved out with his girls, and . . . well, we don't really see them much."

"Are you all right?"

"Yeah, yeah," Corrie said, wiping her face. "I don't usually prattle on like this, but . . . what else are we gonna do while we wait to get where we're getting, you know? You hungry at all?"

Eana laughed. "I feel like I might never need to eat again after all they've fed us. Which is funny, given how in the hold—"

"Yeah," Corrie said.

"We're gonna be all right?" Eana asked. "We got blessed by the saints."

"We did," Corrie said. "Let's get some rest, hmm? We don't need to do anything but rest right now, as long as you need. Right now, we're safe."

CHAPTER FIVE

THE FOLKS ON THE SHIP had cleaned and repaired Corrie's uniform, bringing it to her like it was fresh off the hot press. Corrie was shocked how good it still looked. After all she had been through, she would have thought restoring it was impossible. But here it was, crisp like new, the red and green of the Maradaine City Constabulary. It had been her pride and honor to wear, the legacy of her family and name. Carrying on the work that Papa died for.

What would he have thought, knowing she had gotten her sergeant's bars at nineteen? She hoped he would have been proud of her.

Their hosts made a few gestures and signs like they wanted her and Eana to get proper dressed and come up to the top deck of the ship. She had been up top a few times—the crew never acted like they didn't have free rein to go wherever they wished on the ship—but there was only so much looking at the wide stretch of empty horizon that interested her. It was lovely, it was spectacular, but she had seen it.

Still, she got dressed—they had even polished her boots—and Eana did the same. Her work dress had been reduced nearly to rags over the course of the slave hold and the ocean, but the folks on this ship had either reconstructed it or rebuilt one from scratch. It was a lovely blue and white dress, making her look almost like a River Patrol girl.

Saints, where the blazes were the River Patrol that night? If they weren't stopping a boat full of abducted kids, what blazing good were they doing?

Back to the point, the two of them looked sharp, presentable, and dignified, like respectable Maradaine professionals, not escaped slaves that had been dragged out of the ocean. Wherever they were going, surely looking decent and proper would go a long way in finding their way back home. Eana had even gotten her long chestnut-brown hair under control, tying it into a Patyma braid with a set of blue and white ribbons that matched the dress.

"I used to do that with my hair, when I had it."

"Yours has been growing back nice," Eana said. "Almost not looking like a street boy."

"Shut it," Corrie said with a laugh. "I had gotten pretty used to the short cropping. Maybe I'll just keep it that way."

"You make it work," Eana said. "I don't think I could."

One of the women who had been attending on them came into the cabin and gestured for them to follow.

"What do you think this is?" Eana asked as they came through the hallway after their hostess.

"I'm guessing we've made it to wherever this ship is going to."

"And we can get back home from here?"

The poor girl had been putting on a brave face since they had arrived on the ship, but her resolve was clearly breaking. Fear was plain in her eyes.

"We'll figure it out. You grew up on the river, right?"

"Yeah."

"Then you know ships from all over come to Maradaine, and ships from Maradaine go all over the world. No matter where we are, there will be a way to get home."

"You're sure?"

"Of course," Corrie said as she went up the steps above deck. "Everyone wants to go to Maradaine. It's the grandest city in the world."

The skyline she was greeted with when she came into the sunlight belied that claim, in every way Corrie could imagine.

The city they were approaching was beyond spectacular. They were approaching what appeared to be two separate islands, both which were completely covered in buildings and towers, towers that rose higher than Corrie had ever seen in Maradaine. Buildings laid in with glass and pearl and gold, which all shone in the glinting sunlight as the ship passed between the two islands. The surrounding straits were filled with ships of every size, every design, sails and flags of every color.

"Do you see a Druth ship in all those?" Eana asked.

Corrie squinted to try to see further, and pointed in the distance. "Look! You see the Druth flag on those?"

"Yes!" Eana said. She grabbed Corrie with excitement, wrapping her arms around her. "Never thought I'd be so happy to see that."

As they went through the strait, they approached another island and what seemed to be a jutting piece of the mainland—at least there the sweep of dense metropolis went as far as Corrie's eye could see. And spanning from the mainland to the island was a bridge that made the Great Maradaine seem small and petty in comparison.

"What city is this?" Eana asked.

Corrie didn't know for certain, and her own pitiful studies of geography wouldn't have been much help, but Garten's blabbering had stuck with her, resurrecting a few bits of knowledge of the eastern world. She didn't know too many cities in this part of the world, but if they had been going up the Imachan coast, only one place she had heard of could possibly match what she was seeing in terms of grandeur and majesty.

"It's the Mocassa."

CHAPTER SIX

CORRIE WISHED SHE KNEW MORE about the Mocassa—or more correctly, had paid better attention during those lessons. She knew it was a huge city—was it the capital of Imachan? Or just the biggest city out here? Or was it some separate city-state that wasn't part of Imachan? That sounded vaguely correct, but that could just be something she had mixed up with one of the other grand cities of the world.

A few other city names poured out of her memory: Kyor, Rekyashom, Rek Nayim, Trisdé, Vedix, Clwythnn . . . not that she had any idea where they were. Wait, no, Clwythnn was in Waisholm. She was pretty sure.

"So what's next?" Eana asked.

"Those Druth ships are anchored near that set of buildings. Maybe we've got an embassy or trade enclave or something. I guess when we get off and get inspected by whatever they have for customs—"

"Customs?" Eana asked. "How will that work?"

"I'm just guessing," Corrie said. "Look at those ships—small cutters. You see them?"

"Yeah," Eana said.

"A lot of those with the same design and build, and they seem to be escorting new ships toward that set of docks. And there's a bunch of those same ships around those docks. And we seem to be heading toward it." Indeed, the crew of this ship were running around like mad folks, setting sails and tying ropes and a half-dozen other things that Corrie didn't understand.

"It's pretty close to the Druth ships!" Eana said excitedly.

"Yeah," Corrie said. "Maybe that's a whole enclave, like the Little East, where the foreign ships dock, deal with local officials, that sort of thing."

"I'm glad you know what's going on."

"I really don't," Corrie said. "Just . . . just trying to do what my brother does. Using my eyes, using my head, making decent guesses about what I'm seeing."

"It's pretty smart."

"If you say so," Corrie said.

One of those cutters approached the ship as it came closer to the port, and ropes were thrown down, and in moments they were secured to the docks. Only now Corrie realized they had been on the top deck for a couple hours.

Their hosts came over and gestured for them to stand near the gangplank, but made them stop when Corrie tried to go down. Not quite aggressively, but there was a firmness to their demeanor which Corrie felt had been a slight shift from their earlier timidity.

Hairs on her neck went up. Something was rutting wrong.

She held Eana's hand and gave it a reassuring squeeze. Maybe it was nothing, but her instincts screamed that trouble was looming over their heads.

Several of the other members of the crew lined up, holding papers and binders, and a handful of uniformed men came up on the ship. It was definitely a uniform, even if it looked nothing like the Constabulary coat of green and red. All five of them—machies, surely, with their rich brown complexion and thick beards—were in the same matching brown and white wraps, which almost looked like dresses, open in the front to show off their bare, hairy chests. Not something Corrie really wanted to see.

She also noticed the long blades at their hips, as well as sets of iron shackles.

One of them—flair and plumage on his hat marked him as an officer, surely—came up to one of the crew and asked a question in some guttural language. The crewmember returned with a handful of halting words, showing his papers. The officer hissed to one of his men, who approached, and that man and the ship's crewman had an animated exchange in the language of the ship. Then he started looking over the papers.

After a few more exchanges that Corrie couldn't understand, going over the papers of the rest of the crew, the machie officer, the translator, and the ship's crewman approached Corrie and Eana.

The crewman spoke with a lot of excitement, showing several papers.

The officer said something to Corrie.

"I . . . I don't know what you're saying."

He looked to his man, who shrugged.

"None of you speak Druth Trade? That's all I rutting speak."

More confused exchanges between them all. The crewman presented more papers. The officer looked to Corrie like he expected something.

"I'm a citizen of Druthal," she said. "Sergeant Corrie Welling, in the Maradaine Constabulary. I don't have any papers or anything, nor does she. Come on, none of you speak Trade?"

The officer gave her some heated words she couldn't understand.

"Druth," she said tapping her chest. She could still see one of those Druth ships in the distance, and pointed to it. "If you get me there, it'll be fine."

The officer took the papers from the crewman, shook his hand and bundled them up. He moved up closer to Corrie, looking over her face carefully. Then he reached in and opened her mouth with his fingers.

"Hey, hey," she said, batting him away. "Keep your machie fingers out of my rutting mouth!"

He frowned, and then moved over to inspect Eana.

Corrie shoved a finger in his face. "Do not touch her."

They may not have shared language, but her point seemed to have been made clear enough. He stepped back, hands up, palms out.

"Good," she said.

He held out the papers that the crewman had given him. It was a bunch of squiggles and lines to her, written in machie or tyzo or both.

"I don't know what that is," she said.

He tapped it vigorously with one hand.

"Yeah, yeah," she said, taking it. "I don't know what this is."

He held out the other to Eana, who cautiously took it.

"Now what?" Corrie said. "Can we find someone who speaks rutting Trade? Druth?"

"Druth," the officer said, almost as a growl. He gave a wave, and then his other men came over, shackles out.

"Corrie!" Eana cried.

Corrie made a quick decision. These were proper officers here, she should respect that. Treat the system with respect, get through it. "Don't fight them," she said, presenting her wrists to them. Let them know she was complying, going peacefully.

The officer seemed to recognize that, and gave a nod of respectful acknowledgment.

At least, that's how Corrie took it. Maybe for the machies, he was making fun of her.

Either way, in a moment, she and Eana were shackled, led down the gangplank, and brought into one of the buildings, where they were immediately put into a cell.

CHAPTER SEVEN

THEY WERE IN THE CELL through the night, and, mercifully, left relatively alone. Whatever this was—and Corrie was determined to figure out just what the rutting blazes this was—the folks keeping them locked up in here weren't abusing them. Food and water was brought twice, and it was decent enough. Corrie had no palate for this machie food, but it was fine enough. Cold, spiced meat, flat bread, some sort of paste. She ate some and let Eana finish the rest.

The girl was a wreck. She ended up crying herself to sleep.

Corrie couldn't sleep, she kept an eye out. She'd guard Eana through the night, and beat the rutting piss out of anyone who came to mess with her.

While they were alone in the cell, there were other cells in this block, some of them occupied. None of the others in there looked Druth. Still, Corrie had to try.

"Hey, any tossers here speak Trade?" she called out. "Anyone?"

Nothing.

Corrie had dozed off somewhere in the night, woken by the guards coming with a morning meal. This came with something that resembled porridge, though Corrie didn't care for the spices, and what Corrie thought was tea but was definitely not. Dark and bitter in its warmth. She didn't hate it, though.

When meals were done, guards came and collected trays, and then escorted everyone out of all the cells.

"Hello?" Corrie asked when the guard took her out and led her and Eana down the hall. "What is going on? Does anyone speak Trade?"

No one answered as they were taken out of one building, into the bright light of the morning and led across the complex on the dock.

"There are Druth ships right down that way!" Corrie shouted. "I can see them! Just—HELLO! ANYONE! DRUTH WOMEN RIGHT HERE!"

One of the guards got in front of her, and Corrie braced herself for a backhand, and would give back as hard as she could when it came.

Instead, the guard just frowned, and pulled her along.

"What are they doing to us?" Eana asked.

"Hopefully just taking us to an official of some sort. Like a judge or such." Corrie was saying that more to quiet her own panicked heart. This rutting machie nonsense could be anything, and there was no way of knowing if it would be decent or fair.

They fed you in the cell, no mistreatment or abuse there. She had certainly seen folks in the Constabulary do worse with some of the sewage they had brought into the cells. Maybe it was warranted. But she knew damn well that nothing she had done, and certain nothing Eana had done, warranted being locked up.

All they did was escape a situation they never should have been in.

They were led into the next building—her and Eana and the half-dozen others who had been locked up with them—and brought up on a stage, in front of a small crowd. Was this how they did trials? Was this how justice worked here?

Rutting blazes.

She had read about the Inquest, the horrors before there was a proper system of law and law enforcement in Maradaine. Sham trials, mob justice. Hangings for entertainment. Did these people still do that? There was nothing on this stage that looked like it was for execution or torture purposes. Were the people in the crowd here to see humiliation?

They brought the first woman of the other prisoners forward, and then one guard stood next to her and read off a whole litany of something—not that Corrie got a damn word—from the book he had. When he finished, he stepped back, and another person—this one not in the same kind of uniform, but with the bearing of an official—stepped up on a block and started shouting. Shouting and pointing. Pointing to people in the crowd as their hands went up, as he shouted more. Shouted the same thing again and again.

Familiarity locked in.

"Is this a rutting auction?" she shouted. "By every damn saint, are you selling us at a rutting slave auction?"

The guards and the crowd all got agitated, some of them scowling or snapping at her. The auctioneer tried to get moving again on selling the one girl.

"No!" Corrie shouted. "No rutting way, this is not what you are rutting doing—"

One man from the crowd stepped forward. "Miss, calm down until it is your place."

"Do you rutting speak Trade?" Corrie asked. "Will you tell these bastards that we are not rutting slaves, we are Druth citizens, and we will not be sold!"

His eyes went wide, and he came up on the stage, launching into a flurry of machie nonsense. It took Corrie a moment to realize he was shouting at the guards and the auctioneer. Multiple times he said, *"Rhj reyy 'hilo chol_ach?"* to them.

"What the blazes—"

"No one explained to you?" he asked Corrie.

"You're the first person who has spoken Trade since we got here," she said. "No one explained rutting anything."

He spat to the floor. "Terrible. *ipp 'u ah'ra lheh!* You have failed in the eyes of God!" This was again to the folks in uniform.

"Please, sir," Eana pleaded. "What is going on? Are we being sold as slaves?"

"No, no, child," he said, looking at Eana with what seemed to be kindly eyes. Or maybe Corrie wanted to see that. He looked like most of the other machs here. Dusky complexion, dark eyes, dark hair, big, wild beard. His beard and hair were streaked with white, though. "But you have incurred a debt, yes?"

"A debt?" Corrie asked.

He snapped at one of the officials, who presented a sheath of papers. The same documents that the folks on the ship had given to the custom guards. He thumbed through them. "You didn't pay for your passage on your ship?"

"Didn't pay?" Corrie asked. "That's not how it rutting went."

"I only know what this claims," he said. He said a few things back and forth with the others. "You arrived on a Gunjari ship, and the crew claimed your bill was due. This debt of yours was assured by the Trust of Mocassa, which now holds your debt lien."

"I don't even know what half of what you said. I don't even know what Gunjari is."

"That doesn't matter," he said. "You were transported on a ship, yes?"

"Yes, but—"

One of the officials started to speak, and he snapped at them. "I am sorry, miss, that they did not bother to lay out the particulars to, or even seek out someone who spoke your language to communicate with you."

Corrie bit back her anger. This man wasn't at fault. "I appreciate that."

"Let me tell you what's claimed here," he said. "The two of you owe for passage on the *Seinjeu*, where you received a private room, deluxe treatment."

"But we—"

"Ate many premium meals, with additional fruit and sweet courses."

"We never—"

"Had clothing repaired, ruined bedding, menstruation care . . ." He muttered in machie. "This is bordering on absurd."

"We were adrift at sea and they rescued us," Corrie said.

"Yes, I see," he said. He showed her the sheet. "They're even charging you for rescue services, and time lost for straying from course."

"They're charging us?" Eana asked. "But we never agreed—"

He scowled. "Agreed isn't the issue. They claimed you incurred these charges, and the agent of the trust confirmed them and confirmed your acknowledgment."

"We never acknowledged anything!" Corrie said. "We didn't know they planned to charge us."

He conferred with the others. "I'm sorry," he said after a moment. "But they say your debt is valid and must stand, unless you deny that the services rendered in the claim are false. Did they not render these services?"

Corrie was about to argue, but the truth of it was, they had received those services. They had relished them. She had had no idea a bill was being tallied, but the price—

Whatever price, she had promised to Saint Veran. And the trickster had brought that due.

"No, they were rendered. But we were treated falsely by the Gunjari, and by these officers of the trust. Neither one rutting told us a damned thing about cost or debt."

"That has no bearing, sadly," he said. "So this is where you find yourself, at the debt market."

"Which is?"

"The trust of the city doesn't find it useful to hold your debt and take responsibility for your standing until it's paid. So the title of your debt is up for sale, which we negotiate here."

"So you—all of these bastards—are here to buy us? How is that not a slave auction?" She was shouting again.

"It isn't," he said. "We aren't buying you, we're buying your debts, which are then owed to us, with the collection of interest upon it."

"How is that—"

"Wait," he said as the crowd grew restless, murmuring louder. "I will see what I can do."

He waved his finger at the crowd, shouting a bit more in machie nonsense. Then more at the officials. This went on for several minutes, and most of the officials looked put out, and the man who was interceding on their behalf grew heated. Corrie wasn't sure what it all meant, but she hoped his "see what I can do" wasn't another damned trap. She had endured enough trickery.

"You two Druth girls are together?" he asked after some exchange.

"Yes," Corrie said, taking hold of Eana's hand.

He nodded. "Then I will buy the claim of your debts. It is more than I planned to spend, but . . . I have pity for you both. And I suspect I will get my value back with you two."

Corrie had no idea what he meant, but she already knew she didn't like it.

CHAPTER EIGHT

CORRIE STILL HAD NO RUTTING idea what the blazes was happening, though she had the feeling in her gut that, despite that one fellow's protests to the contrary, she and Eana had just been sold into slavery to these Imach bastards.

If that turned out to be true, she'd make sure to at least choke the life out of him before this was over.

Not until you get Eana out of this sewage. Corrie didn't care what happened to her. The family had surely already presumed she had a last ride, and sat a mourning for her. But more importantly, that was her job. Put her life in place of the innocent, the civilian. That was Eana right now. Her duty, protect the girl.

She couldn't do something as easy as sacrificing herself to petty ends.

Not yet, anyway.

She and Eana were led off the stage, out the door and to another building in the compound. The fellow who had bought them followed along.

"So you own us now, is that it?"

"No, I told you," he said. "I am the steward of your debt."

"And who the blazes are you, again?"

"My apologies," he said. "In the chaos of sorting all that, I did not foster proper introductions. Very poor on my part. My name is Nalaccian Assema. And you two Druth flowers are?"

"Let me make one thing really rutting clear," Corrie said. "You call either her or me a flower or a jewel or a treasure or beauty or anything that comes in the neighborhood of those words again, I'm going to punch you so hard, they find your teeth yesterday."

He swallowed hard. "My apologies. I am . . . not fully graced in the nuances of your language. I meant no disrespect."

"See to that," Corrie said.

"Might I be blessed with your names?"

"Sergeant Corrianna Welling, of the Maradaine Constabulary," Corrie said. "'Corrie' or 'Sergeant' are acceptable."

"Absolutely, Sergeant," he said. "And you are?"

"Eana Mellick," Eana said. "It's just Eana, really."

"Charming," he said. "I understand your anger, Sergeant. It's well earned. And I will not resent its misdirection toward me. But try to remember I am not the source of your discontent."

Not fully graced in the nuance, my piss.

"So what happens now, Nally?" Corrie asked.

He scowled slightly. "You're going to dislike it."

"I'm sure."

They came into a new building, which reminded Corrie of a hospital or the infirmary of the stationhouse. It had that same sense of gruesome necessity.

Plus there were tables with a trays of sharp-looking tools next to it.

"The blazes?" she asked.

"You'll both be fitted with debt bolts, and tattooed to show the extent of your debt."

"We will what?" Corrie felt her voice go up an octave as she made no attempt to hide her anger.

"Part of how the system is maintained is the indebted are publicly marked to be easily identified."

"Why?" Corrie asked, hoping just the tone of her voice would strike everyone dead as the others pulled her and Eana to tables.

His face screwed up in thought. "Once we finish here, you'll have liberty within parts of the city, with some restrictions. These markers are so those restrictions are imposed."

"Free within the city?" Corrie asked. "We can't leave?"

"Not until the debt in settled."

One of the other machies pulled her onto the table, rolling up her arm.

"And how much is the debt?"

"It is three thousand kessirs, for each of you."

That meant rutting nothing.

"Is that a lot?"

"It is a sizable debt," he said. "Mind you, originally, the debt was six thousand seven hundred on each of you. I argued for you, that the ill consideration of the folks of this facility, the lack of fair treatment, was a cost they incurred. A grievous wrong. And for that, your debt was marked down."

"But how much is three thousand?" she asked. "What does that really rutting mean?"

He scratched at his graying beard. "If you are fortunate and can choose jobs well, work wisely, and live with thrift, taking into account interest and fees, you could pay that off in, I would guess, four years?"

"Four rutting years?" Corrie shouted, and she was so angry, so rutting focused on this piss-drinking bastard, she didn't even realize the machies were clamping some blazing thing into her ear until the pain hammered into her. "What the rutting blazes?"

"That is the debt bolt," he said as her hand went to the cold metal gadget that was attached to her ear. "I advise you not tinker with it."

"What the—"

"The marker that you are indebted. It will stay on your ear until your debt is paid. Wear it honorably, there will be no difficulty."

"What do you mean honorably?" Eana asked, her face a complete terror as the machies came over to put hers on. Now Corrie could rutting see it, the one they were about to put on Eana. It was a tiny monstrosity of brass and copper, a little box with clamps and a keyhole.

"If you attempt to remove it without proper key, or otherwise tamper with it, the springs inside with release and . . . it will tear off your ear."

"No!" Eana cried. At that moment the machies grabbed her head and attached it, and Eana wailed so much it broke Corrie's heart.

"That is rutting barbarous," Corrie said. "She's a child."

"In our law, she is old enough to bear debt and work," Nalaccian said. "Would she not work in Druthal?"

"Yes, she would," Corrie muttered.

"I understand your pain, child," he said. "It is important you wear this with dignity and honor. As I said, trying otherwise, it would rend your flesh, and that shredded space where your ear had been would make it obvious to anyone you were a criminal."

That word hit deep. Corrie rutting understood that. "I will be no criminal," she said hotly. "If this is the law here, then I will rutting abide." She took off her uniform coat and rolled up her sleeve. "Ink my arm, I guess."

"I'm grateful you understand the gravity," Nalaccian said. He gave a nod to the folks working the tattoo needles, and they got to work on her arm, and then Eana.

"And I guess, after all this, I owe you or something?" she asked him.

"Well, of course," he said. "I have paid for the stewardship of your debt, which is now owed to me."

"So I need to work to earn off my debt, hmm? Work for you?" Her stomach broiled thinking where this was going.

"There will be options."

"Hmm. Plenty of options for two young foreign girls who don't speak the language, I'm sure." She had a sense what he had in mind. "And if we don't . . . cooperate? Don't earn off our debt to you?"

"Then I revoke stewardship, sell back your debt, take some loss. The size and scope of your debt will jump, of course. It will be a terrible cycle for you. I have seen it."

They finished the tattoos, which seemed to be mostly elaborate hash-marks. Hers and Eana's were identical. The same debt, three thousand kessirs. Whatever that was.

"And now we're free?"

"You're at liberty, within certain parameters," he said. "Free would be a lie."

"So we are slaves."

"You are . . . how to put this in Druth terms. You are prisoners. Prisoners of debt, with the city serving as a very ample jail."

That hurt Corrie, deep in her heart. "So where are we expected to bunk, then?"

"Let's be off," he said. "I'll show you the way."

CHAPTER NINE

T HE MIDMORNING SUN WAS ALREADY oppressive when Corrie and Eana came out of the compound into the city street. Corrie still wasn't sure exactly what the facility had been: a customs and immigration center, a jail, an auction house for the indebted—it seemed to serve all those functions. That didn't make much sense to her at all.

The street out here was not very inviting. High sandstone walls loomed over the narrow road, and the only activity were heavy wagons, pulled by creatures that were definitely not horses or mules. Ugly, misshapen things to her eye. Big than horses, with a rising humped back that made riding seem impractical, none of the sleek beauty that a horse had.

"Come, we need to move," Nalaccian said, leading them down the narrow space left in the street not taken up by the wagons, only wide enough for them to walk single file. "We cannot get a pullcab in this part of the city."

Corrie pointed down the other direction. "There were Druth ships that way, weren't there?"

"Druth, Waish, Kieran," he said. "It's a protected enclave for Trade Nations ships."

"Why aren't we going there?" she asked. "Are there Druth officials there?"

"I do not know the details of its operation," he said. "But I believe that enclave serves as Druth territory, and therefore, is outside of the bounds of the city. You cannot go there."

"But they could—"

"Sergeant," he said sharply, "you can write petitions to send to Druth officials, but you cannot enter or demand audience. I am sorry. They will not admit you."

He was moving very quickly through the narrow space, turning at an intersection and crossing between two beast-pulled wagons with such clearly practiced skill he did it without thought. If Corrie didn't know better, she would have thought he was trying to lose them, but it was obvious the way he was moving matched the style and pace of the other pedestrians she could see. This was just how people walked in this city, it seemed. Corrie managed to keep pace, but Eana was lagging.

"Hey!" she called out to him. "Slow down!"

He stopped and looked back, scowling. "My apologies, I did not realize the girl was lame."

"She's not lame," Corrie said as they caught up. "We just don't know where we're going, or how those carriages move, and you're just barreling on without us."

"You will not succeed in this city if you do not learn how to move with it."

"Neither of us want to succeed," Corrie said.

"We just want to get home," Eana said. "There's Druth ships right over there."

"You will not be allowed into the enclave," he said, tapping at his ear. "As I said, you will have liberty, but restricted."

"But maybe there's someone in there we can rutting talk to?" Corrie asked. "I mean, I don't blazing know, maybe they can pay off the debt for us, and we can go home and settle accounts there?"

"I've not heard of anyone doing that with any success," Nalaccian said. "It's been my experience that the Druth who utilize that enclave are the ship crews, petty administrators. No one with the free capital to pay off your debts in a lump sum, especially with little systemic structure to guarantee return."

"Which you have here?"

"We have this very system you find yourself in. Come, this is not the conversation for the middle of the street. A little farther to be out of the shipping district, and we can get a pullcab across the sea bridge. There we can speak further."

He led them—walking with what was clearly a deliberate slowness on his part—through a few more blocks of warehouse compounds and streets packed with heavy wagons, to an open plaza, filled with human activity right to the ocean shore. The sharp salty tang of sea air hit Corrie's nose.

Eana's nose was on something else.

"What is that?" she asked. "It smells so good."

"You all haven't eaten," Nalaccian said. "Please forgive my foolishness." He led them to a cart stand where a fellow was grilling some sort of meat, smothering it with a sauce and rolling it up into flatbreads. Corrie felt a pang of memory—it was not unlike the fast wraps from the cart outside the Constabulary stationhouse in Inemar. Her brother Minox practically lived off those wraps.

Nalaccian had a brief exchange with the cook, coins passed hands, and soon hot food was delivered to Corrie and Eana. Corrie was about to tuck in, when a horrid thought crossed her mind.

"This isn't some other trap, where you bought the food and therefore we get further in debt?"

"No, no," he said. "This food, it is a gift from me. I will also pay for our pullcab and tolls across the bridge, freely and openly. I will not treat you dishonest, Sergeant. Once we have the two of you settled, you will, of course, incur living costs, which you must attend to as well as paying your debts—"

"You figured that into your 'four years,' right?"

"Most certainly."

That was something at least. "Thank you for your gift," she said. This man had, so far, been kind to them—to a point where she definitely had her suspicions of his motives—but kind, nonetheless, and her mother would be deeply cross with her for not showing proper gratitude. She would not drop her guard, but there was no need to be rude over slights that, so far, had only manifested in her imagination.

Corrie had no idea what the meat in the wrap was, and the sauce was somehow cool and creamy yet outrageously spicy in ways she was not prepared for, but it was far better than she had been expecting it to be. The spiciness forced her to take her time as she ate, which was clearly not an issue for Eana. The girl wolfed the thing down in a flash.

Nalaccian had made some whistling sounds and hand gestures, and two strapping young men—shirtless and muscular to the point of distraction—came over pulling a vehicle that looked like a cushioned bench on two wheels.

"This is a pullcab, I presume?" she asked.

"Is that not what you would call it?" Nalaccian asked. "I have never been to Maradaine, but I did travel to Korifina in my youth—how I learned your language—and that is what they call these there."

"Never been," she said. She knew Korifina was the southernmost city in Druthal, in the Archduchy of Scaloi— that much of geography lessons had managed to stick with her—but she had never been nor knew what they did there. It had never occurred to her that Korifina would be that different from Maradaine, just smaller.

He gestured for them to get into the pullcab, and Corrie helped Eana step up into it before taking her own seat. Nalaccian let them get settled before he got in place, almost making a point of sitting in a way that minimized physical contact with either of them. He passed a couple coins to the men and told them something in their native tongue. The two of them ran like a bolt out of a crossbow, pulling the cab with them. They went straight toward a wide road, which ramped up onto an enormous bridge.

This was clearly the same bridge Corrie had seen from the ship, and as they crossed it, its scope was even more incredible. The whipping ocean wind washed over several lanes of human traffic going across this gargantuan construction. Corrie was astounded how orderly it was. The Great Maradaine, as well as the other bridges crossing to the north side of the city, were chaotic messes of wagons, pedalcarts, horses, and people in each direction, hustling and crashing into each other on a regular basis. Here, the roadway across the bridge was painted with clear lanes, and each lane kept a specific direction, with traffic that maintained a certain speed.

They were in the lane all the way at the far edge of the road, which was populated entirely by pullcabs with their running pair going full tilt. Corrie was impressed that the young fellows had the kind of stamina to maintain that pace. Perhaps that was just what came from pulling people about all day.

"So we're leaving the city to go to that island?" Eana asked.

"This is all the city," Nalaccian said as he gestured vaguely in every direction. "The four islands and three mainland districts all form the Seven Boroughs of the Mocassa."

"And the Mocassa is the capital of Imachan?" Corrie asked.

He shook his head. "I forget your Druth folk do not understand this part of the world. Imachan isn't a nation like yours is. Roughly speaking, what you think of as 'Imachan' is several kingdoms and principalities, including this city, which is essentially a state unto itself."

"Wait, the Mocassa is its own country?"

"Not exactly," he said as they approached the far end of the bridge, descending down a spiral ramp as the various forms of traffic started to converge. Nalaccian shouted something to the runners, and they jerked hard to one side and went down a different ramp.

"What was that?"

"I told them to take the *chahmmah* ramp. It costs more but moves quicker. We'd be stuck here half the afternoon otherwise."

"You are pretty free with money."

"I have much, I earn much, I should use it as I see fit."

"Earn much," Corrie repeated. "I wonder about that."

"So, we are coming into the borough of Jachaillasa. This is where you two will be living."

"Why do we have to live here?" Eana asked. They had reached the street level, and here things looked like the Machie section of the Little East. Here, this rutting city was matching Corrie's expectations. Teeming with bodies, winding roads, muslin tarps covering street seller stands, and buildings of brown and red stone.

What jumped out to Corrie the most were the windows.

Every building had windows, but they were just holes cut into the stone—no glass, no bars, no anything. Between that and the rough stonework on these buildings, any fool could climb up and get in any room they wanted.

Not very safe.

"So you want us to live here, in Jachai," she said.

"Want is not the right word, I don't think," Nalaccian said. "I have space in one of my debthouses here that you can claim, and I give you a deal on the rent as you are under my charge. You are at liberty to seek other living quarters, if that is what suits you, but you will have difficulty finding place that will give you the same fairness."

"And why would we?" She nodded, tapping at the monstrosity on her ear. "It's this, isn't it? Landlords would consider us a blazing bad risk, and either be scared off or hike up the price, right?"

"You speak in ways, Sergeant, that I did not hear much in Korifina. Is such profane speaking more common in Maradaine?"

"It's common to me," she said. "Rutting deal with it."

"I am not bothered, for we often hear much worse from coarse folks here. Especially in this part of the city."

"Is this a bad part of the city?" Eana asked. "Are . . . are we going to be in danger?"

"It is not that bad," he said. "I choose to keep a home here, which I stay at most of the time. But it's also . . . there are, what is the word?"

"I don't know," Corrie said.

"There are a series of laws in place, called *tumm imrihirri.* It details who can be allowed to live in which parts of town. You have two different *rhizhi* upon you. Restrictions, yes."

"We're only allowed to live certain parts of town because we're indebted?"

"And also foreigners. That is the larger factor in play. We're going to the sector of Jachaillasa that is specifically for you."

"So we're to live in the Little East, is what you're saying." Corrie chuckled at the irony of that. Of course, it made sense. In Maradaine, Imachs and other foreigners lived crammed together in the one part of the city they were allowed. Now it was her rutting turn to be crammed in somewhere here.

Nalaccian barked a few more orders, and the pullcab turned a curve and came to a stop. "Come," he said, getting out and giving coins to the runners. "We are here, your new home."

The house was unremarkable from the outside, just like every other one on this street: reddish-brown stone, several stories high, incredibly narrow. All the buildings here were tall but absurdly narrow; every house was maybe three or four armlengths wide, but she noted five floors' worth of windows. And between each house was what could charitably called an alley, but Corrie imagined she could only get through it if she turned sideways and held her breath. It was as if they had tried to pack as many of these lean, looming homes on the street as possible.

"Come, come," Nalaccian said, waving them toward the doorway. There was no actual door, just a hanging curtain. Looking up, Corrie noted that, like she had noticed before, none of the windows had any glass or bars, and she could see clearly into the rooms on the second floor, and imagined it was just as easy to see inside from even higher. She looked at the house across the street, and it was clear: anyone on the higher floors could easily see inside.

She also noted who she could see in Nalaccian's house. There were two young women—in loose blouses with bare arms—engaged in what Corrie presumed was kitchen activity on the second floor. A floor above, another young woman—with rich Ch'omik-black skin—sat in the windowsill with her bare leg dangling out for the world to see. Yet another woman of smoky complexion leaned out of a fourth-floor window and shouted to someone across the street.

A house full of young women. Whistles blared in Corrie's head. This was exactly what she feared.

"Corrie?" Eana asked. She had pressed herself against Corrie; side, her small hand digging into her own. She knew what she was seeing, too.

"Get ready to run," Corrie whispered. Tear her ear off, lock her away forever, she would not submit to this, and she would fight like blazes to protect Eana from it as well.

"Nally," she said sternly. "I'm not taking a step inside that doxy-house of yours. I will not let you peddle our flesh, regardless of what debt we may owe you."

"Peddle your—*ip' ĵavv a*—no, not at all, Sergeant. That is not what this is."

"You're telling me this house full of women—women who owe a debt for you—isn't you running a rutting brothel? That's not how you expect us to earn our keep and pay our way?"

"No!" He glanced up to where she was pointing, the chomie woman with her leg out the window, and sighed. "I can see how it looks that way. And if any of the other *ghehfuczahn* who were there at the auction had bought your debt, that may well have been your fate."

"But not you?" Corrie asked. She kept her grip clutched on Eana's hand. "Because you're so much more noble?"

"I would not use that word," he said. He sat down on the stoop. "Listen to me, sergeant. I am not a charity here. I purchased the steward-ship over your debts so those others would not, and I do expect to profit from that enterprise. I will profit from renting space in that house to you, as I do from all the people who live in there. You will have to work, and likely work in hard, unpleasant ways to manage all your responsibilities. I will not deny any of those things. But what I will not do, not ever, is dictate to you what work you must do. I am not charity, but I am not cruel."

"So this is not your doxyhouse?" Corrie said. "We won't be expected to roll anyone to pay our debt to you?"

"Expected, no. If that is the work you choose to do, that is your busi-ness. I believe that is how Hanakhla up there earns her way." He shouted something up to her that wasn't Trade, and didn't sound like his native tongue either. She responded in kind. "But as I said, her business. You earn your way *your way*. Have I not made it clear, you are at liberty to the city. I want you to thrive, I want you to pay your debt, make profit for me, and be free to get back to your homes as soon as you can."

Corrie scowled. She didn't trust it, not really, but there was enough selfish interest in what he said to at least make it believable. If he had tried to sell her that he was some saint, watching over the poor indebted girls of the Mocassa just out of the best intentions of his heart, she would have run like a prize horse with Eana in tow.

"Is it safe?" Eana asked quietly.

"Safe as we can hope it to be," Corrie said. If they were stuck here, they needed a place to live, and it wasn't as if they had better options.

As of right now, Nalaccian was the only person in the whole blazing city who they could even consider friendly. What rutting choice did they truly have?

"Come," he said. "Let's acquaint you with the house."

CHAPTER TEN

INSIDE THE HOUSE WAS, IF nothing else, an escape from the
oppressive heat. It was surprisingly cool, with a rich breeze coming
through the main room. Though it seemed like the whole floor was one
long room, with only half walls breaking it into sections.

Nalaccian stripped off his shoes and stockings, placing them in a
piece of furniture by the entryway that was clearly intended for this.
Many other shoes waited in the niches of the furniture. Another piece of
furniture had cloaks and wraps hanging on it. Clearly this section of the
house was for storing away the clothing that wasn't supposed to be worn
inside the house. The foyer of the family house back in Maradaine was
the same—everyone was supposed to hang their belts on the hooks and
store their crossbows, handsticks, and irons in there. Never in the house
proper, Mama insisted.

Seemed that was the way with shoes in this place.

Eana slipped off her shoes and put them away in one of the empty
niches. Corrie's boots didn't fit easily, though, so she left them on the
floor next to the furniture.

Nalaccian went into the next chamber, where the main feature was a
stairwell than was, unsurprisingly, incredibly narrow. These Mocassans
did not like to waste space with steps much bigger than the width of a

foot. Corrie was certain she'd fall and crack her neck going up or down those.

"Heya! *Ah'ra ar reyy?* Srella?"

A woman yelled back in some machie nonsense, which Nalaccian gave back, and more shouting between them ensued, which grew increasingly heated.

"She really is very kind," he said, as if in apology.

"And she is?" Corrie asked.

"She is Henik ab Srella." A young woman—easily just about Corrie's age, maybe a bit older—clomped down those narrow steps like she was born to it. *"Aftu ļuahl ach puilįvv?"*

"These girls are Druth, don't speak in *imachai* in front of them, Srella. It is rude."

"Hmm," Srella said. "You Druth girls are, how you say, lost cats? He likes to pull them out of alleys." Her accent was thick as butter, but not Imach. Nor did she look Imach.

"And where are you rutting from?" Corrie asked.

"Corrie!" Eana squealed. "Be nice!"

"I'm very rutting nice."

"Druth girls, indeed, wonderful," Srella said. She came down the rest of the steps and clapped Corrie on the arm. "I am Henik ab Srella Ariska Miezhta mik Giowen lek Ni vil Ousnaa sim Jiul, but Srella is fine enough. I am sorry for your burden."

"Burden?" Corrie asked.

Srella tapped the debt bolt on her own ear, and held up her bare arm, showing her own tattoo, which looked much larger than Corrie's. But while Corrie's and Eana's consisted of a lattice of open honeycomb shapes, Srella's had over half of hers filled in with blue. "We all must do what we can."

"You also owe—"

"We all owe, here, friend," Srella said. "But there are worse fates, hmm?"

"Apparently so," Corrie said.

"Is this it?" she asked, turning to Nalaccian. "You brought two lost cats to share our home, and we won't see you for at least another round of blood?"

"I'll be about," he said. "I'm always more around when I bring new guests."

"Guests, as if we have choice." She scoffed. "My apologies, Druth girls, I mean no shame upon you."

"Not sure why it would be shame," Corrie said.

Eana clutched onto Corrie's arm. "Did we do something wrong?"

"No," Corrie said. "Is this where we live now? I mean, we don't seem to have much rutting choice here, but if this is where we live, let's get it set."

"Get it set?" Srella asked. "I don't speak your language as well as I thought."

"I rutting mean—" Corrie felt her temper rising up, and ground her teeth to hold it down. "I mean, Eana and I have been through quite a bit today—quite a whole blazing lot for a month, frankly—and I don't want any more rutting games. We're living here, hmm?"

"So he says," Srella said.

"It is your best option for today, if nothing else," Nalaccian said. "A few days from now, you can decide for yourself something else. But this is an option for you, Sergeant."

"Thank you," Corrie said begrudgingly. "Thank you for being the least rutting horrible person in this city."

"An honor," Nalaccian said with a bow. "I must be off."

"I knew it," Srella said. "Go. I will teach them the rules of the house."

"Blessed day to you both. *Ghehahi zha ip'.*" He collected his shoes and went off.

"Rules of the house?" Corrie asked. "Besides leaving shoes at the door, what is there?"

"I am guessing that you did not come to the Mocassa with intent," Srella said.

"Not at all," Corrie said.

Eana suddenly opened up, words gushing out of her. "We were abducted, shoved onto a ship, kept locked in a hold with other kids and such, and they were going to sell us as slaves, but Corrie got free and fought the slavers but there was a storm and the ship sank and we ended up on a shoreboat and this other ship picked us up and treated us nice until we got here, where they said we owed them a debt for all the nice stuff and I *just want to go home*."

The tears came like a crashing wave that washed over Eana. Srella wrapped her arms around the girl, making soft cooing noises.

"Ya, yes, blessed air, let it out. Tragedy you have been through, yes. We will not put you through that here. I know."

"Thank you," Corrie said. Her own tears were on a knifepoint in her heart, but she didn't let herself break, not yet. She had to hold it together.

"You never shared your names, friends," Srella said.

"Corrie Welling," Corrie said.

"It is a pleasure, Welling," Srella said. She looked down at Eana, holding the girl's face in her hands. "And you, sweet air?"

"Eana. Eana Mellick."

"Eana, not—I am a fool, I forget you Druth name yourselves backward. You are Corrie, then. Though I heard Nalaccian call you sergeant. This is . . . title of some sort?"

"Rank in the City Constabulary."

"She's an officer," Eana whispered.

"You are a law officer," Srella said. "We've never had one of those here."

That was an odd thing. "Like, in the city?"

"In the house. Come, come. This floor is just for coming and going, dumping your filth."

"As in the water closet?" Corrie asked.

"Not sure what that means," Srella said. She pointed past the half wall, which then led to another doorway outside. "But there are pots and seats back there for your filth, and cleaning it out is one of the house chores."

"Like a rutting stable," Corrie said. Eana, however, ran back there and dropped behind the half wall. At least they didn't expect people to do their business in front of the world and everyone.

"I thought a city this big would have running water," Corrie said.

Srella made an odd noise, and then nodded. "I figured your meaning, of water closet. We had those in Giowen as well. But not here. Not that they could not do it, but they take water very seriously here. Almost sacred. So the idea of sullying it with your filth is . . . horrifying to them."

"I guess this is the rutting desert," Corrie said.

"I have been here too long," Srella said with a sigh. "Are you finished, girl?"

Eana came back out, fixing her skirt. "Sorry. I didn't realize I had been holding it since the auction."

"Let's meet the rest, come," Srella said, going up the tiny stairway. Corrie let Eana go first and walked behind, keeping one hand extended to grab the girl if she slipped. Corrie couldn't imagine running down here in the middle of the night needing to piss, but that was how it was done, apparently.

Srella called out in another language as they came up on the next floor, which had that same narrow, long structure, with half walls marking the separations. The front of the floor was clearly kitchen, where another woman was hard at work grinding something into a paste. The center room, with the stairways, also had a long table that was only knee high, surrounded by cushions on the floor. The back section, above the filth stable, looked almost like a water closet, in that it had water spigots on the wall. A gauzy curtain blocked her view of the whole room, and someone was behind the curtain, scrubbing their arms.

"Here is what's called the *ghose'a*," Srella said. "Kitchen, eating, and washing, for everyone."

"How many women live here?" Eana asked.

"The two of you will make eleven." Srella looked up the stairwell and shouted in another language. "Most of them do not speak your tongue."

"I figured you were the only rutting one," Corrie said.

"There in the kitchen, that's Basichara," Srella said. *"Basi, chehrr ḷutte, slah imyya. Atte reyy fyahllmu Eana. Oleeh reyy fyahllmu Corrie."*

Basichara—also with a bolt on her ear and tattooed arm—looked up from her work, raising an eyebrow. *"Imyya ḷutte vaff zehw gheh'. Rine reyy ibhorr uarai."*

"Pleasure," Corrie said. "What did she say?"

"That you're overdressed," Srella said. "She said you'll die from heat."

"That's true," Eana said. "But this is all we have."

"Seeing how part of our debt involves fixing these clothes, I'm keeping my rutting uniform."

"You can take the coat off," Eana said quietly. "We're . . . we're home right now."

"This isn't—"

"You know what I mean," Eana said.

Corrie muttered some choice profanities under her breath and took off her uniform jacket. She was sweating a river, and it did make the heat a bit more bearable.

Two more women came down the steps: the chomie woman Corrie had seen in the window, and a brown-skinned woman with hard, dark eyes. Both debt-marked and bolted. The chomie openly sneered. *"Reyy rhe u ļu'um?"*

"Chehrr berrirri. rhehzhar reyy. Corrie tu Eana."

"Hanakhla, right?" Corrie said.

Hanakhla squinted at Corrie for a moment, and then smiled broadly, tapping at her eye. *"I gehgha."*

"What was that?" Corrie asked.

"She likes your scar." Srella had a further exchange with Hanakhla, who gave nodding approval to Corrie.

"And she's Pumesticolomikal," Srella said. "She's from one of the provinces in the Turjin Empire. We all called her Pume. She only speaks a little Imach." She had a brief exchange with Pume in what was clearly a completely different language.

"Better than my none," Corrie said. "This is going to be rutting challenging."

"Right," Eana said. She glanced at a slateboard that was on the wall over the table, covered in symbols and scrawls that made no sense whatsoever to Corrie. "I presume that's important?"

"That's the house chore board," Srella said. "Which I maintain."

"Gonna need to learn how to read Imach," Eana said.

"You said there were eleven girls here?" Corrie asked. "Six of us here, and whoever is behind the curtain. Where are the rest?"

"Working," the woman behind the curtain said. She came out into the main room, rubbing her half-naked body with a drycloth. Corrie had never seen a woman like her in her life—not just her impressive physique and powerful arms. She had skin that was somehow both chomie dark and tyzo golden at the same time, but with short blond hair and eyes so strikingly blue they stood out from across the room.

But what stood out most of all was the tattoo on her arm. All the girls here had tattoos like Corrie and Eana, but this woman's went all the way up to her shoulder. How much rutting debt did she have?

"That's Maäenda," Srella said, her voice softening for the first time.

"You speak Trade, I guess," Corrie said.

"Smart one," Maäenda said. "You're having them bed down in our chamber?"

"That . . ." Srella stammered for a moment. "It made the most sense."

"Right," Maäenda said. "Corrie and Eana from Druthal. We're up on the top floor, in back side." She then asked something of Basichara, who responded with a snap. "I guess we're eating soon. How is it by you? You two need to rest, or ready to get to it?"

"Get to what, exactly?" Corrie asked.

Srella had another exchange with Pume and Hanakhla, who then went downstairs. "You're going to need to work, of course, to earn for your *wugerhe*—rent and meal costs here."

"Room and board," Corrie said.

"Hmm?"

"In Druthal, it's called 'room and board.'"

"That's a mouthful. But it's three and half kessir every *mnu*."

"*Mnu?*" Eana asked.

"It . . . not quite Druth word. You say 'week'? Similar, but *mnu* is nine days."

Corrie nodded, though she still had no idea how much a kessir really was. "So we need to earn that and keep up the house? And you assign that stuff?" She pointed to the chore board.

"I don't assign. You accept tasks, and if you do them, that's discounted from your *wugerhe*. But if you accept, you better well do them, hear?"

"Don't try to scare them, Srella," Maäenda said. "This is all, I'm sure, fearful enough."

"Yes," Eana said meekly.

"Follow me up," Maäenda said. "I'll show you where to bunk and all."

"Thanks," Corrie said.

Maäenda went up the stairs, giving some last command to Srella—and it felt like a command—and Srella's demeanor lost all its edge. There was something to the dynamic Corrie couldn't quite put her finger on—but her head was still swimming with the new situation, new faces, every other language she was hearing. As much as she wanted to investigate further, figure out all the secrets going on in this house, she was not in the rutting mood for it.

"You don't speak any Imach?" Maäenda asked as they went up.

"Not a word," Corrie said.

"How did you expect to get on here?"

"I didn't," Corrie said. "We were abducted and on a slave ship, we escaped as the ship went down, got rescued and delivered here, but with this debt we're rutting saddled with. We didn't make a single goddamn choice to be here."

"Mercy," Maäenda said. "You're going to want to work some jobs that bring in actual money, I presume."

"Yeah, well, Nally said we'd be at it about four years to pay our debt, and I want to prove him blazing wrong."

"Good spirit. Here." She brought them to back side of the floor. The strong breeze went through the floor from their window—looking over an open market square, filled with people shouting and barking at each other—giving the space a cool, fresh feeling. There were cloth mats on the floor—clearly they didn't use actual beds or bunks here—and clothing and other personal affects in neat, folded piles on the ground. Corrie didn't mind sharing the space, of course. Saints, she had always shared a room with Alma and the cousins. Before the twins moved out of the house, there had been six of them in that room. And since Corrie used to work the night shift, she had learned how to sleep in the day, with everyone quietly moving in and out.

She'd be able to handle this fine.

Could Eana?

"Thank you," Eana said quietly. "This is all . . . all very kind."

"We're all on the same ship in this one," Maäenda said, grabbing a shirt from what must have been her pile. She started to get dressed, in a style that Corrie couldn't identify. Nothing like anything she had seen on patrol in the Little East. This woman was definitely a mystery.

"So, right now, since you don't speak the language, your best bet is going to the labor market in the morning."

"Labor market?"

"It's a square about a half mile from here. Anyone who's looking to hire someone for a bit of odd work—usually hard labor, you know, or at least tedium—they'll go looking there."

"I'm good to go now," Corrie said.

Maäenda shook her head. "No point, hmm? It's in the morning when the people who are hiring come for it. You'd just waste your time standing around. That's why I'm here right now, I didn't pick anything up today."

"You don't have a regular job yet?" Corrie asked. "How long have you been here?"

"About two years," she said, rubbing at the tattoo on her arm. "There's good days and bad ones."

Corrie look back over to the narrow stairway. "Those go up to the roof?"

"Yeah," Maäenda said. "I'll sleep up there sometimes. Good view of the stars."

Corrie went over and start to go up. "And the whole rutting city, I bet."

"You aren't going to jump, are you?"

That knocked Corrie across her senses.

"What? No, of course not."

"I mean, it's happened."

"I got no plans of that," Corrie said. "I got this far because I wasn't rutting about to give up, that doesn't stop now." She went up to the roof.

She was glad Eana didn't follow her, in part because she hadn't had a moment alone since—saints, she couldn't even remember when. And she hadn't been more than twenty feet from the girl since this began.

But she was right about the view. From here, she could see this part of the city, sprawled out before her: narrow tenements like this one, and towers and fortresses and grand homes, and a breathtaking stretch of water with even more city beyond it.

"Four rutting years," she muttered, letting the tears flow, finally. "You got me, Saint Veran, you certainly got me. I said any price and this is a rutting price, isn't it? But, by blazes, I will not be beaten by this fetid rutting boil of a city. I'm going to work and I'm going to get myself and Eana back home to Maradaine. You'll see. You will rutting see, you blazing jerk. But I've got a job for you, and you're going to do it without any tricks, you hear? You've had your rutting fun, and now you've got to give Mama and the rest of the family a sign. Make sure they know I am rutting alive, and I am fighting my way to get home to them. I am getting the blazes home. You hear me? I am getting home."

She heard a scuff behind her, and turned to see Maäenda. Anything Corrie had resembling resolve shattered, and the tears turn to a wail, loud enough to be heard on the street below, a sound of such horrific mourning that anyone who heard it would know the pain that ripped her soul apart.

She couldn't even stay on her feet, and her knees gave out. She would have fallen onto her face there on the roof, but Maäenda was there, catching her in those powerful arms. Corrie let herself fall apart completely, melting into Maäenda, who had the good sense to say nothing at all—no words could matter right now—and just let Corrie be held.

CHAPTER ELEVEN

CORRIE WOKE UP IN THE gray light before the dawn, her body covered in sweat. She should have taken a cue from Srella and Maäenda when they slept in their skivs, which was not a practice in the Welling household. Not that Corrie had any nightclothes, or anything other than her uniform. Nor could she do anything about that until she got work and made proper money.

She was surprised it was still very warm in the house, even without the sun up, and air flowing through the open windows. She slipped out of the sleeping chamber, careful not to disturb Eana or the others, and made her way carefully down the three flights of steps to the horse troughs. Picking a relatively clean spot to relieve herself, it was clear that maintaining dignity was not a high priority here. From her vantage point, she could see out the back door, across the tiny patch of scrub grass through the broken fence into the house behind this one. Into their horse troughs, specifically.

She went back up one story to the—what did Srella call it? The *ghose'a?*—to figure out the washing area. It showed they did, in fact, have running water here, in that the spigots at face level would spray like a hard rain, but she had no soap or drycloth. She managed to rinse off her body, which felt pretty damn good in this blazing heat—how was it this hot this early?—and just put her shirt and slacks back on over her damp skin.

It wasn't until she finished getting dressed that she realized there was a woman sitting on one of the cushions in the center room, nibbling on fruit and flatbread, and staring at Corrie.

"Ach chehrr reyy."

"Morning," Corrie said. "Don't suppose you speak Trade?"

"Yhaute!" the woman shouted. *"A gheh ah'ivv reyy druth ri li!"*

Corrie picked out one word there. "Yeah, I'm the new Druth girl. Hope it's exciting for you."

"A e ri li!" This woman seemed far too excited over whatever she was talking about.

"Ehyna ah'ivv ļughur, Meija." Maäenda came down the steps, rubbing her eyes. "It is far too early for her to be that excited. Is there coffee?"

"I have no idea," Corrie said.

"Meija, kh'afe vorr?"

Meija—at least, Corrie presumed that was her name—rattled off too many words too fast for Corrie to ever differentiate them. Maäenda walked away halfway through and went to the kitchen. "Corrie, here." She took a pot off the stove and poured two small cups of black liquid. "You get this in Druthal?"

Corrie took one of the cups that Maäenda offered. "There's a couple shops of it in the Little East."

"Better than Druth tea, I'll tell you that," Maäenda said. "It makes up for there being no beer here."

"No beer?"

"They don't believe in it," Maäenda shook her head. "Literally, it is an edict in their faith to forsake the fermented."

Corrie sipped at the hot liquid. Dark and bitter, but in a way that did remind her of tea. "That's rutting interesting," she said. This was what they had given her in the cell yesterday.

"I'm glad you're up. We should make our way to the job square sooner rather than later. It is best to be there before the sun is fully up."

"I'm in your hands."

"Ehv tud rhị reyy ishi?" Meija snapped. *"ʹeh rhwegzeh rhi' 'o shi?"*

"Ah'ivv gahbvul rh̲ahch." Maäenda snapped. "But you better be ready to use your hands, Sergeant. Girl like you, doesn't speak a word of the local? Not many options for work."

Corrie sighed and finished her coffee in a single gulp. "Then let's be about."

They went down, got their shoes on—Maäenda's were simple leather slips, which seemed to be the style—and went out into the city. They had gone down two blocks, slipped through an alley and crossed a market square by the time Corrie realized she'd have no chance at all of navigating her way back to the house.

"Is the house on a specific street? You all name streets, number houses here?"

"Streets are named, yes, but I don't know about this house numbering."

"How do you find the right house? Because the do all look the rutting same."

"It's all navigation, hmm?" Maäenda said. She pointed to a bright red sign over one shop. "You see that?"

"Yeah, but I can't read the rutting machie."

"Don't need to. All it says is laundering is done there. But you see that sign, take a right at the next cross, walk through two intersections, count four houses on the left."

"Sign, right, two, four on the left," Corrie said to herself, hoping it would stick. "I mean, if you get work and I don't . . ."

"Right, you need to find your way. You need to learn your way, hmm? Same with your little friend."

"Because we're stuck for four years at least."

"Let me tell you," Maäenda said, stopping in her walk and pivoting to stare Corrie down. "Nalaccian told you four years, and that was a good guess, but that's presuming everything goes well, you know?"

"I'm guessing things have not been going well for you?"

She sighed. "Good seasons and bad. But you see what I got to work with here." She slapped her bare arm.

"That looks like a rutting lot of debt."

"Twenty-seven thousand kessirs," she said. "With the interest, the expenses, the good seasons and bad, I might be free of it in thirty years."

"Thirty?"

"Maybe more."

Corrie could barely breathe hearing that. "That's a blazing tragedy. I can't . . . I won't . . ."

"You don't know how much of one," Maäenda said, leading her into the wide plaza. Filled with street vendors, carts loaded with things Corrie couldn't identify, many of those strange animals pulling the carts, and already so many people despite the sun only just rising over the tenement towers to the east.

It wasn't lost on Corrie that this place made the marketplace on Promenade look like a quaint country fair. Plus there were folks with every skin and hair color that Corrie could imagine in the world. One factor stood out among many of the women Corrie saw.

"Should we have our hair covered or something?" Most of the women she saw had elaborate wraps or shawls hiding their hair.

"That's another thing of the faith, to varying degrees," Maäenda said. "If our hair was long, it would be an issue, but yours is short enough not to matter."

"You know why my hair's so short?" Corrie asked. "Because machie slan in the Little East tackled me and chopped it off."

"That'll happen," Maäenda said. "Why do you think I keep mine so close cropped? Now, your little friend, when she starts this—"

"I'd blazing prefer she didn't."

"There's a lot I'd prefer that isn't happening. When she starts this, she's going to have to choose to wear a cover or close crop. I'd advise the latter. Easier to deal with in this hot dusty air."

One woman pulling a cart almost crashed into them, stopping just in time as she looked up and locked eyes on Corrie. The woman's clothes and complexion marked her just as much a foreigner as Corrie. The type Corrie had seen plenty of in the Little East.

"Kher o togh toj phum, arsakor."

Not machie, and the last word popped out hard, one Corrie knew pretty damn well.

"I ain't your sister, miss. Move along."

The woman peered at her with dark eyes. *"Aue naaja vaueat, xaa auear raueruenvour thikaueagh kher. A mu kher auiauir thikaa knouzui.* The dead have called."

Corrie grabbed Maäenda's arm and moved away fast. "Let's keep going."

"All right—"

Corrie all but dragged Maäenda along until they were halfway across the plaza, even though Corrie had no idea where they were going. That didn't matter, just getting away from that woman.

"What was that about?" Maäenda asked.

"That woman was Kelliracqui, or maybe Racquin. Same difference."

"I don't really know what that means. She acted like she knew you or something."

"No, not at all," Corrie said. "My mother is Racquin, so I've seen her type around before."

"You knew what she was saying."

"Just that she called me '*arsakor.*' Little sister. But she was laying down a grift that I'm not rutting taking up."

"A what?"

Corrie didn't have time to explain Racquin tricksters and the scams they played. "She was playing up an old Racquin superstition. It's nothing. Let's get going."

Maäenda looked at her with an odd regard. Confusion. Maybe even pity. Corrie didn't need any rutting pity right now. She pitied herself enough just fine. "Come, this is the place."

The place was a wooden platform—almost like a stage for street theater—in the middle of one part of the plaza. Several people were already there, taking a place on the platform, holding up small slate-boards with machie writing on it. Maäenda grabbed two boards and a piece of chalk from an old machie lady who was minding them.

"What can you do?" Maäenda asked Corrie.

"I'm a rutting constable."

"Yes, but—" she shook her head. "Skills, girl."

Corrie understood. "I'm a good shot with a crossbow—"

"Do you have a crossbow?"

"No."

"Give me something else, then."

"I can fight with a handstick or bare fists."

Maäenda glared at her. "Are you looking for fight ring work?"

"Is that a thing here?"

"I have been in cities on every continent known, friend. It is a thing everywhere. It is usually terrible. You might make money, but it is usually as much a slavery as the debt. Is that the work you want?"

Probably rutting not. "Put that I can handle myself, like, as a law officer, without implying I'm looking for fight ring."

"That might require more subtlety than my command of the Imach language or the space on the slateboard holds. Personal guard, I will put."

"Fine."

"What else?"

"I was horsepatrol, so I can ride horses . . ."

"You know animal care?"

"I mean, of course. I would tend to the stable stuff. My pop—"

"Animal care is good, if you know it. What more?"

"Whatever else requires strong arms and good hands, I suppose."

"Sure, sure," Maäenda said. "And I write that you do not speak the language." She handed Corrie the slate with machie scrawling all over it. As she started to write her own, she said, "Now get up there and hold up your sign."

"I'm trusting you here," Corrie said. "If this actually says I'll doxy or some sewage like that, I will crack your blasted skull."

"I bet you would try," Maäenda said with a flash of grin.

"Don't doubt me, friend," Corrie said. She noticed a few folks were milling about, checking out the various workers standing on the platform. "Hey! Hey!" she called out. "Good Druth girl right here, check it here, check it!" She held out her slateboard so people could get a better look.

"What are you doing?"

"Getting attention," Corrie said. "I've only got one thing working for me right now, and it's this smart, loud rutting mouth."

"That's not the only thing you got."

"If nothing else—hey, hey, come on, buddy!—it puts those eyes on me instead of those deadweights down the stage."

"Not how it's really done," Maäenda said.

"We all got to work some grift, you know?" Corrie said. "Hey, hey!" she shouted at one fellow walking with a woman, the two of them both wearing richly embroidered robes. "This is what you're looking for."

"This word grift seems to have a host of meanings," Maäenda said.

The robed couple stopped in front of Corrie, in intensely whispered conversation as they examined her slateboard.

"Yeah," Corrie said. "Do you speak Druth Trade? Honest girl needing to work here."

They said something in machie—so probably not—and Corrie held her sign closer. "Come on, she wrote I don't speak machie, but I'm strong, all right?"

"They want to know about your animal skills."

"I know horses, had one under me from when I could walk. Always took care of my mounts. I know what it takes."

Maäenda said something to them, and then they had a full exchange.

"They have a full day of work for you, maybe work for the whole *mnu* if you work out."

"Nice," Corrie said. "And what do they pay?"

"Two kessir fifty a day." Maäenda shrugged. "It's pretty good, I'd take it."

"Sure, sure," Corrie said. "How do we—?"

"Put your slate down and go with them."

"Right," Corrie said. She hoped this was all legitimate and above the water. She really had no idea. She hopped off the stage. "Let's ride."

The man gave Maäenda a coin and started to walk away.

"What was that for?" Corrie asked as she followed after.

"Broker fee!" Maäenda said, with a big, joyful grin. "Go, work! See you at the house tonight!"

CHAPTER TWELVE

CORRIE FOLLOWED ALONG BEHIND THE couple, who seemed to barely acknowledge her presence. They walked and chatted in a manner that she interpreted as amiable, stopping at one point for an extended exchange with another couple they encountered on the street. None of them acknowledged Corrie directly, though the woman made a small gesture that seemed to communicate they had hired her for something. So they were still aware of her following them.

Corrie did note that their interaction with the other couple was very explicitly divided: the men talked with each other, and the women stepped to the side to converse separately. She presumed they were Imach—or perhaps Mocassan was the better term. Or maybe some other form of machie. Not that Corrie had any clue how to tell the difference between any of the wide variety of peoples she had been meeting.

Except that Kellirac woman, who spooked the blazes out of her. She didn't need or want to see that woman ever again.

The street conversation ended, and the woman gave Corrie a little gesture to follow again, which she did for several more blocks. She really had no idea how to tell the neighborhoods apart, how she could get home from here, but remembered what Maäenda had said about navigation. Find her way back to the plaza, the red sign, then the rest was simple. In theory. She looked around, finding the landmarks she could remember, using bright colors that stood out from the browns and tans and sandstones that dominated the city here. Which was odd, in that they didn't seem to shy away from vibrant reds and blues and yellows in the clothing, in the cloth tarps over the shop carts, and certainly all the foods she saw for sale were extraordinarily colorful. They passed a spice merchant, where the seed-and-powder-filled bins were bursting with color and aroma.

They crossed a busy roadway completely into a different neighborhood. Now there were wider walkways, homes with walled yards and metal gates, and trees with green and purple leaves, the likes of which Corrie had never seen. They reached one of the gates, and once they were inside, the man immediately cut off and made for the house, while the woman touched Corrie on the arm and guided her toward another structure. A barn or stables by the look of it.

And the smell.

Saints preserve her, they weren't yet within twenty feet of the thing and the stench was ready to knock her down.

"So what's the rutting story?" Corrie asked, covering her face with one hand.

The woman gestured vaguely in the barn. *"Imermea ri rik uafuc egh lehvinh."*

"Yeah, that doesn't help," Corrie said. "Though you don't rutting know what the blazes I'm saying, either."

"Mnisyi mnubh ah'ivv agh," the woman said, pointing at the barn with an irritated expression.

"I guess I sighed up for the sewage work," Corrie said. "Let's see to it."

She went and opened the doors of the barn, and the stench—so much worse with the doors open—hit her like a punch in the face. "Dear God and every saint," she muttered.

There were several animals in there—two ponies and five other beasts that were sort of like sheep, but with very different fur and horns.

And so much filth, like she had never seen before. So much that the animals—who also looked underfed and underwatered—had it caked into their hides.

"Oh, no," she said, going up to one of the ponies. "This isn't good."

The poor thing trembled at her approach, but it stayed still enough that she was able to stroke it. "All right, let's help all you fellows out, all right?"

The woman watched Corrie for a bit, silently, as she let all the creatures out of the barn into a small fenced paddock behind it. Deal with the most obvious things—get them out of there. There was a dry trough and a well pump, which took Corrie a minute to figure out, and she was able to fill it up, and each of the animals greedily crowded around it to drink. The not-sheep started grazing on the plants in the paddock, and the mistress didn't seem put off by that. The last thing Corrie needed right now was to get in trouble or lose a job because the animal ate some prized plant.

She went back into the barn, opening up doors on both sides to get air flowing through the thing. She was already glad she hadn't worn wear her uniform coat, as it was hot as blazes and the sun was still barely getting started going across the sky. She stripped off her shirt down to her chemise top, and then wrapped the shirt around her face so she wouldn't completely lose control of her stomach while working in there.

The woman came a bit closer to the barn, her face disapproving. *"Radd ah'ivv dheh mnuw sskeyo ayya te. I ehshehff ach shirr iad. 'o wa dahyf a'uagh."*

"I don't know what you said, lady," Corrie said. "I'm just trying to do the work here, you know?"

The woman took half a step closer, and said, *"Ah'ivv fuc tig mnuw, eh u bhehw ach 'o berr tud."* She shrugged, like whatever she had just said made things acceptable.

"So, clean out the waste and sewage, hmm?" Corrie asked. "Make this a decent place for those poor creatures?"

"A gheh ach ehshehff berr gha. Wa ghehraull ad 'o."

"All right, whatever. I'm just going to make the best out this mess for those poor creatures."

She worked through the morning, one stall at a time, taking breaks to check on the animals. She found a pile of something that was the Imach equivalent of oats—at least she presumed they were—and fed the ponies. Both of them were good boys, once she got them at ease with her.

The other animals—the not-sheep—seemed happy enough as the pranced and played about the paddock. She wanted to get them all cleaned up, brush them out, but she hadn't found a brush yet. Maybe if this work would continue, she'd find something to work with.

One of the not-sheep was female and was heavy with milk. Corrie wasn't sure what to do about that. Milkmaid was not a job she had ever done. And surely someone had been milking the beast up until now.

Though perhaps that person was no longer available, for whatever rutting reason, and thus Corrie was here.

After a bit of searching, she found what looked like a clean bucket, coaxed the creature to come close, and gave milking her best try. The animal seemed very happy at the idea, licking her face as she did it. Poor thing must have been in agony. She had only started to get a hang of it when the mistress came a bit closer with a concerned expression.

Corrie held up the bucket with a small quantity of milk. "Should I keep doing this? She seems desperate for it."

The woman gave Corrie a gesture that seemed to mean, "Yes, continue," and so Corrie did, filling up the bucket until the animal had no more milk left. Once that was done, the woman gestured for Corrie to hand over the bucket, and took it inside the house.

Corrie went back to work in the barn, shoveling out filth for the rest of the afternoon, really only starting to make headway with cleaning it out. At some point, the woman came back outside, making gestures to get the animals back into the barn. Corrie did that, making sure they had water and hay for the night, if nothing else, and closed them up.

The woman seemed satisfied, if nothing else, and handed Corrie a few coins. She then gestured toward the gate.

So the day's work was clearly done.

Corrie put her shirt back on, pocketed the coins and left the property, the woman shutting the gate behind her. Corrie then made her desultory journey first back to the plaza, keeping her hands in her pockets, wrapped around the coins. She had no idea if pickpockets were a problem in this city, but saw no need to take chances.

What she also saw none of was anyone she would clearly identify as a law enforcer or peace officer. Maybe she didn't know how they were identified here, but she would have thought it should have been obvious.

"Green and red is bright for a reason," Pop had said. "Brass badges shine for a reason. To be spotted easily, even from far away. Stand out in the crowd."

If this city had them, she didn't see them.

She found the plaza, and then the red sign, and then the route back to the house as Maäenda had laid it out to her, arriving as the sun was setting. Her feet ached, her shoulders were sore as blazes, and the skin on her arms had turned a rather disturbing shade of pink.

Plus she was covered in animal filth and smelled of it.

She stripped off her boots as soon as she was in the house, and deciding that since propriety of any sort as she defined it was clearly not an issue with these people, also took her shirt and slacks off as she went up the stairs, going straight into the waters room.

The spray of water wasn't much, but it was cool and refreshing.

Eana came around the curtain. "Good day?"

"I worked, so I suppose so," Corrie said.

"Srella told me there can be a lot of days where there is no work, so that's probably very true." She handed a rough wooden bucket to Corrie. "Soap and sponge, by the way. And I've got a drycloth for you."

"Bless you," Corrie said, taking it. "And you?"

"Learned most of the way things go in this house, did some chores as I could with Srella. Which should lower my rent."

"Good," Corrie said, scrubbing the filth off her skin, which was far too red and tender for her liking. She must have baked in the Imach sun.

"But that's not going to be enough," Eana said. "I'm going in with you tomorrow to wherever Maäenda took you. I need to work too."

Corrie sighed. "I rutting well know. I wish you didn't—"

"I worked in the house, sewed nets, helped with the boats. I'm fine, Corrie."

"I know," Corrie said. "I think it's rutting unfair on both of us. But, fine. Tell me there's food because I am famished."

"Dinner is almost on. Hurry up washing, and we can all eat with the household."

Eana left the waters room, but her last words hit Corrie in the center of her heart. How many meals with the household had there been at the Welling household without her? What were they all thinking and feeling now? She missed all of them. Even Oren, the tosser.

She held her head under the spigot, washing away the tears with the filth and sweat. She would find her way back to the family. And, if nothing else, she would find a way to let them know she was still alive, as soon as she rutting could.

CHAPTER THIRTEEN

F OR THE NEXT FOUR DAYS, Corrie woke up before the sun, as did Eana, Maäenda, and most of the rest of the household, and they went to the plaza together. For each of those days, the wife had returned to the job platform and gestured to Corrie to follow her. She went to their household, took care of the animals and cleaned out the stables, and got paid in coins at the end of the day. The work was hard, and at the end of each day Corrie was feeling every muscle and bone in her body, but she felt some small amount of pride in what she was accomplishing. Saint Veran had challenged her to pay the price he had demanded, and she had risen to it. Doing the work, paying the debt. She wished it wasn't necessary, but there were far worse ways to do it besides caring for some animals.

She actually kind of liked the work.

Eana had gotten work at a fabric mill of some sort, where she was embroidering patterns with, as she described it, an army of young girls with nimble fingers.

"I think the rest of the girls are a bunch of gossips," Eana said as they were settling down after supper. "I mean, I don't know what they're talking about, but it has the sense of gossiping. And I gather most of them are coming from the same place."

"Like, the same neighborhood?" Corrie asked.

"Maybe? Or maybe a dorm for them all? They didn't come from the jobs market like I did."

"You feel safe there, though? The work is fine?"

"I used to make and repair fishing nets for my dad and uncles, so it's kind of like that? I mean, it's hard, hot work, and they're really strict about stopping for water or the latrine. But it's fine. And one of the supervisors speaks a little Trade, so I'm not lost."

"It's good work," Maäenda said, already half asleep on her bedroll. Somewhere downstairs, Srella was still puttering about. Corrie noticed that she didn't tend to come up until everyone else was asleep. "It pays pretty well, but they only want the girls with the small, nimble fingers."

"Which I have," Eana said proudly.

"Just don't let them get crushed in one of the loom shuttles," Maäenda said.

Eana was quiet for a moment. "Well, now that's all I'll think about."

"You'll be rutting fine," Corrie said, nudging the girl with her foot.

Eana reached over and grabbed Corrie's foot, giving it an affectionate squeeze. "We're doing all right, hmm?"

"Yeah. Hey, Maäe," Corrie said.

Maäenda picked her head up and gave her a quizzical eyebrow. "Is that an attempt at endearment by truncating my name?"

"Sure," Corrie said. "I mean, none of you all call me Corrianna."

"I didn't know your proper name was Corrianna," Maäenda said. "What is so pressing it keeps me from dreams?"

"How do we pay rent, pay our debt, all that? Does Srella collect it, does Nally come out here every week, or *mnu*, or whatever?"

"You have a very interesting looseness with people's names," Maäenda said. "It might be a source of trouble for you."

"I'm used to rutting trouble," Corrie said.

Maäenda scowled. "Please do not attempt endearment with my name. It does not sound good to my ear."

"What kind of name is Maäenda, anyway?" Eana asked.

"The one my mother gave me," Maäenda said, with the kind of finality that stated no further questions would be tolerated at this time.

"We all have long days tomorrow," Corrie said, moving to blow out the candle. "So let's—"

A scream from outside the window pierced the night. A woman's scream. Corrie was on her feet in a trice, pulling on boots and her uniform coat.

"What are you—" Maäenda asked.

"Someone needs help," Corrie said.

"You don't know what is happening."

The screaming woman continued, no longer a single cry, but hurried, frantic words. Pleading.

"I don't know what she's saying," Corrie said, coat on. "But I'm guessing it's not 'thank you, sir, continue what you're doing.'"

She bounded out of the room, jumping down each set of narrow stairways to the floor below. She reached the kitchen within a few heartbeats, where Srella was sitting under the washtap as if in prayer.

"What—" Srella started as Corrie charged in.

"Trouble," Corrie said. She glanced around the kitchen and spotted what she wanted—the hard wooden pin that Basichara used to roll dough. Good, solid, not unlike a handstick. Armed with that, she went down, and out the back door of the latrine.

Maäenda was on her heels as Corrie focused her attention toward the source of the screams. Somewhere in the next street over.

"What are you intending?" Maäenda asked as Corrie charged in that direction, through the cramped alley between two houses.

"Saving a life, I hope," Corrie said. She checked her coat pocket. Whistle was there. Good. She took it out and brought it to her lips as she came out of the alley.

A machie woman was being set upon by three men. Swarthy fellows, and big ones at that. Corrie gave a shrill blast of her whistle, and all three men turned their attention on her.

"Leave her alone," Corrie said.

The men all scowled and went back to grabbing the woman, looking like they intended to drag her into a house.

Corrie blew another whistle blast. Out of instinct, it was a backup call, which was pointless. Any backup who knew that call was half a world away.

"Stand and be held!" Corrie shouted. "That woman is not to be further molested."

"Temmi 'ivv dhi, te ayya!" one of the men said.

"He said to shut your mouth," Maäenda said quietly. "We should get inside before—"

"Tell them what I said," Corrie said. "Final warning."

"What?"

"Tell them this is their final warning."

Maäenda said, *"Rayya nu rheh dhah orehllehrh vdoahvall."*

That made the men laugh, and one of them let the poor woman go— the other two held on to her arms—and he came striding over to Corrie, balling his hand in a fist.

Typical rutting idiot. Showing off his punch, probably always relying on his size to intimidate. He thought being strong meant he knew how to fight.

Corrie stepped to the side and drove a kick into his knee, sending him down to the street with a resounding crack. He cried out in pain as Corrie cracked the rolling pin across his back.

"Hurts, don't it?" she asked. She grabbed his arm and twisted it being him, pinning him to the ground with her knee. "Now, are you boys going to let her go?"

They did that, but only to advance on Corrie. She hopped up, keeping one foot on the first fellow's neck. Captain Cinellan would not approve of that sort of force, but she wasn't in Maradaine. She had no backup, unless Maäenda was up for some tussle, and she needed to subdue or discourage these fellows on her own. It wasn't going to end with these boys getting ironed and dragged to the stationhouse.

But the girl had been let go.

"Maäenda," Corrie said quietly. "Get that girl out of here somewhere safe."

"What are you—"

"I've got these boys," she said.

Maäenda reached out to the woman with a few quick words, and like a rabbit she dashed out and took that hand, and they were both down the alley. Corrie flipped the pin into a better grip while bringing up her guard.

One of them reached out to grab her, slow and stupid. These rutting brutes moved like cows. She danced back from his grasp, and took three quick hard jabs at his chest and neck, before whipping the pin into his tenders. He dropped, groaning and gasping.

Papa had taught her that move when she was seven, and it never stopped being useful.

Cracking her neck as she took a few steps away from the third one, she gave him a little smirk. "You think you got anything better?"

On the balls of her feet, she hopped away from his wild punch. These guys were not used to a girl who fought back.

"A reyy 'ivv batbal!"

"I'll show you some batbal," she said back, cracking him across the chin with the pin. That didn't put him down, and he managed a heavy cross into the center of her chest, knocking her off her feet.

She didn't stay on the ground, though. She rolled back and popped back up. This guy came at her again, though his two friends weren't getting up any time soon. So it was just her and him.

Normally, she'd stay in it. She'd make sure a bastard like this one was ironed up and brought in. Not another night free on the street for him. But she didn't have that luxury. Or that authority. She was just a crazy Druth girl with a stick. For now, she had to settle for just getting their victim away. She was safe, and that was what mattered.

All Corrie had to do now was not let these boys follow.

She had one advantage. This fellow looked like he was already getting winded.

"All right," she said. "Let's see what you got."

Then she did one thing she'd never have done as a constable in Maradaine.

She ran away.

The brute came after her, as she expected, and she led him around the block away from the debthouse. She kept running, glancing back to make sure he was following her—he was, as were his two blasted pals, both of them stumbling in their attempt to keep up.

"What, not so rutting easy with a girl who hits back, is it?" she taunted them. She knew they didn't understand, but she didn't blazing care.

Three blocks from the debthouse, it was time to get rid of these boys. As they struggled to keep up, she spotted what she was looking for: one of those way too blazing narrow alleyways between two houses. Full charge, she ran right into one, and it was a blazes of a tight squeeze. She let herself get a bit scraped against the stone as she pushed through, though. Halfway down, she glanced back, and sure enough, those idiots were trying to get to her, but couldn't rutting fit.

She got out the other end into the back garden of that house.

"So long, pissdrinkers!" she shouted as she ran off into the night.

She got back to the debthouse to find everyone awake. They were huddled in the common floor, all around the girl, who was a crying mess.

"Sorry about your doughpin," she said to Basichara as she handed back to her. All the women in the house were staring at Corrie, in what she took to be astonishment. "Is she all right?"

"She is, how do you say—spooked," Srella said. "But unharmed."

"Good," Corrie said. "Does she need an escort home, or does she want to stay here?"

There was a brief exchange with Srella and the girl. "She wants to get home or her father will presume that she had been assaulted and turn her out."

"Lovely," Corrie said. She took the doughpin back. "Guess I'll be needing that."

"I will go with you," Maäenda said. "So you can find her home and your way back."

It was not far to the girl's house, where her family quickly shuffled her inside, and gave odd glares to Corrie and Maäenda. Corrie noted that the house was close enough that they surely had heard her screams. Everyone on the rutting block must have.

"I do not understand," Maäenda said as they made their way back. "Why would you risk yourself to rescue a stranger?"

"Because I'm a blasted constable," Corrie said. "That's what I do. Blazes, it's the work I'd rather do, if I could."

"Very strange," Maäenda said. "But it is commendable."

The next morning she went back to the estate, cared for the animals for half the day, and then the man came outside with no pants on, piss-whistle dangling in the wind. Then his wife screamed at him, and they argued. Then they tore their remaining clothing off and rutted like cats in heat right in front of Corrie. Once that was done, he went back inside, the wife gathered herself, gave Corrie an absurd amount of coins, and sent her to the gate.

At dinner at the debthouse, she told this to Srella and Maäenda. One of the other girls—Ibareska?—started talking to Srella at length, and then Srella nodded.

"She says the same thing happened to her at that house," Srella offered. "And she heard that others have had the same thing. That couple, it is the thing they do."

"That would have been good to know about," Corrie said. "I wouldn't have gone along with that job if I had."

"Apologies," Maäenda said. "I didn't know."

Ibareska offered something else, which Srella translated. "She says, that job is done for you now, they won't come back. Be glad they paid well for it."

"So I need another job?" Corrie asked.

"You need another job."

CHAPTER FOURTEEN

THE OTHER WOMEN IN THE house—at least the ones who didn't speak Trade—gave Corrie a different regard after the night rescue. Corrie didn't have a rutting name for it, because it wasn't quite respect, and it wasn't fear. A mix of both, with a hint of approval.

Except from Hanakhla, the Ch'omik doxy, who clearly found great mirth and amusement in Corrie's presence. She spoke to Corrie with excited animation—though in Ch'omik or some other language that neither Srella or Maäenda knew.

That regard, whatever it was, paid off after a couple days at the job platform. The first new day there, as had been predicted, the woman did not come for Corrie, either to care for her animals or watch her and her husband roll each other. That suited Corrie fine, but she did feel bad for the animals.

No one picked her up that day, or the next, but the third day—she was getting rutting tired of this process, but Maäenda and the other girls seemed accustomed to it, so Corrie would adapt—she was waiting with her slateboard, and one of the other girls came down the platform to stand with her, guiding a new boss along with her. She made several gestures to Corrie.

"The blazes is this?"

Maäenda listened to it all. "There's a job she wants, but the fellow needs two girls, one to be the guard on the door. She's saying you would be very good for the job."

"Guard the door for what?"

Brief exchange. Corrie was growing to hate being so reliant on Maäenda to know what was going on.

"She's got a job for a show of some sort?" Maäenda offered. "I think she's gonna dance for some gentlemen, if you get me. Maybe a bit of—"

"I get it," Corrie said. "So, what, I'm basically her protection detail?"

"I think so," Maäenda responded.

"What's her name?"

"Hezinaz," Maäenda said.

Corrie almost called the girl "Hezi," but remembered Maäenda's admonition about shortening girl's names. "Hezinaz? Corrie," she said, tapping her chest. She hopped off the platform. "Let's go, hmm?"

If nothing else, it was work that sort of came close to being a constable. So that was something.

"So," Corrie said as she walked along with Hezinaz. "You aren't getting a rutting word I'm saying, are you?"

Hezinaz laughed nervously, and gripped Corrie on the arm. She then held up her fists and mimed a fight, and nodded enthusiastically.

Saints help her, if this was really some sort of pit fighting work, she'd kill Maäenda. But even that was work, at least. What was that thing Minox had busted up? Something about a ring for fighting a bear?

Corrie did not want to fight a bear, or whatever the machie equivalent of that was. Not having it.

They reached what Corrie presumed was their destination, what looked not unlike a pub. Didn't smell like one, though. What was that joint in Machie town? Coffeehouse. That was that smell, but more. Richer and smokier. Not unpleasant. As Hezinaz went inside, the man who had hired them gestured for Corrie to stay at the door. He spoke to her, as well as big gestures, which she interpreted as "guard the door, don't let anyone in."

Corrie could do that.

She glanced inside, to see it was full of men, young and old, sitting at cramped tables, drinking coffee and smoking something that smelled quite different from Minox's Fuergan tobacco. Hezinaz was led to a small stage, and a couple of men with instruments joined her up there. After a moment of conferring, they started to play—jaunty and lively, in an unfamiliar way—and Hezinaz started to dance.

Corrie had been braced for the salacious, if not just plain depraved. Saints knew there were several places in Maradaine for men to see that sort of thing if they wished. But that wasn't what the dance was. While it had a certain sensuality, there was an underlying sense of it also being . . . wholesome. The men clapped with the music appreciatively, and they were enjoying the show on its own terms. Corrie found herself enjoying the performance herself. Hezinaz certainly had the skills, the moves. Corrie could never dance like that, certainly not in front of people.

Her attention was so much inside the coffeehouse, she almost didn't notice the five people storming up to her, rage in their faces.

"Whoa," she said, holding up her hands. "Can't get in, folks."

The five of them—three men, two women, all machie, all wearing matching green sashes and headwraps—did not seem the slightest bit deterred by Corrie. The moved to force their way through.

Corrie planted her feet in the doorway and squared her shoulders. The front of the five, at first, just pushed at her, but she didn't budge. But if she had to hold against them if they got more violent than that, she'd have a problem. She didn't see how she could possibly fight all five at once, let alone do that in a way that also kept them from coming in.

"Hey now," Corrie said, pointing a finger at the person who pushed her, praying that an authoritative tone and firm posture could overcome the language barrier. "It's just people enjoying a show. Move along."

"Dhah eh rhuj gheh ip' tu a'all reyy!" the leader shouted. The other four looked at him with deference, even reverence. But they didn't charge at her, not yet. So she was having some effect. That, or they were following procedure.

Blazes. Procedure. Matching sashes and headwraps. Was that the uniform? Were they the machie equivalent of the Constabulary? She had no idea.

"Unless you have a writ or other official documents, I can't let you in," she said. She slowly reached in her pocket for her whistle, the only thing she had on her that could be even close to a weapon. None of them had crossbows or handsticks, but they did each have a knife at their belt. She had no easy way to deal with a knife fight right now, so she didn't want a sudden movement to spook them into drawing.

The leader stepped back, his dark eyes narrowing. *"Bho beghehvah-gri'o reyy. Slah ehv ap zha ip' bho aftu gehreyy."*

"Maybe so," Corrie said, presuming he was throwing out some disparagement of her character. "But I've been hired to hold this door."

One of the other men whispered something to the leader. Corrie noted a look in his eye, like he understood what she was saying. Maybe he did.

"Let's not make this difficult," Corrie said, making eye contact with that one. "Everyone gets to go home with all their teeth."

The music stopped inside, and Corrie dared a quick glance. It looked like the dance was done. Hard to say if it finished as it was supposed to, or if this had been sufficient disruption to stop it.

The leader of the group spat at Corrie's feet, and all of them walked off. Corrie let out a breath. She wasn't sure how she would have handled that if it had come to blows. Not to mention, she wasn't certain if she was on the right side of the law on that. She needed to find out who those folks were, and what, if any, authority they had.

She needed to rutting find out how things worked in this blasted city.

Hezinaz came up behind Corrie, grabbing her shoulder and squeezing with affection. Corrie looked back and Hezinaz winked, held up a bag and shook it. The jingle of many coins.

"We done?" Corrie asked. "Not bad. Sorry those folks ruined things." She gave a gesture to the departing people.

Hezinaz's eyes went dark, and she almost growled. *"Ppeh atud. Sanh p'o lijh."*

"You said it," Corrie said. "Let's get home."

CHAPTER FIFTEEN

I T HAD BEEN WEEKS—OR *mnus* or whatever the rutting blazes they wanted to call it here—and Corrie was livid with herself that she had been so focused on working, on getting her situation settled, that she hadn't thought about the Druth Embassy, or about going there for help. What kind of rutting idiot was she not to even think of these things? It had left her brain until Eana mentioned it.

"So where is this rutting embassy?" she asked. "Where we landed? In that enclave?"

"I've got no idea," Eana said. "One of the others at the shop mentioned that it existed. Shouldn't we check it out?"

"Damn right," Corrie said. "Maybe they can sort out this whole debt sewage and get us home."

"Doubt it," Srella called from down in the latrine.

"Didn't ask you!" Corrie shouted down the steps.

"Maybe you should!" Srella yelled back. "Because I'd tell you that the embassies are all over in Teamaccea, and you will be very challenged to get there."

"Teamaccea?" Corrie asked.

"The mainland district across the bridge," Eana supplied.

"Where we first landed?"

"No, that's Mahacossa. There's seven boroughs—"

"I don't need a rutting geography lesson, girl," Corrie said.

"You do if you want to get there," Srella said, coming up the steps, spade in hand. "Instead of gabbing about this, you could help me clean up down there."

"So tempting," Eana said. "I mean, to shovel up everyone's sewage."

"It's very lucrative on the chore board."

"It needs to be," Eana said. "Especially since I don't know what these girls are eating. But I see what it is doing to them."

"I know what the food in this city does to me," Corrie said. "Not any slight on what you or Basi are cooking. I'm actually fond of it. My insides have a different rutting opinion."

"Hmm," Srella said. "Point is, you need plenty of money to spare to get across the bridge into Teamaccea. Can you afford that?"

"Can we not afford it?" Corrie said. Thinking it over, she leaned in closer to Eana. "But maybe I should go alone first if there's a toll."

"You always want to do that," Eana said. "I am all right here. I am managing."

"And I'll check it out. How do I get there?"

Maäenda came down the stairs. "I'll take you to the bridge," she said with a sigh. "I have a bit of business out there."

Srella's hand went, almost involuntarily, to touch Maäenda's shoulder, and then she pulled back. "Are . . . are you sure?"

"I have been putting that off," Maäenda said. "If you're free, Constable, we can go right now. But bring some spare coin."

Corrie scoffed. Not that she had much to spare. She had gotten paid well for the stable job—such as it was—and the door guarding job, and Eana was getting by all right. They had covered rent and board for this *mnu* and next, and paid Nalaccian enough to stay ahead of the interest. They hadn't given him everything, on Srella's advice. "If you have more, hold on to it for the lean times. There will be lean times."

So what could she spare? She grabbed a few coins that were half-kessirs and a few more that were fekkins, which were like tick coins back home. Hopefully that would do.

As they walked through narrow streets, Corrie felt compelled to say something to Maäenda. "Hey, listen. I wanted to just say, I really rutting appreciate the help you've given Eana and me in all this. It's been . . . I don't know how we would have made it through without you."

Maäenda chuckled drily. "I try to remember what it was like when I was you. And Srella was there for me."

"How long have you been here?"

Maäenda tightened her lips and said nothing. Clearly not a question she wanted to answer.

They approached the bridge—another grand, spanning monstrosity, another marvel of engineering that was far beyond Corrie's ken. This bridge had guards—yellow coats, epaulets, and braiding, long blades at their hip, looking like proper officials—who were checking papers, taking tolls, and opening up the gate at the foot of the bridge for each person to pass. It was not an efficient process, and there was something of a line. Several different lines.

"You want to be over there," Maäenda said, pointing to the end of one line. "When you are done with this, I will be down at those docks over there."

"That could be hours," Corrie said. "First the line, and how do I find the embassy without you—"

"I can't help you with that," she said. She sighed, looking at the bridge and the sprawling salt water between them and the mainland. "I am forbidden to cross the bridge."

"Why?"

Maäenda tapped the massive tattoo on her arm, and then walked off toward the dock.

The line Corrie had been directed to was long, but it seemed to be moving quickly, which was a small comfort. Except, as she got closer to the head of the line, it was clear it moved quickly because most people were barred from crossing and sent away. Efficiency came from the fact that they accepted their rejection with grace.

Corrie wasn't planning on accepting it with grace.

"Hey," she said as she reached the front.

One guard looked at her, then at her arm. *"Rhuf?"*

"What?"

The man sighed, like he was already upset. *"Rhuf. Hill frrosh tu zhi kessir."*

The only word she got there was "kessir."

"Sorry, how much?" she asked.

The first guard looked at his companion, who screwed his face in thought. After a moment, he said haltingly, "Papers. Or ten and six."

"Sixteen?" she asked. "It costs sixteen kessir to cross?"

The one who seemed to know a bit of Trade nodded, and pointed to her arm. "No papers? High debt. High toll."

"That's blazing ridiculous!" she shouted. "I need to get to the Druth Embassy? Over there? Druth?" She tapped on her chest.

The one who spoke Trade just shrugged, and the other one unceremoniously shoved her to the side so the next person could go.

"But—"

"Papers or money!" He shooed her off.

The next person in line was similarly dismissed, and then said something to Corrie that felt like it was some sort of commiseration.

It was clear, short of barreling her way through, there was no crossing this bridge today. She certainly did not have the money to spare sixteen kessir right now. She'd have to figure something else out.

She made her way down to the dock, where Maäenda was arguing with some man, while another one—a very large one who had that same official look as the fellows on the bridge, stood in front of her to prevent her from walking out on the docks. Corrie couldn't make out a word of it, and as she approached, the large man held out an enormous hand to stop her from coming up.

"Everything all right?" she asked.

"Just taking care of the business," Maäenda said. She returned to the language she had been speaking, and this continued for a bit.

"Druth girl," the man on the docks said. "Tell your friend to stop being foolish, she could be free."

Maäenda scoffed and spat at his feet. "If I did that, I will never be free." She stormed off, stopping just before the rickety steps back up to street level to look back, her face full of sorrow, longing. She took in a deep breath and started up the steps. Corrie ran over to her.

"What was—"

Maäenda clutched Corrie's hand and squeezed.

"Corrianna," she said. "Please lead me back to the house and ask nothing of me whatsoever. I cannot be seen weeping in the streets."

Corrie had no idea what had just happened, but did as asked, holding Maäenda's hand as the woman's cracked, leathery skin turned white at the knuckles. Despite that, Maäenda showed no emotion on her face as they went, until they got inside the house. Even then, Maäenda took off her shoes, went up the stairs to the kitchen, and promptly dropped to her knees, wailing like Corrie had never heard.

Srella was there, almost diving to the floor to catch Maäenda before she fell completely, wrapping her in her arms as hot, screaming tears erupted from her.

"Hey, hey," Srella said, followed by something in another language. Not machie, but maybe the same one Maäenda was using on the docks.

"Is she—" Eana asked, coming down from the upper floors. The other girls in the house had all looked in at the commotion.

"*E'hja!*" Srella shouted, waving them off. "She just needs to cry it out. Let me to her."

"Why does she—" Corrie started.

"Let me to her," Srella insisted. "It's not your concern."

"But—"

Maäenda had completely collapsed to the ground, going on in what Corrie presumed was her own language.

"Just be about your own lives," Srella said. "I will tend to her. This is what happens when she goes to the docks. She will be fine in the morning."

Corrie and Eana went up to their room. "What happened?" Eana asked.

"I don't even rutting know. Some guy told her she could be free if she just did something, and she said she'd never be free if she did, and . . . the rest wasn't something I understood."

"Rutting blazes," Eana said. "I bet he wants her to marry him or something, and he'd pay her debt. It's huge."

"Maybe," Corrie said. "And watch your rutting language."

"Watch yours."

"Yeah," Eana said. She sighed. "Speaking of, I am starting to pick up on the local tongue. I'm able to talk a little to the girls I work with."

"That's good," Corrie said. Blazes. That was something she was going to have to work on if she had any hope of paying off these debts. Especially since she shouldn't keep relying on Maäenda.

CHAPTER SIXTEEN

F OR EIGHT DAYS, CORRIE WENT out to the job platform, and
no work came her way. It was more than a little discouraging.
Eana was still working, and Maäenda was claimed most days, as was
Hezinaz. By midmorning, most of the folks on the platform would
leave, but Corrie stuck around as long as she could stand the heat, which
usually became unbearable around midday. She'd return to the house,
and since she was there, she powered through whatever chores Srella
put on the board.

Not that she could read the board. But she'd ask Srella for a task,
and Srella was pleased to give her one. She did all the sewage that she
never did at home. Washed clothes and blood cottons, beat out bedding,
scrubbed floors, and cleaned out the latrine troughs. She peeled nuts and
trimmed roots and ground seeds into spice powder. Her fingers were a
mess of cuts and calluses.

Saints, no wonder why Aunt Zura was always in a rutting mood.

On the eighth day, after the others had all gotten work, she was
about to go back when the Kelliracqui woman from the other day came
right up to her, staring at her close and hard. She was so close, Corrie
could see the woman had one brown eye, while the other was as blue as
the sea. It was more than a little rutting unnerving.

"Phua rhu jash? Maa raruinvour ffaja mou soh, arsakor."

"Yeah, I don't speak Sechiall, lady," Corrie said. "And I told you, I'm no rutting sister to you."

"We are all daughters of Jox and Javer," she said with a heavy accent. "You are lost in this place, but the dead still can find you. I can—"

"Back yourself rutting up," Corrie said. "Or I will wallop you."

"You are not ready. Children rarely are." The woman stepped back and started to walk away. She turned her head back to Corrie and spoke again, and Corrie would have sworn her voice was deeper and accentless. "You'll get it next time, Crasher."

Corrie's heart stopped for a moment, ice chilling her bones. Did she just—no, she must have misheard. She must have—no. Impossible. No.

She wanted to call to the woman, shout at her. Clock that stupid blue eye out of her head. But her throat froze, and the woman had vanished into the crowd.

She must have heard wrong.

She was pulled out of her reverie by a cry in another language—not Imach, not sure what it was—but unmistakable in tone and meaning. A cry for help.

She centered in on where it was coming from—an alley behind one of the coffeehouses in this plaza. She made her way over there at her best pace, pushing back the dark thoughts the Kelliracqui woman had evoked, and put on her constabulary face.

Corrie rounded into the alley, where four machie bruisers were surrounding a skinny dark-skinned boy—chomie, most likely—looking like they were about to stomp his skull into the ground.

"Hey now, what's all this?" she said with as much authority as she had.

The boy looked up and locked eyes with her. "Please!" he said in clean Trade. "Help me."

These bruisers all had a good foot over height and fifty pounds of muscle over her. She couldn't possibly take them all in a brawl, not in this tight space, and not successfully enough to help this kid.

"Oh, it's you," she said, putting on her best authoritative voice. She hoped her tone would translate beyond her words. Maybe a one of these toughs also spoke Trade, so she had to give a bit of show. "You know we've been looking for you." Shoulders high, chin up, she pushed her way through the toughs up to the kid, acting like she completely belonged there.

One of the toughs said something harsh to her, which she ignored as she grabbed the kid—though seeing his face close, it was clear he was more her age or older, but he was so skinny and short, he seemed like a kid—pulling him up to his feet.

"I don't know what your beef is, friend, but this man is wanted for questioning."

"Rhị add rheh?"

The kid looked at her, and his eyes narrowed a bit, and then he turned to the tough, rattling something off.

"You tell him I'm taking you, and if he's got issue, he can take it up with the Druth Embassy."

"Druth?" one of the other toughs asked.

"Yeah," she said, pulling the kid out of the circle of toughs, while he kept talking fast. "But I need him now, so scrat."

Tone and authority seemed to have been enough to stop those boys in their tracks this time, as she dragged the boy out of the alley and led him off like he had been put in irons.

Once they were a block away, he let out a sigh. "Thank you, thank you so much," he said as he fixed the round fur cap on his head.

"Tell me that I didn't just save a thief or some sewage like that," she said. "Or that they were legit officers of some sort."

"No, no," he said. "I had made a mistake thinking they were Osadi when, actually, they were Kutiqari, so I had said something which in Osad Abu is a playful jest, but a more dire insult in Kutiqar, and . . . they did not take it well."

"Well," she said, brushing the dust off his shoulder. "I've probably made a dozen mistakes like that since I landed here."

"Druth," he said with a smile. "Let me guess. Maradaine City. South side?"

"That's right," she said. "You been there?"

"Never," he said. "Oh, I'd love to see it. I love to speak your language!" He offered his hand. "My name is Nas'nyom. I'm a linguistics student at the Mocassan Conservatory."

"Corrie Welling," she said. "Indebted former constable from Maradaine."

"I cannot thank you enough, Corrie Welling," he said. His eyes sparkled a little. "Or, perhaps—you bear the debt marks, you were on the work platform today?"

"Yes," she said.

"And you don't speak the languages here, do you?"

"No," she said sharply.

"Well then, I can thank you enough. You need to learn Imach. I will teach you."

CHAPTER SEVENTEEN

NAS'NYOM WAS NOT CH'OMIK, CORRIE would learn over the next *mnu* of instruction, but Jelidan, which was not something her previous education had properly prepared her for. Before she came here, all she had been taught was that the Jelidan Cities were a stretch of primitive, savage people to the east. She wouldn't have even been able to find it on a map.

At one point in his language instructions, Nas'nyom actually brought a map, showing her where they were in the world, with the Mocassa among other Imach Nations, Ch'omikTaa to the north across the empty desert, and the Jelidan states along the coast to the southern borders of the Kieran Empire and Fuerga. They had gone up to the roof of the debthouse, working each evening on her language until the sun had sunk too low to read anymore.

"Of course, 'Jelidan' is an incorrect name that comes from the old Kieran," Nas'nyom said. "From *jelida*, which meant 'monstrous.' A term that was applied to dozens of different cultures that bear only the most superficial of similarities."

"You hardly seem like a rutting primitive savage," Corrie said.

"Well, I'm from Tekir Sanaa." He pointed to the city marked on his map. "We value learning, spiritual enlightenment. Some of the cultures that fall under the canopy of 'Jelidan'—especially the ones closest to the

Kieran border and the Ch'omik states—are quite aggressive and warlike. And some engage in atrocious practices. But they might say that certain Druth or Imach or Tekiri practices are atrocious. Perspective and understanding is crucial."

"So why would you leave your home to come here?"

"I won the honor," he said. "It is challenging to travel out of Tekir Sanaa, there is only one Fuergan family that will land on our shore and trade with us. There is an intense competition each season to win the honor of passage on the ship to other parts of the world. But I studied, I worked, and was declared worthy. To be here, learning all the great things the conservatory can teach me? All the languages and other secrets it holds? I can't imagine a greater joy than fulfilling that destiny."

"Yeah, well, I was always destined to be a horsebound stick," Corrie said. "Not like the Royal College was coming to my door."

"You sell yourself short, my friend," he said. "You are very bright. Now: *rhj add ad mnuw gheh mizahn?*"

Corrie took each word in: What do do like for eating? No, what do *you* like for eating? She thought through her response.

"Ti' lheh chahrrehf mnuw slah Acseria bhah'h mizahn." I like to eat Acserian pork wraps.

"Sah lheh chahrrehf mnuw slah Acseria bhah'h mizahn," he corrected her. "Remember, it's like 'I' and 'me.'"

"I saw with my eye, *sah* is I, she gave the tea to me, *ti'* is me," she said.

"See, that's very clever," he said. "You should—"

"Who is this?"

Nalaccian came up the stairs, his face as red as it could be with his brown skin. One of the other house girls—Osecca? The one Corrie almost never saw—hovered right behind him, her face accusing.

"Nally, this is—"

"Sergeant," he said sharply. "You are allowed to stay here, under this roof, at a very reasonable rate, because I allow it. I do not expect you to abuse my hospitality."

"What are you—"

"This man!" Nalaccian shouted, pointing an accusing finger at Nas'nyom. "He has no business here."

"I should go," Nas'nyom said, gathering up his things.

"Wait, wait," Corrie said, stepping between him and Nalaccian. "You have a problem with me bringing a man here, or bringing him, specifically?"

"Yes to both. You are not to have guests, especially degenerates like this endarkened beast."

"Whoa!" Corrie said. "Ease it down. He's just teaching me Imach so I can get along in this *fucmilehddi* city and get a decent job so I can pay off this debt to you!"

Nalaccian gasped. "You would teach her language like that?"

Nas'nyom stifled a laugh. "I did not teach her that word, your grace."

"Do you know what that even means, Sergeant?" Nalaccian asked.

"I've got some inkling," Corrie said. "You want us to go to a rutting coffee shop for me to study, I will."

"In the future, yes. Do not bring him here." His rage had cooled, but he still scowled hard at Nas'nyom. "He has no place in this house."

Nas'nyom had gathered his things, and Corrie led him down the flights of stairs to the exit. She couldn't help but notice that as she went down, Hanakhla glared at her, knives from her eyes. Did she have the beef with Nas'nyom? With Jelidans in general? Maybe she and Osecca had squealed to Nalaccian.

At the door, Nas'nyom put his shoes back on. "There is a coffee-house near the campus where we can work undisturbed. Meet me tomorrow there at fifth star."

"I'll have to find campus, but sure," Corrie said. "Don't worry about Nally and his—"

"I am used to it," he said. "Many people in this city hate the foreigners they can look down on. I—" His face lit up. "You need to work, yes? A job to pay off your debt?"

"I really need one," she said. The past *mnu* had given her a bit of grunt-and-shoulder work, but nothing that lasted more than a day.

"I may know of something for you. Oh, why did I not think of that before?"

"What is it?"

"New plan. Meet me at that coffeehouse—it has a sign of three birds over the door—at first star."

"That's when I need to be on the platform to get a job," she said.

"This is to get you a job," he said. He bowed his head to signal his departure. "And one that should last and pay well."

She bowed her head to him in his fashion. "If you think so, I'm rutting game."

"Then to tomorrow."

CHAPTER EIGHTEEN

C ORRIE WASN'T SURE WHAT NAS'NYOM had planned for her, but instinct told her to be prepared. If this was an opportunity for a real job, the sort of job she actually wanted, then she needed to take it seriously. So she washed her uniform, checked it for any stains or tears—no, it was still in good rutting shape, thanks to the bastards on the ship—and pressed it as crisp as she could manage with the things she had on hand at the debthouse. Meija seemed to get what Corrie was doing and came to help.

"*Rh̞arh mna'iyy reyyeh' ayeju 'o gheh l̆ahli.*" Something you— saints above this language had far too many ways to say "you"— for care . . . and burn?

"Right," Corrie said. "I don't want to burn it. *Ge l̆ahli 'o̞.*"

Meija laughed at that, probably because all Corrie managed to say was "No burn want." Which was better conversation than she could have managed with Meija a month ago.

Still, with Meija's help, she got her uniform into good shape, and she looked as crisp as a cadet just being minted to patrol. She felt pretty good as she left with Eana and Maäenda, until Hanakhla started shouting at her from the window.

"What is that about?" Corrie asked.

"Thought you were learning the language," Maäenda said.

"I'm learning Imach. Not whatever she's shouting."

"It's Taanis, one of the Ch'omik dialects," Maäenda said. "And she's probably saying nothing worth knowing."

"How many languages do you speak?" Corrie asked. Nas'nyom, apparently, was fluent in nine, four of them being Jelidan tongues, and had a solid grasp on eight more. Corrie couldn't even imagine such a thing. That kid was smart as anyone she had ever known, but apparently also dumb enough to say insulting things in coffeehouses to big guys.

"Four," Maäenda said. "Mocassan Imach, Fuergan—whatever Srella's version of it is, Druth Trade, and Ocean Keisholm."

"Ocean Keisholm is your native tongue?"

"My mother tongue, I suppose."

"Maäenda, where are you from, anyway?"

"From the sea, of course," she said.

"What?" Eana asked. "Like the River Screamers in fisherman stories?"

"The what? What are you on about, girl?"

"They're magical creatures that live under the water and—"

"*Puösha*, no, girl. I'm a person like you. Live under the water, what nonsense."

Eana continued to ask questions, but they had reached the point where Corrie had to turn off to the west to get to the Mocassan Conservatory of Knowledge. She'd have to learn the secrets of Maäenda's life from the sea another time.

The coffee shop with the three birds was easy enough to find. The part of town around the conservatory wasn't unlike the parts of Aventil near the U of M campus, or the High River neighborhood near RCM. Younger people, a certain vital energy in the streets. Vibrant shops, raised voices.

And there were a wide variety of faces here. It wasn't all machie, but a mix of machs and tyzos and piries and chomies, and she would have sworn a couple Poasians.

But no Druth folks, not that she saw.

The coffeehouse was crowded and tight, and smelled nine different ways she couldn't describe. Voices in a half-dozen languages. She could pick out hints of Imach in it all, catching a word here and there that she understood. Maybe she was starting to get it.

"Corrie!" Nas'nyom called her over to a table. "You take it sweet?" He had mugs of coffee on the table, where someone else was sitting with him—a brown-skinned woman. She didn't look machie or Turjin like Pume, especially with the stone-lined metal studs embedded in her brow. Corrie wasn't sure who she was or where she was from.

"I'll take it however you have it," she said, sitting down.

"This is Hanetlaxa," he said, indicating the woman. "She's a cook."

"Hi," Corrie said, offering her hand. The woman looked confused and just grabbed it like it was a dead fish.

"She doesn't speak Trade," Nas'nyom said. "She's Xonacan."

Corrie nodded, trying to remember the map. Xonaca was a small continent—or was it a large island?—between here and the tyzo continent. She didn't know more than that.

"So, what's the score? You don't want to get me a job as a cook."

"No, no," he said. He said a bit to Hanetlaxa in what Corrie presumed was Xonacan, and then they had a whole exchange for a while. It was a bit rutting awkward to just sit through this conversation, and this lady probably felt the same way when they were talking in Trade. She sipped at her coffee, hot and bitter and sweet, and oddly the one great thing about being here in the Mocassa. Once she got home, she would probably still go to that coffee shop in the Little East. Even if they did act rutting strange about women being in there.

Not here, though.

Maybe that was tied to the Mocassa being a real different place from the rest of Imachan. Nas'nyom had tried to explain it to her, how there were ten different nations here, each with their own customs and laws, and the idea of it being one country was just stupid and rutting wrong.

She was learning that a lot of her ideas about the world were just stupid and rutting wrong.

"Good," Nas'nyom said. "So, Hanetlaxa works for a rich Xonacan family, who live just a few blocks from here. They have a daughter who is a student here at the Mocassan Conservatory, and they want to hire someone to be her bodyguard."

"You think that's a job I can do?" Corrie asked.

"Are you kidding?" Nas'nyom said. "You're perfect. And Hanetlaxa is ready to take you over there. Do you want to try for the job?" He asked something to the woman, who responded quickly. "Ninety kessir a *mnu.* Can you beat that?"

Corrie let out a low whistle. She couldn't. And she couldn't do the math in her head, but she figured at that rate of payment, she could pay off her debts that much faster, and get home that much sooner. She drank down the rest of her coffee.

"Well, let's rutting get over there."

Another extended conversation with Hanetlaxa, and the woman made a noise that sounded like agreement, and they got up and left, following her.

"Listen," Corrie said as they walked a few steps behind the woman. "I don't rutting know any blazing thing about Xonaca. How out of my depth am I here?"

"What do you mean?"

"I mean, for one, I don't speak Xonacan."

"There isn't 'Xonacan,' as much. There is an overarching Xonacan language family, with nine core languages, including Tchoja, the language we were speaking—two of the most common ones you encounter outside of the continent—"

"See, that's one of those rutting things I don't know." Corrie sighed. "You know, Nassy—"

"I recognize you do that out of affection, but that means 'died in one's sleep' in my own language, let alone the dire insult it is in several Imach dialects—"

"Nas'nyom," she said, hitting that damned glottal noise that she never got right hard out of spite. "You chose to come here. You want to learn about . . . all this. I never wanted that. I had a simple life in Maradaine and the rest of the damn—"

She choked hard on the words.

"Corrie," he said. "I will help you through it. They are an educated family, they speak Imach, and I am pretty sure also Trade. At least the daughter does. She's a student of the world."

"I never asked to be a student of the rutting world!" Corrie said. "And now I'm learning how much sewage I had in my head about it."

"About the world?"

She chuckled ruefully. "If I'm being honest—" She looked at him, those rutting earnest eyes of his that pierced right into her heart. "And it's hard to be honest, but I thought Maradaine was the rutting center of the world, and everywhere else was full of primitive pissheads who could manage a boot buckle—"

"Hardly fair."

"Complete rutting idiocy!" Corrie said. "From the Gunjari ship to seeing the city to every person I meet from every part of the world—"

"The Mocassa truly is the crossroads of the world."

"So here's me, Druth idiot, stuck here unless I can get a job from people from a place I ain't never heard of until, frankly, today."

His hand touched her shoulder. Saints, that was the most comforting contact she had had since—

Since she had last been home, the night she was taken.

Something cracked, and there in the middle of the street, tears just fell out of her. She grabbed Nas'nyom and pulled him tight to her, gripping her arms around him.

"All right," he said quietly. He patted her shoulder. "I'm not sure what all is happening, but it's better to happen here and be done when we go inside."

"Sorry," she said, pulling back and pulling the rein hard on those feelings. "I got it together."

"This is the house," he said. He pointed to a large estate house, with a great stone wall surrounding it. Atop the corners of the stone wall were strange statues, the likes of which Corrie had never seen before.

"Once again, tell me about rutting Xonaca."

"What can I say in the moments before we knock?" he said as they came up to the door. "Several invasions and occupations, often the battleground of other people's wars. Deceptively primitive looking since they mostly work with stone and soft metals, but—"

"But?"

"I'm thinking. Eight primary nations, each led by a matriarch, oh, and this family are from a deposed sub-matriarch and are here in exile."

"What?"

That was all he said before they were at the main door of the house

—a mansion, truly—which opened straight away. A large bruiser of a fellow, brown-skinned, with several stones embedded in his face. Rings in the nose and lips.

"Hi there," Corrie said.

He just grunted, and Nas'nyom started speaking rapidly. There were glares and shrugs between the bruiser and Hanetlaxa, and he stepped back to grant them entrance.

The house was astounding, Corrie had to give them that. Intricate pieces of art—wood and stone carvings—filled niches along the walls. Plus there was a giant stone head, a slender wooden statue of a woman, and flowers.

So many flowers.

A woman came into the room—she didn't just enter, she strode with a regal bearing that Corrie hadn't even seen in Druth nobility. And her outfit was a burst of bright yellow and orange, colors of the cloth as fresh and vibrant as the flowers that crowned her hair. It was oddly refreshing to see, since most people in this city wore dirty shades of brown and red. This woman—easily her mother's age, if not older, but still moving with the ease and grace that Corrie couldn't match—walked right up to Corrie with an odd regard in her eye.

And Corrie's attention then went right to the woman's eye, since her eyebrows were laced with golden rings, a chain that connected to each ear, and held a small blue gem just above her nose.

She spoke—the language was music in her mouth—and Nas'nyom and Hanetlaxa both replied to her, head down, eyes to the floor. This exchange went on for some time, and the woman came up to Corrie, lifting her head up with a finger—every finger had a ring on it—under Corrie's chin.

"You . . . Druth?" she asked. This close, Corrie saw her front teeth were also gold, one with a small gem embedded in it, the others with symbols.

"Yes," Corrie said. "You might have a job for me?"

"Soldier?"

"Constable," Corrie corrected. "Does that translate?"

Nas'nyom made some attempt. The woman seemed to take this in.

"Canoc," she said lightly. The bruiser took note and stepped forward. She pointed to Corrie and said casually, *"Wa xôrtsûtchî."*

Canoc moved closer, eyes narrowing like he was about to do something bad.

"She told him to kill you!" Nas'nyom said. A pointless warning, as Canoc slammed his foot into Corrie's chest, knocking her back. It had been a while since anyone had hit her that hard, but she kept on her feet, stepping back and forcing him to close the distance to her. Which he obliged her with. Good. He might be big and strong, but he was, as Pop used to say, all gallop and no rein.

Corrie dropped low, dodging Canoc's mighty fist. She didn't waste time, hammering a kick into his knee. Best way to take down a fellow twice her size. He dropped down when she kicked him, and so she was able to sweep up on top of his back, using the strength in her legs to pull him to the floor. He lashed out when she had him down, but she was able to drive one heel onto one arm while pulling his other arm behind his back, pushing his face into the floor.

"Let's not, Canoc," she said sternly. She looked over to Nas'nyom, who was standing behind Hanetlaxa, his face terrified. "Whatever went wrong just now, can you clear it up?"

The matriarch clapped her hands in excitement. "Is very good," she said in heavily accented Druth Trade. "I am liking. Canoc, *baŋ ju kahka. Notś' t'ô baŋ î wetśuqe.*"

"So, a test?" Corrie asked as she felt Canoc relax under her grip. She stepped off him keeping her guard up. He pulled himself up and gave her a regard of begrudging respect. She nodded back. "You've got a damn good kick, friend." She doubted he understood the words, but she got a sense he understood the compliment.

"Yes, a test," the matriarch said, as she chose her words carefully. "I am wanting someone . . . to . . . *cîsî?*" She looked to Nas'nyom.

"Guard," he said.

"Yes, guard." She shook her head and looked to Nas'nyom. *"Baŋ are a rîke I cho. Châ we mi juc xo baŋ tśe?"*

"Wîô, kêt' cêceŋtśi."

"Ty'ô qu sha'mitch' baŋ. Ji notś' enwê ty'ô qitś tchîn cha'mitch' cê' ty'ô rîtśe weŋ hajne ty'ô riw. the tśîl rîtś'il sharkaw."

"What?" Corrie asked.

"The test was necessary to make sure you could guard her daughter," Nas'nyom said. The matriarch continued to speak, and Nas'nyom started being right on top of interpreting her. "She says that, as long as Tletanaxia approves of you, you have the job. Every class day every *mnu*, here at first star, go with her to campus and classes, stay with her until her return home. One hun—" He looked back to the matriarch in surprise. "One hundred eight kessir per *mnu*."

"Nice," Corrie said. "Happy to do it."

The matriarch continued.

"She—she wants to know if you . . ." He coughed uncomfortably. "If you like to bed girls."

"Never tried it," Corrie said. "Unless sharing a rutting room with my cousins for my whole life counts." His face told her that this was not a moment to joke. "No, no, ma'am. That is not a thing I do." Not that bedding anyone had been much of a priority for her. Save a few enthusiastic fumblings with Moskly in the station bunks when they were both cadets, she hadn't done any bedding. She certainly wasn't in the mood here in the Mocassa.

"Good," Nas'nyom said in translation. "We need a guard who is focused on protecting her, not distracted wanting to—sorry, there is a certain, shall we say, blunt coarseness to Tchoja that I'm not quite sure how to translate into Trade."

"I get it," Corrie said. "I do my job, ma'am. I'm here for that, not the rolling."

"Very good," she said in accented Trade once Nas'nyom had translated. She pointed off in a vague direction. "Tletanaxia there. Go find."

CHAPTER NINETEEN

"THERE" WAS NOT ANYWHERE PARTICULARLY easy to find on the vague point of the matriarch's bejeweled finger, and Hanetlaxa had to lead her through more hallways to a grand floral atrium—a room with a great glass ceiling, just as hot as the infernal sun outside, but heavy with a dampness that made it feel like a rain might break any moment.

It was rutting insufferable.

Sitting on the dirt floor amid the splendor of dozens of flowers, the likes of which Corrie had never seen in her life, was a young woman of dark brown complexion whose entire attention was on the dead creature in front of her. Whatever it was, it had been cut open like one of the bodies on the examinarium tables at the stationhouse.

"What is that?" Corrie asked.

"It's a Tiqari fruit bat," the girl said absently, twirling the sharp instrument she had been cutting with in her fingers. "I'm surprised it was this far south, but it didn't seem to be able to survive here."

"Huh," Corrie said, crouching down next to her. "So why did it die?"

"That is what I'm trying to determine," she said. She looked up from the work, her dark eyes taking in Corrie. "You're Druth."

"So you are observant," Corrie said. She had piercings in her face, like the mother and Canoc, but hers were bone and stone, though at least one tooth had a precious gem embedded in it. "You speak Trade pretty well."

"Even here, the best books on anatomy are Druth," the woman said. "It was necessary to learn it to study those texts. And I'm guessing you don't speak much Mocassan Imach, and certainly not Tchoja."

"I just learned there was a language called Tchoja about an hour ago," Corrie said. "And I'm rutting working on the Imach." The woman looked up at Corrie with puzzled askance. "Ma'am," Corrie added quickly.

"How interesting," she said flatly. She pointed inside the creature's body. "Do you know what that organ is?"

"That its belly?" Corrie asked. "Looks pretty big. Too big, really."

"Very good," she said. "It is distended. I was about to make an incision to check my thesis."

"Go ahead," Corrie said. The woman raised an eyebrow and the corner of her lip turned up.

"Do you want to know my thesis?"

Corrie would probably not know that word if it hadn't been for Minox. He sometimes rutting threw that word around instead of just saying, "what I think." Fancy talk for people at Unis.

Which this girl was.

"As in how you think it died? It's because something went wrong in its belly, right?"

"Essentially," she said. She sliced open the belly, releasing an awful stench in the process. "As I suspected."

"That smells like rotting fruit," Corrie said.

"Precisely. It was rotting because the creature couldn't digest it. So, somehow, it came down here and ate a local fruit that was not part of its normal diet. Which its stomach could not digest! So it starved to death with a full belly!"

"Mystery solved," Corrie said.

"Except for the mystery of why it was here in the first place," she said. She got to her feet, peeling off the leather gloves she had been wearing. Unlike the matriarch, she was dressed in the browns and reds of the locals, including a leather apron over her dress. "You have the dress and bearing of a soldier. Are you who my mother hired to watch over me?"

"Constable," Corrie said. "And yes. If you agree."

"I'm inclined to, especially since you didn't flinch at my work," she said. "Why is a Druth law officer looking for work in the Mocassa?"

"Because I got betrayed, abducted, thrown onto a slave ship coming to this side of the world, escaped, the ship sank, I got picked up by a Gunjari ship that brought me here, claimed I owed them a huge debt, and now my debt is owned by some hairy Imach fellow who yells at me."

"Thrilling," she said with a hint of joy flashing in her eyes. "And does this story have a name with it?"

"Corrie Welling. Sergeant Corrie Welling."

"Tletanaxia," she said. "First Daughter to the *quqô tśînôsho* of the *tśîtśesh* of Taa-shej, third in the court of the—I'm tired already saying it. You can call me Tleta."

"Tleta," Corrie said. "And Corrie is just fine for me."

PART TWO:

DAUGHTERS OF THE WORLD

CHAPTER TWENTY

THE CAMPUS OF THE MOCASSAN Conservatory of Knowledge—or "Napah Imtau zh'ehv Mocassa" as it said on the arch—was the first place Corrie had seen in this city which had anything resembling breathing room. There were open walkways between the buildings, with spiky bushes lining them, and no one was crowding anyone else as they went from space to space.

There also was not, at this time, any obvious threat to Tleta as they walked through it.

"So if I may ask—"

"Ask questions freely, Corrie," Tleta said. "It is how one learns."

"Not that I'm complaining, but why does your mother want you to have a personal guard?" Corrie was still in her full Constabulary uniform with coat and badge, which she felt helped her look formal and official while walking with Tleta—it certainly got her looks—and Canoc had given her a club that was close enough to a standard hand-stick that it fit in her belt loop. She almost felt like herself for a moment.

"I did explain who I am, didn't I?" Tleta asked.

"First daughter of something, and Nas'nyom—"

"He's the one who brought you? Interesting."

"You know him?"

"I had a few classes with him, when I was learning Druth Trade. I would not think you would be a suitable lover for him."

"Not lover," Corrie said firmly. "I saved his pork one time, and he's been teaching me local Imach, that's all." She wanted to change the subject. "He said you were nobles in exile or something?"

"Not entirely wrong," Tleta said. They reached one building, and Tleta indicated they were entering. "My mother should be the ruling matriarch of Taa-shej, a region in Tchoja, but her half-cousin forced a claim by rite of spear, and my mother chose to abdicate her claim and accept exile in the Mocassa in exchange for maintaining holdings and income worthy of her station."

"So there was a palace coup?"

"This is not a word I learned in my studies."

"You said your mom's cousin overthrew her? That's what we call that. It happened to Druth kings *all the time* from what I remember."

"More nuance, but roughly," Tleta said. "Now the half-cousin is dead and her daughter, Nlâtoca, is the *quqô tsînôsho*. Where the problem lies."

"Nlâtoca is the problem?" Pieces clicked. "Let me rutting guess. Your mother abdicated, but you didn't, so Nlat thinks you might want to come back?"

"There is a fear that she might try to take me back to Taa-shej, where she can force my abdication of claim, and ransom me to my mother for her sources of fortune."

"All right," Corrie said, taking this in. She glanced around the hall they were entering. Plenty of students, most of them apparently Imach. Did she really have the eye to tell Imach from Xonacan? Tleta had piercing and gem work in her face. The house guard had them, too, as well as the cook. Were those easy to remove to be disguised? Corrie had no idea. Still, no one was looking at Tleta in a way that made Corrie consider them a threat. "Where are we going?"

"Upper hall," Tleta said, pointing to the stairs. "The Mocassan Conservatory has integrated teaching, in as much as it is allowed under High Divine Law."

That was a new term. First time she had heard anything about law outside of the restrictions put on debtholders. Something to find out more about later. "Which means what?"

"For all the classes, men and women must stand in different parts of the hall. For these lectures, the men are on the lower floor, and the women in the balcony. This is why my mother needed to find a woman to be my guard, so you can go to all the spaces I do."

Following Tleta up the stairs, Corrie asked, "So, is that what High Divine Law does?"

"An aspect," Tleta said. "Very strange, if you ask me, but even in a great institution such as this, they are subject to the prescriptions of their faith."

Was that why Nalaccian threw a shoe over Nas'nyom being in the house? Was it some violation of religious law? Was religious law what held over this city? Maäenda had talked about head coverings for the faithful, and how fermented beverages were forbidden. But she hadn't seen—

Those bastards with the green sashes. They had a bit of official air to them, the only one in something resembling a uniform besides the guards on the bridge. Was that religious? Were they mad about Hezinaz dancing because it was a violation of this High Divine Law?

"Corrie?" Tleta asked. "Are you well?"

"Yes, sorry," Corrie said, realizing she had stopped dead in the middle of the stairs. "I'm just—there's a lot about this city I still need to learn."

"Learning is why we are in the world," Tleta said. "And I'm going to be late for this lecture."

"Yes, of course," Corrie said, continuing to the top.

The upper balcony was crowded with women, most of whom were dressed in the traditional style Corrie had seen out in the streets: long dresses and head scarves, in muted browns and tans. It was so packed, there was nowhere to move once they came out. Corrie could barely see past the sea of brown robes, and given that Tleta was a bit on the short side, she probably could not see anything at all.

"Is this good for you?" Corrie asked.

"It will do," Tleta said. "I am expected to stand in the back here."

"Why?"

"Because I'm a foreigner."

Corrie heard a gong ring, and then an authoritative voice started speaking in Imach. Corrie picked out a word here and there, which pleased her. It was about the first time she found herself understanding Imach outside of Nas'nyom or her housemates. Everyone on the street spoke like a galloping horse. Corrie leaned against the support column as the lecture went on. She didn't understand much beyond a few words, and had no idea what the lecture was covering, so there was nothing to do but let it drone in the background and keep an eye out for potential kidnappers.

Since that was apparently a thing.

Or maybe it was just a precaution.

Corrie would do as good a job as she could, regardless. At this pay rate, if her sums were right—and they probably weren't, she was terrible at that—she could be clear of the debt in thirty *mnus* or so. What was that, nine months? And she'd be clear enough sooner to cross the bridge into Mahacossa, reach the Druth Embassy, get some help there, hopefully.

Don't forget about Eana. You need to get her home.

Maybe she should put some of this money into Eana's debt.

Keep your eye ahead, head clear, she thought. She hadn't even had a full day of work, not paid yet, so she shouldn't start dreaming of how she would spend it.

But maybe dream of home a little.

Corrie noticed the lecturer using a phrase over and over: *'ac lŏh bheh 'u.* "As you all can see." Corrie knew she wasn't seeing anything down there. She listened more carefully. She missed a lot, but words like *gha*—"look"—and *zahrr osahz gheh*—"give your attention"—stood out.

"Is he demonstrating something down there?" Corrie asked in a whisper.

"I'm trying to listen," Tleta said.

"But are you supposed to see as well?"

"Ideally, but—"

All Corrie needed to hear. She tapped the young woman in front of Tleta and used one of the first phrases Nas'nyom had taught her, one of her favorites that didn't involve profanity: *"Javv, bhos ah',"*

Pardon, step aside. One of the most useful phrases for a constable. The machie woman looked at her, confused. Corrie gave her the best I'm-the Authority-here face she had, and the girl stepped back. *"Bhos ah'.'ñu ahdu 'ugh. Bhos ah',"*

With that, she made a hole that she and Tleta could move through to the front of the balcony, and see the instructor with a human body cut open, pointing out parts inside. Also the men on the floor below had plenty of space to stand apart and all see well.

"That wasn't necessary," Tleta said, though her broad smile showed off another etched tooth Corrie hadn't seen yet.

"You need to see this," Corrie whispered. Though she had no idea what Tleta was studying. Hopefully it was to be a doctor or examinarian or something. For all Corrie knew this was a murder class. Would the machies have a murder class at their university? She had no idea.

"Thank you," Tleta said, and then her attention was fully on the lecture. Corrie's attention went to the other students around them, who were also intent on the lecture, but had a few side glances that said they might also want to hurt her and Tleta. Corrie returned with an expression that told them it would be a bad idea.

She did have a salary to earn, after all.

CHAPTER TWENTY-ONE

"A FOOL I WAS," TLETA said as they left a second class for the day. "I've been missing half the point of these classes."

"Glad to help," Corrie said.

"Though, you told that one woman that I was an *aip 'wirrir*, which I don't think is accurate."

"It means 'princess,' right?"

"I think it has very specific meaning here, which would not apply to me. Let's try to avoid miscommunication where you are translating Druth concepts into Imach and applying them to Xonacan culture."

Corrie nodded, taking the admonishment. "I just wanted to impress upon them you were important."

"I think you did, in that you implied I was blessed with divinity." She laughed a trilling laugh. "I just don't want my fellow students thinking I am claiming to be a prophet of their God or something. Or that I claim any special treatment due to station."

"You have a bodyguard," Corrie pointed out.

"Which is already a bit too . . . what's the word I want? Conspiracy?"

"Conspicuous?" Corrie offered.

"Yes. We are both conspicuous here, no?"

"It's kind of the look I'm going for here," Corrie said, indicating her uniform. "The point of the uniform is to stand out."

Tleta went to a bench in the walkway and sat down, kicking off her sandals and rubbing her feet. "You have a lot of pride in your place in Druth society, don't you?"

"My family is all Constabulary, so, yeah."

"You're following the calling of your family?" Tleta asked. "And this brings you happiness?"

"It's what I've wanted," Corrie said.

"I wish I had that certainty," Tleta said. "I think studying medicine is bringing me happiness. But it is the opposite of the calling of family."

"So let me understand," Corrie said. "Your mother abdicated, you haven't. But if you just want to be a doctor, why not abdicate your own claim?"

"It would be irresponsible," Tleta said. "At least until I have my own daughter."

"That makes no rutting sense." Blazes, she slipped and swore in front of Tleta. She had been trying not to do that. Tleta's face showed that she didn't quite understand what Corrie said, though.

"I was already born when my mother abdicated. So I had the right to my own will, to the claim I was born into. If I were to abdicate now, without having mothered a daughter, any child I have after that would have no choice. I would not want to do that to her."

There were elements of that logic that came from something Corrie didn't understand at all. She chalked that up to just being how things were in Xonaca. *Everything is different in the rest of the world.*

"But you don't want it."

"I don't think I do," Tleta said. "But I sometimes think I ought to want it."

"What, like, storm back into Tchoja and claim your throne?"

"I lost something in there," Tleta said. "Your language seems to have nuance that I did not grasp in my studies. I would do something with weather to sit?"

Corrie laughed at that, and then caught herself. She didn't want Tleta to think she was mocking her. She needed this job. She forced herself to think about how Minox would ask the question. Talk like he would.

"I meant, you would consider asserting your claim?" Corrie asked.

"I don't know. Is it a duty I owe the people? Do I have a . . . for lack of better word . . . divine imperative to the *rînôsho*?"

"Well," Corrie said. "My salary for helping an insurrection or fighting a divine war is *much* higher."

"Noted," Tleta said with a chuckle. "The rest of the day I spend at the library, and then we'll return home. You can stay for dinner or return to your own home."

Corrie was very touched by the offer, but then a sour thought hit. "It —sorry, never mind."

"What?" Tleta asked.

"I'm sorry," Corrie said. "I'm stuck in this rutting debt situation—" she paused, not sure if she should share anything too personal here, as well as curb her instinct to swear every other word. But something about Tleta made Corrie want to drop her guard, even if she was her employer. "I got in this mess due to presuming generosity where it didn't exist. So when someone offers, say, dinner, I'm now thinking there's a hidden price."

"None," Tleta said. "It is our custom to welcome people with our bounty, for food is life, and . . . I don't need to bore you." She hopped off the bench and slipped on her sandals. "Walk and tell me your story."

They went to the library—which was a grand building the size of the Druth Parliament—and Corrie told the whole tale of how she ended up in the Mocassa. On the inside, Corrie had never seen anything of the sort. Rows upon rows of shelves loaded with books, and as they went upstairs two flights, even more books. "The greatest collection of knowledge on the entire world, they say," Tleta said. "Larger than the Universitat Imperia in Oroba in the Kieran Empire, or the Wik-lap-sun in Rek Nayim in Tsoulja. Maybe the Former Imperial Archives in Lyrana, but there's contention on that."

"There's libraries in Maradaine's schools," Corrie said a little defensively.

"Like this?"

"I have no idea," Corrie said. But she honestly couldn't imagine any library anywhere having the scope and scale as this rutting place.

Tleta selected a few books and sat down at a table. "Go on."

"But you're studying."

"I can read and listen to you at the same time. My head works better that way. And I'm as curious as the dead about it."

"All right," Corrie said, and continued, now getting to the point where she was fighting the bastards in the ship's hold, and going on.

"A Gunjari ship?" Tleta asked when Corrie reached that point. "No wonder you were tricked."

"Are they known for that?"

"They're part of Lyrana, which is terrible—" Corrie nodded, remembering those Lyranan tyzos had nearly killed her and Tricky. "But they're, like, the worst part of Lyrana. Because they're officious and precise and meticulous, but they were part of the Turjin empire as well, so they're also complete sewage lickers who don't care who they hurt, if it gets them what they want. Worst of both places."

Sewage lickers was a new one. And that put Corrie at ease about profanity in front of her.

"So you don't like them?"

"You don't know the history of Xonaca, do you?"

"I really don't."

"The short version is nearly every other part of the world around here, mostly the Tyzanian Empire, which became Lyrana and Rekyashom, but also the Turjins, the Fuergans, the Ch'omiks, the Imachs, all of them? They kept sticking their *tsiceli* into Xonaca, the womb of the world."

Tleta held her thumb and forefinger just a couple inches apart, to make it clear what *tsiceli* was in her native language. She laughed heartily, and Corrie joined in.

"Ssst!"

They both looked to seem some tyzo lady—the kind with bright, wild hair, Tsouljan?—scowl at them.

"We are being disruptive," Tleta said in a lower voice.

"Sorry," Corrie said, stifling her laughter.

"I'll tell you more over dinner," Tleta said.

Corrie smiled and nodded, but in the pit of her gut she suddenly became very worried over the idea of what Xonacans ate. Local Mocassan cuisine was already playing enough mess on her insides.

CHAPTER TWENTY-TWO

THEY LEFT THE LIBRARY SHORTLY before sunset, and as they left it was impossible to ignore the crowd engaged in a spirited argument on the library steps. Noting that some of the people involved, as well as half the crowd watching, had knives at their belts, Corrie intentionally guided Tleta away from that.

"It's just a philosophical discussion," Tleta said. "People here will just raise their voices when they do that. It is a passionate place."

"Passionate is rutting fine," Corrie said. "It's when that escalates to them pulling out knives that I get worried."

"Knives?"

"Half of them were carrying openly," Corrie said. "I've seen that plenty here—same in Maradaine, of course—but that doesn't mean we shouldn't have care."

"Huh," Tleta said as they walked through the campus gates. "I hadn't even noticed."

They returned to Tleta's house, and again Tleta offered to Corrie to join them for dinner. "It is offered freely. You are a new addition to who we are, and it is customary."

"I won't disrupt what's customary, then," Corrie said.

Tleta brought her to a dining hall, with a low but grand table made of intricately carved dark wood. Not unlike the eating table at the debthouse, this table only came up to the top of Corrie's shin. The table was decorated ornately with colorful woven mats and floral displays. Tleta's mother sat at the head, with another Xonacan woman about the same age at her right hand, and three young men sat at the far end.

Tleta had some exchanges with her mother, and then said, "You've of course met my mother, Yalititca, *wêcêrîc webet* of Taa-shej."

"Lady Yalititca," Corrie said, bowing her head. She didn't know anything about the proper manners of Xonaca, but she'd put on the best Druth ones she knew how to do.

"And her dear friend Marichua, who has been her strength in this time of exile."

"Ma'am," Corrie said.

Tleta gave a dismissive wave to the three men. "And my mother's current *mitsîrîke*, Potec, Dachec, and—" She struggled with it for a moment. *"ka tś'il baŋ e'?"*

"Machpît," he said with a hurt tone.

"Machpît," she said.

"Mitsîrîke?" Corrie asked.

"How to translate? Lesser husbands? Her harem. I don't care about them. Sit."

Corrie sat on a mat next to Tleta. "Is that . . . typical? And none of them are your pop?"

"My . . . is that a way of saying father?"

"Right."

"He was a true *cêrîke*." Her voice trembled just a little when she said that. "But he stayed in Taa-shej, obliged to serve my mother's cousin when she took power."

There was a lot going on here that went straight through Corrie's ears, but she put together enough to understand that Tleta's pop wasn't part of the scene, and she was not happy about that.

Further conversation on that subject was stopped by the arrival of servants carrying ceramic bowls. One was placed in front of Corrie, filled with a creamy green soup. Corrie took a moment to observe her hosts to see if any prayer or other ritual was demanded before starting to eat. But none of them were, and they were all looking to her.

"Is it on me as the guest to start first?" she asked.

Tleta nodded. "Of course. You are the one being treated here."

Corrie took up the spoon—a large one carved from wood—and sipped the soup. It was surprising; sweet and cool and spicy all at once. Not what she would think it would be, but she had no idea what she was expecting. "Very nice," she said.

They all started eating as well.

"Would that not be the polite thing in Maradaine?" Tleta asked.

"The polite thing in my family house is supposed to be wait for everyone to sit down," Corrie said, "but that actually never happens. So the true polite thing is to wait until my mother and Aunt Zura sit down."

"Honored matriarchs," Tleta said with understanding.

"Not exactly," Corrie said. "But they're the ones who mostly did all the work in the kitchen, so when they sit, it means the meal is actually served."

The men at the far end ate quietly, but Tleta's mother and Marichua spoke animatedly, and then asked Tleta something, to which Tleta responded, and then a bit of back and forth. Corrie kept eating her soup while they did, unable to figure out the flavors behind it. Like nothing she had ever eaten.

Tleta leaned in. "They want to know why it never happens, that everyone in the family sits down."

"Oh," Corrie said, putting down her spoon. She didn't know how much Trade these women spoke, and heard her mother's voice telling her to keep a civil tongue. She bit back her instinct to pepper her sentences with profanity. "Most of the people in my family are work-ing, and we often work different shifts, different times. And, for exam-ple, my brother Minox, he would stay at work very late. So there isn't a time we could all sit together. I used to work the ru—that is, the night shift, so I was always at work when most of the family had dinner."

Tleta translated that to them, and then Marichua said, with heavy accent. "Is that here? Your family?"

"No, that's in Maradaine," Corrie said, raising her voice a bit too much. She realized she had almost finished her soup, and remembered the recurring argument Zura and Mama would have over what was an insult. "Tleta, is it rude if I do finish my soup, or if I don't?"

Tleta looked very confused. "I don't understand. Do you not want to finish it?"

"It's excellent, it's just—so, my mama is Racquin, Kelliracqui, and my Aunt Zura is Acserian. They constantly row over this when a guest is at dinner. According to Mama, if a guest doesn't eat everything offered, that's an insult to whoever cooked the food, the food itself, the work behind buying it."

"I understand, yes. Though we would not take insult in that."

"But, see, for Zura? If you don't leave a bite or two, then you're insulting the hosts that they didn't not give you enough food. So, imagine, you do one thing in Kellirac, that's a mortal insult. You do the opposite in Acseria, that's a mortal insult. I have no idea what the rules are, well, either here in the Mocassa, or with you all."

Tleta nodded. "Like you not knowing to eat first," she said. "Eat what you want, as much or as little, there is no insult."

Corrie finished her soup, as did everyone else at the table, just as another plate was brought to her. This one, she just did not understand. It seemed to be a large vegetable, but not one she was familiar with, that was hollowed out and filled with red things that were chopped up and mixed together, then covered with a white sauce of some sort.

"Tell me about this," she said.

"It is very traditional in Tchoja," Tleta said. "It is called *nos îhas notchîm*, I don't know what to translate that to. The *nos* is stuffed with a mix of *xônê* flowers, fruits, and nuts, and then the *notchîm* is made from other nuts."

"Never eaten flowers before," Corrie said. She picked up the utensil offered, with seemed to have qualities of knife and fork, cut through a piece and put it in her mouth.

It was the best thing she had ever eaten, and in the back of her mind she immediately apologized to her mother and Aunt Zura for even thinking that.

"Is good?" Yalititca asked.

"Very good, thank you," Corrie said, taking another bite. Everyone else started in as well.

After a few bites in silence, Marichua asked, "So, no family here. Where live now?"

"I live in a debthouse near the plaza," Corrie said. "With ten other women in a similar situation."

"Can I explain your circumstances of debt?" Tleta asked. "I want to reassure them that you are not at fault."

"Sure," Corrie said. She ate while Tleta told her story with much animation, which captured the attention of the whole table. She wasn't even finished when the three men were openly weeping.

"Great tragedy," Yalititca said. "We . . . very glad we can help."

"Very sad," Marichua said. "Like story of Maäenda."

That got Corrie's attention. "You know Maäenda?"

Tleta took the answer. "We've heard the story. It's a tragedy of a pure, noble soul, bearing an impossible burden. All over the city, hearts shatter at the story of Maäenda of the Keisholmi."

"Maäenda," Corrie said, again, a bit in shock. "And this isn't a common name in the city?"

"Keisholmi names are hardly common here," Tleta said. Not that Corrie even knew who or what the Keisholmi were. "And none would dare take her name."

"I'm just—Maäenda lives in the debthouse with me. We sleep in the same room, and I never—"

Tleta got very excited, rattled off a lot of words to the rest of the table, who all also got very excited. She then turned back to Corrie. "You actually know her?"

"So you all have heard of her?" Corrie asked.

"She is a living legend, Corrie," Tleta said. "You don't know that?"

"Not at all," Corrie said. "But I would love to hear all about it."

CHAPTER TWENTY-THREE

MAÄENDA WAS ALONE IN THE kitchen when Corrie got home, scowling a bit on her arrival.

"It's very late. Not exactly safe to be walking around out there."

"I was working," Corrie said. "Scored a very good job. But I didn't mean to make you worry, *Admiral*."

Maäenda looked up sharply at that. "Pardon?"

"I'm sorry," Corrie said. "Is it *admiral* or *queen*, because there was some questionable translation at play."

Maäenda almost jumped from the kitchen, grabbed Corrie by the arm and dragged her into the waters room.

"What do you know?"

"Besides the fact that you have a rutting ship?" Corrie said, wrenching herself out of Maäenda's grip. "And you could, apparently, sell it to clear everything on your arm."

"It isn't that simple," Maäenda said.

"That's what that bastard on the dock was saying, wasn't he? Sell your ship, and you'd be free."

"No," Maäenda said, her dark face turning red, tears forming at the corners of her blue eyes. "Do you have any idea, *any*, what that ship is to me? Could you sell the very heart out of your chest?"

"Then tell me," Corrie said. "I spent the night listening to Xonacan women wax on about how brave and heroic you were, putting up your title as collateral so you could take on that debt—"

"Save my people," Maäenda said. "Do you have any idea who the Keisholmi are?"

"No, because you are a rutting mousetrap about who you are," Corrie said. She snapped her fingers tight in Maäenda's face. "I sleep right next to you, and—"

"That does not make us anything," Maäenda said. "I had pity for you in your situation, as we are in the same trap." She held up her heavily marked arm. "But as much as I owe on this, Sergeant, what I owe you is nothing at all."

"Sewage!" Corrie shouted, which got Maäenda's hand over her mouth. Corrie was about to knock her in the head in reply, as Maäenda shoved her against the wall.

"What do you want me to say?"

Corrie shook her head free from Maäenda hand. "I want to hear it from you. They said your crew had been enslaved, and you took on that debt to free them all, but they haven't come back for you. Rather they left you alone with one ship for when you were free."

Maäenda sunk to the floor. Quietly, she said. "Queen is probably a better word that admiral. Or what's the word? What do you call you lower nobles?"

"Like a countess? Marchioness?"

"Perhaps there is no word," Maäenda said. She sighed. "I was an *iktetro* to waterborne Keisholmi, commanding five ships in my mother's fleet."

"Five ships?"

"Before I came here I had never spent more than three days in a row on dry land. But I accepted this burden, this curse, to have the means to free the people under my command. I wasn't . . . it wasn't supposed to come to this. Either my family has abandoned me, or they have met worse ends."

Corrie sat on the damp floor with her. "I imagine my family is *still* turning Maradaine upside down to find out what happened to me. If yours isn't tearing the oceans apart for you, they aren't worthy of you."

Maäenda nodded. "I believe they would. My brother was to take the money we borrowed, go to Mahabassiana and purchase our crew out of bondage, then go to our family holdings in Tekyamir, petition the sea clans for what he needed to come back and free me. A thousand things could have gone wrong."

"And if you sell your ship? That would take care of that debt?"

"If I sell the *Chiishwi*, then I have surrendered everything. Already that crew under my care were captured, enslaved, it is incredibly shameful. I would rather be bound to this island, this debt never paid, then to be at liberty but unable to taste the ocean on the deck of what is mine."

"That . . ." Corrie said quietly, not sure how to take all that. "That's a rutting lot to take in."

"Only Srella knows of this, Sergeant. Please maintain that trust."

"Maybe in this house, but my new employers know about you, and I get the impression you are a legend in some circles."

"The wealthy of Jachaillasa love to tell the story to each other. They imagine what they might do in my place, and pray they will never come to it." She gave Corrie a punch to the arm that Corrie interpreted as being affectionate. "You have a new employer. Is it a good one?"

"I think so?" Corrie said. "It's being a bodyguard to a Xonacan girl who's at the conservatory. Which is at least decent rutting work."

"You think it will last?"

"I rutting hope so," Corrie said.

The next few days went as hoped, with Corrie getting up before sunrise, getting to the Xonacan household in time to escort Tleta to the campus, and staying with her through her routine. There was some variation to that routine, such as the day Tleta went to something resembling a bathhouse to sit naked in a steam-filled room with other women, and then rinse in a cold pool. Corrie wasn't sure of the expected protocol for that. She opted to look over the steam room and take position outside the door where she could act immediately if anything happened. At least one other woman came with a debt-bolted servant who did the same, so that seemed the right choice.

There were also the days where Tleta worked in the vivisection lab, examining the anatomies of a host of different animals. Corrie was reminded of the examinarium at the stationhouse, and the studying her cousin Davis had gone through to become an examinarian assistant. The rows he had had with Uncle Timmothen over that one, because he wasn't becoming a "proper" constable.

Tleta had suggested to Corrie that when she worked in the library, Nas'nyom could come and resume Corrie's language lessons. "No need to tell mother, and it's good for me to work my Trade and Mocassan Imach to listen to you learn."

After one *mnu*, she was paid as promised, and with that covered her rent, made a decent payment to her debt, kept some in saving for the next *mnu*, and dared to use seven kessir to cross the bridge to Mahacossa on her free day. Fortunately, that bridge was cheaper for her than the one in to Teamaccea. This time, she was allowed to cross, and then took nearly an hour to cross the sea bridge on foot, and then find her way to the Druth enclave.

Corrie wasn't allowed to get even close to it. Guards—these looked quite official in their uniforms—made sure she could not cross a certain point, with no singular bit of negotiation. It was forbidden for someone with a debt bolt and markings to even get in sight of the enclave gates. She had prepared for this—Maäenda had warned her—so she had a letter written. She begged for a local woman, paying her a half-kessir for the trouble, to deliver the letter to the enclave, in the hope that someone there would post it back to Maradaine.

She wasn't sure if it actually would work, and it was an expensive gamble. Crossing back to Jachaillasa only cost her two kessir, thankfully, but the whole affair had cost far too much to try again this way. If she was going to send a message home, she needed a better way.

Fortunately, Tleta made it clear she was very pleased with Corrie as her bodyguard, and wanted to continue the arrangement for as long as Corrie was willing.

CHAPTER TWENTY-FOUR

T HREE *MNU* INTO THE ROUTINE with Tleta, and Corrie was
starting to get a hold of how her schedule worked, as well as the
Imach calendar as a whole. Months were not a thing here, but seasons
were, with ten *mnu* per season, and each day of the *mnu* had a name. Of
course, each day—*pe'mi, pe'yhi, pe'ru*—just meant "day one," "day
two," "day three." Learning the language took away the confusion, but
also the allure of mystery.

They were currently in Hafialtar, the "Season of Death." Corrie had
thought that meant it was winter—had she been gone that long already?
—but that didn't seem right. She had lost count, but she thought it might
still be Alasim back home. Maybe it was already Nalithan. Neither Tleta
or Nas'nyom knew enough about the Druth calendar to give her an
answer.

Not that it mattered. It would still be many, many *mnu* until she was
even free to head home, let alone get there.

The day was 597 Pe'rhef zha ghos u Hafialtar, in other words, the
ninth day of the fifth *mnu* of the Season of Death, in the year 597. Corrie
had no rutting idea why it was the year 597 here in Imachan, and that
wasn't a question she was remotely interested in asking. What mattered
was it was *pe'rehf*, so that meant the morning was spent in the vivisection lab, followed by a steam session, then lunch in the topiary outside

the library—Hanetlaxa personally delivered the meal, laying out blankets for Tleta to lie on, and cleaning it all up when Tleta was done—an afternoon class on ethics of medicine, and then studying in the library until around dusk. Tleta clearly liked routine, and stuck to it.

Corrie had noticed that Tleta never spoke to anyone, except Corrie and Nas'nyom, outside of an academic context. She would engage in the classes, she would discuss points with her fellow students, but it was clear after these few *mnu*s that while Tleta had peers, she didn't have friends.

Maybe that's your real job, she thought to herself that morning as Tleta was dressing after her steam. There had yet to be a single incident where Corrie had had to actually intervene as a bodyguard, or that anyone had even seemed a threat to Tleta's safety. At least, not a threat that specifically targeted her.

Most days there had been people gathered in the plaza outside the library, often in heated conversation, even demonstrations, but over the past *mnu* it had taken a specific form that gave Corrie pause. What had been one person up on a step making arguments had become a growing group standing shoulder to shoulder. And they all wore green sashes, with knives at their belts.

This afternoon, there were nine of them, one of them shouting all sorts of things—a lot of words Corrie wasn't getting, but what she did get were words like "horror" and "wrath" and "condemn." Today, that all seemed to be aimed at a Tsouljan woman—Corrie presumed she was a woman, as much as could tell with the loose robe and high-braided yellow hair—who was trying to talk back in a calm tone. That wasn't going anywhere, especially when the nine spoke in unison.

"Let's go around all this," Corrie said, guiding Tleta toward the topiary.

"Why are there so many of them?" Tleta asked.

"Who are they?" Corrie asked. "I had run into some trouble with those green sashes on another job. Are they some sort of militia?"

"I don't know that word," Tleta said. "They've been showing up in this part of the city over the past season or so. Some kind of religious movement—oh, no."

Corrie followed Tleta's gaze back to the library, where the nine green-sashed folks had come down from the steps and were circling around the Tsouljan woman, who had fallen to her knees. Their shouts had changed to red-faced jeers, and more than a few of those rutting bastards were spitting on her.

Every instinct in Corrie's heart was to run into that, but she glanced back to Tleta first.

"I have to—"

"Help her," Tleta urged.

That was all Corrie needed. She charged over, pulling out her whistle and giving it a sharp blast.

"All of you back off!" she shouted—or she was reasonably confident she that was what she shouted in Imach—as she moved in to break through that circle of folks. She kept one hand on the club in her belt, not sure what she would do if she was forced to use it. Blazes, she had no idea if the law was even on her side in this. But there was no one else even looking like a figure of authority here. "You leave her alone."

As she came up to the circle, just the brush of her shoulder against one of them was enough to make them all react. They jumped back like she had been a hot iron, scattering away from the woman. One of them sneered at Corrie and said something about daring to defile them.

"I will do a lot rutting more than defile," she said in Trade, half-drawing the club. She switched to her rough Imach, saying, "You will not bother this woman."

"She speaks like she *fhehrrehgh* the *'alĭ-shehrruzat*," the leader said. A few words in there that Corrie couldn't figure out. "She is *buehmm*."

"She is a member of the conservatory and will not be disrespected!" This came from Tleta, who had come close enough to engage. A pair from the group stepped forward to join the leader, like they were ready to brawl.

"The bunch of you, disperse," Corrie said in Imach in her firmest tone of authority. "Or I will have to disperse you."

"Ťhu eh ehf reyy?" one of the others asked the leader. Is she a . . . whatever *"ehf"* was. He put up a hand to them, as if to silence them.

"The great Hajan will hear of this," he said in Trade. "Remember." With a signal from him, the whole group marched off.

Corrie relaxed her grip on the club and turned to the Tsouljan girl, taking a kerchief out of her pocket. "Are you all right?" she asked in Imach as she handed it to her.

The girl, still on her knees, took it and wiped the spit off her face. "Unhurt," she said in Trade. "Thank you."

"But are you all right?" Tleta asked.

The woman's dark eyes found Tleta, and an uncomfortable, long moment passed between until she said, "No, I do not think so." Her tone, in as much as Corrie could get a sense of it, was that of someone forcing herself to not cry. Like the other Tsouljans Corrie had met—which had only been a few in the Little East—she didn't show emotions on her face in any way Corrie could read. For Corrie, the quaver in her voice was the only clue that she was on the verge of breaking.

"Stay with us," Tleta said. "Unless you need to get somewhere, and we will get you there."

"That is very kind," the woman said. "I should go home to sleep, but I do not think I can right now."

"Are you hungry?" Tleta asked. "Come with us."

The woman took Tleta's hand, and gave her other one to Corrie—she was trembling, likely with both fear and rage—and got to her feet. They led her to the topiary park, where Hanetlaxa was already setting up their lunch.

"We have a guest today," Tleta said. "I hope that isn't a problem."

Hanetlaxa's face told a whole rutting story that Tleta did not seem to notice, but she went to work putting together a third portion.

The Tsouljan girl looked to Corrie. "So are you a mage?"

"No," Corrie said with a laugh. "How did that—is that what *'ehf'* means?"

"Not exactly," Tleta said. "It's, like, magic to be feared."

"Those types fear everything," the Tsouljan said.

"Why did they even think that?" Corrie asked.

"You told them to become clouds or you would turn them into clouds," the Tsouljan said.

Corrie laughed again. "My Imach is still so rutting bad."

"It is getting better," Tleta said.

"Both of you speak much better Trade," Corrie said as Hanetlaxa handed them plates. Corrie had no idea what this food was—sort of like a pastry, stuffed with something that was sort of like cheese—but like everything else she had eaten from Hanetlaxa's kitchen, it was utterly rutting delicious. "Which is downright embarrassing since we are on the other side of the world from Maradaine."

"You are from Maradaine?" the Tsouljan asked. "I have always been curious to go."

"Corrie was a peace officer in Maradaine," Tleta said.

"Corrie is your name?"

"Corrie Welling," Corrie said. "I'm a constable. Or was before I ended up here."

"Tletanaxia," Tleta said. "I will not impose my longer titles on you, you can call me Tleta."

"Ang Rek-Nouq," she said before taking a bite of the food. She made a squeal of delight that shattered the Tsouljan reserve. "*Teng ne riq*, what a delight!"

"I'm glad you like it," Tleta said.

"And I'm very glad you offered," Ang said with a tiny smile. "Thank you for all that you've done."

Corrie shrugged. "It's what any decent person would do."

"And yet," Ang said as she continued to eat, "it was only you two."

CHAPTER TWENTY-FIVE

LUNCH WITH ANG BECAME A regular appointment, as that was when their schedules would intersect. Corrie had wondered why Ang had been planning on going home to sleep in the middle of the day, but the answer was rutting obvious: she was studying astronomy. She would spend her night up in the high observation tower of the library, looking through the lensescope at the moons and stars. It was, according to Ang, the largest, most advanced lensescope in the eastern world, which is why she had come to the Mocassa.

"It was a great honor to be selected," Ang told them at their shared lunch one day. "I love the work, all that I have observed and discovered, though the toll on my mind has been great. I can never sleep as well as I would like. But when I publish my findings, it will be worth it."

"I don't know much about that," Corrie had said. "But I know how working nights can rut your head up."

"I'm so tired all the time," Ang said. "Great blessings for Mocassan coffee."

"I'm with you on that."

"But I'm very fortunate to get to be here now, of all times," Ang said. "Many things are happening in the sky. The *Rekfonwik* put a great trust in me."

"It's rutting amazing," Corrie said. She had, over the course of the lunches, dropped all attempts to curb the more colorful aspects of her speech. "A few months ago, I had barely heard of this blazing city, and for so many people on this side of the world, it's the destination of choice."

"What happened to you is an atrocity," Ang said with compassion. "But I must confess I am glad that it brought you to the Mocassa so we could meet."

Corrie blushed a little—she had to admit, something about the golden tone of Ang's skin, the warmth of smile, her odd beauty, it all made her pulse quicken in ways she couldn't explain. The wild, dandelion-yellow hair in intricate braids was also fascinating. "I would have preferred it without the kidnapping and debt slavery, though."

"Absolutely," Tleta said. "I'll have you know, I am trying to convince my mother to resolve that issue."

"What?" Corrie asked.

"She is being obstinate, though. But I hate that you are here under duress. I want at least one of us to be able to go home."

Corrie felt that blush creep up again. "I don't know what to rutting say to that." She sighed. "Even still, even if I was clear myself, I couldn't leave until Eana was as well."

"Eana is the girl you were rescued with?" Ang asked.

Tleta frowned. "And mother will not hire anyone else. I'm sorry, I would if I controlled the funds."

"You don't have to blazing apologize to me," Corrie said. "You're already doing so much. And Eana has a steady job, she's working, and I'm putting some into her debt as well."

"Corrie, you need to clear your own—"

"I made that girl a promise," Corrie said. "Not to mention to a saint."

"This is about your superstition," Ang said with a dismissive note.

"Let me tell you, I was never a church-going girl," Corrie said. "But on that ship, in that storm, I prayed to Saint Veran that I would pay what it took to get out of there and survive." She held up her arm. "I'm not going to pretend I didn't survive, but at a cost."

"But do you think this saint did that?" Ang asked. "It seems a bit . . . I don't want to say illogical, but . . ."

"Listen," Corrie said. "This world is filled with some strange sewage. Tell me you haven't seen that. I've seen your people do some wild mystical I don't even know."

"Our mysticism is rooted in that which can be questioned and examined," Ang said. "And I am not some mewling *fel* who delves in that. I believe what I can observe."

"I observed a whole ship get shattered by lightning and two people survived," Corrie said. "Maybe there is no God, maybe the saints are not interceding for us, but that is not on me to say one way or the other."

"Those people on the library steps," Tleta said. "They were angry with you about some religious matter." They had not talked about those events since, and the green-sashed bastards had been absent in the two *mnus* that had passed, at least on campus. Corrie had noted them in the streets when she walked to Tleta's home, in the square, near the debthouse. She wasn't sure if there were really more of them, or if she was just noticing them more.

"Who the rutting blazes are they?"

Ang made an expression Corrie couldn't figure out. "They're some sort of fringe part of the local religion, and their leader is very upset about the astronomical work we do here."

"Why would that bother them?"

"I don't know. They called it an atrocity, and when I shot back at them, they . . . well, you saw."

"Corrie scared them off, though," Tleta said with a wide, gemtoothed smile.

As strange as it seemed, here on the other side of the world, in the worst of circumstance, Corrie had found two women, so very not like her in any way, that she could call friends. A small bit of joy in this nightmare, which made it just a bit more bearable.

The next morning, Eana was coughing up blood.

CHAPTER TWENTY-SIX

"I T'S FINE," EANA SAID THROUGH coughs. She struggled to get to her feet. "I'll be fine."

Srella was already stepping up, putting a hand against the girl's forehead. "She is filled with fever."

Basichara, who slept on the other side of the house, stuck her head into their chamber. "Fever?"

"You know one word of Trade, and it's 'fever'?" Corrie asked her.

Basichara continued, now in Imach. *"Dheh ghor ahdugh gheh e'hur. Frahn shre chochegig rh̯ahrigh. U imehshehff lehr reyy."* Corrie got most of that. A disease in the city, in the workhouses.

"What, like a plague?" Corrie asked. "Is the city doing anything?"

"What would they do?" Srella asked.

"We need to get her to a doctor, yes?" Corrie asked.

"No, no," Eana said. "I need to get to work."

"Sewage," Corrie said. "You can barely stand."

"They fire girls if they don't come in," Eana said. "Even if they're sick."

"Doctor," Corrie said, keeping in the back of her head how many times she had been Eana in this conversation, and Mama or Aunt Beliah had been the one insisting she stay in bed. "Is there one we can bring her to? Or bring here?"

"None in this part of town," Srella said. "None who would look at a girl with a debt bolt on her ear, not without a letter from the debtholder. Nor would they come in this home without Nalaccian's permission—"

"His permission?" Corrie asked. "It's that a rutting rule in this place?"

"I just need to work," Eana said.

"Stay in that rutting bed or I will iron you to it," Corrie said.

"Dheh ppeh sdua rin ftu," Basichara offered. *She'll lose the job.*

"She'll lose it if she dies of fever," Corrie told her in her best Imach. "Let alone if she keeps coughing up blood."

Basi shrugged and went downstairs.

"You need to work, no?" Srella asked. "I'll look after her."

"Where does Nalaccian live?" Corrie asked.

"What?"

"Where does he live?" Corrie repeated. "I have no idea, he comes here for rent and payments."

"I . . . I don't . . ."

Srella wasn't going to be any damned help. Corrie when down a floor and went right into the room Hanakhla slept in. Hanakhla was sitting on the floor half naked, rubbing oil into her skin.

"Hey," Corrie said, and switched to Imach. "Where does Nalaccian live?"

"What saying you?" Hanakhla asked.

"Nalaccian. You went to him to—" she had no idea how to say "squeal" in Imach, which is what she wanted. "Complain about Nas'nyom."

"Care I have not Jelidan boar you about babble with," Hanakhla said. Saints, Hanakhla's Imach was as bad as Corrie's, if not worse. She had everything in the wrong order.

"Eana is sick," Corrie said. "I need to talk to Nalaccian."

Hanakhla scowled. "Girl sick?" in Trade.

"Girl sick," Corrie said back. "Doctor," she added in Imach.

Hanakhla took Corrie's hand and led her down to the main floor and out into the street without bothering with shoes. Corrie grabbed her boots as the went out the door and did her best to get them on her feet as they went around a few corners, across the plaza, and into the part of town where the depraved couple who were mean to their animals lived.

Hanakhla pounded on one door, shouting her own language. After a few moments of that, Nalaccian stuck his head out of a window. He shouted something to Hanakhla, who then pointed to Corrie.

"Why are you at my door, Sergeant?"

"Eana is sick, she needs a doctor."

"Then take her to one, if you feel you must," he said. "It is not my urgency."

"Apparently they won't treat her without you allowing it. Just like I can't cross any bridges."

He sighed. "They do keep changing these things."

"Can we—"

"Sergeant, I will have to meet with my solicitor to draw up the papers. In the meantime, I will not complain about any doctor you can get to come to the house." He went back inside.

Hanakhla spat on the ground. "Pay it for he should. Doctor his own."

"Rutting blazes," Corrie muttered. Switching to Imach. "If I went to one, I'd have to pay out of my own wages?"

"Or girl's. Not first to die of high blood. Not in house that. Not in room that."

"Do you—" Corrie was getting flustered, unable to think of the right word in Imach. Saints, she needed Nas'nyom for this. And she needed to get to Tleta—

Tleta.

"I have an idea," she said. "I'll be back at the house soon."

She had ran off, down the road and two blocks away before she realized she had said that in Trade, and surely Hanakhla didn't understand a word of it.

Corrie couldn't waste time dwelling on that. She ran through the streets, weaving past the carts and wagons and going over and under things with ease. When she reached Tleta's estate, she was kind of astounded how much she was adjusted to the rhythm of the Mocassan streets, that she was running through them like she used to in Maradaine when she was a page.

"Corrie," Tleta said as she came out of the house. "Your breathing is quite labored."

"I ran," Corrie said in between heavy breaths.

"Why would you do that?"

"Eana is sick, and—"

"Say no more," Tleta said. "I'll get my bag."

Corrie felt a whole weight come off her heart as Tleta went back inside, emerging a few minutes later with a leather bag, walking at a tight clip.

"Tell me what you know," Tleta said.

"She's got a fever, and she's coughing up blood."

"Tchîmo ty'ô nush," Tleta muttered, and Corrie hadn't learned what that meant, but did know it was one of the more vile things to say in her native tongue. "You said she's been working. Do you know where?"

"Someplace where they have a lot of girls embroidering things?"

"And how many women live in your home?"

"Eleven with me and her."

"Celi ba ty'ô kotś'," was her response. She stopped walking and grabbed Corrie by the shoulders. In the middle of the street, she put a hand to Corrie's head. "And you? Fever?"

"No," Corrie said.

Tleta's fingers prodded Corrie in a few places, some a little too personal. "Sore? Tender?"

"Just rutting annoying," Corrie said.

"Still, you share a sleeping space with her?"

"Yeah," Corrie said. "And two others."

"Disease can live in you for many days, live in your breath, well before you feel sick."

"If you say so," Corrie said. She had no rutting idea about that. "What can we—"

Tleta was already in her bag, taking out a strip of cloth that she wrapped around her mouth and nose. She gave another to Corrie. "It might not make a difference, but if you do have a disease in you, this could keep you from sharing it."

Corrie wrapped it around her face. "How can you tell?"

"I don't even know for sure, yet. Let's get there quickly."

They reached the debthouse, and for a moment Corrie was afraid that Tleta would balk at entering such a place, but she went right in, took off her sandals, and went right up.

"Where is the patient?" Tleta asked in Imach as they came up to the *ghose'a*.

"Who is this?" Srella asked. She and Basi were both working in the kitchen, and Pume was filling buckets with water.

"A doctor," Corrie told her.

"A student of medicine," Tleta stressed. "Where is she, and who has been in close contact?"

"Top floor," Srella said. "And Corrie and I, and Basi saw her. And Maäenda."

Tleta had a moment of pause. "The rest of the household should isolate themselves from those who have had contact. Until I know more. Is Maäenda here?"

"She . . ." Srella's voice trembled. "She went to the job market with most of the rest of the girls. Is . . . could she be sick?"

"I don't know enough," Tleta said. "But someone should get her and tell her to come back here."

"I'll go," Srella said, moving to the stairs. Tleta got in front of her, taking out another strip of fabric.

"Cover your face, just in case," Tleta said.

"In case of what?"

Handing her yet another, Tleta said, "And tell Maäenda to do the same. Do not argue with me."

Srella looked to Corrie. "You trust her?"

"On this, blazes yes."

Srella took the fabric strips and went downstairs.

"Keep with that water, get it to a boil," Tleta ordered. "Corrie, stay down here with that one. I will go up."

Corrie let Tleta go upstairs, and paced around the *ghose'a* for a while. Pume and Basichara exchanged a few words, which was a strange blend of Imach and Pume's language, so Corrie didn't quite follow, but Pume put the full buckets near them and otherwise kept her distance.

"Be still," Basi offered.

"I can't," Corrie said, her hands almost shaking. "I need . . . I need to do something."

Basi took Corrie by the hand and led her over to the kitchen. She put a bowl of some vegetables in front of her and handed her a knife.

"Chop. Thin slice. Do that."

Corrie normally would rutting object to that—she fought Mama and Aunt Zura every blazing time they expected her to work in the kitchen with them. But at this moment, doing anything other than pacing about was perfect. She got to work cutting, let herself get lost in the mindlessness of the task.

Srella and Maäenda returned, Maäenda looking more than a little put out.

"I am supposedly sick?" she asked.

"We don't know," Corrie said. "But it's better to be safe."

"Only because I did not get any work today," she said. "Else I would not stand for this."

Tleta came down the stairs, her mask off.

"I have relative confidence in this not being a disease to be spread," she said. "I have examined her as well as I can, checked her body, looked at her blood with lenses, and that is my guess."

"So what is it?" Maäenda asked.

Tleta saw her, and bowed her head. "Begging your grace, *ikt—*"

"No," Maäenda said firmly. "None of that."

"Of course," Tleta said. "Based on other factors on her body, especially the discoloration of her fingers, I suspect her sickness is caused by something in her work. The dye on the fabric, likely."

"So she's, what, poisoned?" Corrie asked.

"I believe, in essence," Tleta said.

"Many girls who work that place get sick," Basichara said. "Why they always need new girls."

"What can we do about that?" Corrie asked. "What's the law here?"

"Law?" Srella asked.

"How do we get that place shut down? They need to be stopped."

Maäenda chuckled and spoke in Trade. "I forget you have such lofty ideals, Sergeant. That the law would protect people like us." Corrie hadn't even realized how much of the conversation had been in Imach.

"It's supposed to."

"It doesn't," Maäenda said. "The only law here keeps us in this place. In our place."

Tleta stepped between them. "I have made her comfortable, and given her some medicines to bolster her strength, quench the fires of the fever. Little more I can do. But I think she could recover, if she stays clear of that place.."

"Could?" Corrie asked.

"I would not lie to you, Corrie," Tleta said. "I will not give you dishonest hope on this."

"We appreciate that, *mûwkêt'*," Srella said.

Hanakhla came up the steps with Nalaccian in tow. Neither looked happy.

"What is going on?" he asked. "Is the girl sick? What have you done?"

"Had a doctor care for her," Corrie said.

"This woman, she is doctor?" he asked, pointing a finger at Tleta.

"This woman is the one who treated the girl in your charge," Tleta said. "You need to care better for these things."

"Speak not to me in that manner," he said, his bony finger pointing at her. "I am very fair to these girls."

"I have little confidence in that," she said.

"Who are you to speak to me thus?" he asked. "I will not stand for it."

"It's fine, Tleta," Corrie said.

That name got his attention, and he took a step back. "I apologize."

"Not to me," Tleta said. "Pay instead the courtesy to those who owe you."

"You're here," Corrie said. "I imagine you need rent for me and Eana." She dug into her pocket and handed him coins. "That should cover. Now do you have my letter?"

"It is not possible," he said. "There are rules—"

"I told you," Maäenda said. "Who the law protects, and who it stomps."

"Why not?" Corrie asked. The shipping enclave may have already failed, but if she could get to the embassy, it could change everything for her. "It's on you, you know?"

"Not without a bond," he said. "I do not make these rules."

"A bond?" Corrie asked.

"A backer to your debt," Srella offered. "Who promises to take on your debt should you run away." She squeezed Maäenda's arm, who reflexively pulled away, silent. The honeycomb lines on her arm already told the whole story.

"If the girl is fine, I will go," Nalaccian said. "The rest of the rent is due—"

"The House Yalitizia, *tśîtśesh* of Taa-shej will bond Corrie Welling," Tleta said. "Give her liberty to all seven boroughs."

Nalaccian stared at her in disbelief, and then nodded his head. "She will have passage papers by sunrise tomorrow." He handed Corrie back the coins, adding in a quiet voice that sounded full of shame. "Rent is not due until tomorrow."

He left down the stairs. Hanakhla stalked upstairs, and Pume—who Corrie had barely noticed was still sitting unobtrusively in the corner of the *ghose'a*—scurried up after her.

"Thank you for Eana," Maäenda said to Tleta. "Your kindness is noted."

"Yours is legendary," Tleta returned. Maäenda made a dismissive scoff and went up. Basichara and Srella went back to working in the kitchen.

"You . . . you didn't have to do that," Corrie said.

"No, but why wouldn't I?" Tleta asked. "It's only a risk if you run from the city. I trust you not to do that."

"But the rutting—"

"Corrie," Tleta said gently. "We should get to campus and class now. You do have a job to do."

CHAPTER TWENTY-SEVEN

OVER THE COURSE OF SEVERAL DAYS, EANA'S FEVER went up and down, and she couldn't possibly go to work. Not that Corrie would let her, and she made damned sure that Srella and Maäenda had her back on that. Tleta gave her tisanes and tinctures to help Eana recover, but said, "the key thing is that she rest, gain strength, and stay out of wherever she was working."

Nalaccian came the first morning to collect rent and debt payment for the *mnu*, and Corrie paid for herself and Eana. Nalaccian did keep his word, and presented Corrie with liberty papers, granting her passage over any bridge into any borough of the city.

"This is only for you, Sergeant," he said. "And you are clear of the consequences of the bond?"

"My debt goes onto Tleta if I skip off," she said. "I ain't going to do that, and you rutting well know that."

"My knowledge is not infinite," he said. "There are many mysteries of the human heart to which I am not privy. I will not presume to know what you will and will not do."

"Sure," she said. "Tell yourself that."

He shrugged. "I hope that is useful to you. But I do not think you will get the relief you seek."

It was another few days before Corrie could make use of her letters, and in that time Eana's fever spiked again. She didn't argue staying in bed now, and Srella was taking care of her, bringing her food and water, and emptying out the buckets of sewage. A damned perfect nursemaid.

"Let me cover your rent, at least," Corrie told Srella as she got ready to leave for the bridge. "You're doing so much . . ."

"I keep the house going," Srella said. "What kind of person would I be if I let her starve and sit in her own filth?"

"You're kind of a terrible Fuergan," Maäenda joked from the kitchen. "I thought your people believed in profit."

"If I were a good Fuergan, by their standards, I would not be here with debt on my arm," Srella said with a scoff. "I am happy to be the person I am."

Maäenda gave her the barest hint of a smile. "I'm happy about that too." The two of them both looked like Nyla every time she came home with some suitor and sat in the parlor with him. It was obvious there what Nyla wanted her fellow to do, and it was just as blazing obvious with these two.

"Saints, rutting kiss already," Corrie said as she drank down the last of her coffee. Both Maäenda and Srella sputtered some confused sounds —Corrie couldn't swear if it was language or not—as Corrie bounded off down the stairs to leave. Let them stew on that for a while.

Corrie made her way to the bridge to Teamaccea, realizing that she was definitely getting her feel for the layout of the city, knew how to make her way around. Moreover, now that she knew how to read Imach, she could use the street signs. That made a huge rutting difference.

She got in line at the bridge, and waited in the same line as before. Again, it was a long line that went quickly, which surprised Corrie. Why did so many people come to the bridge, attempting to cross, but expecting to be turned away? What was going on there?

Unresolved mystery for now, as Minox liked to call it.

She got up to the guards.

"Letters or fee?" they asked in Imach.

She presented her letter, which they gave a small amount of scrutiny to. After a moment, the guard waved her through.

The walk across the bridge was a long slog, which she had expected, but for that walk she was treated to the spectacular view of crossing a wide swath of water—ocean, really. It was truly incredible, and she wondered how the blazes the Imachs had built something like this. It was far more impressive, and just rutting bigger, than the Great Maradaine Bridge. She remembered Papa telling her about how that was built, what went into it, the massive labor of engineering and resources. "The pinnacle of achievement right there, Crasher," he would say.

He would tell her so many things back then. She wondered what the blazes he could say to her now, were he able. Would he tell her she was rutting everything up, or be proud of how much she had done? She had no blazing idea.

She wiped her face, not sure if it was sea spray or tears.

It was late morning by the time she reached the other side of the bridge, and Teamaccea was like a whole other city. Not just in being yet another grand, astounding metropolis, but it looked totally different. Here, the architecture gleamed. No sense of dull sandstone or brown here. Buildings rose in high towers that looked like pearl and glass had been spun together. Here, the colors were brighter, in the clothes, the shops, the people.

And here, something very different caught her eye as she crossed through the entry plaza: constables.

Or at least, folks who were clearly the local equal. There were several folks in matching uniforms of yellow wraps and ochre belts, and blades at their hips. But more to the point: she knew their bearing. The way they walked, the way their eyes moved about, taking in everything. It went beyond words or culture, it was a universal language that she knew all too well.

So why were there constables in Teamaccea but not in Jachaillasa?

Another unresolved.

But for now, she went up to one.

"Pardon?" she asked in her best Imach. "I understand the Druth Embassy is near here. Could you tell me where it is?"

He looked at her with an initial jab of harshness, like how dare she interrupt him, but once he took her in with his eyes, his expression softened.

"It is down four blocks that way. On Street Shcholl."

"Thanks," she said, giving him a salute.

He mimicked the gesture and smiled back.

A universal language, indeed.

She followed the direction to Street Shcholl—everything here was very well labeled—to the gate of a building that looked almost exactly like one of those fancy houses in East Maradaine.

Saints above, it was so beautiful to see that.

She went up to the gate and pulled the bell cord as hard as she could.

After a moment, a fellow in Druth Army uniform came out of the house to the gate.

"Can I help you?" he asked in Imach.

"Yeah, I need to come in," Corrie said in Trade. "Talk to the ambassador or someone."

His eyebrow went up. "Oh, you're Druth. Sorry."

"Born and raised in Maradaine," she said. "Can I come in?"

He looked at her, confusion crossing his face. "Hold on, let me find out." He went back inside.

That seemed odd.

She waited at the gate for more than a few minutes, starting to pace back and forth with impatience. Some rutting nutter came up to her, asking in Imach about visiting Maradaine, if it was as interesting a city as they had heard. She tried to answer politely, and then the fellow started asking about the best brothels in Maradaine. She then used some of the choice Imach invectives she had learned in the past few months and chased him off.

She felt pretty damned good about that, and then looked back to the embassy, to see some bloke in a fancy suit looking aghast.

"This is the girl?" he asked the soldier as they approached the gate.

"Yes, sir," the soldier offered.

"Sergeant Corrianna Welling, of the Maradaine Constabulary," Corrie offered. Time to get as formal as possible.

"You are a constable, hmm?" the official asked. "Not just some costume you put together?"

"No, sir. Sergeant at Inemar Stationhouse, in the Grand Inspection Unit under Captain Brace Cinellan."

"Very well, yes," he said. "But what does that have to do with me here?"

"Are you the ambassador?" she asked.

"I'm the attaché to the ambassador. He's far too busy to come to the gate for . . . petitioners."

"Listen," Corrie said. "I've got a real situation here, and I need your help—"

"You certainly do," he said. He reached through the bars of the gate, and his hand brushed on her ear, and the went down to her arm, lifting it up so he could inspect the tattoo. "Yes, indeed, quite a situation."

"Which is why I need your help—"

"Listen, young lady," he said sharply. "We can't be helping any random person who comes wandering up to our gates."

"Are you rutting kidding me?" she asked, the words coming out her mouth before she could catch them. "I'm not—"

"Whatever misfortune you put yourself in, young lady, is likely tied to your own misdeeds . . ."

"Misdeeds?" she asked, her voice going up an octave. "I was blazing kidnapped—"

"But kept your uniform the whole time," he said derisively. "Quite a tale."

"How do you—I can't believe—" she sputtered. "I'm a citizen of Druthal!"

"I'm sorry, my dear," he said in a tone that made clear he was anything but. "But as long as you have those on your arm and ear? You're not."

With a dismissive wave, he turned away and went inside. The soldier had the decency to look appalled, silently mouth an apology and go in himself.

Corrie rang the bell a few more times, and shouted herself hoarse. Eventually the soldier came back out.

"I'm real sorry, miss," he said. "They're telling me I need to expel you with force if you don't leave quietly. Please don't make me do that."

"Listen," she said, pulling the letter she had already written out of her pocket. "If nothing else, can you all send this back to Maradaine? My family doesn't even know I'm alive." She held it through the bars of the gate.

The soldier hesitated, and then took it. "I'll see if I can get it in the next pouch." He glanced at it. "Keller Cove girl, huh?"

"All my life," she said.

"Shaleton, myself," he said. He glanced about. "Listen, you got to be off, they're watching. But, are you safe? Are they making you do anything, you know, unseemly?"

"I'm rutting fine, along those lines," she said. "But I want to go home."

He nodded. "All right, I'll do what I can. Be off now."

"Thank you, um—"

"Penkins, miss."

"Penkins. You're a credit to your uniform."

She went off before she put him in a tough spot. No need to make trouble for the one bloke who was being decent.

She had made it only a block back toward the bridge when a hand grabbed her on the upper arm. She grabbed it by the wrist, was about to throw the hand's owner to the ground when he spun her about to face him.

Young Druth man, dressed like a gentleman. Like the sort who ran money houses or law offices.

"Can I rutting help you?" she asked.

"As a matter of fact, Sergeant Corrianna Welling of the Maradaine Constabulary," he said with a voice as smooth as Mama's gravy. "You most certainly can. And that could put me in a position to subsequently help you. So let's sit over there and have a coffee, hmm?"

CHAPTER TWENTY-EIGHT

CORRIE HAD NO IDEA WHAT to make of this blasted fellow, but she kept her eyes on his hands as he brought over mugs of coffee and sat down.

"I appreciate your time, Sergeant," he said.

"Then don't rutting waste it," she said. "What the blazes do you want?"

"I also appreciate you've made no attempt to curb your profane tongue," he said. "I know that means you're not putting on a front for me."

"Who the blazes are you?"

He sipped at his coffee. "Moriel. Lieutenant Moriel, of Druth Intelligence."

"You're a spy?"

"Spy implies that my role is . . . clandestine. And while I do interface with folks here in east who do have that role, mine is far less romantic."

"Which is?" she asked.

"My desk here is about information. Coordinating it. Many bits of information—what people want, what people need—come across my desk."

"What does this rutting have to do with me?" Corrie asked. "Can any of this blather get me back to Maradaine?"

"Maybe it can, Sergeant," he said. He spread his hands like he was already apologizing. "I have very limited authority and funds to work with, but the ambassador does listen to me. If I have cause, I can get him interested in something."

"Something like?"

"Petitioning your debt release," he said. "It would be something he might do for a friend of Druthal."

This was spreading some thick butter, and Corrie didn't trust it one damned bit. "Would you get to the rutting point, Moriel?"

"What is fascinating is, before you arrived at our gate today, it had been my plan to establish contact with you. So you saved me some time."

She stood up. "I'm done with this sewage."

"All right, all right," Moriel said. "Sit down, I'll tell you."

Corrie didn't want to, but if there was any chance this could help her get home, get Eana home, even a little sooner, she should hear it out. She sat down and sipped the bitter coffee.

"I've had a lot of odd directives from home in the past few months," he said. "I'll be honest, I don't know the wheres and whys of it all. But I have instructions."

"And they involve me?" Corrie asked. "Do they know I'm alive? Does my family—"

"It's not about you, Sergeant," he said bluntly. "I'm sorry, but no. I have been asked, however, to place an operative in the Mocassan Conservatory, in the hope of getting information that the Central Office deems valuable."

"Right," Corrie said. That made sense. What had Tleta said about the library? Largest collection on the continent? There was probably a ton of things in there Druth Intelligence wanted to know. Not to mention the place was filled with people from all over the world, so of course a spy would be interested. "And that's how you know about me? One of your folks spotted me with Tleta?"

"Your role as bodyguard to Miss Tletanaxia did get our attention.

But my orders are for something specific. Namely, my superiors are interested in astronomical and astrological information."

"Astro—" Corrie started. It clicked. "You mean Ang."

He nodded. "My operatives have made multiple attempts to make a connection with her, to gain access to her work. The woman seemed impervious to all usual social methods of infiltration, and a more . . . blunt approach would be less valuable."

"Blunt?" Corrie asked. "What, like knocking over the rutting head and dragging her into a basement?"

His expression told a lifetime of stories.

"None of that sewage, not on my watch," she said.

"I would not prefer that either," he said. In other blazing words, he didn't rule it out.

"If you even think—"

"But that's the beautiful thing, Sergeant," he said. "Because you have become friends with Miss Rek-Nouq. You have access. You can be that asset."

"If you think I—"

"Just imagine, Sergeant. Nothing violent, nothing untoward. You could simply convince Miss Rek-Nouq to come here and take a very generous offer. Central Office wants her to willingly come to Maradaine. I certainly can imagine, if she does, there will be room enough on the ship for you and Miss . . . what is her name? Mellick. Eana Mellick. I imagine after all she's been through she is . . . anxious to get on that ship. And if you can make that happen, I'm certain we can make it happen on our end."

CHAPTER TWENTY-NINE

C ORRIE DID NOT GO STRAIGHT home after crossing back into Jachaillasa. She wandered over to the Mocassan Conservatory, walking around watching the students on the campus, wondering which, if any, were Moriel's spies. She couldn't rutting believe that after all this time, in the embassy they had known exactly who she was, what was going on with her, and they had done nothing. This whole damned time, she had been left out in the dry.

Rutting bastards.

But they were bastards who could get her and Eana home.

Blazes.

It was times like this she could use a beer, and there was nothing of the sort in this stinking city. Just coffee, which she did not need to drink any more of. Her hands were already starting to tremble.

She was in half a mind to find a fight to start, just so she would have something to punch. That sort of thing would get a person ironed and pinked back in Maradaine, apt to spent a couple nights in the station-house cell to cool off. Who would stop her here? What were the real consequences? There seemed to be no real law officers, except the guards at the bridges. Maybe those freaks with the green sashes, whoever they were. But actual law? She still hadn't seen it, not here in

Jachaillasa. But they did have them across the bridge in Teamaccea. What was with this rutting city?

She found herself in the middle of the grand plaza near the house— Imrrehzull Rḫah it was called, she now knew—and sat down on the job platform. No one was here, of course. The sun was setting, not a time for anyone to look for jobs. Certainly not the kind offered here. But it was the only real place for someone to sit down here. Other than on the campus, there were no benches anywhere.

Folks here were not the sitting type, maybe.

She'd literally kill right now to sit down at a normal size table and have a beer and a striker. To talk to the rest of her family. Saints, even Oren, the tosser. Any of them would help her figure out what to do. Or just make her laugh.

She really could use a laugh.

Someone sat down next to her and handed her a meat wrap from one of the food carts. "You look like you've had a day, Crasher."

A cold chill hit her spine. That was her father's voice. That was how he talked. "Crasher" was his name for her after the incident with his horse and the barn.

But the person next to her was the strange Kelliracqui woman.

"You've got half a click to run or I'm gonna wallop you so hard," Corrie said.

"So you aren't ready," the woman said, her thick accent coming through now. "I had thought you were, by the look of you."

"Ready for what?" Corrie asked. She was still holding the meat wrap. The Kelliracqui woman had her own, and she took a hearty bite out of it.

"To talk to your dead," the woman said through her chewing. "Don't you know? Didn't your people—you don't have your people do you?"

"No, I—shut it. I'm not rutting talking to you—"

"You've never met a *thikaavh* before, have you?"

"A what?"

"A Caller," the woman said. Her voice shifted, somehow getting even more of an accent. "Eat, would you? You're all bones, girl."

"What the blazes was that?"

"That was . . . Sezki. You know Sezki?"

"I do not," Corrie said. "The blazes are you on about?"

"Sezki . . . D'Fen. That's it. She had a boy named Minox, and when he grew up, had a daughter named . . . Amalia."

Corrie jumped to her feet. "The blazes you know that?" That was Mama's name, and Mama's father was Minox D'Fen. Corrie had never met him, but that was who her brother was named after.

"She told me," the woman said. "But . . . no, she's gone. The dead come and go, talk when they want to. When they think you need to know something."

"And my great-grandmother wants me to eat this?"

The woman chuckled. "Enough that I bought it for you. If you really don't want it, I'll take it back."

"She made you buy it?" Corrie asked, looking at the wrap. It was like most of the meat wraps in this town: flatbread, thin-sliced spiced meat, and the creamy, fiery sauce. Almost, but not quite like the fast wraps Minox was always eating from that cart outside the stationhouse. She was hungry. Blast it, she took a bite.

"There you go," the woman said. "When the dead ask, they are very persuasive. And since I first spotted you, they've been quite annoying."

"Sure," Corrie said, not really buying this. She had seen some strange things in her time, but this sewage sounded like some Racquin grift. "You know I'm not really Racquin, don't you?"

"You are your mother's daughter," she said with a shrug. "And your father's. He's the one really struggling."

"How?" Corrie didn't want to believe a word of this, but still she asked the question. Why the blazes did she do that?

"He's worried about you, and the strong emotions, they . . . they make it harder for me to hear the call. I need to sit in quiet, tune into the call, really connect. Maybe we should go back to my tent?"

That blew some whistles in Corrie's head. Everything about this screamed danger, and Corrie had had more than enough of that for today, for her whole lifetime.

"No, ma'am," she said, handing over the half-eaten wrap. "I think I know where I need to go."

She did not go home, instead heading back to the campus. She went straight to the library, waving at the librarians and docents who gave her odd regard as she went through. They had seen her enough to think she belonged, and no one would try to kick her out. She made her way to the stairwell, and went all the way to the top to the scope observatory.

Ang was inside, as she normally would right before sunset. She would usually spend her nights holed up in here, observing the sky through the enormous lensescope that dominated the room. Corrie had never seen anything like the thing, bigger than the Inemar Stationhouse.

"Corrie," Ang said when she saw her. "Whatever are you here for? Is everything all right?"

"Not at all," Corrie said. "I've got a real jam here, and I need to talk to you about it."

"If I can be of help," Ang said, sitting down at her desk. "What's the problem?"

"I went to the Druth Embassy today, to see if someone could help with my situation."

"Sensible," Ang said.

"And maybe they can. They say they can, but . . . there is a price."

"One might presume," Ang said. She was taking notes as she talked. Corrie was fascinated that the girl could seem to be able to write in her notebook while keeping her attention entirely on Corrie. "I take it the price is different than the terms of your debt? And it is one that disquiets you?"

"It rutting well does," Corrie said. "They want you."

Ang stopped writing. "What do you mean?"

"I mean . . . they want me to convince you to come to the embassy, and then they'll take you to Maradaine."

"And your method to entice me is to tell me plainly?" she asked, "It certainly is a methodology I respect."

"I wanted to be honest with you," Corrie said. "There's something hinky about it."

"My knowledge of your language clearly isn't complete enough to understand 'hinky,'" she said. "They are interested in specifically me?"

"Yeah," Corrie said.

"Quite curious," she said. "I do appreciate your candor and alerting me. Unless this is a prelude to using force to compel me."

"Not at all!" Corrie said. "Though I'm not sure if they wouldn't."

"Why would they be interested in me?" Ang asked idly. "Is it the comet?"

"The what?"

"Right now the forefront of my work is involved in confirming the existence of a comet that should be visible, if my observations and equations are accurate, at the change of the year."

"I don't know what a comet is," Corrie said.

"It's an uncommon astrological phenomenon. Several cultures attribute spiritual meaning to them, and they might cause shifts in how magic operates. That is part of the nature of my study."

"Listen," Corrie said. "I don't think this business is right at all. I don't know why they want you. My gut tells me it isn't for your own good. But if it is something you're interested in—"

"It could help you," Ang said. "I won't dissemble, Corrie. Right now my work here is critical, and in a critical phase. I have no interest in Maradaine or any other part of the world until that has eased down. I regret if this causes you difficulty."

"No, no," Corrie said. "I ain't interested in giving you any grief. I don't need their tricky deal."

"Capital," Ang said. She took Corrie's hand and gave it an affectionate squeeze. "So you will keep me safe from your own government?"

"If I rutting have to," Corrie said. "I won't be part of you getting hurt."

"Very well," Ang said, a bright smile coming. "I need to get to my observations. I'm making a presentation tomorrow, and I must prepare. You are welcome to stay . . ."

"I should get home and to sleep," Corrie said. "See you tomorrow."

"Until then."

Corrie got home, and the debthouse was largely quiet, as it usually was this late. Corrie felt exhausted, and wasted no time going up to her room. Srella was in the midst of sponging off Eana's brow.

"How is she?" Corrie asked.

"Her fever is up again," Srella said. Eana seemed asleep, but was also whimpering and moaning loudly. "The tincture isn't as effective."

"Tleta said that might be a possibility," Corrie said. "So how do we cool her down?"

"I don't know," Srella said. She looked like she was about to say more, but stopped to regard the mist coming with her breath. "Is it colder?"

"Yeah," Corrie said. The room was definitely colder.

Freezing.

A flash of frost filled the whole room. Srella jumped to her feet. *"Ghehof!"* she said.

"Magic?" Corrie asked. "That wasn't you?"

"Was it you?"

"No!" Corrie said. "I can't do any of that business. But if it wasn't either of us—" She looked down to Eana, now covered in a thin layer of frost. She looked peaceful, too. No more whimpering. Like the freezing of the room had made her more comfortable.

"Then it was her," Srella said.

Rutting, blasted blazes.

Eana was a mage.

CHAPTER THIRTY

E ANA'S HEALTH IMPROVED SIGNIFICANTLY AFTER that incident, and she was back in the kitchen the next morning, eating up a storm. Corrie and Srella didn't tell anyone else what was going on, and Corrie wasn't sure how to broach it with Eana, if she even was fully aware of what happened. While everyone else ate or got ready for the day, they went up on the roof.

"Look, I know that things about mages and magic can get really rolled up in Maradaine," Corrie said. "My brother's a mage, and he never had proper training, never joined a Circle, and it's caused him a mess of trouble. How do things work here?"

"I'm not sure, but . . . I think they really don't," Srella said. She shrugged. "I never heard much of it back home, but there most mages got recruited for training and then worked for hire. It's considered a good fortune because you're near certain to make income."

"But not here," Corrie said.

"I never even heard," Srella said. "People don't talk about it. Magic. At all. Like it's—"

"Taboo," Corrie said. "Rutting, blasted blazes. Like, she could be in trouble? Just for existing?"

"I don't even know," Srella said. "Let's talk to Maäenda. She might know."

Corrie wasn't sure. "Can she . . . I don't know a blazing thing about where she comes from. What she would think."

"I think it's a normal part of life there."

"Are you rutting sure?"

"It's never come up!"

The debate over whether or not to bring Maäenda in was ended as she came up on the roof.

"What has you two so worked up?" she asked. "Thank my spirits you're talking in Druth so the rest of the girls don't know what is going on. But what is going on? What might I know?"

"If—" Corrie started, trying to think the best way to phrase it. "If someone had magical ability here, in the Mocassa. What would their options be?"

"Depths below, it's Eana, isn't it?" Maäenda asked.

"I didn't say that," Corrie said.

"You didn't have to," Maäenda said. "It's not like you would be having a secret conversation about Pume."

"I might," Srella said.

"Shut your slap hole," Maäenda said. "Eana's just chatting away with Basi and the others right now."

"I don't know if she's aware of it," Corrie said. "She . . . she was in the throes of fever when she did it."

"This is the dumbest conversation," Maäenda said. "First, we talk to her. How long do you have before you need to go to Tletanaxia."

"Maybe half a bell," Corrie said. She corrected for Mocassan time. "Quarter-star."

"That isn't enough . . . but, fine, I'll . . . I'll have that talk with her."

Corrie paused for a moment. "We . . . we're talking about the *magic* talk, right?"

"Rutting yes!" Maäenda said.

"Just making rutting sure!"

"Both of you calm down," Srella said. "I'm losing my brain."

Corrie took a deep breath. "Really, I want to know, how much . . . trouble could she be in, here?"

Maäenda sighed. "It's not good."

"How not good?"

"I'm no expert, but there's a whole holiday about ousting the Mage Kings? And I think 'a mage should be struck until dead' is in their holy text."

"WHAT?"

"It depends on who you ask, how you translate, different sects interpret it—"

"What about the sects *here* in the Mocassa?"

"I can tell you, I've never heard of a magic school here," Maäenda said. "At least not in Jachaillasa. Maybe in one of the other boroughs."

Corrie sighed. "There's a weird Kellirac woman who keeps bugging me, and she has power of some sort. She might know something."

"That woman just wants to swindle you and take your money."

"I marked her for that the first moment," Corrie said. "But she does have something real."

"I would avoid."

Corrie knew Maäenda was right. "I can probably ask Ang safely. Tsouljans respect magic."

"You're sure?" Srella asked.

"Of that, I'm rutting sure."

"I have a few people I can talk to discreetly," Maäenda said. "Surely this is not the first girl to find her magic in this city."

"I need to go," Corrie said. "We'll gather information and talk it out tonight, hmm?"

"A plan," Srella said. "Go."

Corrie hurried down the stairs, grabbed one of Basichara's pastries as she said goodbye to Eana, and was down the last flight, boots on, and charging through the street in the space of ten heartbeats. She finished the pastry—spices and honey and nuts—as she hurried along, and reached the Xonacan household with time to wipe the dust off her boots before she knocked.

"How's the day treating you, Canoc?" she asked as the large man let her in. He responded in Xonacan, she had no idea what. But there was that smile from him that always made Corrie feel that, even though they didn't understand each other, they understood each other. "Can't argue with that."

He chuckled and went off. In a few minutes, Tleta came down to the house foyer, dressed in her usual style that accented the sedate Imach browns and tans with the splash of color provided by a feathered hat. The feathers, Corrie had observed, were a common fashion accessory for Tleta and her mother, but today's feathers, for the first time, were green and red.

"Are you matching my uniform, Tleta?"

"I noticed that you definitely stand out a bit conspicuously in the crowd," she said. "So I thought I'd join you today."

"Some people do wear green in this city," Corrie said. "But a bright red does seem to be right out. Their reds are all muted, dull."

"Which is tragic," Tleta said. "Let's be off."

The streets were especially crowded as they walked to the campus. Corrie wasn't sure why that would be, but after everything that had happened in the past day, it put her on edge.

"Is everything all right?" Tleta asked. "You seem out of sorts."

"Something is happening today," Corrie said. "Is there a holiday or something like that today?"

"Not that I'm aware of."

"Stay at my arm," Corrie said, noting the crowds were getting even denser as they got closer to campus. People were pressed up against each other, pushing their way along.

Tleta grabbed onto Corrie's arm and looped it with her own. Which was good, because she could have easily been pulled away from Corrie and dragged off by the flow of the crowd. Corrie still wasn't convinced that anyone was actually trying to hurt or abduct Tleta, but if they were, this would be a prime opportunity.

"What is going on?" Tleta asked, holding herself close to Corrie. "Can we even get to campus?"

"We will," Corrie said. She pushed her way through the people, now hearing lots of angry shouting from the direction of the campus.

"What is—" Tleta said, and then she gasped. *"Shâc nâs ty'ô."*

Corrie had no idea what she just said, but she definitely understood the sentiment behind it.

The street through the campus grounds was filled with a marching parade. Dozens upon dozens of men and women. All of them with that green sash.

CHAPTER THIRTY-ONE

THERE WAS NO WAY TO get onto the campus without crossing through the stream of green-sashed folks.

"Maybe we should go home," Tleta said.

"If you want, we will," Corrie said. "But you shouldn't be denied your studies because of this."

Tleta squeeze Corrie's arm. "I don't want to miss my class."

"All right," Corrie said, taking Tleta's arm like she was one of those ladies at the dress shows that Nyla loved to go to. "On my lead."

"Please," Tleta said.

Corrie stepped into the street, leading Tleta with her, and walked straight into the parading march of people. As she did, she held up her hand to the oncoming folks, using her best Imach and authoritative voice. *"Mi bhahv, gahpe'hi. Bhos 'hoff."* One side, people. Step away.

That had been enough to pause the parade, and make a gap they could get through. They were almost across the street when someone shouted in Imach.

"You dare? You interrupt the *ahmua*? B'enelkha comes, *qaysh*, and you *rehll* her path?"

"Qaysh, qaysh, qaysh!" many of them chanted.

"Ignore them," Corrie said, pulling Tleta across. They were off the street, through to the campus grounds. Not that it made much difference, because it was clear the parade was coming onto the campus. As Corrie led Tleta to her lecture hall, they saw more and more of those green-sashed freaks gathering outside the library.

"What do you think they're doing?" Corrie asked as they came inside.

"I have no idea," Tleta said. "But I'm worried about Ang."

Of course. She would still be in the library, and whoever these bastards were, they definitely had a mad-on about Ang. That wouldn't do at all.

Saints, why was everyone so rutting interested in Ang? What was so fascinating about her work?

They went upstairs to the class balcony, but today it was nearly empty. The floor below as well. The lecturer, standing in front of his slateboard, looked very put out.

"It seems we have a *rhahw'alĭ* here today," he said. Corrie wasn't sure what that one word meant. "And as a result, we all forget this is a place of learning."

"I have not forgotten," Tleta announced from her place on balcony. "I don't care about whatever that is."

"I appreciate that, miss," the lecturer said. "I appreciate the few of you who take this seriously. Let us continue with the working of the *Nerrĵ*, which is located—"

The lesson continued, but Corrie's ear was on the outside, where she could hear the crowd growing, getting more agitated, more aggressive. Building to something. Shortly before the lecture was finished—and Corrie had the sense the teacher had given up early—a great cheer came from the outside that made the windows shake. As she guided Tleta out, she wasn't sure what to expect, but she had a distinct sense that it would not be good.

The library square was packed, and someone was giving a speech. It was too far away to make out the details, but after every few lines, there was another cheer.

"We should get you out of here," Corrie said.

Tleta just said one word. "Ang."

"She'll be fine, she has the sense to—"

Tleta smacked Corrie's arm and pointed. "Ang!"

Corrie looked again, and while the packed scene was too chaotic and full to make out details among the sea of green-sashed folks, the flash of dandelion-yellow hair could be spotted from all the way across the grounds. She was on the library steps, surrounded.

Blazes.

"I can't leave you—"

"Yes, you can, she's all alone."

"All right," Corrie said, pointing to the bathhouse. "Go in there, go in the hot room, or a closet, or whatever, and bar the door until you hear me call for you."

Tleta nodded and ran inside.

Corrie checked her uniform, drew out her club, and strode over with her chin high. As she got closer, she moved people in her path with a firm arm, saying, "Step aside, make a path, clear it," in Imach as she went. Thanks every saint, they responded to that authority. Of course, these people seemed almost in a rapture, so focused on what was happening on the steps that they barely noticed Corrie pushing her way through.

She made it near the front, and could finally see the center of the attention. A woman was on the steps—Corrie would guess as old as Mama, but she had a certain regal bearing that made her almost ageless. And while she had the green sash, hers was decorated with golden embroidery. More of note, unlike most of the Imach women Corrie had seen around town, this woman's head was uncovered, her hair a long tumble of midnight glory.

She pointed an accusing finger at Ang, who stood stiff and trembling. Her chin was high and her expression defiant, but tears were running down her face.

"This woman dares to think she can unlock the secrets of heaven! This woman believes the mystery of God is an equation she can solve!"

"You don't—" Ang started, but jeers drowned her out.

"But we are here to beg you, foolish girl, do not unlock heaven! It is not your place to solve God!"

"You—" Ang tried again.

As Corrie forced her way through the last few people, the woman strode over to Ang and grabbed her by the chin.

"What *uaḷuvv* you have to think you should do this," she said. "Who told you this was your place?"

"I will not—"

"God will bring punishment down upon you. Fire will rain down."

The crowd started chanting for fire. *"Rhirrazh! Rhirrazh! Rhirrazh!"*

Then someone threw a burning book onto the library steps, and everyone started screaming.

No time to wait. Corrie slammed through the last few people in front of her, not caring if she hurt any of them as she knocked them to the ground. Now was not the time to worry about that.

Simple math. Fire took precedence.

Corrie jumped out and stomped on the book, smothering the flame before it got any farther, and as she did that, she gave five hard, sharp bursts with her whistle.

The Riot Call.

Not that it meant anything to anyone in this city. But she knew how to send that whistle call, so the trill overpowered any shout or cry. For just a moment, she had all eyes on her, and she had to use it fast.

She just hoped she had the language for it.

"Get back!" she called out. "All of you step back and stand down or face consequences!"

The woman looked to Corrie and let go of Ang's face. "Who do you think you are, little girl?"

"Sergeant Corrie Welling," Corrie said, tapping her badge. The word she used for "sergeant" was *"uarho"*—"high officer," roughly. Claim authority here. Take it from this woman. What would her brothers do? Or Tricky? What would Pop do? "I'm going to need to see some papers from you, ma'am. Identification. Permits. Please produce that immediately."

"Papers?" the woman asked incredulously. "You're asking me for papers?" She looked out to the crowd like she was in charge.

Corrie was not going to let this woman be in charge, not until, at the very rutting least, Ang was safe.

"Was I unclear?" Corrie asked. She looked out to the crowd, and pointed her club at them all. "I've put out the call, and every single one of you is liable for damages and battery here. All of you will face severe consequences if you do not stand down."

That was at least enough for the crowd to give a hint of pause. They all seemed to withdraw just a tiny amount.

"You do not have the authority, High Officer, to demand of me—"

"Are you part of the faculty here, ma'am?" Corrie snapped back. "Do you have any right to cause such disorder on the campus of the Mocassan Conservatory of Knowledge?"

"I have been appointed by God—"

Corrie stepped forward, not giving any ground to this woman. "I am going to need to see some papers from you, ma'am, to that effect. Identify yourself."

Some fool from the front of the crowd stepped forward. "She is B'enelkha Hajan, the blessed prophet of the new word! She calls us to end the heresy—"

Corrie shut him down with a whistle blast. "I did not call on you," she told him. She recognized his rutting face, though. The one who had been harassing Ang the other day. "I've already got your number, fella, and you're going to face irons and charges if you don't shut your rutting face!"

She didn't say "rutting," but a word in Imach that was *far* more offensive.

The crowd gasped.

But that was the weapon she had. Like Pop had taught her. "When they're stronger, when they outnumber you, when they want to grind you down, words are all you got, Crasher. If the other pages give you guff, you send them reeling with your mouth. They never expect that from a young girl like you, and if you send a shock into their skull like that, you make them forget everything else."

That had gotten her through when the other pages tried to bully her, through her cadet years when they all hated her, and kept her on target when she was riding the dark each night.

And right now, it had shut up B'enelkha Hajan for a moment.

She spun back on her. "Now, I already have cause to bring up charges of harassment and battery on this *honored* student of this fine university, Miss Hajan. Whoever you think you are, whatever *appoint-*

ment you claim to have, you have no jurisdiction here. You have no right to harass people here."

B'enelkha Hajan slowly stepped up to Corrie, looking her up and down. "This is the Druth girl who chased you off before, isn't it?"

She glanced over to the fool Corrie had snapped at. For a moment he looked back and forth, like he couldn't decide which of them he was more afraid of.

"Yes," he said quietly.

"I won't ask again, Miss Hajan," Corrie said, even if she had no idea how she would back any ultimatum she made here. "Either show me you have permission to assemble here, or be off."

"My permission comes from the divine," Hajan said. "I am called to this. It is a sacred duty to end the heresy in this city."

"So, nothing," Corrie said. Before Hajan could say anything, Corrie turn to the crowd. "Clear off and go home *immediately*, or so help me God, I will make sure every single one of you will get locked up in the darkest hole I can find on this island!"

That, amazingly, was enough to make most of the crowd scatter like rats. Corrie was shocked it had worked so well. Almost all of them ran off. The only ones who didn't were the fellow who had bothered Ang the last time, and a few of the green-sash folks around him. Maybe half a dozen. And in the mood Corrie was in right now, she was more than ready to knock in the teeth of each and every rutting one of them.

"You invoked the name of God against me," Hajan said quietly. "That was a grave error. His wrath is not yours to command."

Corrie stepped closer. "The wrath of God isn't what you should worry about right now," she said. "Now clear off while I still let you."

Hajan turned back to Ang, pointing at her. "Your blasphemy will not go unpunished. Both of you. Your attempt to unlock the heavens will crash it down on our heads! And you!"

She spun around to face Corrie as she walked down the steps to her followers.

"You will regret today, 'Sergeant' Corrie Welling."

She said 'sergeant' in Trade, with an exaggerated attempt at a Maradaine accent. Then she spun back around, her black hair flowing like a cape, and stalked off.

Ang's hands were on Corrie, with almost flailing desperation as her trembles devolved into a full body shudder, and tears turning into wrenching sobs.

"Hey, hey," Corrie said, clutching onto her. "I've got you, come on. Let's get you out of here."

As Corrie led her out of the square and to the bathhouse, Ang broke like a dam, words pouring out of her with her tears. "They said I was a goat who deserved to be carved up. That I should be stripped naked and dragged through the streets."

"That's never going to happen," Corrie said. "We got rid of them."

"This time."

CHAPTER THIRTY-TWO

THEY FOUND TLETA IN THE bathhouse, where she had locked herself in a changing room, just as Corrie had told her to. "I feel terrible for leaving you alone, though."

"You stayed safe," Corrie said. "That's my job here."

"But I'm not your job," Ang said.

"Maybe not the one I'm getting paid to do," Corrie said. "But it's who I rutting am, and nothing will change that."

"Can you help me get home?" Ang asked. "I don't want to walk alone in the street."

"Of course," Tleta said.

Ang's home was an apartment in the same sort of high, narrow building that the debthouse was. But as soon as they arrived, it was clear she was no longer welcome.

"You are heresy," an Imach woman in the doorway hissed at Ang. "I will not have that business under my roof."

"But—" Ang said.

"No!" the Imach woman said. As a young man threw crates and books and clothes out of the third-floor window, the woman at the door went on. "I have heard what you do, and you should die in the street!"

"You are a wicked rutting slan," Corrie told the woman, and threw in a few more choice words in Imach that Nas'nyom had made it clear she should never use. While Tleta comforted Ang, who was beyond the capacity to make rational noises, Corrie collected her belongings strewn in the street, chasing off the thieving boys who were trying to make off with a few books. She got everything together into something resembling order in three crates.

"Where will I even go?" Ang asked. "Where is safe?"

"My home," Tleta said. "I will demand that Mother takes you in, and make an outrageous fuss if she refuses."

They got to Tleta's home, and Corrie felt some small ease once they were inside, protected in stone. Yalititca made something of a stink, and Tleta, as promised, made an outrageous fuss. At some point Marichua came into the room, and then there was a whole three-way fight, which Corrie understood absolutely none of. She couldn't even figure out where Marichua was in the row, be it standing with Tleta, against her, or just airing grievances about a completely unrelated matter.

While they argued, Corrie and Ang waited patiently in a sitting room near the garden. Ang was still trembling, but her tears had stopped for the moment.

"Do you think they would protect me at the embassy?" Ang asked quietly.

"Maybe," Corrie said. "I mean, I know it's in my rutting best interest to just tell you yes, but . . . blazes, I don't know what they would do about all this." For all Corrie knew, Lieutenant Moriel was behind this to put pressure on Ang.

"They want me to go to Maradaine?"

"They say," Corrie said. "But . . . it all sets whistles off for me. I don't trust them being something good for you. I don't know why they want you, but . . . I've got a bad feeling."

"You don't trust your own people?"

"The ones who clobbered me and locked me on a slave ship were my people. Not just Druth, but brothers in Green and Red."

"Your own kin?"

"Not literally," Corrie said. "But fellow constables. People who should have been doing the right thing. So, yeah, my trust in my people is low. Especially when they put a price on helping Eana and me."

"How is your friend?" Ang asked. "She's been sick?"

"Actually, that's a real question for you. She . . . it looks like she's a mage."

"What blessing," Ang said. "She has many opportunities ahead."

"In this town?" Corrie asked. "Or would they treat her like you?"

Ang's face fell. "Of course. That could be a danger."

"My very thought," Corrie said. "You wouldn't happen to know where a girl like her could learn how to control her power in this city?"

Ang frowned. "Not in Jachaillasa. There is a *teknosom* in Mahacossa, like . . . what is the word in Trade? Monastery?"

"There's a Tsouljan enclave in Maradaine. My brother tried to learn magic from them, but it didn't go well. Plus there was the murder."

"I cannot swear they would be helpful," Ang said. "I can send word and ask? With discretion."

"That could be helpful," Corrie said. "Thank you."

Ang took Corrie's hand and gripped it tight. "Anything you need, my friend."

Tleta came in with her mother and Marichua. Her mother stepped forward and said, through gritted teeth in rough Imach, "You are welcome guest to our home."

"Thank you, ma'am," Ang said.

"We're having dinner soon," Tleta said. "Corrie, are you staying here?"

"For dinner, or staying for good here?"

Her mother made some aggrieved noises.

"For dinner. You can't stay here. There are laws about where indebted can stay, you know."

"Right," Corrie said, which set some clockwork spinning in her brain.

As Tleta's mother and Marichua went off, there was a knock on the door, and after a moment, Canoc presented Nas'nyom.

"You are here," he said with relief when he saw Corrie. He gave bows of regard to Tleta and Ang, with greetings each in their native tongue. "I have heard such stories about tumult on the campus. They said the Druth girl started a fight with the Sect of Hajan. What did you do?"

"With the who of what now?" Corrie asked. "Those nutters were about to kill Ang, and I scared them off."

"The Sect of Hajan," he said. "Do you have any idea who they are?"

"Besides hating me?" Ang asked.

"Who are they?"

"They follow B'enelkha Hajan with an impassioned zeal," he said. "I think it's madness, but she started preaching in the streets about a year ago, and more and more people started following her. She talks about how the people in the Mocassa are not true enough in their devotion to God. That a day is coming, the year will end with God swallowing the sun and burning the sky with fire, and only the faithful will survive. More and more people think she's a true prophet. Her sect grows every day!"

"The year will end with what?" Ang asked, and suddenly she started to laugh. Laughing so hard, she lost her footing and ended up on the floor. "By the grace of light, she says—that I would unlock heaven . . . swallow the sun . . ."

Tleta got down on the floor with Ang. "What is it? What's so funny?"

"That's why she hates me," Ang said. "Because I—it's so absurd—that damned woman."

"She's very dangerous," Nas'nyom said. "And they say you made her very angry, Corrie."

"I shut her thing down," Corrie said. "And I'd do it again. I don't care if God does whisper in her ear."

Ang caught her breath again. "Well, she must know what I know, and that's why she wants to shut me up."

"What do you know?" Tleta asked.

"What all my work has been leading to right now," Ang said. "In a couple *mnu*, there will be an eclipse of the sun."

"Which is?" Corrie asked.

"One moon moves in front of the sun," Ang said. "And the same day, right before the new year begins, is when the comet will be its most visible." She laughed again. "Swallow the sun, burn the sky with fire."

"So she's right?" Corrie asked.

"It's an astronomical event that is predictable," Ang said. "Which is why she was on about me 'unlocking heaven.'"

Corrie understood. "Because if you tell people that, you rob her of her power. You were supposed to make a presentation!"

"Which I never got to," Ang said. "Because . . ."

Corrie swore. "So that's why she made her fuss today. Rutting slan. I should—"

"What could you even do?" Tleta asked. "How could you do anything?"

"She already did so much," Ang said.

"I got lucky," Corrie said, the ideas swirling in her brain locking together. "I faked my way through enough bravado to scare down the crowd. I doubt I could pull that off again. If I'm going to keep you—both of you—safe, and this . . . cult is going to keep up assaulting you, I'm going to need some authority here."

"Authority?" Tleta asked.

"Exactly. And it amazes me, while there's clearly law in this part of the city—like where I'm allowed to sleep."

"Which is absurd," Tleta said.

"But there isn't an institution to enforce it. Maybe for the people who own buildings and debt, but nothing for the people. And that's got to change."

"What do you think you're going to do?" Nas'nyom asked.

"I'm going to figure out how to start a constabulary on this island."

CHAPTER THIRTY-THREE

NIGHT HAD FALLEN BY THE time Corrie got back to the debthouse, and while she had eaten at Tleta's house, she was hungry again when she came in. The house was quiet, but someone had left a lamp burning on the entrance floor, and another up in the *ghose'a.* Corrie took advantage of the time to herself to strip out of her sweaty uniform and wash it and herself under the spigot. Saints, that felt good. She helped herself to flatbread and the collection of sauces and pastes in the icebox, sitting in the *ghose'a* in her damp chemise and skivs and feeling quite happy with herself and what she had managed to do today.

She, for once, got to be a proper constable. Stopped things before they turned into a riot.

Pop would have been proud if he had seen her.

While washing up, Osecca came home. She stopped dead in the middle of the *ghose'a,* staring at Corrie like she had almost never seen her before. No, staring at Corrie as if she was a dog on hind legs, washing at the spigot. Like something she couldn't even believe.

"Something wrong?" Corrie asked in Imach.

Osecca snorted and went upstairs without a word. Corrie ignored that. Too much to think about.

She had been lucky today, really, and if those zealots of Hajan had wanted to tear her up, they would have. She needed to be better prepared. Ang and Tleta had their reservations about her creating a constabulary in the borough, but it had to be done. She needed to do it.

Though she should find out why it didn't exist already. That was rutting strange, but she knew damn well she shouldn't presume only she knew how to do things. The fact that Jachaillasa didn't have some form of street-level law enforcement was messed up, but she needed to learn more. That was one thing Tleta said, and she agreed.

No going off like a wild horse with no rein.

As she was eating, she heard someone come down the steps, and then Maäenda stuck her head out of the hole of the stairwell.

"Your day all right?"

"The things I would do for a cold Druth beer," Corrie said. "You?"

"It's been a day," Maäenda said, coming down. "I've not directly spoken to Eana about . . . you know. I was hoping you might have some answers for her before we really, you know, broach the subject."

"I do not," Corrie said. "What did you tell her?"

"That she shouldn't go back to work at the weaver hall, because she'll just get poisoned again."

"Very good. She probably still wants to work more."

"Shouldn't she?"

Corrie sighed. "Of course. She rutting has to. I just wish she didn't have to." She saw Maäenda's eyes go to the floor. "You know exactly what I mean by that."

"Yeah," Maäenda said, sitting with her. "I took this on so none of my people had to."

"If I had known it was an option, I would have done the same," Corrie said. "And gotten her on the first ship back to Maradaine."

"No offense, but from what I know of Druth ships, that might not be the safest thing for a girl on her own."

Corrie took that in. "Rutting blazes, that's probably true."

Maäenda shrugged and grabbed a piece of flatbread. "I mean, I've not met a lot of your people, but the ones on the sea?"

"Fair," Corrie said. She leaned in closer. "So what do your people do with mages?"

"Typically, if one of the Keisholm are born a mage, we . . ." She paused. "I won't bore you about the whole history of the Tyzanian Empire and then Rekyashom—"

"Wait, are your people from Rekyashom?" Corrie asked. "Because I never heard about the Keisholm before, but I have heard of Rekyashom. Don't know a damned thing about it, but I heard of it."

"It's more complicated than that, but the Rekyashom are the land-bound kin to the Keisholm. Both our peoples are who we are because of the empire, which was very big on putting people in their boxes."

Corrie thought she had a grasp on what Maäenda was getting at. "As in, ocean people and magic people should be kept separate?"

"Right," Maäenda said. "Everyone was valued in the empire, but you were put to your best use. Even now, that mindset remains with us to our core."

"I mean, my family is pretty much all Constabulary, so I get it."

Eana came down the steps. "Is she telling you about all that again?"

"Again?" Corrie asked.

"Look, I'm pretty sure you told me all your stories," Eana said. "So almost anything you say is again."

"Just for that, I won't tell you about staring down an army of zealots on the library steps today."

Maäenda raised an eyebrow. "You what?"

"It was a day."

"And mine was boring," Eana said, going to the icebox. "But I am rutting starving."

"Language," Corrie said. "People will say I'm a bad influence."

"You are a bad influence," Eana said.

"Saints, she really has my number," Corrie said.

"She really does," Maäenda said. "I'll let you two talk."

She went up, and Eana came and sat down with a bowl filled with nine different things. She started eating with a ravenous abandon that Corrie was familiar with.

"Quite the appetite," Corrie said.

"I must be making up for having just broth when I was sick," Eana said. "I am doing all right, yes? Not sick anymore? Because Maäenda and Srella tiptoed around me all day. Like I was going to burst into flame if they got too close."

"Not impossible," Corrie said.

"What?"

Corrie took a deep breath. "Something is going on with you, and we're going to have to figure out how to deal with it."

"Something?" Eana asked. "Cor, you're scaring me a little."

"A little rutting scared probably is a good thing," Corrie said. "You feeling any different right now?"

"Different how?"

"Like—rutting blazes, I don't even know how to have this conversation."

Eana started to laugh. "I thought we went over this when I got my blood on the ship."

Corrie laughed despite herself. "Not that one."

"Then what?"

Another breath. This was harder to say that Corrie had thought. "I think you're a mage."

Eana paused mid-bite.

"A what?"

"A mage. As in you can use magic."

"Why would you think that?"

"Well, you made the room as cold as winter last night."

"You're exaggerating."

"Actual ice, Eana."

Eana stood up. "But . . . I mean, wouldn't I know? Shouldn't I—I don't even know."

"I don't rightly know."

"You!" Eana pointed an almost accusatory finger at Corrie. "You have a brother that's a mage!"

"Yeah. And his situation was weird. He didn't get it until he was already older than me, already a stick. And he was never properly trained. So . . . I just know what I saw. But he has an appetite like you do now."

"I just barely ate when I was sick."

"And now you're always hungry, right? Because that magic, it burns through your gut."

"Don't say that!"

"Eana—"

"Haven't I been through enough?" she cried. "Saints, with every rutting thing we have gone through—kidnapped, drowned, bought, sold, poisoned—can I get a bit of a break?"

"Eana!" Corrie said sharply, but trying to keep her voice down. "Your hands!"

Eana stopped and looked at her hands, which were glowing bright orange.

"Blazes, I'm a rutting mage."

"It's all right," Corrie said, getting to her feet and taking the girl in an embrace. "Cool your head now, ease down whatever makes your hands glow. Most important thing right now is you get a handle on this."

"Handle," Eana said. "Right." She looked at her hands in confusion. "I'm not entirely sure how I'm doing this."

Corrie muttered a few choice swears. She had never had a proper conversation with Minox about this. He had never wanted one. It was a thing he absolutely hated to talk about, even with her. "I don't rightly know, myself."

Eana closed her eyes, and the glow around her hands cycled through a few colors, got brighter and dimmer, and then finally subsided.

"There you go!" Corrie said.

"Maybe," Eana said. "I don't rightly know how I felt my way through that."

"The real question is, can you keep it, you know, off?"

Eana looked at her funny. "There's something you really aren't telling me, isn't there?"

"You know how, back home, a lot of folks really don't like mages?"

"Do I. Saints, my father might drown me in the river if he found out."

"Here it's apparently worse."

It was Eana's turn for a few choice swears.

"You're sure?"

"It's what I've heard," Corrie said. "Now, Maäenda and Srella know, but they're both from places that don't get their skivs yanked up over magic. Same with my friend Ang, she's Tsouljan."

"Tsouljan?"

"Let me tell you, Tsouljans know all sorts of mystic sewage. She says there's an enclave or something here, and they might have someone who could help teach you how to use it. How to keep it in check."

"Right," Eana said. "Because that's the real thing, hmm? I have to keep this in check. Things weren't rutting terrible enough, now I got to keep this bottled up, and I don't even know rutting how."

Corrie took her into her arms again. "Hey, hey, I'm right here, and we're going to get through this, hear? We are."

"I can't work now, can I?"

Corrie shook her head. "Maybe not for a bit. But you stay here, do chores for the house with Srella, and I will handle your payments."

"You shouldn't—"

"We are together, Eana," Corrie emphasized. "You and I against this whole blazing city."

Eana started crying, and grabbed Corrie so tight they both fell back down to the floor. Corrie held her, letting the girl sob, for as long as it took.

CHAPTER THIRTY-FOUR

ON TLETA'S NEXT DAY IN the library, Corrie went looking for any books she could find on the history of the city, the laws, how the laws were enforced, and how the city was organized. Everything she found was dense and heavy, making her head swim.

Then Nas'nyom came with a handful of books for her, which laid things out very plainly and simply, which was very helpful given her Imach reading level.

"Thank the saints you found these," she said.

"It was simple," he said. "Those are schoolbooks to explain it to children."

She felt like she was being sassed, but she didn't care. "Just what I need."

As she read through the books, she got the basics down, and Nas'nyom filled in details where he could. Centuries ago, each of the seven boroughs of the Mocassa was its own kingdom, and while now they were united as the Mocassa, that distinction was never lost. There being only some form of official guard on the bridges made sense now: they weren't law enforcement, they were border patrol.

"Here's the part I need," Corrie said, flipping through the book, hoping she was reading her Imach correctly. "Jachaillasa never had a lord or king or however this word *oeh* translates."

"'Little King' is a reasonable translation," Nas'nyom told her.

Corrie kept reading, "Because the people of the island always resisted, that none should command them but themselves."

"How does this help you form a police force?" Tleta asked, though she looked a little put off by the whole exchange. She was going through anatomy texts—in Trade, Corrie noticed—and Corrie had noticed that she had been having a hard time focusing on her own work since the day of the demonstration.

"Here we are," Corrie said, flipping through the pages. "'The people make the law, and that they would stay together to enforce the law and see it enacted.' That's it?" She did not like that answer, but going through the book, there wasn't much more for her to work with. "What does that mean?"

Nas'nyom's eyes went to the ground. "You remember the day we met?"

"You mean—" She thought about the brutes beating him up in that alley. Did Nas'nyom break the law there? Was that what she stopped— Mocassan justice? "What did you do?"

Nas'nyom looked in every direction rather than meeting Corrie's eyes, and finally said. "And God did again look down upon the world, and saw men lay with men in the manner of wives, and he did again grow displeased. 'See how they fail me,' God said. 'Why should I suffer them to live?'"

"The blazes is that sewage?"

"From the Book of Sorrows in the Bahimahl'Ima. A whole book in their holy text where God names reasons why humanity should be destroyed."

"So," Corrie said, letting the meaning of the verse sink in. "They tried to kill you because you like to roll with other men? That's the law here?"

"Barbarous," Tleta said absently.

"It's not, strictly speaking, the law here," Nas'nyom said. "If you want to get into what is the law, essentially the only thing is the proclamation, 'And as it is spoken by God, so it shall be the law of man.' And what it says in the Book of Sorrows can be interpreted many ways."

"Seems pretty clear what they think of folks like you," Corrie said.

"Because you don't know the whole passage. The Book of Sorrows is a series of calls and responses, where God looks at the world, sees something in humanity that displeases him and announces he will therefore destroy the world."

Tleta sighed heavily. "How is God a him?"

"That's what it says," Nas'nyom said.

"The Imachs have a god that gives birth to the world, but is a him?"

"It isn't my holy book," Nas'nyom said.

Corrie wasn't going to get into this, though she knew well enough that God was neither he nor she, God was all and everything, beyond the finite thoughts of male and female and anything in between. At least, that was the Druth outlook, and it was not a fight she had any interest in having right now.

"Anyway," Nas'nyom continued, "then the angels step up and defend humanity, and God decides not to destroy the world, until he sees something else displeasing. The whole book goes on for some time with this cycle and is quite tedious."

"And how is this relevant?" Corrie asked.

"Because different parts of Imachan have different interpretations of the book. And some regions and sects just pick which parts work for them. But one of the big schisms in the Imach faith revolves around which part matters more: the displeasure of God, or the angel's defense."

"Which means what exactly?"

"Just like I told you when we met. I thought those gentlemen were Osadi, who usually take the outlook of the angel's defense. But they were Kutiqari, who feel—at least in terms of men who lie with other men in the manner of wives—that it displeases God and the offender should have penance placed upon him."

"Why do I get the feeling that the Kutiqari only choose some of the displeasures to act on?"

"Because they do," Nas'nyom said. "But that represents the core of the law here. Sin is crime, crime is sin, as interpreted by whoever serves as a holy one, within the expression of their faith, as their devotees would act."

"So let me get this straight," Corrie said. "If that B'enelkha Hajan is a prophet, and has her zealots, her interpretation of sin is law, and anything they do is enforcement of the law." She swore a few times in Trade, Imach, and Xonacan.

"Language, Corrie," Tleta said. "If you're going to say that word, say it correctly. Roll the tongue more."

"She's right," Nas'nyom said.

"So she was in the legal right, as blazing messed up as that is. Blazes, is there a thing in that book about music or dancing?"

"Some Imach Nations have restrictions on both," Nas'nyom said. "The Mocassa is not one of them, because most of this city takes a rather reformed, progressive view of faith and its interpretation."

"But not Hajan."

"But she doesn't hold sway over the city, or even the borough. Which is important. Her word is not law."

"Whose is?"

"The people."

"But she's . . . people. Her followers are people."

"Anything that would affect the freedom of the people must be decided by the people," Nas'nyom said. He thumped his thumb on the book Corrie was reading. "The people make the law, the people see it enforced. Enforcement of the law is a law is a collective act. People step forward and act."

"The justice of the riot, which is rarely actual justice," Corrie said. She remembered stories of the way mages and other "unsavories" were strung up during the Inquest in Maradaine. "So how do I use that to just ends?"

"Especially if she wants to make a proper constabulary force?" Tleta asked.

Nas'nyom slid another primer book to her. "You make your case in front of the Jachaillasa Council of the People. Which meets every third *Pe'rhef*. The next one is in two days."

CHAPTER THIRTY-FIVE

T HAT NIGHT, NALACCIAN BROUGHT A new debt ward to the house whom he had acquired earlier that day. Near as anyone could tell, she was from somewhere in northern Lyrana, and no one could talk to her. Nalaccian said he believed her name was "Njien", but there was no way to confirm that.

"Does she even know what's going on?" Corrie asked Nalaccian.

"Your guess is as good as mine," he said. "But she will adapt. Look at you. Your command of the local language is admirable."

"I could bring Nas'nyom here to help her," she said.

"That is the sullied Jelic boy you brought here, yes?" Nalaccian said with a voice that dripped loathing. "I would prefer he not enter these walls."

"He speaks, like, eighteen languages," Corrie said, making up a number. "And understands them better than anyone. Girl can't work if she doesn't even understand what's going on."

While they were having this conversation, Pume—who Corrie had barely ever heard more than two syllables from, always kept her eyes to the floor—started shouting at the new girl. And she gave back as well, though even to Corrie's ear, they weren't speaking the same language at all.

"This is the fun you bring us," Corrie said, putting her body between the two women. Quick glance at them both, neither had a weapon.

"You are the most challenging ward I've ever taken on, Sergeant," Nalaccian said. "Can I leave this in your capable hands?"

"Saints above," Corrie muttered. Switching languages, she called out, "Hey, Hanakhla, can you get Pume out of here?"

Hanakhla, who was largely minding her own business in the kitchen, put down her food and scooped Pume up, throwing the angry woman over her shoulder and taking her up the stairs.

"I see I can," Nalaccian said, heading down the steps.

"Before you go," Corrie said, urging the Lyranan girl to sit. "I need something else from you."

"From me?" He shook his head. "Why do you feel so entitled to make requests?"

"I guess it's how I'm built," she said plainly. "The Jachaillasa Council of the People. It meets in two days, yes?"

His face screwed up in confusion. "Why does that interest you?"

"I need to go and present something to them."

That got him back up the steps. "What in the name of God would you have to present?"

"There's no proper law enforcement in this city. No one protecting people. So I'm going to propose they make a constabulary happen."

"Why would you want to do a thing like that?" he asked.

"Too many times I've already stepped in to save folks when no one else did. Something should exist in this town."

"I don't disagree," he said. "But who pays for these police?"

"Who pays for anything here?" Corrie asked. "City taxes?"

Nalaccian gave a small prayer, and sat down next to Corrie. The poor Lyranan girl looks utterly perplexed. "So, yes, the council has a treasury, which is generated from taxes on properties."

"So there is money to pay for such a thing."

He frowned. "I couldn't speak to how much. Though if people pay what I do in taxes . . ."

"Now, are there people on the council permanently? Or does everyone present vote, or . . . how does that work?"

"You really have been looking at it," he said. "Everyone present has a voice in the vote, but you can't just walk in and make a proposal. You need a floor sponsor."

Rutting blazes. "How do I get that?"

"Only a tax-paying property owner can sponsor someone to the floor. Which I am."

"So you could—"

"I could," he said. "And for the record, I like that you have an idea like this. I can tell you, unless you are convincing, people resist it. But you are very good at convincing when you want to be."

"So would you?" Corrie asked.

He shrugged. "If you are amenable enough to help Miss Njien here get settled and working, I would."

"I'm gonna call on Nas'nyom."

He sighed again, very annoyed. "If you must."

"Thank you," she said. "I do appreciate it."

"Good. I like being appreciated. And I should be appreciated more for all I do, but I am not a man of greed." He patted Miss Njien on her freshly tattooed arm, and went off.

"So," Corrie said, looking at the terrified woman. "Njien is it?"

"Kyet?"

"Njien?" Corrie asked, which exaggerated hand gestures. Then to herself. "Corrie."

"Corrie?" she asked, though her accent lost part of it.

"Right," Corrie said. She got up and called up the stairs. "Who else is here?"

Hezinaz came down the steps. "Why are you yelling?"

"We have a new girl here," Corrie said. "Njien here is going to need to be set up."

"And why is that my problem?"

"Just . . . stay with her while I go get someone to help translate with her."

Hezinaz was clearly put out, but said, "Fine. Be quick."

Corrie dashed out across town—it was already well after dark—to the house by campus where Nas'nyom rented a room. That house was much like the debthouse—absurdly narrow, amongst other tall, thin houses. She yanked the bell cord and stepped back.

Some old man stuck his head out the window. "Don't want any!"

"Not selling any!" Corrie called back. "Where's Nas'nyom?"

"What trouble has that *raanharho* caused now?"

That was a bit much, Corrie thought. Though she had to acknowledge, not too many months ago, she wouldn't have hesitated in saying the equivalent back home.

What a difference those months brought.

"Just rutting get him," she said.

The man grumbled and went back in. A few minutes later, Nas'nyom emerged, tying up his vest as he came out, shoes barely on. "What's going on?"

"How are your Lyranan languages?"

He shrugged. "I'm excellent with Old High Tyzanian, and the prime Lyranan dialect is based on that. Beyond that . . . not much?"

"We've got a new girl in the debthouse, no one can talk to her, and I don't think she knows what's going on."

He let out a low whistle. "That is very challenging. Of course I'll come help."

They hurried back, and Corrie couldn't help but notice that in his neighborhood she was seeing little groups of two or three people wearing Hajan's green sash. They weren't too conspicuous, but there were enough small groups to make her nervous. Not that they were doing anything but standing on corners or sitting in coffeehouses talking. But her instincts for trouble lit up seeing them again and again.

All the more reason to get some proper policing in this town.

They got back to the debthouse to find Hezinaz teaching Njien a dance, while Basi and Meija clapped.

"How are we?" Corrie asked.

Hezinaz made an odd sound. "I have no idea, but it was what I could do without talking. She seems less scared, but . . . only a little?"

Nas'nyom had already sat down with Njien—which made Basi and Meija frown a little, but they all turned to Corrie while Nas'nyom worked.

"What was this you were telling Nalaccian about talking to the council?" Basichara asked. "Making a police force?"

"That's the idea," Corrie said.

"But why?" Meija asked. "Don't you know?"

"Know what?" Corrie asked. "Listen, I don't know why this place doesn't have an constables or something like that. I just know that I've stepped up and done it because it seems there is no one else."

"We remember," Hezinaz said. "That night, before you learned how to talk—"

"I could always blazing talk."

"Talk in a civilized tongue," Hezinaz said. "We remember you ran out to help that girl. Would that be what this 'constabulary' of yours would do?"

"That's the idea," Corrie said.

"Here's what you have to know," Meija said. "This city had a rich bastard, like, forty years ago, who hated the religion and everyone who practiced it. So he hired a bunch of mooks, and made uniforms and talked a whole talk about keeping people safe, but it was really just his plan to knock out all the religious leaders and force the faith out of the city."

"And that didn't work, I presume?"

"No, because the people rose up against him," Hezinaz said. "Because on this island, the attitude is we take care of ourselves, take care of our own."

"That's what any good constabulary should do," Corrie said. "My pop always said, we're serving our neighbors, taking care of them. Everyone takes care of each other, that's the ideal."

"Good," Basi said.

"Because people here will be against anything that sounds like you're going to impose on them. That's what you'll be up against," Meija said.

Hezinaz added, "Your whole fight is going to be against the current. We only like it because we've seen you."

"Hezinaz told us how you kept those folks at the door when she danced," Basi said.

Hezinaz was already familiar with them, right. "You had those bastards pegged back then." Corrie asked. Both Meija and Basi gasped at the Imach word Corrie used there.

"They showed up about a season before you got here," Hezinaz said. "Rather, that woman they follow showed up, started preaching in doorways. Then folks joined up with her. Just a couple fools, they would make a ruckus anytime I had a dancing job. But then there were more and more, they kept growing, and they caused enough trouble at any event I tried to work. They're a menace is what they are."

"But what do they want?"

"Destroy people having a good time, you ask me," Hezinaz said. "I have no idea why anyone would follow that woman."

"Heard her once," Meija said. "I have no idea where she gets her scripture from, because it's nothing I read."

"She's trouble, all right," Corrie said. "Which is part of why we—I need to do this."

Hezinaz put one hand on Corrie's chest. "This is what you need. You go there, you show them your heart. Show them the girl who is willing to fight *for* the people here, with the people here, you have a chance."

Corrie wiped at her eye before tears formed. "Thanks. I . . . I wouldn't have known any of that. I'm glad you've got me on this."

"Hey, if you succeed, that means more jobs," Meija said. "That's always good for all of us."

"I hope so," Corrie said.

"Sorry," Nas'nyom said, getting to his feet. "I'm not on real solid ground on this, but I've got some basics with her."

"Could you communicate?" Corrie asked.

He helped the Lyranan woman to her feet. "This is Saa Njien, but you call her Saa. She's from the city of Sai Mikal in Zhai Zrao Province in the Zygranian part of Lyrana."

"Is that where Gunjar is?" Corrie asked.

"That's right," Nas'nyom said.

Corrie kept her grumbling about the Gunjar to herself.

"And there's a girl from Zagaral here?"

"I don't know," Corrie said. "Where the blazes is Zagaral?"

"It's part of the Turjin Empire."

"Right, Pume."

"There's a lot of longstanding enmity between Zagaral and Zygranian Lyrana, and—"

"No, I already tore Pume off of her," Corrie said. "Does she under-stand what happened to her?"

"I didn't get it all," Nas'nyom said. "She's actually quite well educated, so she knew enough Old Tyzanian to—it doesn't matter. I think her family left her as collateral in exchange for goods for a trade venture. But then the marker was sold, and that then became debt on her? I may have missed nuance."

"That's rutting monstrous," Corrie said.

"Common tale," Meija said. "That's what happened to me."

"Same," Basichara said. "Srella too."

"Rutting blazes," Corrie said. "Let her know she's safe here, but she has to work to pay her rent and debt. But we'll help her with that."

"I'll take her to the platform tomorrow," Hezinaz said. "And we can put her in my room with Hanakhla."

"We'd have to. The only other space is with Pume," Basi said. "And, mister, umm . . ."

"Nas'nyom," he offered.

"I suppose it's fine if you come and help her learn how to talk enough to get along and such. But if you touch any of the girls, I will let Hanakhla snap you apart."

"Not a worry there, miss," he said.

Corrie kept a chuckle to herself.

"Good," she said. "Let's all get some sleep, hmm?"

The other girls went up while Nas'nyom explained things to Saa. Then she came up to Corrie.

"Nifei," she offered.

"What is she saying?" Corrie asked.

"Thank you," Nas'nyom offered. "Say *'ongkea.'*"

Corrie did, and then Saa went up behind Hezinaz.

"Thank you," Corrie said to Nas'nyom.

"My pleasure," he said. "I live to make communication easier. And you have some work to do on that."

"What do you rutting mean?" she asked. "My Imach has gotten pretty good."

"It is 'talking with friends in the kitchen' good. You're not at 'make a speech in public' level yet, and if you're going to do that the day after tomorrow, I'm happy to help."

Speech in public. Rutting blazes. She hadn't really thought about what that meant. That would be hard enough in Trade. She swallowed hard and nodded. She needed to do this, especially if those blazing Hajan cultist incidents were going to keep escalating.

CHAPTER THIRTY-SIX

ANG'S EYES WERE RED WITH tears when Corrie arrived at Tletanaxia's home, and her yellow braids were more of a tangled nest.

"What's wrong?" Corrie asked.

Ang's eyes were downcast. "I received word from my superiors at the *teknosom*."

The Tsouljan enclave here. "I take it they didn't have good news."

"No," Ang said. Corrie gave her some space to fill in any details, but she didn't say anything for some time.

"What did they say?" Corrie finally asked.

"That I have a lot of work to do, and I need to pay attention to that, not to Druth girls who have nothing to do with my work." She wiped her face. "That the work I'm doing is the most important thing."

"I'm sure it rutting is to them, but—" Corrie started, then realized how harsh she sounded. "Sorry. It's not your rutting fault. Those bastards there—"

"I am answerable to them," Ang said in a clipped tone. "On levels you cannot understand."

Corrie took a step back. "Maybe I don't," Corrie said. "But that doesn't make them not bastards."

"You wouldn't know. You cannot know what pressures are on me, what expectations is part of who I . . . who we are, as a people."

"I don't," Corrie said. "I just know that decent people help others. That's what makes them decent. But if they don't want to, I'm sure they got their reasons, but they shouldn't be giving you guff for wanting to."

Ang looked down again. "I won't be staying here anymore. I will go to the observatory and spend all my time there, day and night. Up there, I will be fine, and finish this very important work."

"That . . . that doesn't sit right with me, Ang."

"I have been wasting too much time with social engagement. That has been made clear. And I cannot be allowed to fail."

"Saints almighty, Ang, you . . . are they sending someone to protect you, at least?"

"What do you mean?"

"That rutting—that rutting cult is still going to target you."

"If I stay inside they won't see me."

"They know where you are, though. Tell me your masters are at least sending a guard for you. Come on, I've seen them back at the Tsouljan compound in Maradaine. They've got their hair dyed red."

"None of the Vil are spared for me. They have their tasks of import, like I have mine. We all do our part toward our tasks, toward our purpose."

That sounded like some sewage, but Corrie could tell it was sewage that was buried deep. The kind of stuff that comes from being told something a thousand times as a kid so you rutting believe it.

"All right, but I'm going to keep making sure you're safe, even if they won't."

Tleta came out. "Are we ready for the day?" she asked.

"Yes," Corrie said. "Ang says she's going to the observatory and is going to stay there until the work is done."

"That's, what, twenty days?" Tleta asked.

"It's what I will do," Ang said firmly.

"Tell her that isn't healthy."

"I don't think she's going to listen to me," Corrie said.

"This isn't about you!" Ang snapped. "Tleta, explain to her something about duty."

"You want me to—"

"You think I don't know about duty?" Corrie asked. "You think I worked night shifts policing the streets of Inemar because I didn't know what duty was?"

"My family, my caste," Ang said. "You have no idea what it means to have your place in society dictated to you, and—"

"No idea," Corrie said. "I come from eight generations of constables. My family is nothing but expectation. One cousin joined the River Patrol and it's still a rutting scandal!"

"So you should understand!" Ang shouted back. "This is my moment, my—destiny. I can't let some half-cocked zealots ruin that for me."

"And you think I want to let them?" Corrie shot at her. "I'm trying to protect you!"

"What are you even fighting about?" Tleta asked. "She has to finish her work. If that means she stays locked up in that tower for the rest of the season, so be it. And we're going to help her do that."

Corrie forced her emotions down. "Right. Get her work done, and keep her safe. We can do that."

"But the Tsouljan Commission does not want me wasting time with fraternization," Ang said.

Corrie bit her tongue, not wanting to say something in further anger. But Tleta was the one who spoke.

"If I were a coarse Druth girl," Tleta said, "I would say, 'to rutting blazes with them.'"

Ang and Corrie both started laughing. Corrie came closer to Ang and took her hand. "Listen, the Tsouljan Commission can demand as much duty and destiny as they please. But they can't stop us from loving the blazes out of you, hmm?"

"Settled, then. We get you to the library so you can get to work, and Corrie will present her plan to the city for a constabulary force, which will protect the campus from the zealots. I will make sure you are kept fed during your confinement."

"I know some girls who could use the cooking and delivery work," Corrie said quietly.

"All the better," Tleta said. "We will get through this together. And you will do amazing, brilliant work that will make the Tsouljan Commission's eyes bleed for joy." Corrie didn't know what to make of that, nor did Ang from her expression. Tleta obviously took in their confusion. "It's more poetic in my language."

Ang laughed and embraced them both, holding on until Corrie started to feel more than a little awkward about it.

"Let's move," she said as she pulled away. "We're burning up the daylight."

CHAPTER THIRTY-SEVEN

THE DAY OF THE COUNCIL meeting, almost the entire debthouse was waiting for Corrie when she returned home to get ready. All of them had, apparently, formed a plan to maximize her appearance to appeal to her audience. Srella had cleaned and pressed Corrie's uniform jacket. Basichara, Hezinaz, and Meija went to work on Corrie's hair and face painting, while Saa cleaned and polished her fingernails—a thing Corrie had never even heard of before—and Pume painted her hands. Those two had, it seemed, reached some sort of silent detente.

"I never was much of one for this sort of frippery," Corrie said as they worked.

"You are a Druth woman—with debt on your arm and ear—about to propose a very Druth idea to people who are not crazy about either Druth ideas or women having ideas," Hezinaz said.

"If nothing else," Meija said. "You need to look like you are offering respect to them, that you honor the culture here."

"While still projecting strength," Maäenda said as she came down the steps to the *ghose'a*. Corrie had never seen anything like Maäenda in this moment. She was dressed in a pearl-laden viridescent coat, embroidered with blue silken ribbons, and a pearl and jade diadem on her head. Corrie had no idea she even had such things, or where she was hiding them. Blazes, one of these girls could pay off their whole debt with that crown.

"What are you—" Corrie said.

"My name apparently holds some weight here," Maäenda said. "So when you walk in, you'll walk with a queen at your side."

Corrie's eyes must have started to water, as Hezinaz said, "Don't cry! We'll have to start over!"

"Thank you," Corrie said. "Your support means a lot."

"We're all coming," Eana said as she came down, wearing her dress from the Gunjari ship.

"But why—"

"Every voice matters," Srella said. "Everyone who is present votes. So let's start with some votes in your corner."

In a few minutes, almost all of them were dressed as impressively as a handful of women in debt possibly could. Obviously, all of them had some secret stash of clothing—a floral-printed robe or a fur-lined headdress, a silk scarf or just a leather choker—something that showed who they were and where they came from. Corrie, of course, had no idea what everything meant to each of the girls, but she could feel a certain pride coming off of each of them as they came down the steps, ready to leave. Every one of them, while not as outwardly resplendent as Maäenda as Admiral-Queen of Keisholm, shone with her own regality. Corrie could see the high Fuergan lady in Henik ab Srella, the Turjin imperial princess in Pume, the noblewomen of Ghalad, Kadabal and Osad Abu Assein in Basichara, Meija and Hezinaz, the stately reserve of Zhai Zrao in Saa, the glorious warrior of Ch'omikTaa in Hanakhla.

And, of course, Eana, who might have just been a dockside boatgirl from the Trelan neighborhood, but held herself like a baroness. Her hair had the same beaded braids that Meija had put into Corrie's.

"Sergeant Welling!" the call came from the street. "Are you ready?"

Corrie led the ladies down the stairs, coming out into the street to find Nalaccian dressed in his finest dress of orange and purple with a brocade vest. He beamed with pride as all the women emerged from his debthouse.

"I've never imagined," he said with an almost awe-struck voice.

"This is an astounding sight, ladies, and I am honored to see you come together for the sergeant today. I am moved."

"Moved enough to credit our rents and debts for the *mnu*?" Maäenda asked.

His eyebrow went up, and Corrie couldn't quite get a read on him at first. "The least that can be done for a queen of the Dolsholm Sea."

Corrie was genuinely surprised by that. Often she assumed the worst of the man, and that was based on him profiting off of their misery, of course. But she had to admit, of the situations she could have found herself in, it could have been significantly worse.

Nas'nyom stood a respectful distance from Nalaccian, in an iridescent robe and face painting to match.

"Wow, you look like a rutting rainbow," Corrie told him.

"Thank you," he said. "That's actually a very holy and blessed symbol where I'm from."

"Let's get moving," she said, and followed Nalaccian as he led the full entourage through the neighborhood, past the campus, and to an open amphitheater near the island's coast. It actually was a quite sizable place—the sort of setting where a few thousand people could watch tetchball. What did folks play here? Corrie was sure there must be a sport these people loved like they loved tetch in Maradaine, but she hadn't had a chance to find out. Not that she had much opportunity to explore such things.

But it was a reminder of how mad this idea of hers actually was. Here she was, a Druth girl, barely twenty years old, in part of this grand and ancient city, going to tell them how to run their business, which they had done for centuries, and she knew so little about them.

Saints, this was stupid.

"Quite the turnout," Nalaccian said, looking at the crowd that easily numbered a few hundred.

"It's not usually like this?" Corrie asked.

"Well, I've only personally come a few times, when I had something at stake, or an issue I wanted to raise. Maybe twenty people, including the five Council chairs." He pointed to the adorned table with five older men seated at it.

"They're the ones in charge of the borough?"

Nalaccian shrugged. "More accurate would be that they administrate this meeting and, when something is decided, supervise that those called upon to enact that decision perform as ordered. In theory, we're all in charge. They assure it is done. It's honestly a thankless role. The responsibility of power, without the perks."

"And you know about that?"

"In this borough, people with money recognize that the money is the power. Office is for bureaucrats."

Corrie kept her grumblings to herself. She hadn't paid much attention to the local elections, the politics of the city aldermen, but she had heard more than enough grousing about it from her aunts and uncles.

She spotted Tleta, with her mother and Marichua and the three semi-husbands, seated on stone benches near the front. She went down and sat with them—all of them dressed to every inch of Xonacan nobility, which Corrie thought looked beautiful and terrifying. Feathers and stonework adorned their heads, and heavy black and gray paint across their eyes gave them and almost skull-like appearance. Tleta and her mother both wore capes made entirely of blue feathers, which made them look like a pair of majestic birds of prey.

As the rest of the group sat in the row behind, Tleta asked, "Are you nervous?"

"I would rather fight every single person here with my bare hands than rutting stand up and speak," Corrie said. "But here we are."

Tleta took her hand and squeezed. "No matter what happens, I am proud of you here."

"Thank you," Corrie said.

"And your appearance is divine," Tleta said. "Did your housemates do this to you?"

"I feel like a painting," Corrie said. "It feels silly."

"Divine," she said. With a sly, jewel-filled grin, she added, "But if I had known, I'd have suggested a small emerald in silver for that front tooth."

"Tleta, I'm going to say this with friendship and respect," Corrie said. "There's not a rutting chance of that happening."

Nas'nyom, sitting behind her, leaned forward. "Have you decided if you will speak in Imach, or in Trade, and I will interpret for you?"

"I got to talk in Imach," Corrie said. "If one thing has been made completely rutting clear to me, I have to show I respect these people and this borough. I can't do that and not speak their language."

"I understand."

"But stay close when I speak," Corrie said. "Guide me if I stumble."

"Of course."

At the table, the old man in the center wrapped his knuckles on the box in front of him, making a booming drum sound.

"Order called, order called. Tonight's session of the Council of Jachaillasa Borough, made of all her citizens who so choose to appear, is called to order." He looked out at the crowd with an appreciative nod. "This is quite a good turnout tonight, I am quite pleased to see so many of you today."

One of the other men said, "Even with such attendance, let's keep things civil and brief. None of us want to be here all night."

"Indeed," the center man said. "Let us begin with the examination of old business, and confirming the proper execution thereof. Olleivo, you have a report?"

The man at the end stood up and began to read off his papers—monotone and dry, filled with jargon and numbers. In less than a minute, Corrie's ears were overwhelmed. In three, she realized she was listening to the dullest man alive reciting the most boring thing she had ever heard.

Nalaccian leaned in from behind her. "Settle in for a bit, Sergeant. This part will take a while."

CHAPTER THIRTY-EIGHT

A FTER WHAT MUST HAVE BEEN an hour—or about a half a
star, by the timekeeping here, in as much as Corrie understood it
—the examination of old business came to an end, and the old man in
the center asked, "What new concerns await us?"

Nalaccian stood up. "I would sponsor a speaker."

"Citizen Assema," the old man said. "You are recognized. Who do
you sponsor?"

He signaled Corrie to stand up. "Sergeant Corrianna Welling, born
of Maradaine, under my ward. She speaks with my blessing."

"Your sponsorship is noted. Does any citizen of standing second
this, and can testify to the character of Welling of Maradaine?"

A man on the other side of the seating stood up. "I will so testify."
Corrie had no clue who this man was, but when he sat down, she saw
the young woman next to him. The one she had saved on the street some
weeks ago.

Tleta's mother stood as well. "She is in my employ, and she has
served admirably."

"We thank you, Madam Yalititca," the man in the center said. "We
will hear Sergeant Corrianna Welling, born of Maradaine."

Nalaccian gave Corrie a nudge. She cleared her throat and began,
with the specific phrases Nas'nyom had given her.

"I am grateful for your time and ears, Citizens of Jachaillasa. Please forgive me if I stumble in my speech. I am still learning your language, and I never was the most educated of people back home."

"We hear you and understand, Sergeant," the man in the center said. "Proceed."

"Before I came here, I was an officer in the Maradaine Constabulary, the peacekeeping and law enforcement body in my city. It was my duty and honor to serve, a calling in my family for eight generations." Talk about family and history, they told her. That would resonate. "I've always been proud to wear this uniform to serve the city I lived in. And now, I live here for the foreseeable future."

The man at the far end of the table raised his hand. "Sergeant, could you skip your preamble and reach the point of your speech?"

"In my time here, I've worked as a personal guard to the *tśîtśesh* of Taa-shej, and I've had to intervene several times for the safety of Miss Tletanaxia. But I've also found myself in the position, multiple times, where my sense of duty compelled me to protect various citizens when violence was being acted upon their person."

"You took it in your own hands," one of the men said. "By what authority?"

"That is precisely my point," Corrie said. "That this city needs people to be . . ." She didn't have the word in Imach, and looked to Nas'nyom. "Deputized?"

"Ghe'rho."

She repeated that. "To give them the power and authority to act on behalf of our neighbors, to protect and aid them."

"We all know that power can be abused," one of the men said. "How can we be assured that those given authority will be just, true, and godly?"

Corrie had been expecting a question like that. She pointed to the brass on her chest. "This badge probably doesn't mean anything to most of you, it's written in Trade. But it has my name on it. It means that anyone who sees me performing my duty can also hold me accountable. And I wear this uniform, the Green and Red of the Maradaine Constabulary, so I can be seen easily. So I stand out as an officer of the peace. If the city decides to create a constabulary force, which I sincerely hope they do, it is critical that those who run it maintain accountability, using tools like my badge and my uniform, and watch over their own to prevent abuse."

"Sergeant Welling," the man in the center said. "Are you just proposing that a force be created, or are you proposing that you run it?"

"Primarily the first, sir," she said. "As for the second, if asked to captain, I would be honored to serve. If you only seek my suggestions on how to run it, I will happily offer. Mostly, I just want the opportunity to serve this city like I did in Maradaine, and serve my neighbors by helping keep them safe."

There was, to Corrie's surprise, a smattering of applause at that. Most of that came from her housemates, but it was spread throughout the auditorium.

"Order, please," the man in the center said.

The man who asked her about how to the force would be just, true, and godly raised his hand. "Before we ask the people to vote, I would hear debate and dissent." He pointed to someone in the crowd. Pointed like he had already planned on this person to speak and he was just waiting for an opportune moment, which Corrie found rutting strange. Then that person stood up.

It was B'enelkha Hajan.

"I am gladdened to see such a sense of . . . community here," she said, her voice as fluid and poisonous as quicksilver. "My heart is filled to see the good and godly people of this city come together, especially the brothers and sisters who have joined the faithful of the Anach'Imal. I am ever so grateful that so many people have heard the true word of God, and that our place in this city, in this borough, and in the eyes of God have been so validated. Which is why I so heartily agree with Sergeant Welling."

What was she rutting doing? Corrie looked to her friends, and all of them seemed perplexed. Even Nalaccian looked very confused.

"We do need people to aid this borough, to guide and aid their neighbors on a path that is true and just and godly. Very much so. Such a force must be, we all need to agree, led by someone who speaks with the conviction and truth of God, and who commands the loyalty and respect of those under them. As Sergeant Welling put it, those who run it must keep their people accountable. What is more accountable than the word of God?"

Someone else stood up, wearing the green sash. "The Anach'Imal protect the word of God! They can protect Jachaillasa from the wicked and sinful!"

Someone else, also with a green sash. "The Anach'Imal stand ready and together!"

A third. "We stand, ready to fight, ready to hold the wicked to account, ready to obey the orders of our leader in the name of God."

Mister True and Just and Godly asked, "Is the suggestion put forth that this 'constabulary' force be comprised of the members of the Anach'Imal?"

The man in the center scoffed, "That is patently absurd—"

"I would not presume," Hajan said over him. "But if asked, I would be honored to serve." She looked over to Corrie and gave the barest of a sly smile.

"That is highly irregular," the man in the center said.

"We should put it to vote," True and Just and Godly said. "Does anyone make the call for a vote?"

One of those three green-sashes all called out. "Call for a vote! Make the Anach'Imal the enforcers of laws of God and man in the borough of Jachaillasa! Make B'enelkha Hajan, prophet of the voice of God, our commander in our holy war!"

"Call it for a vote!" the other two men called out.

"Can they do that?" Corrie asked Nalaccian.

"They can, but it doesn't matter if they don't have the votes."

"It is called to vote," the man in the center said. "If you are for this measure, stand and be counted."

So many people stood up, and as Corrie looked around the crowd she realized with dawning horror that they most definitely had the votes. She didn't even have to count. The auditorium was filled with people in green sashes.

"Everyone who shows gets to rutting vote," she muttered to herself. "They packed the rutting meeting."

"So it is voted, so it is done," the man in the center said, though he sounded very unhappy about it. "The Anach'Imal are our force of law, under the command of B'enelkha Hajan."

Corrie looked back to Hajan, whose face was so punchably gleeful. It took every bit of restraint Corrie had not to leap out and show that woman just how punchable her face was.

"How is this possible?" Tleta asked. "How did they do this?"

"I see how," Maäenda said, her voice a low growl. She pointed toward Hajan, and Corrie saw it. Ibareska and Osecca, the only residents of the debthouse who hadn't joined them tonight. They were seated right by Hajan, wearing green sashes.

"I am so grateful," Hajan said as everyone else sat down. "While we are here, and while we are voting, I think it is critical that we know what it means when we say that the laws of God are the laws of Mankind. I would propose we clarify some points."

"Proposal is heard," Mister True and Just and Godly said. And Corrie wanted to kick herself for not seeing it so clearly. This rutting bastard was in Hajan's pocket this whole blazing time. Minox would have seen it. If she had been smarter, had been paying attention, she would have caught it. Seen all the green sashes. She had fouled the whole thing up, and now none of her friends, housemates, or neighbors would be safe. And now she was stuck here, powerless to stop that woman as she made things even worse, and the bastard at the table enabled her. "We should hear the thoughts of our new captain of our constabulary, and vote on her laws."

"God is smiling down on us," Hajan said with an expression of pure bliss. "Truly, a new day is dawning here, and soon that day will burn across the sky, and the righteous shall stand tall! Hear me now as I speak his law!"

CHAPTER THIRTY-NINE

HAJAN MANAGED TO PASS ONLY a few edicts in that session of the council before the center chairman shut the whole meeting down, but the worst and most damaging one was imposing a borough-wide curfew on "foreigners, indigents, and indebted." They would have to be indoors, at designated addresses, by sunset. "For their own safety until the streets are safe from the ungodly," Hajan said.

Corrie couldn't believe what a fool she had been played for. The only thing that gave her a bit of comfort was that most of the girls in the debthouse were just as mad, but their anger was reserved for Ibareska and Osecca.

Those two said nothing, and tried to keep to themselves in their room. Basi wasn't having that, and started a ruckus when they tried to bed down. So they spent two nights on the roof. Srella refused to even let them eat or use the water, and insisted to Nalaccian that he take them somewhere else.

But when he came in two days, it was to clear their debts and remove the bolts on their ears. They left completely at liberty.

"The blazes is that?" Corrie asked once those two left.

"Their debts were covered," he said. "I have no cause to hold them even if I wanted to."

"Covered by Hajan?"

"I imagine," Nalaccian said. "There's little I can do."

Little to be done. Which Corrie understood, given how powerless she was. Her whole life had become a cruel joke. She had to walk the streets filled with green-sashed zealots wearing a mockery of her badge on their chests.

So much of this rutting stung, but the badges were the worst. They were in the same wedge-shield shape that hers was, the same brass color. But instead of a name, each one just said *"Rhehyyu Zha'ima."* Servant of God. Add in that they wore headdresses and scarves, hiding their faces, so there was no identifying any of them.

An army of faceless, nameless zealots on every corner of the borough.

Corrie still walked to Tleta's home each morning, her badge shining, nodding her head to each one as she passed. Eye contact with each one as she passed. She rutting hated them, but they were the officers of law on the streets right now, and she'd show respect. Show them that she wasn't going to break now. She bit onto her tongue with each nod she gave, not giving them a single excuse to come at her. Stay within the bounds of the law, such as it was.

Every time she nodded, they would say, *"Yimm gha."* We watch.

They could watch all they rutting wanted.

Corrie would take Tleta through her schedule. They would go up and check on Ang, looking more exhausted and worn down each day. In addition to meals from Tleta's household, Srella and Basi were making things to be brought to her, and Eana or Meija would deliver them. She was brought fresh clothes, and they were taken back to the debthouse for washing. All of which Tleta paid for—or made her mother pay for, it wasn't clear.

Tleta had to drop one of her late classes, because she wouldn't have been able to get back home in time afterward before curfew hour. She was hardly the only one affected. Many of the MCK students, as well as the faculty, now were subject to that absurd law. Nas'nyom had been quite scarce of late. Corrie hadn't seen him since the meeting night, and she needed to make a point to check on him.

"It will cool down, go back to normal by the end of the season," Tleta said as they walked back one afternoon.

"Why do you think so?" Corrie said. "Those bastards have a taste of power. They won't let go."

"You think I don't know about that?" Tleta asked. "I've already fled one country. This isn't a coup. It's just some bullies blowing their air. Once it stops being new, once it's no longer fun for them to throw around their weight, and it's just work, they'll ease up. Besides, if they become too disruptive, the other boroughs will intercede. They won't push too far."

"It's been my rutting experience that—"

"Hey!" A zealot guard got in their faces. "What language is that?"

"Druth Trade," Corrie answer in Imach.

"Do you both speak a proper language?" he asked. "Or are you stupid foreigners who never learned civil tongues?"

"We can," Tleta said in Imach.

"Then use it in the streets," he said. "Or we will assume you are spreading sedition and heresy."

Corrie bit back a response, and Tleta must have sensed how much Corrie wanted to snap, because she squeezed Corrie's hand while saying, "Our humble error. We will rectify."

Corrie knew it was her fault.

"It's not your fault, Crasher."

The Death Caller had been stalking Corrie's path back home from Tleta's household since the council meeting, and after five days, got in her path and spoke to her.

"I don't have time for you right now," Corrie said as she brushed past. "Stop pretending to be my father."

"I'm not your father," the Death Caller said, keeping pace with her. "But he's been drumming against my skull every waking and sleeping hour."

"What do you want?" Corrie asked.

"Honestly, I want a decent night's sleep at this point," she said. "My own fault, I suppose."

"How do you see that?"

The Death Caller made a sound—almost a sigh, almost a growl— and then said, "I saw you, and thought you could be an easy mark. A bit of Kellirac blood, you knew just enough Sechiall to be aware, and I could work you for a few coins."

Corrie stopped in the middle of the road, dumbfounded by this. She held up her debt-marked arm. "Do I look like I had a few coins to rutting spare, you conniving slan?"

"Hate me if you want," the Death Caller said. "Because I tried to draw on you, find someone among the dead to tempt you with, and that opened a door I can't close any more."

"Sounds like you made your own problem," Corrie said. "Just like I rutting did."

"It's not your fault, Crasher," she said, again with the lower voice. Then the Death Caller knocked her head with the palm of her hand. "Stop doing that!" she shouted out loud.

Two of the zealot guards glanced their way.

"How about we not," Corrie said low, taking the Death Caller by the arm and leading her off. "Let's not get their rutting attention."

"I don't disagree," she said. "I wish I could take it back, I wish I could stop it, but I can't, and . . . I am sorry."

"Well, we all are," Corrie said. "Just leave me alone."

"I can't," she said. "Listen, this is—I don't know what it is, but—"

"I'm not giving you any money," Corrie said. She couldn't believe the rutting gall of this woman. That she would dare to keep trying this— con, charade, whatever it was. She was working some long rutting game and she could go to blazes.

"I don't care, listen!" The Death Caller glanced about, as if to make sure she hadn't again gathered the attention of the zealot guard. "In addition to calling to the dead, I can . . . I can feel when death is coming. Like a little tap to the back of my skull. And right now, it's like I'm being slammed with a hammer. Something is coming, Sergeant, some- thing horrible. And he says—"

"What?" Corrie asked, trying to hold back the anger, the tears. "What do you claim my dead father wants to tell me?"

"He wants you to know he doesn't regret taking his last ride, even though he didn't see you again," she said. "And he's afraid you'll have to take yours soon."

Corrie couldn't take it, and as much as she wanted to wallop this woman over the head, beat her teeth in, the zealots were everywhere. They watched.

Ironic, there would be someone to stop her now in this city, thanks to her.

She stormed off, pushing her way through the crowds hurrying home before the bells of Night Star, before the beginning of curfew. She made it inside just as they were ringing. She shucked off her boots and climbed up the steps to find the whole household sitting around the *ghose'a.*

"We having a meeting?" she asked.

"There's not much else we can do right now," Maäenda said. "Day jobs are drying up. Nighttime jobs are gone."

"And no one wants the zealots to catch them with their *dhatcurr* out," Hanakhla said in broken Imach. "So no one is giving me any work either."

"I'm sorry," Corrie said. "It's my fault—"

"Maybe a little," Maäenda said.

"No," Eana stressed. "We're not saying that."

"She tried to fix something and it got worse instead," Maäenda said. "I've done that many times myself, it needs to be acknowledged."

"But it was that *et'um* and those traitors who really did it," Srella said. "I should have thrown them off the roof when I could."

"Enough," Corrie said. "I am sorry. I thought I could—"

"We thought so too," Hezinaz said. Her voice was hoarse, and her hands were red and raw. "We believe in what you were trying to do."

"We still do," Meija added.

Srella walked over to Maäenda and put her hands on the woman's shoulders, as if to spur a reminder. "Which is why we thought it was so important to be united now. Those of us still here."

"United in what?" Corrie asked.

Maäenda sighed. "It is now very dangerous out there for everyone who isn't one of the Anach'Imal. Especially women. Especially foreigners. Especially indebted." She gestured to the whole group gathered there. "All of us."

"You think I don't know that?" Corrie asked.

Srella gave Maäenda a slap on the arm. "Which is why—"

"Which is why," Maäenda echoed. "Now, more than ever, we all need to watch out for each other. Be there for each other. And be ready for things to go badly."

"They've gone pretty rutting badly," Corrie said.

"And we're going to need you to help us," Eana said.

"Haven't I done blazing enough?" Corrie asked.

"Please," Eana said. She picked up a cloth bag off the table. "We pooled together our money and bought this, one for each of us. We want you to teach us."

"You pooled your money for what?"

Eana dumped the contents of the bag onto the table.

It was full of wooden whistles.

CHAPTER FORTY

E VERY ONE OF THE GIRLS had had a run-in with the zealot
guard over the past few days. Srella and Maäenda had both been
made to acknowledge their heresy by not being among the faithful.
Pume and Saa both got harassed in the marketplace, the food they had
bought confiscated without explanation. Hanakhla had been called a
dozen insulting names and spat on, and had only not lost her temper
with those guards because Basichara had been on hand to get her away.
Meija had been asked to recite a passage from the Books of the Sun to
prove she was faithful.

Hezinaz had gotten it worst of all.

Some of them remembered Hezinaz from the dancing job, and
decided she was sinful, and thus penance was required. So that morning,
a gang of them had grabbed her and brought her to some dank basement.
They stripped her down, forced her to kneel down on all fours in a bed
of salt and recite a prayer of forgiveness, over and over. For hours.
Eventually, once she could barely speak, they grew bored of it all, and
pushed her back out onto the street half naked, throwing the rest of her
clothes in the dirt. She stumbled back home and fell into the washroom
until Basi and Eana found her and cleaned her up.

That was when Eana had decided about the whistles.

"You told me about how you use the whistle calls back in

Maradaine," she said. "How there's all sorts of codes, calling for help, alerting about trouble, saying if someone's hurt."

"And you think if we all have whistles, we can do what?" Corrie asked.

"Be there for each other," Srella said. "Imagine if Hezinaz could have called for help."

Corrie's first thought was that Hezi would have gotten it even worse, and whoever came to help her would have probably been beaten senseless.

"We need to protect ourselves," Eana said. She picked up one of the whistles. "And these, when you use them, have power."

"They have power when there's an actual organization—"

"What do we look like?" Eana asked.

"Ten girls who are going to rutting get themselves killed," Corrie said. "No weapons, no backup, there's nothing a whistle can do—"

"Maybe not if we have each other," Maäenda said as she took one of the whistles off the table. "And maybe not if you can teach us how you do it. I have heard stories about how you've used that whistle. Kept those zealots at bay on campus."

"Saved Nas'nyom," Saa said in halted, heavily accented Imach. She picked up a whistle.

"You kept five of them at the door with nothing but your sheer presence," Hezinaz rasped, taking one. "No weapons, no backup. Not even speaking the language. Just you, hands up, telling them no."

"Someone has to stand up," Basichara said, taking one.

"Someone has to say no," Meija added as she picked one up.

Pume didn't speak, but took one. The rest all took up the remaining whistles.

"All right," Corrie said. She took her whistle out of her pocket. Amazing that this had stayed with her since Maradaine. And they weren't wrong. The thing had saved her and Eana in the middle of the ocean. It had been the only thing she had to get the zealots off of Ang.

Ang. Was she alone tonight? What would happen if the zealots decided to come for her, accuse her of heresy for "unlocking heaven" and drag her out into the streets.

"All right," she said again. "If we're going to do this, we're really going to do this. You all shouldn't go in the street alone. Only in pairs."

"Teach us the whistle calls," Eana said.

"First thing is, we're going to learn them, but we'll do them real quiet. Last thing we need is to get the zealots' attention right now."

"They would hear?" Basichara asked.

Corrie grinned. "If I really blew, you'd hear it ten blocks away at least. Which is what you need. So really rutting blare when you need it, but right now, let's keep it low."

"Low," Srella repeated.

"Now, there's a bunch of calls that don't matter right now—"

"Why don't they matter?" Maäenda asked.

"Because you're not calling for a page or a lockwagon, because those don't exist here."

"Right," Maäenda said.

"So let's focus on what does matter. There are five big ones we'll need. The Trouble Call, the Safety Call, the Injury Call, the Riot Call and the Return Call. That last one is crucial."

"What's that one for?" Eana asked.

"The other four are all about letting people know what you need. You need backup, you need rescue, someone's been hurt, or things are going completely wrong. The Return Call is for acknowledgment. You hear one of the other calls, you give a Return and come running. But you make sure they hear that return so they know help is on the way."

"So what's that one?"

Corrie held the whistle to her lips. "Pay attention, it goes like this."

CHAPTER FORTY-ONE

T HE GIRLS WEREN'T WORKING—THE jobs were just gone at
the platform, so they all started being deputies for Corrie, in her
underground constabulary. Corrie did what she could to help them since
they weren't working. She still got well paid by Tleta's mother, and
convinced Tleta to give some of them formal work, but that had a limit
which was quickly reached. "We can only do so much for them all,
Corrie." She had been more than a little snappish when she said that.

Tleta's patience was strained. Corrie understood—she just wanted to
study medicine and anatomy, and she was stuck in the middle of this
business. Corrie had stuck her in it. Frankly, Corrie was amazed she had
put up with as much as she had.

The streets and marketplaces were nearly empty now, save Hajan's
people at nearly every intersection. Corrie had no idea if it was because
people were staying in, or if the people who *could* get out of Jachaillasa
already had. If so, it meant the only ones left were the poor, the desperate, and of course the indebted.

Corrie would have run too, if she could. Anyone sensible would
have.

Corrie covered Eana's rent, her debt payments, and a bit more. If she
could help it, she'd get Eana clean and on a boat home as soon as possible. Now that she knew Eana was a mage, there was no sense in wasting

time. Especially with these zealots. It was critical to get her back to Maradaine where she could be safe and learn at the University of Maradaine or wherever.

But even with little money, the girls of the debthouse were eager to do whatever they could. And that included keeping an eye on Ang.

Ang had no one else. It disgusted Corrie that the people of her government had put such pressure on her to deliver, to work herself to the bone, but had given her almost nothing to accomplish that. How could they dare to rutting do that to her?

So most nights, two of the girls from the house stayed up in the library tower with Ang. They did little more than sleep quietly while she worked, stayed out of her way. Ang didn't say much about it, but she seemed to appreciate knowing that someone was nearby.

Corrie hadn't slept much at all. Nas'nyom wasn't in his house, and she didn't know where he was. She hoped he had gone to one of the other boroughs, or was just hiding very well. She feared it was worse than that.

Since she wasn't sleeping much, she took every third night with Ang. Tleta, despite her stress, would stay each night Corrie did. Corrie suspected she just wanted to be able to stay in the library all night and do her reading in peace.

One of those nights, it was well past midnight, and Ang was doing calculations at her desk. Tleta had dozed off in the corner, one of her medical texts on her chest. Corrie was sitting in another corner with ink, pen, and sheafs of paper.

Dear Minox—

Today is 597 Pe'zhi zha frrosh Hafialtar here in the Mocassa, which literally means 'Day six of the tenth in the Season of Death in year 597.' Not that I really get why its year 597 here and 1215 at home, but that's how it is. Near as I figure, that's the first of Sholan for you, but who knows what rutting day it'll be when you get this.

That's my way of saying, yeah, I'm still alive, stuck in the Mocassa. Surprise.

Corrie resisted the urge to crumple up the sheet. She had already done that with the last three, and she had gotten the impression that Ang resented the waste of paper.

She had been writing all sorts of letters while up here with Ang, one to everyone in her family. She had a bundle of them ready, if she ever got a chance to put them on a boat bound for Maradaine. Most of them were easy. Mama was tough, but she got through it. Alma and Jace were a bit hard, too. The cousins were pretty easy, same with all the aunts and uncles. Her brother Oren was really easy.

Dear Oren—

I'm alive in the Mocassa. This city is full of jerks just like you. Try not to be such a bastard all the time. Everyone would appreciate it.

Corrie

But writing the letter for Minox was rutting impossible. She wanted to tell him so many things, and she didn't know where to start. Which meant she kept trying stupid things, like talking about the Imach calendar.

"How's it going?" Ang asked.

"Terribly," Corrie said. "How about you?"

"I'm seeing nothing but a blurs when I'm looking at these numbers."

"Break," Corrie said.

"Breaks are not part of the discipline."

"Then your discipline is dumb," Corrie said. "Your head is spinning. Break."

Ang came over and sat on the floor next to Corrie. "Is that Druth discipline? To take breaks during important work?"

"It's funny," Corrie said. "Plenty of times on night shift, I would sneak over to my house to get something to eat, because I knew that it didn't really matter, there were other sticks on duty, I could slip off for a little. But when I knew it mattered—like when my brother Minox was missing and maybe losing his head—wasn't anything that could make me stop."

"Really?"

"Blazes, that day, this scar?" she pointed to her eye. "That was freshly stitched, bandaged over, didn't know if I'd see again, and some"—she chuckled, realizing there was a bit of poetic echo to this—"some Imach fanatics had taken me hostage, and Minox had stopped them just before vanishing. Everyone told me I had been through enough, I should go home and take the rest of day off, but . . . like blazes I was going to do that."

"It must sound crazy to you," Ang said. "But my work here, it feels like that to me."

"Not that crazy," Corrie said. "I mean, I don't get it at all. Why looking at the moons and stars and even spotting this comet or whatever, why it's got so many people riled up."

"You'll see the comet," Ang said. "You can't with your bare eye right now, but in a few days?"

"It'll be impressive?"

"Rather," Ang said.

"But why?" Corrie asked. "Like, why does Druth Intelligence want you, why does Hajan want to stop you? You say the work is important, and I know I won't rutting understand a bit of it, but I believe you. But why is it?"

Ang furrowed her brow. "All right, how versed are you in astrology, magical focal points, and mystical theory?"

"Not in the rutting slightest," Corrie said with a laugh.

"Let me try and break it down into simple terms," Ang said. "This is actually good for me, because I will need to present this to laypeople at the enclave."

"I am pretty much laypeople," Corrie said.

"Which—maybe twenty people on the whole planet really understand what I'm up to."

"That's good, I won't feel like a total idiot."

"So, you're from Maradaine. You were there earlier in the year?"

"Sure."

"And you worked nights. You remember a night where one moon was full, and the other was a crescent, and they crossed over each other to make a winged moon?"

"I do," Corrie said. That had been a bit of a crazy night. Folks had gone a bit wild in the streets, and there were a whole lot of arrests for lewd behavior and untoward mischief.

"So, that crossover? It's impossible. Shouldn't happen."

"It did, though."

"I know it did, but it shouldn't have. And if you observe the night sky, the movements of the moons and stars and planets, there are a ton of little things that *shouldn't* happen but do. And we're going to get one in a few days, if my calculations are right."

"You said the eclipse and the comet."

"Right. Because, like I said, you're going to be able to see the comet with your bare eye. Really big, even. Which you shouldn't be able to do."

"All right, I can get my head behind that."

"Here's the wild thing," Ang said, and just talking about it had clearly energized her. "That's only going to happen here, if I've gotten it right. On Jachaillasa. The rest of the city, the other boroughs, the rest of the world? They won't see what we'll see. They'll get the eclipse to some degree, depending on where they are—that doesn't matter—they'll see that, and will make out the comet, but right here, it's going to be a whole different show."

"Why is that?"

"So there's a thing in the sky—in Tsoulja we call it *tet-lok*. If there's a Druth name for it, I haven't come across it. Maybe no one has published about it yet. But roughly it means 'the Unseeable.'"

"A thing in the sky we don't see."

"Right, but it will do things we can see. So, for example, the winged conversion over Maradaine. You can't see it anywhere else, it's impossible, but you do see it in Maradaine, and that's because the Unseeable is changing what you see."

"Like a dirty window almost?"

"A smudged lens would be a better comparison, but roughly."

Corrie could get her head around that. She remembered a thing her cousins used to do when she was a kid. "And like a lens, it focuses on one specific place. Like using one to make the sunlight set something on fire."

"Right on the line," Ang said. "And part of what it focuses are mystical energies."

"Magic?"

"Magic and more," Ang said. "This is out of my field, but 'magic' is a narrow section of the full scope of mystical powers."

"Out of my field as well," Corrie said.

"But, in theory, positions of the moons, the planets, and especially the Unseeable can have effects on those powers."

It all clicked in Corrie's head. "You're figuring out an almanac for this Unseeable. Where it's going to be, what it's going to do, and where it's going to do it."

"More than that," Ang said. "My theory is that there is more than one 'Unseeable,' and the big moments are when their effects line up and magnify each other. We're going to see if I am right in a few days. I've been making all these observations, all these calculations, and if I've got it right, this eclipse with the comet, here on Jachaillasa, is going to be a very powerful moment indeed."

"Powerful as in, magic will go wild?"

"Magic and everything else," Ang said. "On a titanic scale. And my observations and calculations will help find other moments and places where that will be true."

"And that's got value for Druth Intelligence."

"I would imagine so," Ang said. "And . . . come see this." Staying on the floor, she crept over to the window. Just peeking over the sill, she pointed to the campus grounds below. "You see them?"

The zealots were down there. But no rioting or shouting, not this time. They seemed to be kneeling on the ground in silent prayer, but even stranger, they were kneeling in a pattern that formed a circular spiral. Someone stood at the center of that spiral, and while Corrie couldn't quite make out who it was in the dark, she would bet a month's salary it was B'enelkha Hajan.

"What are they doing?" Corrie whispered as they moved away from the window.

"I have no idea," Ang said. "But they started a few nights ago. And I would imagine, someone more versed in mystical theory than I am might have some thoughts about the shapes they're forming, where those shapes are focused, and how that affects mystical energies."

"And how your Unseeables might magnify that, especially when the eclipse and the comet come?"

"That's what I'm very afraid of," Ang said.

"Do you want us here for that?" Corrie asked. "I could bring out all the girls from the house if you want, in case they get a little too frisky?"

"I would love that," Ang said. "But, no. The Tsouljan Commission has, for once, listened to me. They're sending a few of the Vil from the *teknosom* here for the event."

"Finally," Corrie said. "Your people seem to hang you out to dry, but ask a whole rutting lot of you."

"It's duty and service," Ang said. "You understand that, I would think."

"I do, but it cuts both blazing ways. They have duty to you."

"Which they are going to be here for." She chuckled drily. "Of course, I'm not blind to the fact that they want to be on hand to safeguard and deliver my data."

"That's what they're really protecting."

Ang sighed. "Duty and service."

"All right," Corrie said. She went over to Ang's desk and found the whistle buried under her papers. Pressing it into Ang's hand, she said, "Just remember, you need anything, you just call."

"You see?" Ang said. "You understand very well."

CHAPTER FORTY-TWO

W HEN CORRIE GOT BACK TO the debthouse the following
afternoon, there was a cadre of zealot guards outside the house.

"Hold up," one of them said as she approached. "What business do
you have here?"

"I live here," Corrie said.

"Identify yourself," he said.

"Corrie Welling."

"You knew that," one of the other zealots said to the first.

"We had to confirm."

"What's going on?" Corrie asked.

"We can't let anyone unauthorized go into this house right now," the
first said.

"Who would be unauthorized?"

"We'll ask the questions!" the second snapped.

"But who would be?" the first asked. "Is she supposed to wait here?"

"No, she—but we're supposed to protect—"

"But isn't she—"

"Am I not allowed inside?" Corrie asked, ignoring their foolish
questions. These fellows really didn't seem to know what they were
doing. "Is it a crime scene or something?"

"Why would it be a crime scene?" Saints above, these boys were terrible at this job. Because they knew nothing but fanaticism and cruelty.

"I don't know, but if you're keeping people out, it might be because a crime was committed inside and you need to keep the scene clear to examine evidence. Is that the case?" Corrie knew it clearly wasn't the case, though she was now very worried about all the other girls.

The guards had to think a moment. "No, not . . . not like that. We just are supposed to—"

Corrie had had enough. She stepped back. "Srella!"

Srella's head poked out the window, her usual olive complexion pale and drawn. "Corrie, get in here!"

"I need to get in there, fellows," Corrie said.

"Is she supposed to?" the first asked.

A third member of the cadre sighed. "Yes, she's the one we're waiting for. Go in there, unbeliever."

Helpful but rude. Fine. Corrie went inside, stripped her boots off, and went up the stairs.

B'enelkha Hajan was sitting in the *ghose'a*, sipping at a cup of coffee. "Finally she returns. I thought I would be waiting all night."

"What are you doing here?" Corrie asked.

"Waiting for you, Sergeant," Hajan said. "Your housemates have been very hospitable for heathens. It does my soul good to know that there may be hope."

Srella was in the kitchen, looking like she had been holding a scream inside her throat all day. "Well, I'm here. Srella, go up."

Srella rushed over to the stairs, her hand brushing Corrie's as she passed. "Everyone else is upstairs."

"They're fine?"

"Fine," Srella said and went up.

"Sit, Sergeant," Hajan said. "Have a coffee with me, that we may talk with civility."

Corrie cautiously walked into the *ghose'a* and sat down. No rutting idea what this game was. "No coffee for me, thank you. I won't be able to sleep tonight."

"And how are you sleeping, Sergeant? And more importantly, where? Where did you sleep last night?"

"This is where I live," Corrie said.

"It is, and as the curfew comes down with nightfall, it is where you must be. And you continue to work? No problems there?"

"I'm fortunate to have a good job right now."

"Not all the heathen debtgirls can say that, so quite bully for you, child."

That spiked Corrie's rising temper. "What . . ." she started with a snarl, but then held it back. Anger wouldn't get her anywhere. Fighting wouldn't get her anywhere.

What would Pop have done here? What would Minox do? Get information. Information was her only weapon here.

"Why have you come to see me?" she asked, keeping her temper in check.

"I have been vexed, Sergeant. Positively vexed."

Unhelpful, empty answer. "What about?"

"I am vexed that I have failed you, my dear Sergeant. Failed you in so many ways."

Still empty and unhelpful. "How so?"

"I commend you on the command you've gained of the language, child, in the short time you have been here. How did you do that?"

"I had a good teacher," Corrie said.

"You must have. Can you *please* let him know my prayers are with him?"

That felt like a bait. Had they done something to Nas'nyom? Was she trying to force Corrie to get angry?

"Surely this isn't about my language skills."

"Tell me, Sergeant," Hajan said. "You grew up in Maradaine, yes?"

"Yes."

"Is it as decadent and sinful as they say? Or is there actually decency and godliness, in your own pitiful way?"

"Churches all over town," Corrie said. "And constables on every corner."

"Yes, officers of the law. You are very proud of your position with them. Even now, still wearing your uniform and badge."

"It matters," Corrie said. "I show exactly who I am."

"Indeed you do," Hajan said. "I have been very impressed by

that . . . forthright honesty in your character. As troubled as you are, child, you do not hide your nature. Yes, I think God sees that in you. You may be astray, but I think this speaks well for how you could be redeemed."

"Pardon?"

"Were you raised in the faith of your people?" Hajan asked. "Were you, by the flawed standards of Druthal, a godly woman?"

"I didn't burst into flame when I walked into a church," Corrie said.

"I find myself in a troubling situation, child. When I heard of your plan to bring a policing force to this borough, I knew—God told me in my heart—that I needed to take action. That this would be the way to bring godliness to this troubled place. But I fear I have mis-stepped."

"Oh, I would agree with that," Corrie said.

"I saw you as an adversary, Sergeant, because I feared you—a strange, foreign girl who knows nothing of us—could not be brought to God. It was impossible. But now it is clear, as . . . dedicated and right-eous as my faithful are, they are not yet up to the task of serving God as custodians of the public."

"Again, I would definitely agree," Corrie said. She didn't know where this woman—*do not trust her,* she reminded herself—was trying to take this conversation, but she wasn't completely off the pier if she recognized that her zealots were terrible as constables.

"I am so glad you see things my way," Hajan said. "So let us begin with taking you into the fold with the Rite of Acceptance, and then you can begin with the task God sent you here to do. Leading my followers as captain of our guard."

"The who in the rutting what?"

What Corrie had said, in Imach, was actually far more offensive and vulgar than that.

"Sergeant, there is no need for such speech," Hajan said. "I might have to retract the commendation of your teacher if it included such things."

"Most useful part of the vocabulary," Corrie said. "Let me make something very clear, Miss Hajan. There is no rutting way I am taking the Rite of Acceptance or whatever the blazes that is. There is no rutting way I am taking place in your blasted cult, nor is there any rutting way I will teach your rutting zealots how to be better oppressors of my friends and neighbors, and there is definitely no rutting way I am going to be the captain of your guard. And just so we are perfectly clear, whatever God you seem to think whispers into your bat-filled heart had nothing to do with my arrival in this city. I didn't rutting know why Saint Veran put me on this path, but it is becoming very clear that he sent me to put a stop to you!"

Hajan's glare never broke while Corrie went off on her, and when Corrie finished, a sly smile spread across her face. "I am disappointed to hear that, child, but not surprised. I had little faith that your heathen soul could be saved so easily." She got to her feet. "No, Sergeant, I can see it's going to be a much harder fight indeed."

"I'm always here for a harder fight."

"Are you really, Sergeant?"

Corrie narrowed her eyes, and rising up to meet Hajan's gaze, used one of her father's favorite responses when someone was giving him the business. "Take your swing and find out."

Corrie expected that fight, right here and now. She expected Hajan to call up the zealot guard on the street below. She steeled her nerve, slowed her breath, and shifted her weight to the balls of her feet.

Hajan didn't do that. She just went down the stairs and out of the house, while Corrie stood in the *ghose'a*, with the sound of her pounding heart filling her ears as Hajan and the zealot guard marched off down the street.

"Is she gone?" Srella asked, sticking her head through the hole in the ceiling. "Is it safe?"

"She's gone," Corrie said. "Safe is a whole other matter."

Srella came down and grabbed Corrie in an embrace. "You are very brave, Corrie Welling. Foolish, but brave. Please tell me you have a plan of what you are going to do."

"A plan?"

"To put a stop to her."

"Not in the slightest," Corrie said.

Srella did not look deterred. "Then tell me when you do. In the meantime, I should introduce you to the new girl in the house." She whistled up the steps.

"Does she speak the language?" Corrie asked.

"Several, in fact," Srella said as someone came down the steps. Corrie glanced at them for a moment, and her anger melted away. Despite the traditional robes of Imach feminine clothing, the headwrap and veil over the face, she knew exactly who she was looking at.

"Nas'nyom!" she shouted as she grabbed him in an embrace. "Where have you been?"

"Hiding many places," he said, removing the veil. "With this disguise, I was able to get here, and it was only a few moments before Miss Hajan showed up."

"We hid him straightaway," Srella said.

"So they were after you?" Corrie asked.

"For being of Tekir Sanaa, for not being of the faith, for loving other men, or whatever other hosts of reasons. They had my name and came to my home, and I barely escaped them."

"I am so glad you did," Corrie said.

"I am as well," he said with a toothy smile. "You do not have qualms about hiding a fugitive from the law."

"What they are doing is not law," Corrie said. "Not any that I care to uphold. I'd rather stand for justice."

"Justice it is," he said.

"Then let's hope we can get some without paying too high a price," Srella said. "None of us have much to spare."

CHAPTER FORTY-THREE

ORRIE FOUND EANA ON THE roof of the house, sitting on the concrete floor with several books open around her.

"Studying?" Corrie asked.

"Yup," Eana said. She held her hands together and turned them in opposite directions while pulling them apart. A glowing blue ball formed in her hands.

"Impressive," Corrie said. "Magic books?"

"Books on technique," Corrie said. "Nas'nyom brought them over, said he found them in the restricted rooms of the campus library. Apparently no one is really around to enforce the restrictions right now."

"Wouldn't have thought of that," Corrie said.

"Of course, I can only read a couple of them. And my reading in Imach is . . . not great."

"You and me both, sister," Corrie said, sitting in front of her.

Eana looked up. "You really mean it when you call me that, don't you?"

"We may not be blood, but we've been through enough together, I think it feels blazing on point."

"What about the rest of the girls in the house?" Eana asked.

"I'm not there with them. Maybe getting there, but we'll see."

"The girls that are still here are solid," Eana said. "The sort you want in a jam with you."

"They are in a jam with us. But still, we saw with Ibareska and Osecca, everyone might be in it for themselves."

"Maybe," Eana said. "I think if any of the other girls were like them, they'd have left."

"None of them have the options," Corrie said. "Pop would say, 'everyone's a friend in the cell, and a stranger on the street.'"

"And we're in the cell?"

"Ain't we just?"

"You really don't trust these girls, after all they've done?"

"Trust?" Corrie asked. "Whether or not I trust them doesn't matter. If it comes to it, I'll stand next to any one of them, stand in front of them all to keep them safe, because that's my—" Corrie laughed. "I was about to rutting say 'that's my job.' But it ain't, is it?"

"I don't think it's ever stopped being your job, Cor," Eana said. "You know you don't have to take care of me, right?"

"I made a vow to a saint," Corrie said. "And if I've learned one thing in all this, those things need to be taken seriously. That means I don't ever stop taking care of you, not until you walk through the door of your father's house, hear?"

"Heard," Eana said quietly. She turned one of the books to Corrie. "Does this stuff about finger movement make sense to you? The book is Lyranan, I think, but it's got a lot of intricate diagrams."

"I don't know a damn thing about that. My brother never learned anything proper, so I don't know if finger movements matter."

"And this one, it's got a really good description of how to feel the magical energy and channel it. Reading it, and then trying it, it's like—" Eana looked up at the stars and grinned. "It's spending your whole life thinking you couldn't walk, and then just learning that your shoes were too tight."

"You're wearing shoes right now?"

Eana shifted her legs out from under her to shove her feet in Corrie's face. "My shoes are *off* and I'm free!"

Corrie batted them away, laughing. "Your feet are nasty."

"Yours are no better."

"I'm not sticking them in your face."

"Thank Saint Hesprin."

"Shut it."

"Make me."

"I will!"

Corrie grabbed Eana and wrestled her down, like she and Ferah used to when they were girls. Eana, cackling, pushed Corrie off of her, and they both fell back on the floor, howling with laughter.

The frivolity grew quiet, and after a minute of just listening to the sounds of the night, Eana asked, "We're in a lot of trouble here, aren't we?"

"You heard Hajan came here?"

"I saw her, and dashed up."

"She's got my number. And I didn't exactly hold my tongue with her."

"I'm shocked."

"Shut it."

"So now what?"

"Every day, we keep trying to make it through, until we don't," Corrie said.

"Right," Eana said. "But something is coming. Maybe it's just learning about how my magic feels but . . ." She let herself trail off.

"But?"

"The magic, it's like pricks on my skin. And the past couple days, it's like I'm lying on a bed of needles."

"Well," Corrie said, sitting up. "Ang says there'll be an eclipse and a comet tomorrow. So it's going to be a big day."

CHAPTER FORTY-FOUR

CORRIE WOKE UP BEFORE THE sun came up. Back home, it was Sholan the 4th, 1215, basically any other day. It wouldn't even be morning there, Ang had explained to her once, showing her something with a lamp and a globe, but Corrie didn't fully get it. But if it was morning, on Sholan the 4th, it would be another day where Mama and Aunt Zura were up before the sun, just like Corrie was now. They would get down to the kitchen and start making biscuits and frying salt pork and using the fat to make potatoes.

Uncle Timmothen would come down shortly after to sit out front with the morning newssheets. Which one he'd read first depended on if Aunt Emma hadn't beat him down. They would argue and snipe over the news, especially if there was a story about the suffragette movement. Ferah and Edard would be stumbling in with the dawn, if they were both still stuck on night duty. The rest of the house would be running around with taking their turns in the water closet, getting ready to go out to work, Nyla and Alma the first ready. Alma would be going to her last year of prepatory. Then Oren, the tosser, would be off to his station-house. Jace, too. Saints, the day she was taken, Jace had made patrol-man. Aventil was a mess of a neighborhood for him to be patrolling, but he seemed so happy with that beat. He was with good people.

Aunt Beliah would try to bring a plate of breakfast out to Evoy in the barn. Hard to say if Evoy would take it. Corrie hadn't even seen him in so long, long before she had gotten taken. Maybe the family had finally brought him to an asylum. She honestly didn't know why they hadn't yet.

And what would Minox be doing? Last she knew, he had been put off regular duty for a hundred days, so he could learn more about magic and maybe not be declared a danger. Those hundred days had long passed. How was he doing now? What was he doing?

Had they sat mourning for her? Were they all going on with their lives, accepting that she had taken her last ride, and that she was gone? Had they long since given up?

Here, it wasn't Sholan the 4th. Here, it was 597 Pe'rhef zha frrosh Hafialtar. Ninth day of the tenth *mnu* of the Season of Death. The last day of the year. Tomorrow was 598 Pe'belavh. The Day of Beginning.

A holy day.

But today was the day, according to Ang, that things would really go wild.

Corrie went down to the troughs, did her business, then up to the water room to wash off. Srella and Basi were already in the kitchen. Saa and Pume in the *ghose'a*, eyeing each other warily as they silently prepared themselves; Saa cleaning her fingernails, Pume oiling her arms.

"Anyone working?" Corrie asked.

"Besides you?" Basichara asked. "Not that I've heard."

"Maäenda had a lead on something," Srella said. "One of the wealthy families up north needs extra hands to clean and serve for something. She was going to try to get as many of us the gig as she could."

"Safe?" Corrie asked.

"We'll all go with whistles," Srella said.

Saa and Pume both held up their whistles.

"If Eana goes, keep a very close eye on her," Corrie said. "Today might be . . . odd."

"Odd why?" Srella asked.

"Things are happening in the sky today," Corrie said, deciding there was little need to explain it further.

"I hear this," Basichara said. "That is probably why the wealthy are having a party."

"Makes sense," Srella said.

"And it might affect magic," Corrie said. "At least, this is what I hear."

"Ang said it?" Basichara asked as she flipped flatbreads on the hot griddle with her bare fingers. "Tsouljans know these things."

"Ang knows these things," Srella said. "She is very smart."

"Just keep an eye on Eana, please," Corrie said. "I don't want her, I don't know, exploding or something."

Corrie went up and got dressed—most of the rest of the girls were rousing and in the process of getting themselves together. Eana was still asleep—she had been up late going through the magic books—and Corrie wanted to let her sleep.

Dressed and back to the kitchen, Corrie found coffee and a few *dyokah* rolls—flatbread with a sweetly spiced soft cheese rolled like a cigarillo—waiting for her. She happily ate them all, said quick goodbyes to the girls who were around, and went out to Tletanaxia's home.

Half a block from Tleta's house, Lieutenant Moriel all but jumped out of an alley and got right in Corrie's face.

"What kind of stupid are you?" he asked.

"Good to rutting see you as well," she said, stepping around him.

"Do you have any idea what you've done?"

"I didn't know you cared, Lieutenant."

"All you had to do was bring in Rek-Nouq. You could have done that, and you and Miss Mellick would have been on a boat home weeks ago."

"Bring her in?" Corrie asked. "Like she was a fugitive?"

"She's a valuable asset."

"She knows that, and she doesn't want to be your valuable asset."

"So you talked to her about it?"

"Yeah, and she wanted nothing to do with it."

"Then you didn't do a good job of it, did you?" he asked. "You didn't sell it."

"Sell it?" Corrie asked. "The rutting blazes did you think I am?"

"A loyal Druth citizen who wanted to get home. And you've all but ruined your chance to."

"All but?"

"The mess this neighborhood is in is all your fault, Welling. You wanted to start a constabulary? What were you thinking?"

"That I wanted to protect my friends and neighbors here," she said. "That's what I do."

"Instead you opened a door for that mad witch to take her madness to the next level here. And it's going to get worse."

"Worse how?"

"I've got a file on B'enelkha Hajan as long as my arm," he said. "She is going to—it doesn't matter."

"Like blazes it doesn't," she said.

"Listen, before things go to the sewers, just get Ang Rek-Nouq, and get her to the Druth Legation. We've got a safehouse for you all there, and then—"

"Wait," Corrie said. "I know there's the embassy in Teamaccea, and the trading enclave in Mahacossa, but . . . where is there a legation?" Not that she knew the real difference between any of those.

He pointed down the road. "Three blocks that way. The Royal Coat of Arms on the gate."

Corrie could have fallen over dead at that point. "There's a rutting Druth Legation in this part of the city and no one rutting told me?"

"It's right there," he said again. "That's where my main office is."

Almost within a rock's throw of Tleta's house. How could she have missed that? How could she not have known?

"Get Ang, get her there, and we will get you out of this city *today*. And we really need to today."

"Because of the eclipse?"

"Among other things," he said.

"And how would we?"

"The HMS *Queen Mara's Pride* is ready to launch for Maradaine, docked at the southern tip, by the bridge crossing to Mahacossa. I plan to be on it before the sky darkens, and if you get Rek-Nouq, you can be on it, too."

"Eana, too?"

"Certainly," he said. His lip curled in an infuriating smile. He knew that would tempt her. "If you have any sense, you'd get out now."

"Ang doesn't want to come," Corrie said. "And maybe I don't either."

"Foolish," he said. He started to walk off. "We're clearing everything out of there, and I'll be gone by midday. That's how long you have."

She let him leave. He was right about one thing: she was all kinds of stupid. Especially since she was going to let him go and blow up the best chance she'd have to get home.

But the price was Ang. She could easily string up the girl and haul her in, which was clearly what he expected Corrie to do. But she wouldn't do that. She could never do that. She was a constable, not a damned spy.

She reached Tleta's door, which swung open hard and fast, and Tleta stormed out at her, shoving Corrie down to the dirt.

"I should have known!" Tleta shouted "A rutting spy!"

CHAPTER FORTY-FIVE

"I'M NOT—"

"I just saw you," Tleta shouted. "I saw you talking to that bastard!"

"Lieutenant Moriel?"

"Oh, yes, him," Tleta said. "Glad you two are so familiar. I should have rutting known. I should have—*shâ weŋ ty'ô tś'il nitt shôwapno hêx* —you seemed too good to be true, and I should have known!"

"Hold on a rutting minute!" Corrie shouted, switching to Trade because she was too worked up to think and talk in Imach at the same time. "I've met that man twice and I've liked him neither time! I don't know why you hate him but believe me, I'm right there with you!"

"That's exactly what a spy would say!"

"How do you even know him?"

"How—" Tleta stopped and sputtered more in her native tongue. "Why do you think—how do you—we're stuck here—can't you—"

"What are you even talking about?"

"Who do you think backed the coup that ousted my mother? Who do you think backed my cousin? Who do you think you're supposed to be protecting me against? *Druth Intelligence*, you stupid, insipid girl."

"I had no idea!"

"Of course you didn't!" Tleta stormed away, toward the market bazaar square. Corrie chased after her.

"If I did—hey stop!" Corrie caught up and grabbed Tleta's arm. "If I did, if I was under him, do you think—"

Tleta wrenched her arm away and charged off again.

"Do you think I'd be dumb enough to talk to him right under your window?"

Tleta stopped and turned around.

"Fine," Tleta said. "Then what did he want?"

"Something I'm not going to do," Corrie said.

"Oh? And what is that? Oh, wait, it's bringing Ang into him. Which you've been working her for."

"What?"

"You thought I was asleep, but I heard you talking to her about it!"

"Then you heard that it wasn't going to happen!"

"That's how all the spies work!" Tleta was really in a fury. "Tell you lies to make you think they're on your side."

"Hey, now," Corrie said. "I don't know what rutting went down in Xonaca, or how Moriel or Druth Intelligence was involved."

"Will you shut your mouth?" Tleta shouted. "I cannot believe I fell for it. Fell for you! With the whole 'I'm just a simple girl with a filthy mouth' act!"

"That is not a rutting act!"

Out of nowhere, someone jumped over and grabbed the both of them by the arms.

"Ladies, please, perhaps not in such a public place!" It was the Death Caller, looking like a fire had been set in her belly. "You need to get somewhere out of sight for this conversation."

"Let me go!" Tleta said, yanking her arm free. "I am done listening, done being treated like a child! And I am done with you!"

The Death Caller's expression shifted, as did her voice. "Crasher, you've got to get out of here."

"Stop that rutting game right now," Corrie said. "I do not have time for your grift right now."

"It's not a—" she said in her normal voice, and then her head snapped in the other direction. "Corrie, just grab your friend and hide, there's no time—"

"Tleta!" Corrie called. "Let's get inside and—"

"And nothing!" Tleta said as she turned away. "I'm going home before—"

Before didn't happen, as a cadre of zealot guard came running at them, knives and sticks out.

"All of you! Hold fast!"

"Easy," Corrie said, switching back to Imach. "Everything is fine."

"No, it isn't. You all are clearly speaking sedition and sacrilege!"

"We are not," Corrie said. "There's no need—" The zealots grabbed all three of them and bound their hands their backs.

"You were speaking in foreign tongues to hide your blasphemy! You must be taken in for inquest and penance!"

CHAPTER FORTY-SIX

THE ZEALOTS HAULED THEM—CORRIE, Tleta, and the Death Caller, who kept thrashing her head back and forth as they went—through the bazaar, and down a dark corner to a building that looked like it had been a coffee shop in the recent past.

As they were brought in, Corrie saw it definitely had been a coffee shop—the tables and chairs stacked to one side, the dishware piled to one side behind the counter—but the main floor had been repurposed. There were several devices that were clearly designed to bind and abuse people, a few whips, a brazier of glowing coals, a bed of salt, and a few things Corrie did not recognize at all.

"What is this?" Tleta asked.

One of the zealots smacked her across the face. Corrie jumped forward, even though she had her hands bound behind her, and smashed her head into his gut. Two of the other guards pulled her off him. Then they forced the three of them to their knees. Then another zealot—whose green sash had a few yellow chevrons on it—came out from what would have been the coffee shop kitchen.

"Have you brought malefactors before me?" he asked.

"We heard these three speaking in foreign tongues, in words of blasphemy and sedition."

"Very troubling," he said. "You three, you have been charged with serious sins."

"Not crimes?" Corrie asked.

"The same thing, in the eyes of God," he said. "State your names, malefactors."

"You have no—" Corrie started before she took a smack to the face. She was angry, terrified, worried for Tleta, but in the front of her mind was the strangest feeling of all: annoyance. She was annoyed by the lack of proper procedure or respect to rights and process. They hadn't set up a proper stationhouse, but just took over a coffeehouse and made it into an improvised torture room. What kind of policing, what kind of justice was that?

She spat out blood and looked back up at this fellow with his fancy sash. "Pathetic."

He grabbed her chin. "State your name, sinner."

"Corrianna Welling, Sergeant in the Maradaine Constabulary."

"And you, savage?" he asked Tleta.

She scowled, and said, "Tletanaxia, First Daughter to the *quqô tśînôsho* of the *tśîtśesh* of Taa-shej, third in the court of the Tchoja, the Children of the Sky, and the jewel in the eye of all Xonaca, the mother-land of all people, whose womb is ever fruitful."

Fancy Sash glanced at one of the other zealots. "Are we writing this down? We need to write this down."

One of the others got a stylus and a pad and starting jotting things down. Then Fancy Sash went to the Death Caller.

"And your name?"

The Death Caller's face turned up to him, but her eyes were clouded and white.

"It's Adisslana, silly. You know that."

He stumbled back. "How did you—"

"You've gotten so old, Nassir. How long since I saw you?"

"That's not possible . . ."

"You said you were coming back, Nassir, but you never did. I had gotten so hungry. You said you were coming back. Why didn't you come back?"

"What is this blasphemy?" he shouted. "Is this a witch?"

The Death Caller's head snapped to one side, her eyes went clear. "She's the one who wanted to talk to you. Do you have an answer for her? Do you want to tell Adisslana why you left her to die?"

"How dare you say her name!"

His fist cracked down across the Death Caller's face, knocking her down. She looked up at Corrie and winked, saying in Trade, "Stay sharp, Crasher."

"You three are full of blasphemy," he said. "But you have a glorious opportunity now. The opportunity to endure your penance, speak the holy words of acceptance, and become worthy of the Light of God."

"That isn't going to happen," Corrie said.

"You might rethink that, Druth woman," he said. He took a set of metal tongs and removed one of the smoking coals from the brazier. "Because the Light of God is the only chance your soul has. Today, the world burns, and your flesh shall be forfeit. So your soul must be prepared, so it is worthy of the Light of God. The only way sinners such as you can achieve worth is through fire and pain. And you shall be made to repent and submit, so that you may be saved. Today is the last day, for the world will turn dark, the sky will burn, and God will call us the worthy to our reward."

Two of the guards grabbed Tleta pulled her to one of the infernal devices.

CHAPTER FORTY-SEVEN

"HEY, HEY!" CORRIE SHOUTED AS the guards pulled Tleta to
her feet. "Your God is nothing but a piss-drinking bastard! A
tosser who couldn't find his own whistle with both hands!"

"You dare!" Nassir said.

"Every saint over Druthal makes your God lick the sweat off their
backside!"

"What blasphemy!"

"Your God is a knob-swallowing, carpet-scraping, sewage-stained
pig-rutter!"

The guards threw Tleta to the floor and grabbed Corrie. Good, a
little time bought.

"You should not speak in such ways," Nassir said. "We shall show
you. The fire is coming."

"It is coming," the Death Caller said. "You don't know how much
it's coming."

"Shut your mouth, witch!"

"You have no idea!" she cackled. "No clue what is coming for you."

Nassir kicked the Death Caller in the face. She, still on the floor,
started to seize and shake. Her whole body convulsed, limbs flailing as
much as they could with her hands tied behind her back.

And then she stopped completely.

"Is she dead?" one of the guard asked.

"Maybe," Nassir said. "If so, she has been judged by God, and found wanting." He turned to Corrie. "And now it shall be your turn."

"Can't wait," Corrie said. "What weak sewage does your God have for me? Whipping? Branding? You boys going to strip my clothes off first so you can knock your whistles at me?"

That last one took him aback. "We are men of God, not depraved monsters."

"Hard to see the difference."

"She is full of fire," one of the guards said.

"Burn it out of her!" another shouted.

"Gentlemen," Nassir said coolly. "That's not how you handle a fire. We need to douse it."

As if those words had told them all they needed to know, the men holding Corrie pulled her to the ground, and two more got on her to hold her down. Then another covered her face with a cloth.

"You bastards are going to eat—" Corrie started, but that was as far as she got.

Suddenly she was drowning, covered in water, crashing over her. She couldn't breathe, couldn't see, and everything shut down in her brain besides the dear and certainty she was about to die. She was back in the ocean, getting pulled down in that storm, no Eana to pull her onto the boat. No chance—

Then the water stopped. She could breathe. The cloth came off her face, to see Nassir crouched over her, staring at her from above. She could see one of the other guys with a bucket.

"Do you wish to repent?"

"I . . . wish . . ." Corrie wheezed out. She looked up and locked her eyes. "I wish I wasn't still so thirsty."

The cloth covered her face again, the water crashed on her again. She tried to hold her breath, tried to be ready, but there was being no ready, not for this. Her mind couldn't stay calm and centered. She knew she was on the floor in an old coffee shop, a bucket of water being poured over her, but her instincts, every emotion, told her she was in the middle of the ocean, that she was drowning.

"Stop it!" Tleta shouted. "Leave her alone!"

"You'll get your turn!" one of them said. "Don't you worry!"

They had stopped pouring, but the cloth stayed over Corrie's face. "You run out of water or something?" she called out.

"Do you wish to repent?" Nassir asked. "Repent and submit, save your soul!"

"My soul is already saved," Corrie said. "And I'm paying the cost for it."

"You wish to pay?"

"I already am," Corrie said. "Your God can't claim me, because Saint Veran already has that marker. Have your God take it up with him."

"The insolence!"

"Damn right!" Corrie said. And the water started again.

She couldn't handle much more. She tried to hold a piece of herself together, keep it strong. Hold off against these bastards. Keep them on her, leave Tleta alone. Hold off long enough to . . .

She couldn't think of a plan while drowning. She couldn't do anything but pray for it to end.

Pray for it.

Please, Saint Veran, I shouldn't ask . . .

"Gentlemen," she heard a new voice say.

No, not a new voice. An old voice. Speaking in Trade.

"You will stand and be held, and I will charge you to get your hands off my daughter."

"What is she—" Nassir said as the water stopped. "I thought she was dead."

"And the dead have answered."

Corrie, still pinned to the floor, heard a scuffle, which evolved into a brawl, and then there was a shout from somewhere, and several people running off.

The cloth came off Corrie's head, and there was the Death Caller. But somehow, in her face, her bearing, very much not.

"You all right there, Crasher?" she asked in a way that was utterly, completely, unmistakably Rennick Welling.

"Pop?" Corrie asked.

The Death Caller pulled her up to her feet. "We've got to get you out of here. The whole sewage pipe is about to burst in this town, kid."

"What are you talking about?" Corrie asked.

The Death Caller started untying Tleta, and as she did, her expression and body language shifted. In a creaky voice, she said, *"Koɓ tś'il wa wi riw, ty'uwichac. ris cewto i notś'."*

Tleta got to her feet, shaking off the ropes as she touched the Death Caller's face. *"Ty'o tśêtch'?"*

"Tché," the Death Caller said before her demeanor shifted again. "If everyone of them could be quiet—"

"Are you yourself now?" Corrie asked her.

"Yes, for the moment, but—it's like the door broke open." She rubbed at her head as she stumbled away.

"She brings out the dead?" Tleta asked.

"So she claims," Corrie said. "But she's also a half-tick swindler who uses it to play games with people."

Tleta nodded. "Among the Xon'Osta, there are many with the gift. And she's now . . . your father?"

The Death Caller switched back to Rennick. "She is, but now's not the time to reckon that."

"Why did they all run away?" Tleta asked.

The Death Caller went over to the door, walking and moving just like Pop. "Because it's begun."

Corrie and Tleta followed her outside to dim, gray light. Above them, the sun had somehow been chipped away, and a great ball of orange flame tore across the sky.

And the throughout the streets, the army of the zealot guard howled with madness and ecstasy.

PART THREE:

A DAY OF BURNING DARKNESS

CHAPTER FORTY-EIGHT

"WHAT IS—" CORRIE STARTED, EVEN though she knew the answer.

"The eclipse and the comet," Tleta said, her voice somehow both awed and subdued at the same time. "It's incredible."

"Painful is what it is," the Death Caller said.

"Ang said it would amplify magic and every other bit of blasted mystical strangeness," Corrie said. "I guess that means you as well."

"Everybody wants to talk, everybody wants *out*," the Death Caller said, her trembling fingers scratching at her neck. "Your father most of all."

In the street around them, the zealot guards had lost their damn minds. They were crying to the sky, rending off their clothes, and going into houses and dragging people into the streets.

"Maybe he'd be useful right now," Corrie muttered. "We can't stay out here."

"I don't think we can just go back inside, either," Tleta said. She reached out her hand and grabbed Corrie's. "I'm sorry."

"It's fine," Corrie said quickly. "We don't have time to rutting get into it now."

"Still—"

Corrie grabbed her and pulled her back into the narrow alley. Some of the zealots had, in their howling madness, gone into the shop next to them and dragged out the shopkeepers. With savage abandon, they shouted the whole time.

"God's judgment is here! The fire has come! All but the faithful will burn! Repent and submit! Repent sinners in the face of God's wrath!"

These shouts were accompanied with kicks and pummeling. Ferocious. Animalistic. Cruel.

"They're killing them," Tleta cried. Corrie held her back as Tleta's instincts to move toward the injured kicked in.

"And then us if we get in it," Corrie said. "We need to get somewhere safe and—"

Three whistle blasts—short-long-short—pierced through the air. Then again. That was—

"Trouble Call," the Caller said, back to Pop's bearing. "I don't have a whistle, Crasher. They need—"

"A Return Call, I know," Corrie said. Blazes. Blowing that whistle would get every zealot in a block on their backs. But Pop—rutting blazes, she couldn't start thinking of this Racquin huckster as her father —was right. She had to do it. But she also had to keep Tleta safe.

"You—" she said to the Death Caller. "Keep my pop on top, or you'll be channeling yourself. He'll keep you alive."

"Funny, seeing how he died on the job," the Death Caller said.

"Tleta, keep with me, pasted to my left hip. I'm going to take the lead, but—"

The Trouble Call again. And some zealots and taken note, running off in that direction.

"Call back," Tleta said. "That has to be your friends."

Friends. Corrie hadn't really thought about the girls in the debthouse that way, but it was apt. At least in this moment.

"At my hip," Corrie said. "We move as one. Ready, Pop?"

"Make the call," the Death Caller said.

Corrie took out her whistle and blew out: short, long, short, long. The Return Call. Help is on the way.

She dashed out of the alleyway, drawing out her club. She raced down through the bazaar, in the direction of the whistling, back to the fancier neighborhood where Tleta lived. A pair of zealots tried to grab her, but she brooked no nonsense now. Two quick knocks sent the first down, and the Death Caller made short work of the other. Not missing a beat, they kept their pace to a row of walled houses.

The gates had been bashed in, and the zealots were dragging people though the street. Well-dressed, well-appointed people, the very wealthiest best of Jachaillasa, reduced to victims of this fervent riot.

It was a riot.

Whistle calls came again, from the far side of one house. Corrie didn't hesitate. Guard up, club raised.

Last time she had been in a mess like this, her hair had gotten chopped off, nearly lost her eye. But not today. She pushed through, knocking back anyone who jumped at her. Fortunately, these zealots were in such a state, they barely cared. They wanted to tear up everything, everyone, and so none of them took any specific interest in her. If they had piled on her, she wouldn't have been able to hold them off.

She forced her way, dragging Tleta and the Death Caller along, to a path behind one house wall, then down the path to the source of the whistling: the back gate. As Corrie got closer, she saw the gate had been chained shut, and people were pressing against it while sending out the whistle calls. She saw Meija and Saa first, both pressing hard against the gate to no avail.

"I'm coming!" she shouted. She got closer and saw that just beyond Meija and Saa, Hezinaz was behind them, and just past them, Maäenda and Hanakhla, who were fighting like blazes to keep the zealots off the rest.

The house behind them was on fire.

"I'm here!" Corrie shouted. They had to get through the gate and get out of there, but Corrie couldn't see a way to get that chain off. But Saa and Meija had pushed hard enough to make a bit of a gap in the gate.

"You two, grab that side of the gate and pull," Corrie ordered Tleta and the Death Caller. As they did, Corrie shoved her club into the gap, and levered it has hard as she could, forcing a few more inches of give.

"Can you get through?" Corrie asked.

Meija tapped Saa, who tried to push her tiny body through the narrow gap between the metal and stone. When she cried out—pain, frustration—Tleta abandoned her spot pulling at the gate and moved to pull Saa instead. With a hard yank, she got Saa free, scratching her up and tearing her dress in the process. But still: out of there.

"Come on!" Corrie said, pushing her lever harder, trying to force another inch.

"I'll never fit!" Meija said. Hezinaz was already stripping off her outer robes, down to her underdress. While she tried to get through the gap, a jagged edge of the gate tore through her underdress and scratched across her belly, and Tleta headed down the back path by herself.

"Where are you going!" Corrie shouted.

Tleta had gone to one of the wild plants growing on the path and ripped it out of the ground. Meanwhile, Saa worked to pull Hezinaz through, all while Corrie's arms burned with pain and exhaustion.

"Come!" Saa cried as she got Hezinaz out. The tear and scratch had turned into a serious gash, bleeding down Hezinaz' stomach.

Tleta came back with the plant she had torn out of the ground. She threw it down and stomped on it a few times, and then picked up one thick leaf.

"What are you doing?" Corrie asked. "We have to—"

"I know," Tleta said. She squeezed at the leaf, letting the rank juice within cover her hands, and then she rubbed it on the gate and wall around the gap. Wiping the last off on her smock, she reached through to Meija. "Come on!"

Meija took her hand, and Tleta pulled her through the gap. Meija came straight through, the juice greasing her up enough to slip with relative ease.

"Maäenda!" Corrie shouted.

Maäenda pulled one zealot off Hanakhla. "Get them out!"

"It's just you two left!" Corrie said.

Maäenda said something in a language Corrie didn't understand, and shoved Hanakhla at the gate. Hanakhla pushed her way through the gap, not taking or needing help, ignoring all the scrapes against her arms and legs as she got through.

Corrie's arms gave out, losing her grip on the club, and the gap closed just as Hanakhla was out.

Maäenda knocked down the last zealot who was trying to grab her. The tide of zealots coming at them in this corner of the household had only been stemmed due to the fire blazing like mad behind her. Corrie couldn't even see farther through the smoke and heat.

"Hold on!" Corrie said, signaling to the other girls to help her pull the gate again.

"Corrie!" Tleta shouted, pointing to the end of the path, where a couple of zealots had taken notice of them.

Maäenda saw as well. She reached through the bars of the gate and touched Corrie's face. "See you on the other side. Run."

"But—"

"Run!"

The girls all started to scatter, Hanakhla and Saa helping Hezinaz. Corrie was loathe to let go of Maäenda, but a squad of zealots were coming.

"On the other side," Corrie said, and prayed that Maäenda meant literally the other side of the house. Maäenda went into the smoke, and Corrie raced off after the rest.

"Where are we going?" Meija asked.

"My house," Tleta said. "It's nearly a fortress."

CHAPTER FORTY-NINE

TWO BLOCKS. THEY JUST HAD to go two blocks.

"Keep tight," the Death Caller said. "Shoulder to shoulder. Formation."

"Who is that woman?" Meija asked.

"Her father," Tleta said.

"What?" Hezinaz asked.

"Long story," Corrie said. "But she's right. Hanakhla and I take lead, Tleta get in the center and help Hezinaz. The rest of you at the rear, keep frosty."

"On it, Crasher," the Death Caller said. Her head snapped to the side and she said. "I'm sorry, but he's just—and now the rest of—" Another snap. *"Tien ta nei shao mai!"*

Saa's attention perked up at that. *"Ke tsa?"*

"It's gone," the Death Caller said. "I can't be too close to anyone right now, they all want a word."

"Pop, keep it in line in there," Corrie said. Not that she had any sense of what was happening or how it worked, but if anyone could keep some sense of order among the spirits of the dead all trying to talk out of the Death Caller, it was her father.

They pushed to the next street, which was oddly calm. But only because it seemed like the zealots had already crashed through here and torn everything up, and had moved on to more interesting targets. There were a few shops and homes here, and the street had no sign of any residents beyond the torn clothing on the ground, and smears of blood on the walls.

It didn't help that the sky was growing darker—the sun was nearly gone, and the fiery red of the comet cast everything in a bloody shade. Maybe the zealots were right. The city looked like judgment of the divine had come down on them.

"How long is this supposed to last?" Meija asked.

"A few hours, maybe?" Corrie answered, though she had no idea. "We just have to get through it. Once the sun is fully back, and the comet out of sight . . ."

"Everything will calm down," Tleta said with a sense of authority.

"Including my head," the Death Caller said.

Hanakhla made a signal, made everyone move back. "There are a lot of them around the corner," she said. "I heard someone giving orders."

"Hajan?" Corrie asked.

Hanakhla shrugged. "Maybe."

Of course that slan would be in the middle of this. Reveling in it.

"Through there, one at a time," Corrie said, pointing to one of the absurdly narrow alleys. "We come out right across from her house. I'll take the lead."

Corrie squeezed through the narrow passage, one slow step at a time, since that was the fastest she could manage. If those zealots came on either side, they'd be pinned. *Please, Saint Veran,* she prayed, *there's nowhere to run.* If he put her in the middle of this, as some divine prank, as a test for her, a price for her life, he wouldn't have . . .

What did her mama always tell her?

"The saints know how much weight we can carry, and that's what they put on our shoulders."

That always sounded like sewage, but it was the only comfort Corrie could find right now.

She crept, slow and quiet, every little noise making her heart jump. Even her breathing seemed too loud. The zealots would hear, they'd come.

And she could definitely hear them. Their madness was clearly filling the market square and eatery courtyard between here and the campus. Too damn close.

Corrie emerged from the alley, Tleta's house in sight.

The zealots were in sight as well. End of the road, backs to them. Focused on someone speaking. Too far away for Corrie to make out words, but not too far to recognize the voice.

Hajan.

Hanakhla came out, then Meija, Hezinaz, Tleta, and Saa. As the Death Caller emerged, Tleta shouted, "No!" and ran toward the house.

Corrie swore, not bothering to see if the zealots' attention had come with the shout, but chasing after Tleta. Then she saw what had prompted her friend's outcry.

That great big wooden door had already been knocked open.

Tleta was inside, shouting in her native tongue, running through the house. She had good cause to be wild: On the floor of the antechamber, Canoc was dead. Stabbed several times.

"Quiet!" Corrie said catching up to her. "We don't know who's here."

"My family—"

"Might be dead," Corrie said. "Or worse. And their killers might still be here. Let's be careful."

"I'm not going to abandon—"

"We won't," Corrie said. "But let's be smart about it."

Tleta nodded, though she looked like a fire was burning inside her. "How?"

"Listen up," Corrie whispered. "What do you hear?"

Tleta closed her eyes in concentration. "No madness, not in here."

"So the zealots came and went, probably. But some might be lurking about. Who all is in the house, and where would they hide?"

Tleta nodded. Quietly, she led Corrie up the stairs—stairs that were blood-streaked, like a body had been dragged along the floor. They went farther into a bedchamber, where two of Tleta's mother's husbands—or whatever they were—had also been killed. The pool of blood and the drag marks made Corrie think the third had been injured and dragged off.

Tleta crept up to a wooden door and cautiously knocked.

"Cêtch? Jû tś'il ty'ô."

The door opened, and Marichua—her face bloodstained, her hair wild—came out. She grabbed Tleta in an embrace. *"Esse notś' ceɲi tś'ich ɓaɲ cîke!"*

Tleta asked Marichua something, and in teary sobs Marichua replied, while Corrie kept an eye on the hallway, the stairs. No one seemed to be coming for them, or were still in the house.

They got what they came for.

Tleta's wrenching cry confirmed that.

"They took your mother?" Corrie asked.

Tleta nodded, but was otherwise incapable of responding. She half collapsed, her weight on Marichua, who herself almost collapsed on Tleta. The two of them stumbled out of the bloodstained room, and Corrie led them downstairs.

They found the rest of their group in the antechamber—Hanakhla and the Death Caller covering Canoc's body with a cloth, both of them whispering quiet, respectful words.

"This place isn't safe either," Corrie said. "Not for long."

"What about our home?" Hezinaz asked, dropping to the floor. On seeing Hezinaz, her scraped stomach, Tleta suddenly straightened up and went to the other room. She returned with her bag and got to work on Hezinaz' wound.

"Probably not—oh rutting blazes."

Meija must have grasped what occurred to Corrie. "Srella and Basichara are still there. Same with your Jelic friend, and Eana."

"Pume as well," Saa said quietly.

"Are they going to be safe?" Hezinaz asked.

Hanakhla stood up straight. Displaying a command of Imach Corrie hadn't previously heard from her, she said, "The aristocrats at the party had spoken of many being wary of the Anach'Imal, and how they had made plans to escape to one of the other boroughs. And I heard a bit more of the speech that witch was making in the street. Take the bridges, she said. Push them all off, kill the unholy, for we burn in God's grace."

Corrie couldn't quite process that, let alone Hanakhla proving to be a solid asset all of a sudden. That didn't matter, the woman could have her secrets. "So there isn't a safe place in Jachaillasa."

"Maybe the bridge to Rasendi," Hezinaz suggested. "Or a boat."

"Doesn't Maäenda have a boat?" Meija asked.

"That is not an option," Hanakhla said. "No boat would take us, with debt marks on our arms and ears."

"Maybe one," Corrie said. "Everyone stay here, try to get that door closed, and protect each other."

The Death Caller perked up, her demeanor back to Pop's. "Cor, what are you thinking?"

"We need a boat," Corrie said. "And Lieutenant Moriel has one that was supposed to leave today. Let's hope he's still in the legation."

CHAPTER FIFTY

CORRIE SLIPPED OUT OF THE Xonacan house, creeping over to a wall and climbing up. Thank the saints Imachs made nothing smooth. Anyone with hands could climb up this wall. Though at the top, she remembered their preferred method of discouraging folks from scaling walls into the fancy homes: broken glass was embedded all along the top of the wall. Challenging to climb over without being slow and careful.

But slow and careful was all she had right now. The crowd of zealots and more was growing, and she couldn't risk the street in front of the house again. There was no way she could walk through there without being seen again.

Perched precariously on the top of the jagged wall, she could see the raging crowd in the bazaar and beyond. Fires burning everywhere. People running and shouting. Even in the worst riot in Maradaine, she had seen nothing like that.

And above her, the sky was near black, the sun just a sliver. And the red comet burning across the sky made it feel like the world was ending. Ang had said it, and despite being told what would happen, Corrie had not been prepared for the sheer majesty and terror of it.

She could hardly blame the city for going mad.

She crawled over the wall and dropped down to the alley, and praying that none of those mad zealots would catch her—though she still had her club and was more than ready to use it—made her way to the back of the Druth Legation.

She still couldn't rutting believe that this—whatever the blazes a legation was—had been right rutting here all this bloody time. How had she not noticed? There was a gate on the back wall, and right there—right blazing there—was a royal seal of the Druth Throne.

She had been so focused on just surviving, day to day, making the money she could, paying off the debt, getting home, that she just hadn't noticed it.

That gate was ajar, the latch broken. Not a good sign. She could only pray that Moriel, or someone, was still here.

Going in, there was a manicured lawn, like in the parks in Maradaine, with a garden of hedges and flowers, but it had all been trampled and smashed. And splattered with blood. Looking around the yard, there was blood everywhere.

Corrie whispered a prayer and went into what was probably a kitchen door.

In the kitchen—completely torn apart and ransacked—there were bodies. Three of them, boys Corrie's age in army uniforms. From the Scallic 10th, if she read the patches right. She doubted these boys had ever expected to die here.

She didn't plan to, either.

She grabbed a knife off the counter and moved through the household.

"Hello!" she called out in Trade. "Anyone still here?"

"Who's there?" an older woman called out, voice muffled. Perfect Trade. Sounded Scallic.

"Sergeant Corrie Welling, ma'am."

"Sergeant?"

A closet door opened, and a woman in a classically Druth dress tumbled out. "Oh, thank every saint," she said as she pulled herself up. "I was certain I was going to die." She looked Corrie up and down. "How did the Constabulary get here?"

"Ma'am?" Corrie asked "I'm afraid there is no Constabulary, just me."

"You, but how did—oh." She pointed at Corrie's ear. "They put one of those things on you, hmm? You're one of those girls who got in a bit of a brine."

"You could say that, ma'am," Corrie said. "Is . . . did Lieutenant Moriel make it? There are some soldiers in the kitchen who . . ."

"Poor boys," the woman said. She thought for a moment. "Moriel? Oh, that cacksagget."

Not the word Corrie would have used—since she wasn't an old woman from Scaloi—but an apt description. "He said he would be here, but that was before . . . all this."

"All this, indeed," she said. "My apologies, Sergeant. In the heat of apocalypse, I lost my manners, quite unforgivable."

"I fully understand," Corrie said.

"Nonsense," she said, extending her hand. "Marchioness Endilara Idonna of Iscala, Envoy of His Majesty, the King of Druthal."

Corrie took her hand and made some effort to curtsey as she kissed it. "Sergeant Corrie Welling of the Maradaine Constabulary, such as I am."

"You are here, and you maintained your uniform, which speaks to your credit, Sergeant. Can you report what is happening in the streets? The staff officer just shoved me in a closet with barely an explanation, and that was the last I knew."

"It's chaos, ma'am," Corrie said. "There's been an eclipse, and there's a comet in the sky, and the members of one cult are acting like it's the end of the world—"

"Absurdity," the marchioness said. "So they're the ones making a ruckus out there."

"Ruckus is underselling. Dragging people into the street, killing those they consider blasphemous . . ."

"Hmm," the marchioness said, rubbing her chin. "Do we wait it out? I think there's a few bottles of wine in the cellar . . ."

"I'm afraid I can't ru— I can't do that, ma'am. I have people I am responsible for, and I'm hoping to get them out of here."

"Here, being? The borough, the city, the country?"

"Any and all," Corrie said. "Moriel said something about a diplomatic ship leaving for Maradaine today."

"Did he?" the marchioness asked. "How terribly interesting of him. That ship wouldn't happen to be the *Queen Mara's Pride?*"

"I think he did say that."

"Bastard," she muttered. "That's my ship, Sergeant. No wonder he was pushing me to leave today."

"So where—" Corrie started to say when she heard something shatter. Glass. Window. "They're coming back."

"Why would they—"

Something else clattered above them.

"Where is Moriel?" Corrie asked. "Could he still be here?"

"He was locked up in his Letters Room when the trouble started—" The marchioness was interrupted by a bursting sound from upstairs. A wave of heat and light flashed from the stairwell. Corrie grabbed the marchioness around the waist and pulled her over a couch as the blast of flame washed over the place where they were just standing.

"Where?" Corrie asked. "Where is he?"

"Upstairs," she said in a haunted voice, looking at the burning stairway. The marchioness swallowed hard and grabbed Corrie's wrist, pulling her down a hallway.

"Are there back stairs?" Corrie asked.

"No," the marchioness said, stopping just short of the kitchen. She opened up a panel in the wall, revealing a narrow alcove. "Dumbwaiter to the upper floor."

Saints above and sinners below. "That's the only way up there?"

"I'm afraid so, Sergeant."

Corrie stripped off her jacket, handed it to the marchioness and clambered inside. Blazes, it was a tight fit, but she managed to squeeze herself in. "Send me up."

"Right." The marchioness looked at the controls, her face screwed up in concentration. "There's a bell pull up there to signal. Let me know when you need to come down." She started turning a wheel, and Corrie went up.

Corrie sat, confined in darkness like a coffin. *Don't let this be my coffin,* she thought. Not for rutting Moriel.

The dumbwaiter came to a stop, and the door opened to roaring flames filling the hallway. Corrie fought down the instinct to grab the bell cord immediately. Holding her sleeve over her mouth, she clambered out, skittering away from the worst of the flames.

"Lieutenant!" she shouted with what little breath she could draw.

One door—heavy with multiple latches—opened, and Moriel, his hair askew, stuck his head out.

"Sergeant, whatever are you doing?"

"We need to get out of here."

"Do you have Miss Rek-Nouq?"

Corrie couldn't believe that. "No. The city is falling apart, and we need to rutting go."

"Blasted saints," he said, and ducked back into the room.

"What are you—"

He came back out, arms burdened with leather satchels.

"Are you mad?" she asked.

"Very important documents, must be securely delivered to Druthal. Are the soldiers ready downstairs?" He strolled over to the dumbwaiter like he was barely aware of the fire raging throughout the upper floor.

"They're dead, Moriel."

That took him back a moment. "Quite unfortunate. Tell me the marchioness is safe."

"She's waiting to lower the dumbwaiter back down. But we need to go."

"Yes, it is rather pressing," he said lightly. Corrie wasn't sure if he had gone mad or if she had. He loaded the satchels into the dumbwaiter, which took up most of the room in there.

"We won't fit with those."

"Well, of course not. We're not both going to fit at all. But I do insist those reports are the most critical thing, of the three of us, to reach the *Queen Mara's Pride* and make it back to Druthal with the marchioness."

Corrie didn't have time to argue. She cranked the wheel and sent the dumbwaiter down. "You are tragically stupid, Lieutenant."

"I just have the security of the nation in mind."

In a moment, the dumbwaiter came back up, empty. At least the marchioness understood, and Corrie hoped the woman had the sense to find it all as utterly stupid as she did.

"Excellent," Moriel said, getting inside. "Now, again, in order of priority . . ."

"Fine, fine," Corrie said. The fire was too strong and thick—most of the hallway and the entire stairwell were engulfed, and it had surely spread downstairs—to want to waste a second in conversation. She cranked the wheel again and down he went.

Corrie counted the seconds, pulling her blouse over her face, waiting for the dumbwaiter too return.

It didn't.

Rutting blazes.

She cranked it up herself and climbed in. Reaching out, she pulled the bell cord and prayed.

Nothing.

Rutting Moriel should rot in eternal flames.

Of course, she was about to go up in flames any second. She hopped out of the dumbwaiter and cranked the wheel as much as she could to make it go up higher. Struggling to get any breath, she raised it high enough to expose the shaft down into darkness.

Corrie got in, grabbing the cable as best she could so she could lower herself down. At least in the shaft, the air was cooler and a little fresher, rising up from the cellar below. As fast as she dared, she went down, hand over hand, feet braced on the shaft. Even still, it was hard to find her breath, and her head kept wanting to spin.

"Hold it together, Corrie," she said to herself. "You didn't go through all this to die in a fire in a dumbwaiter shaft in the Mocassa. This is not going to be your last ride."

Her foot hit a board that gave a little. The panel door. She kicked it open and clambered out into the hallway.

Moriel and the marchioness were gone, but her coat was still there, discarded on the floor.

Corrie scooped it up and ran as fast as she could, through the kitchen and out the back, into the cool dark of the eclipsed day. She stopped for just a moment to fill her lungs, though the smoky haze still pervaded the air.

She continued two more steps out of the back gate and collided with the marchioness, her face stricken, blood spattered over her face.

"Sergeant!" she cried out. "The lieutenant said you had died in the fire, but . . ."

She pointed to the body in the street. Moriel, an axe buried in his chest.

"How—" Corrie asked.

"Some madman just ran up, struck him and ran off." Her voice trembled. "Please, Sergeant, you're my only hope. If we can get to the *Queen Mara's Pride*, we can leave this infernal city."

"I can't, not without him," Corrie said. She pointed to her ear.

The marchioness scoffed, and scurried over to Moriel's body. She searched in his pockets and pulled out a few papers. Handing them to Corrie she said, "By the power invested in me by our King, Maradaine the Eighteenth of Druthal, I am designating you a diplomatic courier with the rights and authority implied."

"I don't know if we needed the whole rutting ceremony there," Corrie muttered.

"In moments like this, ceremony is all that matters. It keeps us sane and civilized."

Corrie shrugged that off. "Follow me, close at my hip."

"As you say, Sergeant."

Corrie led her down the alley, back out to the street—nearly everything was burning, and the howling and shouts of the zealots filled the air. Corrie wasn't seeing any of them right now, but she heard them in every direction.

She hurried back toward Tleta's house, where right at the door Hanakhla was holding the line with Canoc's spiked club against two zealots. Corrie drew her own club and dashed in, knocking one down, giving Hanakhla the space she needed to go on the offensive against the other.

"You all right?" Corrie asked her in Imach.

"I fought with my mother's mother at my arm," Hanakhla said with a smile. "It is a glorious day."

Corrie looked over to the Death Caller, who was bracing herself against the wall, a greenish mist circling around her.

"We all good?" Corrie asked the rest of the group, huddled in the foyer.

"We need to get out of here," Tleta said. "Do you have a plan?"

Corrie gestured to the marchioness. "She has a boat we can get to."

The marchioness gestured for Corrie to come closer. "Sergeant, who are these people?"

"They're people who helped me when I first got here, and they are with me."

"But, Sergeant, they're . . . foreigners." She said that last word like it was the kindest word she could let herself use, but still dripping with disdain.

"So are we, ma'am. And I'm not leaving anyone behind."

The marchioness took that in and nodded. "Commendable. I am in your hands, Sergeant." She looked to the group. "I am Endilara Idonna of Iscala, Envoy of His Majesty, the King of Druthal. I have a ship we can escape this city with, if we can get to it."

Everyone else scowled as they gathered themselves, but Tleta stepped forward and extended a hand to the marchioness. "Tletanaxia, First Daughter to the *quqô tsînôsho* of the *tsîtsesh* of Taa-shej, third in the court of the Tchoja, the Children of the Sky, and the jewel in the eye of all Xonaca, the motherland of all people, whose womb is ever fruitful. On behalf of all of us, I thank you."

"Oh, jolly good," the marchioness said, taking her hand. "Peerage."

"Enough of this rutting sewage," Corrie said. "Stay tight on me, Hanakhla take the rear, eyes everywhere, watch each other's backs, and let's get moving. It's the end of the world out there."

CHAPTER FIFTY-ONE

THE ZEALOTS HAD MOVED ON from this neighborhood, it seemed, having all but burned it out, leaving a trail of dead. This set of blocks were largely folks like Tleta's family—folks with money, often from other parts of the world.

Corrie led the group through the grand plaza, which her instincts told her was going to be dangerous. Wide open, little place to hide, and trouble could come from any direction. But the zealots were not being very methodical or strategic in their chaos.

Corrie checked over the people in her charge. Tleta looked like she was staying on her feet by pure force of will, like she made herself keep walking just so Marichua could see her being strong, and thus be able to go on herself. Marichua looked shattered, half dead. She moved in a dazed shuffle, bolstered by Meija and Saa, who for their part, were holding up well, save the scrapes and smudges. Hanakhla was a rock, taking up the rear, and looking like she was eager for someone to give her an excuse. Hezinaz stayed in the center of the group, able to walk unaided, but keeping one hand on the bandages Tleta had applied to her stomach. Corrie hoped Tleta's ministrations would be enough; a wound like that was apt to fester and turn sour. If that happened, Hezinaz would likely die. The marchioness also clung close to the center of the group, keeping herself close to Corrie's back.

And then the Death Caller, who stayed at the front of the group with Corrie. She twitched with each step, as if she was constantly cycling through personalities. Corrie was almost afraid she'd break her neck.

"You all right?" she asked. "Are you, I don't know, you?"

"Impossible to answer that," she said. "So much death right now, so many wanting their voice, and . . . the power in this day. It's . . . like being caught in a torrential river. A flood in a storm."

"Because of the eclipse and comet?"

"It would seem."

"Thank you for everything you've done . . . I can't imagine this is rutting easy."

"No it rutting isn't," she said back, her voice shifting. "Sorry, I just . . ." She trailed off and stared off to the south.

"What is it?"

"Death," she said, pointing. "So much death in that direction."

"You can sense it?"

"I can feel it coming. Crasher—Corrie—miss . . ." She snapped her head back to the center. "I feel the people who have died, but I can also sense that more will die. There is power being drawn here. And with it comes death."

"You can sense that?"

"And more, it seems." She stopped walking for a moment, taking a deep breath. "I don't know exactly what happened while you were gone, but"—a twitch of head—"you need to stay on task, Crasher. What's the next step?"

"Is she all right?" the marchioness asked.

"Not really," Corrie said. "We make a path to the debthouse, and from there to the dock."

"The house?" Tleta asked.

"Hopefully it's a safe haven between here and the docks. And no matter what happens next, we should get these other ladies there. It's their home. What happens next, we'll see."

"It highly irregular," the marchioness said. "But I will happily give safe passage to anyone who aids in helping me to my ship."

"Three blocks," Corrie said, switching to Imach. They had reached the laundry shop with the red sign, the one Maäenda had used to help

Corrie navigate home when she first got here. She still used that as her marker, from here take a right at the next cross, walk through two inter-sections, count four houses on the left.

Saints, please let Maäenda be all right.

"How fast can we move?" She looked to Hezinaz.

"I'll keep up," she said.

"Good, because—" Corrie started, and then noticed movement through the plaza. Not just movement. Marching. "Get down, every-one." She directed them all to hide behind the overturned carts.

"What is it?" Tleta asked.

"A lot of people coming through. Let's see who they are. Maybe—"

"Rescue?" Tleta asked. "Proper authorities coming from Teamaccea?"

"No," the Death Caller said. "We need to move. Death and more is coming."

"Stay low until—"

Then Corrie heard a voice. A voice she had already grown sick of.

"The time of fire is upon us! God has darkened the skies and sent his holy messenger to burn across it! This is the sign!"

Hajan. Corrie dared a glance over the cart to see her, walking with a small army behind her.

A call came up from all around. "This is the sign!"

Including in hushed whispers from Meija and Hezinaz.

"What?" Corrie asked.

"We must do as God demands! We must show him who is worthy to be chosen! We must step forth!"

"Step forth!"

People were coming out into the street, toward the growing crowd around Hajan as she walked in rapture through the plaza.

Meija stood up.

"Step forth!"

Hezinaz mumbled the same words, her face clammy with sweat.

And the Death Caller was pounding on her skull. "We must go, go, go."

Corrie couldn't disagree. "That way, turn right, two blocks. Move, and we'll—"

The Death Caller and the marchioness went first, with Tleta—who glanced at Corrie in urgency as she went—following quickly with Saa and Marichua. Hanakhla was trying to pull Meija back down, while keeping an arm around Hezinaz, who was trying to stand up herself.

"The holy fire shall burn the sin out of the this city! Make it all burn!"

"Make it all burn!" the crowd shouted.

"Make it all burn!" Meija shouted, and she ran toward the crowd. Corrie grabbed her ankle before she got too far, making her fall flat on her face.

Hezinaz was trembling, muttering, "Burn burn please no burn burn."

Hanakhla had apparently heard enough, and threw Hezinaz over her shoulder and dashed after the rest.

Meija was thrashing and clawing, moving as if she didn't even care that Corrie held on to her foot. She was trying to drag herself closer to Hajan and her crowd, like she was unable to even consider doing anything else.

"Meija!" Corrie snapped at her. "What is rutting wrong with you?"

"It has to burn, burn out the sin, we are all full of sin but God will judge us worthy or we will burn and we will deserve it . . ."

Corrie dragged Meija toward her, flipping the girl on her back. "Get it blazing together! If they—"

"Infidel!" Meija shouted. "The unholy must burn!"

No rutting time. Corrie cracked her fist against Meija's jaw, knocking her head into the dirt. Thankfully that quieted her cold.

But she had gotten attention.

As Corrie got on her feet, she saw many of the crowd—and they were carrying torches, goddamn it—were all staring, glaring, pointing their fingers.

All but Hajan, who gave the slightest smile and nod to Corrie.

"Unfaithful! Infidel!" they shouted.

"Sorry, Meija," Corrie whispered as she scooped the unconscious girl up and threw her in a brigade carry over her shoulder. Time to run.

Even carrying Meija's potato-sack weight, Corrie caught up to the rest in no time. And the crowd was right behind, except those who got distracted when they decided to use their torches on one of the buildings.

"Go! Go!" Corrie shouted.

They all broke into a run, around the corner, through the rows of narrow houses, all of them in turmoil. Fires in the street, people being dragged out, beatings and shoutings.

"We're not going to make it!" Tleta called out.

"One more block!"

"To what?"

Corrie wasn't even sure. There was no reason, given what was going on all around them, to expect their house would be a safe place. The opposite, if anything.

But she had to go. Eana was there. If their chance to get out of this infernal city was here and now, she couldn't leave Eana behind.

They reached the house, zealous crowds on their heels. Corrie, even carrying Meija, was ahead, and went right for the door.

Instead of getting inside, she bounced off of it. Like she had hit a solid wall where the doorway was.

"What the rutting blazes?" she asked. As the rest of the group piled up behind her, she touched the air of the door way. A jolt of blue energy splashed at her.

"We can't—" Tleta started, but Corrie wasn't hearing it. She stepped back and shouted up to the window.

"Eana!"

Srella stuck her head out the kitchen window. She immediately started babbling in her native tongue, and then. "Eana! They're here!"

The blue haze danced away. Corrie carefully crossed the threshold, this time passing without difficulty.

"Come on, come on!" she called, and everyone else poured into the house, going up the steps without bothering with shoes for once.

Zealots were right on their heels, and when the last one of their people—Saa—passed through the doorframe, one of the zealots grabbed her arm. She shouted, and Corrie heard Srella call something at the same time.

The blue haze flashed in the doorframe, and as it did, the zealot suddenly found himself separated from his hand. He screamed and fell back, and as he writhed on the ground, other zealots pounded on the empty space of the door, unable to pass.

"What—" was all Saa said before she wrenched the disembodied hand—still clutching her arm—and threw it into the latrine troughs.

Corrie followed Saa up the steps, to the crowded *ghose'a* and kitchen, where she dropped her burden of Meija's limp body, and then fell to the floor herself.

Only once she could catch her breath did she assess what was going on in the house.

Srella, Basichara, and Pume were all surrounding Eana, who was glowing blue, sweating and breathing heavily. All three of them were investing themselves in keeping her upright, giving her water, and preparing food for her.

"Eana?" Corrie asked. "Are you—"

"Tired but fine," she said weakly. "But all my attention is on the doors."

"She's been keeping them out," Srella said. "It was amazing, but—" She glanced out the window. "You seem to have drawn them to us."

"Not my plan," Corrie said. She pulled herself up and checked on Meija, who was still out cold, but shivering and muttering.

"What happened?" Basichara asked.

"We came across Hajan and her crowd," Corrie said. "And when Hajan preached, people were repeating it, and Meija and Hezinaz started rutting repeating it with them as well."

"Like they wanted to join the zealots," Hanakhla said.

"What?" Srella asked.

"Like we're telling you. Hajan's words pulled them in."

"Impossible," Basichara said.

"Today is full of the impossible," the marchioness said quietly. "How long can we hold out here? I presume only the child's magic is keeping the rabble out, and that can't last long."

"Long enough to blazing regroup, get our feet," Corrie said. "We have a—"

"Is it true?" a voice called from up the stairs. Feet pounded down and Maäenda—looking like she had crawled through the blazes and fought every sinner, covered in soot and singes—came down and wrapped Corrie up in her powerful arms. "The currents have pulled us together."

"You made it," Corrie said, holding Maäenda tightly. "Thank every rutting saint, you made it."

"And pulled our keeper out of his own trouble," Maäenda said as she pulled out of the embrace. "Nalaccian is resting upstairs, and Nas'nyom is tending to his injuries."

"Injuries?" Tleta asked.

"His arm is broken, among other things," Maäenda said. "I had no chance to be gentle when I rescued him."

Tleta nodded, and after a moment of hushed Xonacan whispers to Marichua, went upstairs. Marichua just slumped down to the floor.

"And now?" Maäenda asked. "What are we doing, and who are our new friends?"

"Lady Marichua of . . . somewhere in Xonaca," Corrie said. "She was a close friend of Tleta's mother, who . . ." Corrie wasn't sure how to finish that.

"Of course," Maäenda said. "And, you, miss?"

The marchioness found her feet. "Endilara Idonna of Iscala." She then got a good look at Maäenda and bowed. "And I am deeply honored, Eminent Lady of the Eastern Seas."

Maäenda waved that off. "No time for that. And you rescued that, what did you call her, grifter?"

"It's complicated, but—"

The Death Caller suddenly jumped to her feet, and her eyes glowed green. In a voice that sounded like it had been scraped from the bottom of a barrel, she began to speak in a language unlike anything Corrie had heard.

And then Hezinaz and Meija began muttering it as well, despite both of them still seeming to be unconscious.

"What is that and how can it rutting stop?" Corrie asked.

"I was hoping you could answer that." Maäenda said.

Nas'nyom popped his head through the hole of the stairwell. "Is she speaking Ancient Moreshkan?"

"What the blazes is Ancient Moreshkan?"

"Language from two thousand years ago," he said. "No one uses it except scholars. Though some of the texts from the Bahimahl'Ima derived from works written—"

Corrie didn't need more than that. Turning on the Death Caller, she said, "Imach, please."

The Death Caller didn't change her rhythm or tone, nor did her empty expression falter, as her language seamlessly shifted from one to the other. "—the end of the sun, the end of the sky, as the fire of God burns across us. And so they looked down up the world, which God could destroy any day he chose, and this was the day—" She, and the other two, all screamed and collapsed.

Pume cried out, and then said something very excitedly.

"What, what is it?"

Nas'nyom was with it. "She said, the words they are saying, it's part of the book of Vatka, the Turjin god of destruction."

"Oh, good, I was thinking that sounded like a happy thing," Corrie said.

"It's also like the Book of Moons in the Bahimahl'Ima," Basichara said. "Where mankind, as God's instrument, joins him in the skies in the end of the world."

"That seems apt," Srella said. "Is that what this is? Is it the end of the world?"

"I refuse to believe that either the God of Imachan or of Turjin is coming to end the world today," Corrie said.

"The sky is on fire," Basichara said.

"It's not the end of the world!" Corrie shouted.

"You're going to hear that—see them all recite that together? See what's happening to her"—Basichara pointed to Eana—"and not think that something profound and . . . world-shattering isn't happening?"

"It's an eclipse and a comet," Corrie said. "Which Ang predicted. As is the boost to mystical energies. Why Eana's magic is stronger right now—"

"So much," Eana said.

"The Death Caller is channeling dark things. And maybe even Hajan can twist the minds of the faithful." She realized what that meant. "Meija and Hezinaz. They're believers in the Imach faith."

"Meija follows her devotions," Hanakhla said. "Hezinaz is a bit more negligent."

"But she does believe," Basichara said.

"Which must be why Hajan can twist them. And rile her people into this frenzy. It's not the end of the damned world, but those bastards out there, they rutting think so, and they're willing to tear the city apart and kill us all to make it happen. So we need to survive and get out of here."

"Get out how? Where?" Maäenda asked.

"Ang said this whole effect is just going to be on this island," Corrie said. "So we get off it. Get far as blazes as we can."

"The north side of the borough is completely engulfed," Maäenda said. "And the bridges to Teamaccea and Oreifal have been claimed by the zealots. Probably the Rasendi bridge as well."

"The south?" Corrie asked. "The bridge to Mahacossa? The docks by that bridge?"

"I don't know," Maäenda said.

"If any place in this borough is still protected at all," the marchioness said. "It's the docks of the southern port and the Mahacossa bridge. You should know, Eminence, the joint garrison on those enclaves. My ship is waiting there."

Corrie nodded. "We stick together, all of us, get to the docks, get to the ship, and get the blazes out of here."

"To where?" Srella asked.

"My ship is bound for Maradaine."

"Home?" Eana asked through tight teeth.

"Anyone who helps get us to the docks is welcome on my ship," the marchioness said. "I will happily grant any of you safe passage."

"To go to Maradaine," Maäenda said derisively.

"If it is safe, I will happily drop anyone who prefers to stay here off at Hussua Island, or any reasonable port on the journey to Druthal. But we should move before—"

A crazed person leaped through the kitchen window and grabbed Pume. Twisting her arm behind her back, he brandished a knife to plunge into her heart. But Pume brought up one leg at an almost impossible angle to block his arm, while twisting the rest of her body in ways that

Corrie would describe as inhuman, until suddenly she was on top of him, leg wrapped around his neck, choking him. Then with another impossibly limber motion, kicked his knife arm so he stabbed himself in his chest. He dropped down to the floor while Pume effortlessly landed on her feet.

"Hot damn," Corrie said in an awed whisper.

Eana moved one hand toward the window, which shimmered with blue light. "Whatever we're going to do, let's do it quickly. I can't hold all this much longer."

"I'll get your stuff," Corrie said. "Everyone else, get what you need, let's get the injured and otherwise incapacitated ready to move, get whatever you can use as a weapon, and let's be on the street in five clicks of the clock."

Several eyes looked to Maäenda, as if in confirmation. "Don't look at me, she told you what to do. Let's get on it!"

CHAPTER FIFTY-TWO

CORRIE WENT UP TO HER room, hopefully for the last time, gathering the few effects she and Eana had acquired. Not that there was much to be sentimental about—a few articles of clothing, mostly. Though Eana had a small box tucked into a corner, with a scrap of cloth, a few splinters of wood, and a link of a chain.

The last remnants of the slave ship that had taken them.

Corrie didn't know why Eana would ever want mementos of that rutting ship, but she respected that it wasn't for her to decide. She scooped that up, as well as her only additional personal items: the letters she had been writing to her family, bundled together with her practice journal and charcoal pencil tied in.

Maäenda came in, gathering her own things, as well as Srella's. "I supported you down there, but this plan is madness."

"I'm open to a better one."

"I do not have a better one. And I imagine Eana is the only thing keeping the birds from gnawing the flesh from our bones. So we cannot stay."

"Honestly," Corrie said, turning to Maäenda, "I'm not a girl with a plan. I only got the chevron on my coat for being too dumb to know when to go home. I'm just running on worn-down shoes now."

"That is not true," Maäenda said. "Eana has told everyone in this house how you became sergeant. We know who you are, what you will do."

"What did she bloody tell you?" Corrie asked. She barely remembered telling Eana that story. Though in the five days on the lifeboat, and the time on the slave ship, she had told a lot of stories. Some of them just to make the time pass, to use her voice to keep the girl awake and alive.

"Your brother was missing, you had been put into the hospital, and you stayed on duty, scouring the city, insisting on keeping working until he was found and safe."

"Yeah, well . . . it was family," Corrie said. "It just happened to impress the captain."

"It takes a lot to impress a captain," Maäenda said. "Especially at your age."

"Says the lady who lives in a debthouse but has noblewomen bow to her," Corrie said.

"We do not choose what we are born into," Maäenda said. "Our families of birth do so much to define what is expected of us. But what we do with those expectations, that is what defines who we are."

"You're getting awfully full in the head right now, lady," Corrie said. "Too many people bowing to you."

"I came too close to dying on dry land today," Maäenda said. "That has led me to heady thoughts."

Finishing gathering their things, as well as Eana's and Srella's, they went down one flight where Tleta was finishing her ministrations on Nalaccian. That, or some form of torture. Corrie had heard the man shouting in pain as she came down.

"Everything all right?" she asked, sticking her head in the bedroom where she tended to him.

"It will be," she said.

"She has gifts in healing arts, but detriments in kindness," Nalaccian said. "Is it as bad as I fear outside?"

"It's worse," Corrie said. "We need to move before they decide to burn this house down."

"They already burned mine," he said. "I was quite fortunate to escape with my life."

"What's your plan?"

"Apparently joining you in the escape from this part of the city, if I am welcome," he said.

"Of course you are," she said. "No one gets left behind."

He smiled ruefully as Tleta helped him to his feet. "I knew you were a good investment."

"Don't make me rutting regret saying that."

"No," he said. "We must flee from here, and for your health and safety, you most definitely must get off this island."

Corrie nodded as she helped him to the steps. While he was able to walk, it was clear that his arm was causing him enough pain to make him move slowly. "I have no great urge to stay, especially now."

"I say this as a warning, Sergeant. With the loss of my house, and surely other properties, once the chaos settles, markers will be called on me. My assets will be claimed and redistributed."

"Great saints," Corrie said. "You might end up with a debt bolt on your ear."

"You are not hearing me," he said.

"He means our debts," Maäenda said as she came down. "His claim to our debts will be taken by others to settle his accounts."

"I have striven to be a kind and fair steward to each and every one of you," he said in his descent to the *ghose'a*. "Most of the other debt stewards in this city would not do the same, and I would have no power to protect you. Your claims will go to other holders, who will do with them —do with you—as they please. So you cannot stay in this city if there is a means to escape."

The room had an unsettling quiet for a moment, no one wanting to make eye contact.

"That is the rutting plan," Corrie said to break the silence. "Or perhaps it would be better to die in this madness."

Pume started to speak, at length, and Nas'nyom, sitting unobtrusively in the corner, began to translate.

"There is no situation where we dare still be on these shores when the day returns. It will return, and when it does, those who lost their minds in anticipation of the end of time will see their zeal turn sour on them. The failure of the world to end will make their fervor curdle, and they will then lash out, and the destruction and death we are seeing now will be visited on this city sevenfold. And if Vatka in his infinite cruelty deems that we would survive that, then yes, the vultures would swoop in, claim ownership over our debts, our bodies, our souls. I will stand free on the ocean when next I see daylight, or die by my own hand. I heard the stories of those who did not escape Gustivakh in time, I will not be one of those."

"Gustivakh?" Corrie asked.

Saa spoke up. "A city on Turjin's western coast. The whole city burned to the ground."

"Then let's not be standing rutting about," Corrie said. "We go out the back door, through the alley to the main avenue on the other side. We stay together, we stay armed, we stay alert. No one left behind."

"What about them?" Srella asked, pointing to Hezinaz and Meija, still out on the floor. "Do we carry them? Do we dare wake them?"

"Her soul is clear," the Death Caller said, pointing to Hezinaz. She didn't speak in her own voice, but in Imach with an accent like Hezinaz had. "She had her *dhageh ahi* when she was seven, but never her *ghehrre'i geh.* So Hajan's call could grasp her but not hold. She will be no threat now, but keep her ears bound when we walk." She touched Hezinaz on the forehead, and the girl woke with a gasp. And then she burst into tears, holding on to the Death Caller like a lost friend.

Corrie didn't even know how that made sense, but nothing rutting did today. "And Meija?"

The Death Caller looked up, still holding on to Hezinaz. A change in her tone. "Her soul still fights with itself. This host can hold it at bay, so she can walk, but that will take her focus. Tell your father he cannot take control in this fight."

"Your father?" Maäenda asked.

"It's far too long," Corrie said. "Pop, or—" Corrie couldn't rutting believe she was having this conversation. "Stay the blazes down so this lady can help Meija, hear?"

The Death Caller switched again. "I hear, Sergeant. Quiet Call from here out."

Saints, that was blazing unnerving. It was too real, and that scared Corrie more than anything Hajan and her hoard of zealots might bring.

The Death Caller switched once more, and with a green glow around her body, helped Meija to her feet. Meija's face was blank, her lips silently muttering, but she moved only when the Death Caller guided her.

"All right," Corrie said, brandishing her club. "Everyone stay close. Let's go."

They slipped down the stairs, and Eana—who let herself be carried by Srella and Maäenda down the stairs—held up the shields, dropping the back doorway so the group could start to leave. A few of the zealots were already in the back garden, but Hanakhla, Saa, and Pume made short, brutal work of them. The rest filed out, Corrie staying with Eana to go last.

"That's good," Corrie told her once Tleta helped Nalaccian out the back. "Let's go!"

"I let it go, those bastards swarm in here," Eana said, nodding to the zealots still pounding at the solid air at the main door. "And I don't think I can walk and hold it."

"Let it go and run," Corrie said. "I've got your back."

"I know you do," Eana said. "But you've got to—"

"On my count, drop and run, hear?"

Eana winked. "Aye, Sergeant."

"That's the right answer," Corrie said. "One, two, three . . . run!"

Eana let go, and her body half collapsed when she did. Corrie was right there to grab her and haul her along out the back door, while four of those bastards came raving at them. They got out the back door, and one of them grabbed hold of Corrie's shoulder. She pivoted and clubbed him straight in the face—his expression one of pure ecstatic mania. Even being smashed in the face, he never lost the look of wild joy, as if nothing had made him happier than trying to tear Corrie limb from limb. Another blow with her club, keeping him in the doorframe to block anyone else getting out, she hammered onto the arm still holding on to her, snapping the bone. Even that didn't deter him.

"Clear!" Eana shouted.

Then another hand grabbed her—Maäenda pulling her away from the house—and a wave washed past Corrie, like when the ocean had tried to swallow her, knocking the zealot and his compatriots back into the house. Then another wave made Corrie's bones shake.

Then the house shook, and while the zealots inside were still getting to their feet, faces full of rapture and chaos, it collapsed into rubble and dust.

Corrie looked back to Eana, still holding up her trembling hands, sly grin on her pale, sweat-covered face. "Didn't think I had it in me."

She wavered and stumbled, and Corrie and Maäenda grabbed her before she collapsed. They hauled her along to the rest of the group, and the sixteen of them pushed together down the avenue through the dark, burning day.

CHAPTER FIFTY-THREE

A S THEY PUSHED FARTHER SOUTH, encounters with the zealots became fewer and fewer. But as they went, behind them the city burned. Fire and smoke in every direction, and with the unnatural night of the eclipse, it was almost impossible to find their way, even on the main road to the southern docks.

Maäenda took the lead, navigating as if by pure instinct. "The sea is this way," she whispered. "I always know how far she is."

For several blocks, they went completely unmolested. It was almost eerie in the quiet of it.

That quiet was shattered when they approached the Plaza Bazaar of the Mahacossa bridge, filled with the pitched frenzy of a full battle. It was almost impossible to fully determine who was fighting who, and to what end. Bridge guards were desperately holding a line at the bridge, other guards blocking the gates of the docks, hordes of zealots pressing in from most directions. And in the middle of it all, hundreds upon hundreds of people trapped in the fray, pressed against gates and walls, unable to escape the mindless grind of death. Torn up like meat.

"How the *shagh tudeza* are we supposed to get through that?" Basichara shouted.

"Even if we did—" Corrie said, ushering everyone into the comparative safety of an abandoned shopfront, from which they could see the full madness without getting pulled into it. At least not right away. "Get through it to what?"

"We must," the marchioness said. "The ones at that gate to the docks, see? Under the sign of the falcon? Druth Naval Guard."

Corrie saw them, holding that gate shut as if it meant their lives. Which it probably did. "And?"

"They will obey me and let us in, if we can reach it."

"There's no way—"

"I can do it," Eana said.

Corrie looked at the girl, who from all appearances could barely stand. "Don't say you can—"

"We hold together, tight and fast, I can protect us all," Eana said. "Then we push through that gate."

"Do you have a better idea?" Tleta asked.

"I'm really tired of that rutting question," Corrie said. "All the ideas today are bad ones."

"That's a truth," Maäenda said.

Meija's muttering started to grow louder.

"Too many people, too much happening," the Death Caller said.

"We need to—" Corrie started, and then Meija shouted.

"The heretics are here! Burn them all—"

That was as far as she got before Hanakhla knocked her down. But the damage had been done. Many of the zealots turned toward their group.

Corrie stepped to the front, club at the ready. *Please, Saint Veran. This is your chance, let her get home.*

As the first of the zealots closed in on her, she brought up the club, to find an arm wrapped around hers at the elbow. Another arm on her other side. Tleta on the left, Srella on the right.

"Don't—" was all she said before the zealot crashed into her.

Or, rather, crashed into the wall of blue energy around her. She turned her head to see all the group clustered together close, arm in arm, with Hanakhla carrying Meija, and Maäenda carrying Eana, whose hands and eyes burned blue and bright.

"Go!" Eana shouted.

"With me!" Corrie shouted. "Stay together!" And moving forward, she called out the march, left and right, left and right, just like she had been made to do in her cadet years, put on parade detail. The zealots pounded on the ball of energy around them, screaming like mindless maniacs as they clawed and hit. With each strike, Eana shouted as if she had been hit.

"Are you—" Tleta called out.

"Just . . . Keep . . . going . . ." Eana said.

They pressed through the crowd, like fording a river, Eana's shield forcing the others to flow around them.

"Too many," the Death Caller said. "All the dead . . . all the dead . . ."

"Hold it together!" Corrie ordered.

A few more steps. Push them all through. Don't let go of anyone.

"We're going to make it," someone whispered.

Another step, the shield clanged against the gate. Corrie noted the two naval officers at guard on the other side, both with terror in their eyes.

"Hey, seaman," Corrie said. "Open up!"

"The blazes?" he said. "Who the—how did—"

"Just open the gate and let us in—"

"I can't possibly!" he said.

His partner shook his head vigorously. "We'll be killed."

"Seaman!"

"I can't open the gate for a motley group of debtgirls!" he said. "Even if one of you is Druth."

The marchioness pressed her way in the group close to Corrie.

"Seaman," she said with all the authority her rank and title afforded her. "Do you have any idea who I am?"

"Ma'am, yes ma'am," he said with a bow of his head.

"Then open this gate and let us all inside."

"Hurry!" Eana shouted.

The two guards looked at each other in a panic, and then one of them grabbed the latch and opened it up. The press of the crowd alone pushed the whole group through—all still wrapped up in the bubble of Eana's magic—and the guard slammed and latched the gate again.

Eana let go and they all collapsed on the ground.

"The blazes is this mess?" a naval officer asked as he came charging over. "We can't be letting any of these folks onto the docks, or—"

Corrie got to her feet and helped the marchioness up, and that stopped the man cold.

"Your Grace," he said with a bow of his head. "I had no idea."

"I trust you've been waiting for me to launch, Lieutenant," she said. "I have arrived with my people, so let's be about it."

"About it?" he asked. "Ma'am, your Grace, we . . . we're ready to leave once you're on board, but . . . we cannot take these people on the *Queen Mara*."

CHAPTER FIFTY-FOUR

"A ND WHY THE RUTTING BLAZES not?" Corrie asked.
"Who the depths are you to speak to me like that?" the lieutenant asked.

"Sergeant Corrie Welling, Maradaine Constabulary," she said
sharply.

"The sergeant and her deputies here have safely delivered me
through this madness to here," the marchioness said. "And I have designated her as a diplomatic envoy, and I will happily do that to every
single one of the fine people if that is what it takes."

"It's just," the lieutenant said, lowering his voice. "The *Queen
Mara's Pride* is already a bit overloaded."

"With whom?"

"When that madness out there first started, several people—before
we locked the gates—several people offered us money for passage off
the island."

"That is not my concern," the marchioness said. "These people
could have easily abandoned me, but they did not, and I will not serve as
proof that Druth honor and hospitality ranks lower than any other part of
the world. Make room, Lieutenant, and with all due haste."

"Lieutenant, that gate isn't gonna hold!" one of the guards said.

"How many are you?" he asked. "Sixteen? I can take, I don't know, maybe a dozen."

"This is to Maradaine?" Tleta asked.

"To Korifina, then Maradaine," the lieutenant said.

"What is happening?" Basichara asked.

"He's saying the ship is full, he can't take us all," Corrie said. "But I think that's sewage."

"And this ship is going to your homeland?" Basichara asked.

"We'll let people off on Hussua if you want," the Marchioness said. "Or anywhere we can stop on the way back to Druthal."

"Please," Basichara said. "If I can be free . . . if I can see Sebahra again . . ."

"We'll take as many as we can," the marchioness said. "Fit them all."

"You all have to go," Nalaccian said. He pointed to the gate, which was straining at the hinges.

The lieutenant swore colorfully. "Fine, everyone aboard. Go, go!"

The marchioness waved everyone forward while the lieutenant shouted out orders to his people, having them get to the ropes, load the last crates, and be ready to sail in ten minutes. Tleta led Marichua on board, Hanakhla carried Meija. Basichara and Hezinaz. Pume and Saa. Nas'nyom and Nalaccian, with a polite, sad nod as he helped Eana weakly make her way up.

Corrie noticed Maäenda stood firm, tears in her eyes, Srella holding her shoulders.

"The blazes is wrong? Let's go!"

"I can't," Maäenda said. "I have . . . I have nothing but the honor of my name, and I lose that if I take to the waves under another flag."

"What?" There was no time for this sewage.

"I cannot sail on a Druth ship," Maäenda said. "But I helped get you all here, and that's what matters."

"You are rutting kidding me," Corrie said.

"She's not," Srella said.

"You have no strictures," Maäenda told Srella. "Get on that ship and be free, like I never can."

"Are you mad?" Corrie asked.

"No," Maäenda said. "But I am Keisholmi. And in this, maybe it's the same thing."

"Go," Srella told Corrie. "While you can."

"While I—" Corrie couldn't believe it. "Aren't you coming?"

"I can't leave her," Srella said, looking at Maäenda and caressing her face.

"You'll both be killed, or . . ."

"Perhaps," Maäenda said. "But I'll not dishonor my heart or my flag."

"And I'll not leave my . . ." Srella stopped on the word. She closed her eyes, welling with tears. "I will not leave my love."

"You finally said it," Maäenda said with the hint of a smile.

Looking at Maäenda, Srella said, as if the saying the words had broken something free inside her, "I love you too much, Maäe, too much to even comprehend not staying with you, wherever we are, whatever fires we face, as long as it's together."

"I know," Maäenda said.

"You're both rutting insane," Corrie said.

Srella smiled sadly and kissed Corrie on the cheek. "Go. Be free. We'll find a way to survive."

"How will you—"

Maäenda scooped Srella up in her powerful arms. "I can do nothing less. I cannot sail under another flag, but I do long for the water. We'll see you on the other side."

Before Corrie could say anything else, Maäenda ran at one of the empty docks, and both of them let out a sound of absurd joy as she leaped into the ocean.

One of the hinges of the gate snapped, and Corrie didn't wait a moment longer to get on the ship.

CHAPTER FIFTY-FIVE

Corrie found Tleta on the bow of the ship, looking ruefully at the city. The sailors around them shouted and ran about, tying and untying ropes, bringing up sails.

"How are you, all things considered?" Corrie asked.

"Oddly sad that I will not get medical letters from the Mocassan Conservatory of Knowledge."

"Really?"

"That's what's on my mind," Tleta said. "But I imagine it's the simple loss that I'm . . . letting myself think about."

"Marichua?"

"Oddly excited at the prospect of Druthal. She's with the noble-woman, and they're already chatting up as best they can given their lack of proper shared language."

"That's nice," Corrie said. "The rest?"

"Settling in best they can. Save her."

She nodded to the Death Caller, who was pacing about a short ways away, muttering all the while.

"I think she'll be fine once the eclipse passes, or we're out of the range of its influence," Corrie said.

"You may be right," Tleta said. Corrie was amazed by the air of resigned calm Tleta had right now.

"But are you going to be all right?"

Tleta shrugged. "Lost a home and a parent. I've done this before."

"When you fled Xonaca?"

"First time is a tragedy," Tleta said. "Soon it will be a comfortable shoe."

"Tleta—"

"Stop, Corrie, I'm fine—"

"There's no way you can be fine. Not after . . ." Corrie didn't want to say it out loud.

"Probably not," Tleta said. "And soon enough, the rush of all of this will end, the truth of it all will crash upon me like a great wave, and I won't be able to even stand. But by then we will be well on our way to Maradaine, and . . . a ship is a good enough place to fall apart."

"I'll help you stand."

"Tell me that Maradaine is a good city," Tleta said.

"It's a sewage hole," Corrie said. "But it's mine, so I love it. And I'll help you love it."

Eana came over to them both, still pale and pasted with sweat, but with a satisfied grin and one hand behind her back. "I have a surprise for you, Corrie."

"I really don't think I am up for anything resembling a surprise," Corrie said.

"You'll like this one," Eana said. Corrie was amazed by her good cheer, even though she looked like she could barely stand. Though, of course, they were here. On a Druth ship, bound for Maradaine. Bound for home. "I remember what you told me about sitting on the porch of your house with your cousins after your shift, and I know you've been craving it here, so I checked with the sailors. And it *is* a Druth ship, so . . ."

She brought her hand out from behind her back, revealing a metal mug with a foamy beer head.

"Oh my saints," Corrie said. "They have beer on this ship. Thank every rutting thing."

"And," Eana said with a smirk. She blew on the mug, and Corrie felt a chill of a winter wind. The metal mug was glazed with frost.

"You're incredible," Corrie said. "Have I told you that lately?"

"Like a human icebox," Eana said. "I seem to have a knack for that."

Corrie took the mug. "My brother was like that with lighting his pipe." Corrie took a deep, delirious sip. It was an absolute rotgut piss of a beer, as would be expected on a ship all the way out here, but Corrie did not rutting care, because it might as well be honey and cream. She sighed. "Perfect end to this. Now if they would just—"

Something in the distance.

"Just what?" Tleta asked.

"Shh," Corrie said. She definitely heard something. She walked over near the gangplank. "Did you hear?"

"Hear what?" Eana asked.

There it was again.

Faint.

Far away, halfway across the island.

Whistle call.

A Trouble Call.

"Someone's calling a Trouble Call out there," Corrie said.

Eana nodded. "I heard it that time," she said. "Far off. Back in the center of the borough."

"How could we hear it from that far off?" Tleta asked.

"If it was blown from up high," Corrie said.

"Like from a tower?"

"Yeah, but who would—"

Corrie realized, like a hammer to her skull, and looked to Tleta, who had hit upon it as well, and they spoke together.

"Ang."

CHAPTER FIFTY-SIX

C ORRIE WANTED TO PUNCH HERSELF. How could she have
rutting forgotten about Ang? She was up there in the tower over
the library, right in the rutting heart of whatever sewage Hajan was
doing. Whatever she was controlling. Of course she was in trouble. And
Corrie had forgotten all about her.

"I have to go for her," Corrie said.

"What?" Eana asked.

"I've got to go, she's in trouble, I—"

"Corrie, that's crazy. We barely made it here. The boat's about to
launch."

As if on cue, the sailors called to push away from the dock.

"Right," Corrie said. "Which is why you stay."

"What?" Eana reached for Corrie's arm, but the sudden action took
too much out of her, threw her off balance. She stumbled and had to
grab a rail to steady herself.

"You can barely stand." Corrie fished her letters out of her pack.
"Listen, Eana, I'm blazing sorry. I said I . . . I said I'd get you home, and
this ship is going to do that. But . . . ." She pressed the letters into Eana's
hands.

"What are you—?"

"The house is on Escaraine in Keller Cove. Welling House. Everyone knows it, just ask . . . and tell them . . ."

"You can't be serious, I can't . . ."

Corrie wanted to say it, but her jaw froze up. She could hold back the tears, but she couldn't and also speak. She snatched the letter on the top of the stack—the one for Minox—and took out her stylus.

Jotting at the end of the half-written letter, she added:

Things have taken a turn, Minox. There's a whistle blowing and I have to take the call. You know how that goes. I've got to take the ride, even though . . .

She hesitated. Blazes, she didn't have time right now.

Even though it's likely to be my last.

But we know that's the job.

Just remember—I was always so proud to do that job, especially when I got to do it with you. And I'm so proud to be your sister.

Gotta ride.

—Cor

She shoved the letter into Eana's hands. The ship was pulling away from the dock. "Get that delivered. I love you. Tell them all I love them. I have to go." She refused to even let Eana respond as she turned and ran, off the side and landing on the dock as the ship pulled away. She didn't—she could not let herself—look back.

Club in one hand, whistle on the other, she started to walk down the marina. She was back at the gate—about to break off at the hinges—when she realized the Death Caller was right with her.

"What are you—"

"You can't do this alone, Crasher," the Death Caller said. Absolutely as Pop.

"Alone I can move quick, be nimble. I'll—"

"Get killed," the Death Caller said, pointing to the crowd at the gate. Now it was all zealots out there, pounding and howling, ready to tear everything down. "I know a little something about that."

"You have a better idea?"

"Yeah." She tapped on her chest. "Tell her."

The Death Caller's head snapped to one side, and she spoke as herself. "No, I . . . I can't do it."

Snap back to Pop. "Yes you can, and you're going to, or so help me—"

"Do what?" Corrie asked.

The Death Caller sighed. "I can do more than just call and channel. It's . . . excruciating. Normally I could barely do this, but . . ." She gestured to the burning, starlit sky. "Today isn't normal, is it?"

Snap to Pop. "Her power is so much more, especially now. And she'd going to use it."

Snap to the Death Caller. "Don't make me."

Snap to Pop. "She brought you this far, when all you ever were going to do was try to swindle her, so by every saint, do it!"

The Death Caller cried out, and then grit her teeth as her face turned beet red. Raising her arms above her head, she formed fists and pulled them down slowly.

In front of her, the air swirled and coalesced, and a fog formed. The fog took shape, vague at first, but then with more detail, to the figure of a man.

Pop.

He was made out of green light and smoke, but undeniably him. Still in his uniform.

Corrie reached out and touched his face.

Touched.

She could see right through him, but he was solid.

"Dad, I—"

He grinned. "I know, Crasher." Then he looked to the Death Caller. "More."

"But—"

"More."

She took a deep breath, and crying out brought her fists down to her sides.

More smoky green figures formed behind Pop. At least a dozen. Two dozen. Corrie lost count. Faces she had seen in sketches hung up in the house. Constabulary uniforms from twenty years ago. Fifty. A hundred. The marina was full of ghostly figures, constables all.

"How is that—"

The Death Caller dropped to the ground, and probably would have cracked her head open on the cobblestones if Tleta hadn't been there to catch her.

"What are you—"

"I'm coming for Ang, and you can't tell me not to," Tleta said. "And I imagine someone needs to mind this woman."

Meanwhile, Pop—standing right there, so real, Corrie's heart couldn't take it—turned to the others. "Friends. Family. I know you all already had your last ride, and you deserve to rest. But my daughter—a proud sergeant in the Green and Red—she's going to need a show of color."

The group of spectral constables all saluted.

"Sergeant," Pop said. "What are your orders?"

"Constabulary!" Corrie called out, her heart almost choking her throat. Until this moment, she thought that on some level the Death Caller had been playing some elaborate trick. But her father was, more or less, standing right there. She was about to go on one last ride with her pop. She looked to the gate, which was about to crack open.

"We've got a rescue mission, and a city full of hostiles. So we flat the streets, clear our path, and march, double time. Are we clear?"

"Yes, Sergeant!" the spectral cadre cried out.

"Then, Officer Welling," Corrie said, realizing she could be talking to almost any one of them as she readied her club, "Would you be so kind as to open the gate?"

CHAPTER FIFTY-SEVEN

T HE SPECTRAL CONSTABULARY CHARGED FORTH. They
went out with handstick and crossbow, irons in hand, and they
crashed into the wave of zealots that came onto the marina. They held
back that tide, and opened a path through the plaza. They pulled zealots
off the folks who still had their heads about them, pinned them down
and ironed them up. And while their sticks, crossbows, and irons found
their marks, again and again, nothing could touch them. They held the
zealots at bay, but for the zealots fighting back, they may as well have
been striking at the wind itself.

"Great mothers of the world," Tleta said as they ran up the open
street. "How is such a thing possible? She holds that much power?"

"It's the comet, the eclipse, and the other things Ang was on about,"
Corrie said. She looked up to the sky, which was now pitch black except
for the red flame of the comet burning across the stars, and the red
burning ring around the black circle where the sun should be. How long
had it been like this? How much longer would it last? It felt like she
would never see the sun again.

The Trouble Call trilled again, far in the distance, but now a bit
clearer, a bit closer.

"Give the Return!" Corrie ordered. "Let her know we're coming."

The constables, still knocking their way through the stragglers as they traveled up the Ftez Tatlehl, the grand artery through the southern part of Jachaillasa, pulled out their whistles and sent the Return. A joyful blast, help is on the way.

Hang on, Ang, Corrie thought.

The Ftez Tatlehl opened up to the Grand Bazaar, which was all on fire. Cries and screams all around.

"We need a path," Corrie said. She pointed to the burning buildings. "And there's people trapped in there."

One specter—with more than a passing resemblance to Uncle Timmothen, but with a great bushy mustache and a uniform that had to be over a century old—stepped forward. "We've got it, miss. Stand firm." He gave a wave, and several of the specters ran into the building. She didn't know who he was—a great-great-uncle?—but he probably lived at a time before the other Loyalties—the Fire Brigade, Yellowshields, River Patrol—had broken off into their own establishments, and the Constabulary did it all. While they pulled folks out of burning buildings, Corrie urged the others to press on.

"Beat through that," she ordered. "Fastest path to the campus." Several of the specters complied, knocking fiery spice carts and food stands—the destruction seemed so pointless—out of the way so they could pass.

"The zealots aren't still here," Pop noted. "You're thinking campus?"

"Hajan and her folks were doing some strange stuff on the grounds the other night. Maybe they've got a ritual?"

"Your guess is as rutting good as mine."

"How—" She had a thousand questions, but she knew this wasn't the time, or the place. They had a mission, and every click of the clock could cost Ang her life. Or worse. She marched double-time as the fires were beat back, the clear shot to the campus grounds opened up.

"I honestly don't know, Crasher," he said, as if that could answer any of her questions. "I just know, right now, right here, I'm with you. Here to answer one more call, because you need me to."

"Is that what you were doing that night?" she asked.

"You know the answer to that," he said.

"You took Minox's posting in Benson Court, so he could go to Inemar," Corrie said. "You went out in the worst part of town."

"And I took every call I heard," he said. "I did it for Minox, and the only regret I had about it was I couldn't also do it for the rest of you."

"Even Oren?"

"I worry about that boy. All of you. Well, not you. I knew you could handle whatever the streets threw at you." Pop's voice cracked a little as he continued. "Eyes up, Crasher. Action ahead."

Corrie glanced over to her ghostly father as he wiped at his face. She knew damn well what he was trying to say, what even now he couldn't quite manage. "Love you, too, Pop."

"I said eyes up," he said, pointing toward the campus gates.

Even in the red light of the comet, it was clear that nearly every door had been smashed in, nearly every book burnt, and dozens of folks in scholarly robes had been nailed to boards. Zealots filled the campus, dragging more and more people out of halls, dragging them across the stone, hanging them up from the trees.

"Monsters," Tleta whispered. Corrie had almost forgotten she was here.

Those who weren't torturing and maiming were gathered around the library, off on the other end of campus. Even from this distance, Corrie could see them, on their knees, chanting, focused on the one person standing on the stairs.

B'enelkha Hajan.

"Constabulary!" Corrie shouted. "Take them all down!"

They charged the campus grounds, the specters tackling and taking down the zealots, getting the victims down off the walls, and putting themselves between the two as they opened a path to the library. Corrie sent off a Return Call.

The response came from the tower on top of the library. Ang was still there, still alive.

Corrie dove in against the crowd of zealots, her father right next to her, granduncles and distant cousins and ancestors of all sorts, standing shoulder to shoulder as they took down the zealots.

"No!" Hajan shouted. "What is this unholiness? Who dares?"

"Hey, Hajan!" Corrie called back as she took down the next zealot in front of her. "On behalf of the citizens of Jachaillasa, I charge you with high crimes against the people. Stand and be held!"

"You! The worst of them all!"

"Proudly," Corrie said.

"You have brought this desecration upon me? These unholy, profane beasts?" She pointed her finger at the specter at Corrie's right, and with a voice that felt like it made the earth tremble said, *"Begone!"*

And the specter slipped away, like the wind blowing smoke.

Sweet blessed saints, what did that mean?

"Take 'em down, friends!" Pop shouted. "Before she can dust you!"

"I abjure you!" Hajan shouted as one of the specters grabbed her. She struck him in the face, adding, *"Begone!"*

And he was gone.

"I've got her," Corrie said, and she pushed her way through to the steps.

"You have no idea what you have, Sergeant," Hajan said. "But you will pay a price, with your very soul. You will pay for this profanity!"

"Not a rutting chance, slan," Corrie said as she cracked her club across Hajan's jaw. "My goddamn profanity is always free."

"Iron her up, Crasher!" Pop yelled, tossing his set of irons to her. As Corrie reached out to catch them, Hajan turned her gaze toward him.

"Foul dead wraith, I abjure thee!"

And Rennick Welling burst apart into a whiff of green smoke.

But his irons landed in Corrie's hand, just as her heart tore into a hundred pieces. Corrie, in pure rage, brought those irons down onto the side of Hajan's head. The woman screamed, the side of her face erupting into green flames.

Three of her goons grabbed Corrie and pulled her off Hajan, toward the library doors. But they only held her for a moment. Corrie had no quarter to give them, no hint of grace for these rutting bastards. She hammered blows with her club and Pop's irons, knocking them all off her.

Whistle bursts from above. Panic call. Corrie looked up and saw Ang, half out the window. Hands trying to push her out.

She turned to the library doors, and Tleta, still half dragging the

Death Caller, who looked like a wet cat, was already there, trying to get them open.

"Latched," she said. "We can't—"

"We have to!" Corrie said. She turned back to the brawl. "I need help with this door!"

The specters charged the steps, moving right through the zealots they were fighting, passing through Hajan as she wailed, holding on to her burnt face. She turned to the ones who were approaching Corrie.

"Begone! Begone! I abjure you, foul spirits! Begone!"

One by one, they burst into nothingness, each before they could reach Corrie. Several of them changed tactics, and grabbed Hajan, trying to hold her down. One spirit rushed past to the door, and grabbed Tleta and the Death Caller, pushing them through the door as if it were water. Then he turned and grabbed Corrie's hand, and Corrie saw who it was. She thought her heart had already been shattered, but this specter was worse, more terrible than she could imagine.

"Evoy?" she asked as he took her hand and pulled her over to the door. Her cousin Evoy, who had all but fallen into madness. Last she knew. "But you're—you're alive, you—"

"I'm sorry," he said as he pulled her to the doors. "Tell Minox—"

Hajan screamed, and in a voice terrible enough to bring down the stars themselves, shouted, *"BEGONE! UNHOLINESS OF ALL KINDS, BEGONE!"*

And a wave of fire exploded from her, destroying every specter in its wake.

"Tell Minox I have the—"

The fire crashed into Evoy—poor, sweet, broken Evoy, Corrie had never been kind enough to him—and he vanished in her arms.

She slammed against the doors of the library.

Alone, pinned against the great wooden doors.

And untold dozens of zealots looking at her.

"Drag that apostate!" Hajan shouted. "Tear her apart, rend the flesh from her bones, and feed me her heart!"

CHAPTER FIFTY-EIGHT

T HEY CAME.

Wild-faced and mad, they came.

Even though Corrie's head was filled with fear and anger and sorrow and rage and terror, all raw and hot, she shoved that deep into her gut. She didn't have time for that.

They came at her, and there wasn't a chance she would survive it. All she could do was stand and hold, last here as long as possible. Hold the door, buy Tleta and Ang a bit of time. Maybe long enough for someone else to come.

No one else is coming.

Still she braced herself against the door, club in one hand, irons in the other, ready to fight her last fight.

The door opened and she fell backward into the library. Before she could even register what had happened, Tleta slammed the door shut again and latched it, just as a dozen of the zealots crashed against it.

"Mi cêtch i chac," Tleta exclaimed as she grabbed Corrie and wrapped her arms around her. "Are you hurt?"

All the emotions Corrie had been bottling up came flooding into her as she scrambled to her feet. Those zealots kept pounding on the door. They were going to kill her. All of them. She, Tltea, Ang, the Death Caller—they were all going to die.

"No," she said, clutching onto Tleta. "But we . . . we're alone."

"The dead?"

"Gone. Hajan, she . . . destroyed them."

"And she . . ." Tleta said, looking to the Death Caller. The woman was sitting on the floor, propped against the wall. Breathing, alive, but her eyes wide, expression blank.

"Hey," Corrie said, crouching in front of her. "Listen up, we've got—"

The woman didn't even react. Corrie grabbed her face and turned it. Nothing.

"She cried out, and then I heard you crying and praying on the other side of the door, and opened it."

"You heard me what?"

"Praying to some saint, said the price was too high."

Corrie hadn't even realized she had been saying that.

"We don't have time," Corrie said, picking up the Death Caller and hauling her over her shoulder. "Ang was fighting for her life up there last I saw. And those bastards will break that door down before too long."

"But—" Tleta said.

"I can only do one thing at a rutting time!" Corrie said. "Let's get up there."

She pounded her way up the stairs to Ang's observatory. Near the top, the steps were streaked with blood, then several bodies. Most of them Tsouljan, with scarlet red hair, but a few of them looked like the library staff. Corrie turned to Tleta and signaled her to be quiet as they continued. Whoever did this was likely still about.

As they rounded the last corner, Tleta picked up a curved Tsouljan blade off one of the bodies.

"You know how to use that?" Corrie whispered.

"I know I'd rather have it than not."

Corrie took a few steps into Ang's lab, which was an absolute mess. Papers everywhere, books piled high, and another body of a Tsouljan red-hair.

"Ang?" Corrie called out as she put the Death Caller down.

Ang stumbled out from behind her desk, looking like she had been through all the wars. Blood streaked over her robe, which was torn and shredded, her yellow braids all tangled and askew. She dropped the blade she was holding and stumbled over to Corrie, grabbing her in a desperate embrace.

"You came," Ang whispered. "I thought I imagined that Return Call."

"I'm here," Corrie said. "I said I'd come."

Ang pulled back a little, just enough to look Corrie in the eye. "Duty and service."

"You know me too well."

Tleta cautiously approached, and when Ang saw her, she grabbed the girl and pulled her into the embrace.

"All right," Corrie said, pulling back. "Are you hurt?"

Ang pulled open her tattered robe to show the bruises on her neck. "A bit. And you two both look like you've had a time."

"None of us are getting hired as window girls any time soon, that's the truth," Corrie said. "What happened?"

"When things were going bad, when the cult first arrived after the eclipse started, they went in and grabbed books, grabbed students, staff, anyone. Dragged them out into the quad, started burning, killing. The rest of the staff got the doors closed, bolted. I kept observing, kept working, and the guards—" She pointed to the dead man on the floor. "They kept their posts, and helped the staff as they moved the most precious books up here. Then that woman arrived on campus."

"Hajan?"

Ang nodded. "She called out for the faithful to destroy the corruption of the outside, burn out the unbelievers. And when she did, the staff —at least some of them—they went mad. Attacking the rest of us, tearing into the books, acting just like—"

"Like they had become her zealots," Corrie said. "Yeah, I've seen that."

"It's this," Ang said, pointing to the observation port in the ceiling, aimed at the blackened sun. "It's driving her power, to the point . . ."

"We know," Corrie said.

"I put out the call as the Vil fought, but the last one . . . he nearly killed me before I managed to defenestrate him."

Corrie looked out the window, but all she saw was the crowd of zealots, forming a spiral of kneeling bodies centered on Hajan. Calmer than before, but that made Corrie far more apprehensive.

"They're up to something, so let's figure out how we get out of here while they do whatever sewage they're pulling."

"No," Ang said. "We can't leave."

CHAPTER FIFTY-NINE

"**P**ARDON?" CORRIE ASKED. "WHAT RUTTING sewage is that?"

"They've already destroyed books," Ang said. "I heard them going on for a while. She called this library 'the very heart of corrupting blasphemy.' She said it has to be destroyed."

"All the more reason to not rutting be here!"

"She's right," Tleta said. "Corrie, this library . . . it's the most extensive collection of knowledge on the continent. Maybe the biggest in the world."

"Yeah, I remember you telling me—"

"There is work in this building, it's irreplaceable," Tleta said. "Knowledge and science and literature and poetry from every part of the world. Some of it, the original, only copy."

"We cannot let them put an end to it," Ang said. "Duty—"

"Duty and service," Corrie said. "You're serious, you want to defend this against them?"

"We have to. It's the only thing that matters." Ang went back over to her instruments. "Plus, I've missed several measurements and recordings. I should . . . I ought to get the data, take down my observations, until the very end."

"Are you mad?"

"No, they down there are, Corrie," Ang said. "They want to destroy everything that the world has worked for. I'm trying to add to it. The work, most of all, needs to be done, and needs to survive."

The Death Caller wheezed out words, despite no movement or change in expression.

"This . . . is . . . the . . . price."

That almost stopped Corrie's heart. She turned to the Death Caller getting in her face. "Is that it? Are you channeling saints now? Or gods, or . . . I don't even rutting know? Is this what you blazing want?" She jumped up to the window, letting go all the feelings she had been holding back, shouting into the burning dark of this cursed day. "Is this what you rutting bastards want?"

Down in the courtyard, Hajan looked up at the tower, literal fire in her eyes. As the chanting around her continued, growing louder and more dissident, she spoke. She didn't shout or call up—almost a whisper —but Corrie heard her perfectly nonetheless.

"Repent, sinner," she said. "Your reckoning is at hand, and your shallow faith cannot save you."

"My faith," Corrie said, in just as low a whisper, but certain that Hajan could hear her. "Is in justice, and I serve that faith like a cloistress. I told you to stand and be held, B'enelkha Hajan, for your crimes against this city, as well as for obstruction of justice. Be ready for me."

"Be ready for the cleansing fire, Sergeant," Hajan said. "The heresy of this place shall be burned out."

It must not be. That is the price.

Corrie wasn't sure if that thought was her own, or came from somewhere else. That didn't matter, though. What mattered was the clarity it brought.

"Corrie?" Tleta asked.

Corrie jumped down from the window. "All right, this is what I'm thinking," Corrie said, letting her mind put the pieces together as best she could. She did not have a mind like Minox or Evoy—

Evoy. How could he . . . is he dead? Or was it a trick, or—

Shove those thoughts down. No time.

"I'm thinking she's behind schedule. She was doing her rituals, building up power, and we charged in here with the specter corps, and that roughed things up. She used power dispelling them, knocking the Death Caller onto the ropes. So she's building again."

"Why do you think that?" Tleta asked.

"Because she's down there, with the kneeling and chanting, instead of sending her freaks to tear down the door and burn us out. She's not going right to doing that for one of two rutting reasons."

"She knows she can wait us out," Tleta said. "We're outnumbered, time is on her side."

"No, it isn't. She's trying to do something there, and it depends on the eclipse. Best I can figure, our best hope is outlasting them. Once the eclipse ends, her power diminishes again, right?"

Ang shrugged. "The math of that checks out."

"You don't know?"

"I have theories, estimates, but . . ."

"Your estimates are all we have. How long for the eclipse to end?"

"A quarter star."

Twenty-five minutes, more or less. She'll make her move before then. Those doors down there won't hold once they set to work knocking them open. "If I'm right, her hold on those folks will break, or at least strain, once the sun is out again. We just hold on until then."

"There is a lot of untested theory here," Ang said.

"You, take your readings. Tleta, you start getting those irreplaceable books and such. Bring as many as you can into here."

"Why in here?"

"Safest place in the building. We've got the main doors down there, another set of doors at the top of the stairs, and the door into here. Those all should buy us some time until they break in here. They'll probably try to get to us before they start destroying the books, but once they do, we'll be in real trouble."

"How so?" Tleta asked.

"This place is made of stone, so it won't burn down that easy, but there's enough paper down there if they light it up, we'll be just as rutting cooked."

"Burn it?"

"Once they get in. And I believe they're going to do that soon.

Whatever is driving Hajan, it is tied to destroying this place. What it represents."

"I did tell you," Ang said. From outside, they could hear the chanting reaching a fevered pitch. Faster, louder, harder.

"Let's be about things," Corrie said. "Take your readings. We've got it."

Corrie left the tower and got to the business of securing the door at the top of the stairs. A bit of makeshift barring was all she could manage. Sewage, but it was what they had.

She got back to the observatory as Tleta came with a handful of books. "From the rare books room down the hall. I always did want access to it."

"What else can we get?" Corrie asked. "I think time—"

"Now, the reckoning is at hand!" The voice rolled through them like thunder. Corrie lost her balance for a moment, her knees giving out. She stumbled onto Tleta, who was just as off her kilter. The Death Caller started to seize on the floor.

"What was that?" Tleta asked?

"I think it means we're out of time," Corrie said.

CHAPTER SIXTY

"WHAT DO WE DO?" TLETA asked as Corrie got back on her feet.

"You help her," Corrie said, pointing to the Death Caller. "I don't know if she's spending the rest of this counting flowers, but she's the only real source of power we have."

"What are you going to do?" Ang asked.

"Stop asking me blasted questions and keep at your work," Corrie said. "If I'm going to get killed saving sciences or some sewage, then do the damned science."

"As you wish," Ang said, with a hint of playfulness that didn't match the mood of the moment. But that cracked through Corrie's armor a little bit.

"And keep each other alive," she said. "I would bet—"

There was a terrible banging sound from below, again and again.

"They're working on the door," Corrie finished. "What I wouldn't give for a crossbow."

Tleta perked up. "There's an armory display on the floor below us. In the archives on the history of war."

"Let's hear it for archivists," Corrie said, walking out of the observatory. "Keep an ear out. If they come up the stairs, regardless of where I am, you shut and bar this door. Move the desk in front of it. Keep them out."

"But if you—"

"Regardless of where I rutting am, hear?"

"I hear you," Tleta said. She brushed her fingers against Corrie's hand. "You stay alive."

Corrie nodded, and went off. She undid her makeshift barricade at the stairwell door and made her way down. No need to be quiet yet. They were bashing away at the main doors, and they'd be in soon. Speed over stealth, at least right now.

The floor below was the fourth floor—it and the floors below opened up, with corridors leading off to different sections of the library —and Corrie could see all the way down to the ground floor. The pounds on the door echoed throughout the library, every crack and snap of wood and metal heard with perfect clarity.

That door wouldn't hold. Corrie took a moment to barricade the stairwell coming up from the third floor. It wouldn't do much besides slow them down, but every minute might make a difference. Twenty minutes until the sun was back. Maybe in twenty minutes the whole thing would be over.

Corrie didn't know her way around the library very well. All she had been to regularly was the anatomy section with Tleta and the observatory. She scanned the signs on the walls, even though it was too dark to read them very well.

Crash.

History. Corrie ran down that corridor.

Crunch.

History of Moirashka. History of the Mage Kings of Moreshkan.

Crack.

History of War.

The room, almost completely dark save the red comet light through the window, was lined with bookshelves, and glass covered display cases in the middle of the room. Corrie wasted no time bringing her elbow down on the glass. She would apologize to any surviving librarians if she needed to.

The display had a few curved blades of various lengths. Corrie ignored those out of hand. "Constables don't go around stabbing people," Pop would say. There was a handled stick—labeled *sapir pe'azh*—not unlike the handsticks of the Constabulary, and something that looked crossbow-like. *Aghaht be'ho.* Smaller, and its shots were more like darts than bolts, but it would do. Last she grabbed a what looked like a knucklestuffer. Slipping that over her fingers, she ran back toward the stairwell just in time to hear the door burst open.

The frenzied mob surged into the library, howling and nattering like wildcats. They tore into the shelves, so intent on getting at the books that they didn't even go to the stairs at first.

Then, amid the rush of bodies, B'enelkha Hajan strode in like the calmest thing Corrie had ever seen. She stood out even more in the crowd, as her body was infused with a sickly violet light. She glanced about, and said quietly, though that same bone-bending power filled her words, "Destroy all this heresy."

She couldn't fight them all, or stop them all. She had nothing resembling a strategy. All she had was herself, one woman against an army, which was about the stupidest thing she could think of. Loading the *aghaht be'ho*, she decided, might as well be stupid. She was probably going to die; she should die like her father and all those others who came back to help her.

Like a damned constable.

She jumped up on the railing so she could see clearly down to the ground floor, aiming her weapon down toward Hajan.

"Attention scoundrels!" she shouted. "You are all under arrest for assault, mayhem, destruction of public property and the disruption of goodwill! All of you stand and be held! Surrender peacefully and you will be treated with civility!"

Hajan looked up. "Find the others."

The crowd swarmed to the stairwell. Corrie didn't let that sway her, even though the thundering sounds of feet and chanting made her heart hammer with fear. She spat that fear back out.

"B'enelkha Hajan! Your crimes against this city will be answered!"

"Your crimes against God shall be! Your reckoning is at hand, and the fire is here for you. I am infused with his power." She lifted off the ground, flying up to the level Corrie was on. "Repent, child, and you may still spend your death in his loving embrace."

Corrie, despite her shaking hand, aimed and took the shot.

The bolt didn't hit Hajan, instead turning to dust in the violet nimbus that surrounded her.

"Repent and love God," Hajan said, floating over to Corrie. "Your sinfulness will be burned out."

"Go to blazes," Corrie said, jumping back off the railing as she dropped the *aghaht be'ho*. Handstick in one hand, knucklestuffer on the other, she stood ready to brawl. "And let the sinners eat your soul."

"My soul has stood in the crucible. Yours must do the same." She floated in close. Corrie hammered blows at her. Left, right, left. Metal and wood. As hard as she could.

Hajan barely reacted to the hits; instead she calmly placed her hand on Corrie's chest.

Corrie's whole body burned from the inside.

CHAPTER SIXTY-ONE

CORRIE LOST A FEW MOMENTS in the pain; every muscle in her body had abandoned her. The haze of burning pain faded, and Corrie found herself being dragged up the steps, the stampeding masses still behind them.

Hajan was carrying her with one hand, like she was a kitten.

"This could have been easy, Sergeant. You could have been part of something glorious, like the others. Instead, you chose to fight against the path of God."

"Fighting . . . for . . . justice," Corrie wheezed out, though she had reverted to Trade. Finding the words in Imach was too much, even as the initial agony faded.

But that fire still burned in her chest, every breath searing her heart.

"Justice is what God gives us, child. And we do what he demands."

"You are a rutting charlatan," Corrie said. "Just another grift, claiming divine right."

"I am flooded with divinity," Hajan said. "God's burning light flows through me."

"You're filled with fire," Corrie said. "In my books, that marks you as a sinner."

Hajan had brought Corrie to the door to the observatory, thankfully shut. Holding Corrie up with one hand, she calmly knocked on the door with the other.

"Corrie?" she heard Tleta call from the other side.

"Tell them to open the door," Hajan said.

With what strength she could muster, Corrie swung a knucklestuffed punch at Hajan, while clawing at the hand holding her up.

"Tell them," Hajan said, largely ignoring the punch.

"Corrie, what's going on?" Tleta called.

"Tleta, do *not* open this door! No matter what you hear, do *not*—" The fire in her chest went from an ember to a blaze. Corrie could not hold back the scream, even as it brought fire from her lungs.

"Corrie!" Tleta shouted.

"Tell her," Hajan said.

"You . . ." Corrie wheezed out. "You will . . ."

"Make it easy on yourself, child."

Corrie found her voice, forced the words out. "You will stand trial for your crimes, and you will be allowed counsel, as is just and fair."

"Foolish girl," Hajan said, bringing the fire again. As Corrie screamed and cried, Hajan went on. "Whoever is in there, I can only assume you have a measure of care for Sergeant Welling. If you wish for her suffering to end, I urge you to open this door."

"Don't!" Corrie shouted, this time in Trade. "Keep it shut!"

"I just want the secrets of heaven," Hajan said. "They cannot rest in the hands of the unfaithful and non-believers."

The secrets of heaven. Ang's data. "You are just full of sewage. None of this is about faith. You want to be able to find places where you can build your power."

"They are my divine right!" Her hand on Corrie's face, and it did feel like God themself was bearing down on her. The scorching pain was too much for Corrie to do anything but scream.

"If I open the door you'll stop?" Tleta asked.

Corrie couldn't get words to her mouth to tell Tleta no.

"Let me in, child, and she will be free."

Corrie could barely move as the door unlatched. As Hajan brought her inside the observatory, she was unceremoniously dropped on the floor, but the burning continued even as Hajan let go. The pain, the fire from deep inside her soul, found voice.

You stupid girl. Did you really think you, an uneducated idiot who dropped from prepatory could do anything about this? Did you think that you deserved those sergeant stripes? You got them because Captain Cinellan felt bad for you. Because of your name, because of your family. Not you. You couldn't even defend yourself enough to keep from getting kidnapped. With children. You're not a constable, but a child. How dare you even think you earned any of it.

"I got this far," Corrie whispered, otherwise unable to move.

Luck. Stupid luck, where you got far more of those kids killed. Eana is lucky to be rid of you. You can't even protect Tletanaxia, and that was your job. You promised her, you promised Ang, and you failed.

Corrie drowned in that voice, in that fire, even as she heard the wild crowd starting to crash their way through the stairwell. They would be here soon, and then it truly would be too late.

Not that she could do a thing to Hajan.

Not that she could do a thing at all.

Stupid, faithless girl. You believe in nothing because you are nothing.

"I do believe . . ."

In nothing.

Then another sound came, piercing the air. A simple sound, one Corrie knew so well, a sound that she knew meant hope for anyone who heard it and knew what it was. That sound was a lifeline of hope and faith and strength that pulled her back up to her feet and sent that voice into the darkness.

A Return Call.

Help was here.

As the zealots charged down the hall, Corrie slammed the door shut and bolted it.

CHAPTER SIXTY-TWO

ORRIE WASN'T SURE HOW MUCH time had passed—it had felt like hours, but it might only have been seconds. Tleta had placed herself between Ang and Hajan, holding the Tsouljan blade too tight and too high, but with determination.

"Stay away from her," Tleta said. "Stay away from the books, from all of it."

"So very bold for a godless heathen," Hajan said. "What do you believe in, child?"

"I don't believe," Tleta said, aiming the point of the blade toward Hajan's throat. "I know. I know veins and arteries, bones and muscles, heart and lungs and liver. I know exactly where to slice to make you bleed out in five heartbeats. I know what to cut so you never walk again. Do not put me to the test, *xôpke*, because I pass every one."

"I'm sure you do," Hajan said. "And you, young Tyzanian? What threats do you have? How do you think you can stop me?"

"I don't need to stop you," Ang said, still looking through her scope. "I just need to wait another minute. Then the moon and the Unseeables will be out of conjunction, the light of day will return, the comet will fade from sight, and the infusion of mystical energies will diminish. This will end."

"It has already ended, child. The world has ended, as you knew it, and it is now the Kingdom of God, the *Nwey'ima* we were promised. I am infused with God's love, God's power, that which He granted to the angels who pleaded for the life of mankind. Now mankind shall plead to me, for I am here as His *zehto-ne'i,* the blessings and judgment of God shall come from me. As shall His punishment."

"What you did to me didn't come from God," Corrie said, limping closer.

"You children still have a chance, to live in God's eternal grace! Just like we gave so many in this city!"

"Like my mother?" Tleta asked, her voice lowering to a growl. "You think you gave her grace?"

"We gave her chance to repent. She chose to condemn her soul to the great Void, the place that is empty of God." Hajan shuddered. "A horror, but those who reject God are, in turn, rejected by Him. The world is full, so very full, of people who will choose that, rather than embrace the light of God."

As she spoke, a beam of sunlight broke through the top of the observatory, filling the room with bright, warm light. Hajan stood in the light, her face ecstatic, and the violet nimbus around her grew. And outside the door, the pounding masses had begun a new chant.

"This power is mine, and it will only grow. Your petty attempts to understand the mysteries of heaven will help me with that, child."

"You aren't getting that," Corrie said, moving to stand by Tleta.

"I am," Hajan said. She called out, with that terrible voice that shook Corrie to her bones, "Tear it all down, my faithful. Tear it down so we might build anew."

The howls and chants moved away, but the pounding continued.

"Now you have a simple choice, faithless girls," she said. "Join me, be one of the Kingdom of God, and give me what I need to make it grow . . . or perish in darkness and damnation as this building falls down on your heads."

Ang answered by taking Corrie and Tleta's hands. *"Nut piqem yup."*

"Bê haxwi muc," Tleta said.

Corrie was surprised that she understood exactly what they each said. "We stand together."

"Then suffer the wrath of God," Hajan said, grabbing Ang by the throat. Ang screamed in agony as her body was engulfed in the violet nimbus that surrounded Hajan. Corrie grabbed Hajan's arm, but she might as well have tried to pry steel off of stone.

Tleta struck with her blade, but it turned to dust on impact.

Hajan knocked Tleta down, and hurled Corrie away with casual swipes of her free hand, while still holding on to Ang. Hajan smiled— the slan smiled!—and said, "I am overflowing with the power of God, child! Did you think your mundane, earthly weapons could harm me?"

Corrie jumped back to her feet, her hand instinctively going to her belt where her crossbow would be, but that wasn't what she found there. Instead it was the answer Corrie needed.

"Oh, Hajan," she said. "You're going to regret saying that."

She leaped, irons in hand—her father's irons, somehow still solid and real in her hand, but clearly neither mundane or earthly—and slammed them on Hajan's wrist.

Hajan let out a scream that might have made God and the saints all weep. Sparks and lightning burst off her as her violet light flickered and faded.

Ang dropped to the floor, wheezing and heaving.

"My children! My faithful! Save me!" Hajan screamed, but this time her voice carried no thunder, no rolling timbre that touched Corrie in the marrow. Everything great and terrible about her had withered into a sad, frantic woman.

The pounding and chanting on the other side of the door had stopped.

Corrie twisted Hajan's arm behind her back and latched the other manacle of the irons. She leaned in and whispered in the woman's ear. "Consider yourself under lawful arrest. Your crimes will be specified, and they will include and not be limited to assault, mayhem, murder, destruction of public property, disruption of goodwill, and most importantly, inciting and encouraging the aforementioned crimes in others. And if they won't charge you with all these crimes here and lock you away in the darkest hole they have, I will drag you back to Maradaine and charge you there."

"No, no!" Hajan said, looking in every direction, frantic as a caged animal. "God has chosen me, I am His vessel, He will not be denied!"

"Science will not be denied," Ang said, getting up from the ground. "You won't—"

Ang did not get to finish her thought, as Hajan bolted forward, shouting, "Heaven will not be unlocked by you!" and slammed into Ang with her shoulder. Before Corrie could grab Hajan, she shoved Ang toward the window, and they both tumbled over the edge.

CHAPTER SIXTY-THREE

C ORRIE DOVE TOWARD THE WINDOW, extending her hand as she went through it. She slapped and made contact, grabbing Ang's hand. The combined weight of Ang and Hajan wrenched Corrie's shoulder, and she would have gone over the ledge herself had Tleta not been there to grab her legs.

Hajan had managed to wrap her legs around Ang, who was barely holding on to Corrie with her one hand. Corrie stretched with her free arm, relying entirely on Tleta's anchor to keep her—all of them—from plummeting to their deaths, and grabbed Ang's other hand.

"I've got you," Corrie said.

"God will not permit it!" Hajan shouted. She thrashed and shook, clearly trying to force Ang to let go without losing her own grip.

"Let go of me!" Ang shouted at her. "You want to meet your God, have at it and leave me out of it!"

Hajan, demonstrating a phenomenal strength, pulled her body up by her legs, so she was looking directly at Corrie. "You cannot save us, Sergeant. We both go to our divine judgment."

Corrie's grip was faltering, and as much as she wanted to deck Hajan in her smug, self-righteous face, she couldn't dare without losing Ang.

After all of this, there was no way she was going to lose Ang.

"Tleta, pull us up!"

"Are you out of your mind?" Tleta yelled back.

"I go to God," Hajan said, and brought her teeth down hard on Corrie's wrist.

Saints above, that hurt. But Corrie held her grip as best she could.

"You think I've never been bitten on the job before?" Corrie asked. "That's an average night shift for me!"

"Corrie!" Ang shouted as her grip slipped an inch. Corrie couldn't hold much longer, especially as blood started to seep from the corners of Hajan's mouth.

"Pull!" Corrie shouted, and flexed her arms as best she could, but she didn't have anything else in her. "Come on!"

And then there were another set of hands on her legs. Another grabbing her waist. More hands on her, pulling all three of them up.

"Got you, *arsakor*," the Death Caller said to her.

More hands came down, taking hold of Ang. Corrie would recognize those muscled arms, covered with debt tattoos, anywhere.

"Come on," Maäenda said. "You're all right."

Hajan let go of her bite. "I will not be judged by heathens such as you. Only God, and He will hold me up." She released her grip with her legs and started to plummet. But then she rose up again, though her face betrayed confusion and fear instead of her previous smug condescension.

"How? What?" she asked as Corrie and Ang were hauled back into the observatory. Corrie turned and saw Eana—sweaty, pale, and being held upright by Srella and Saa. Behind her, coming in, were the other girls from the house: Basichara, Hanakhla, Pume, Meija, and Hezinaz. All of them looked like they had gone through quite a lot of fight. Meija and Hezinaz, especially, looked furious.

"There are people on the walkway below," Eana said, holding up a glowing hand. "I'm assuming you don't want this trash falling on them." She floated Hajan into the room, leaving her hovering, so she could only impotently thrash about.

"How are you—"

"You really thought I would stay on that ship while you went back?" Eana said.

"I told you—" Corrie started.

"Like you, I don't rutting listen," Eana said.

"And we couldn't let you be here alone," Srella said.

"Together," Saa added.

"But how did you—the zealots—"

"Are subdued right now," Basichara said.

"In every sense of the word," Meija added. "But I think quite a lot of them would like to express their feelings to her." She pointed a bloody blade at Hajan, still floating.

"Sharply," Hezinaz growled. "I have quite a few points I'd like to make."

"I'm certain," Corrie said, grabbing Hajan by the front of her dress and pulling her along. "But let's instead make sure she gets proper, public justice."

"Not kill her?" Tleta asked.

"That's not what I do," Corrie said. "Besides, she's far too eager to die for her faith. I don't want to give her that satisfaction."

"God will strike this city down! All of you—"

Eana snapped her fingers, and the hem of Hajan's collar ripped forth and wrapped around her mouth.

"Justice," she said. "But by every saint, I don't want to hear her."

CHAPTER SIXTY-FOUR

"THE SHIP HAD LAUNCHED," CORRIE said as they all worked together to further bind Hajan. "And most of you were on it."

"I gave your letters to the marchioness," Eana said. "And she was very willing to turn right back around and wait, even though the naval officers were quite against it."

"You turned the ship around?"

"No," Eana said. "The naval officers were against it, and the captain quoted some maritime law about authority during hostilities, and therefore her orders had to be ignored. At this point I had gotten worked up enough that the rest of the girls were aware, and when the captain said we were welcome to take the rowboat back, I had them all with me when I got in and magicked it across the harbor."

"Please tell me you did not bring Marichua here," Tleta said.

"No," Basichara said. "And Nalaccian stayed behind, saying if we survived, it would be better if he was off the island for a bit."

"Nas'nyom?"

"He was helping put out a fire on the ground floor," Hanakhla said. "He was very helpful when we arrived here." It looked like that caused her physical pain to say.

Corrie shook her head. "You all . . . you all came back."

"You came back," Ang said.

"She heard your whistle and didn't even blink," Eana said. "I was held up because I had to make sure her letters made it home."

"You could have gone home," Corrie said.

"No more than you could have when you heard that whistle."

Maäenda, satisfied with her knots and gag work on Hajan, said, "And when Srella and I saw your army of ghosts tear through the square, we . . . well, we first checked on what happened in the square, and then we followed as tight as we could, with all of these folks right behind us."

They left the observatory, where a lot of the zealots—and now that things were calm, Corrie noted that a fair amount of them were not wearing the green sash—were mostly sitting on the floor, expressions of utter disbelief on their faces. More were on the stairs. It was as if whatever had driven them into a frenzy had just snapped off, and they had dropped to the floor wherever they were when it happened.

They all perked up when Hajan was being led out into the hallway and down the stairs. Eyes were hard on them all as the group leading her passed by, and whispered mutters followed after them.

"Is that her?"

"She seems so . . . slight."

"Why did we listen to her?"

"Why did we do this?"

"What did I do?"

"Why did she make us do that?"

"I'm going to be sick."

"I'm going to kill her."

"Easy!" Corrie snapped out. "Let me make something clear. B'enelkha Hajan is in custody. She will be turned over to proper authorities, and she will answer for her crimes."

"How?" one man asked. Corrie realized he was the one who had first gotten in her face back when Hezinaz was dancing. "What authorities are there that can take her? Who can make her answer for what she's done? What she . . . what she did to me?" His hands started to shake. "What she made me do?"

"I don't know," Corrie told him. "But we will find someone who can do that, and if we can't, we will make that happen."

"What can even make me whole again?" another asked.

"What can fix this?"

Meija stepped forward. *"'And did you see?' the angel said. 'Amid the fire and plague and famine and horror, there was the man Eh'taja who washed his neighbor's face, and shared his water with him. Though she was hollow-cheeked and ravenous, did Dreiba break her bread and give it to a stranger. Bekara reached out to the man whose body was covered in sores, without fear, and said, let me bring you comfort.'"*

"Faith and quoting the Books brought us to this," one said. "She used that upon us!"

"And as God brought pestilence and disaster to mankind, so we were tested," Basichara said. "Now is still your test."

"Stand together," Hezinaz said. "And stand for justice, so we can heal, so we can rebuild."

The crowd all nodded, and let Corrie pass, leading Hajan out of the library.

"That was pretty brilliant," Corrie whispered to Meija. "I thought it was going to get ugly."

"I wanted to make it ugly," Meija said. "But . . . then I remembered that part of the Book of Sorrows. My father would be quite pleased that study didn't go wasted."

The light of day made it clear how terrible the state of things was on campus. Half the buildings burning, all the gardens torn up, and, of course, the bodies.

So many bodies, it almost made Corrie's heart stop.

"Hey! Hey!" Shouts from across the quad, and a cadre of fellows in yellow and ochre wraps came over. The city guard from Teamaccea. "What's all this?"

"Officers," Corrie said, pulling Hajan along with her. "Sergeant Corrie Welling of the Maradaine Constabulary. I've taken this woman, the instigator of all this chaos, into custody. Do you have authority to take her and deliver her to justice?"

"Do we—" The leader of the cadre looked very confused. "Who exactly are you?"

"She's the one who saved us all," Ang said. "By stopping this woman, who had exerted an unnatural control over people during the eclipse."

"Her?" the leader said, pointing at Hajan. "She did all this?"

"We should take every one of these people and lock them up," another officer said. "Let the Regality figure it all out."

Tleta spoke up. Pointing to Corrie, she said, "This woman is the only reason we are alive. That a crazed mob isn't tearing you limb from limb right now."

"We're supposed to believe that?" the leader said.

Maäenda pushed her way to the front of the group. "Are you questioning the integrity of Sergeant Welling?"

"How do I even know she is who she claims? Or that I should believe what she's telling me."

"Do you know who I am?" Maäenda asked.

"Should I?" the leader asked. Then one of his officers whispered something into his ear, and his expression changed. "My apologies, your Grace."

"Accepted," Maäenda said. "I vouch for Sergeant Welling and any testimony she gives of the events that occurred here today. You will treat is as High Truth."

The cadre leader mulled this over. "All right, Welling, come with us, bring your prisoner. The rest of you, clear off and make space to help the injured."

"I can help the injured," Tleta said. "I am a medical student."

The leader nodded. "Fine, yes. But please, let's otherwise get people who don't need to be here out of here. We'll sort out the rest later."

As they were being led off campus, Corrie saw the chaos in the streets, the consequences of the madness that had infected the borough, but also the folks working together. Putting out fires, helping the fallen, getting people out of the danger. The cadre leader led them all through several blocks until they reached an encampment near the bridge to Teamaccea. He gestured for Corrie to bring Hajan toward one set of tents, while Eana, Ang, Tleta, and the rest of her friends were being led to another part of the camp.

"Go," Maäenda said with a friendly touch on Corrie's arm. "It is fine. We will see you at home."

Home. It amazed Corrie how natural it felt for Maäenda to call the debthouse that, and for the first time ever, Corrie felt it was true.

CHAPTER SIXTY-FIVE

T HE FIRST TWO *MNU* OF the year 598 of the Imach calendar
were a blur of questions and cross-examinations and interroga-
tions. The City Guard from Teamaccea, as well as the Regality of the
High Court of Mocassa, all descended upon Jachaillasa to clean up,
secure the chaos, and determine what the blazes had happened.

Corrie was questioned over and over again. The second time, the
attaché from the Druth Embassy came and verified the documents she
had from Marchioness Idonna, and convinced the High Court that she
should be declared a trusted witness, a *"rhoz ghe'hv berre'i"*—friend of
the judge, literally—in the local parlance. The High Court also agreed
that Corrie had acted in good faith as an officer of law in spirit, and thus
should be treated with the same regard and respect.

Corrie gave the same testimony multiple times, to various authorities
and adjudicators. Tleta was called in for testimony, but Corrie barely
saw her in those days. She was dealing with her own legal matters,
sorting her mother's estate and holdings.

Ang had been completely scarce, as shortly after things calmed
down, a contingent from the *teknosom* rushed in and sequestered her
away in their compound. Corrie wanted to check in on her, but had been
far too busy to have a chance.

The Mocassan Conservatory of Knowledge cancelled further classes indefinitely and shuttered its doors. Of all parts of Jachaillasa, it had suffered the most, both in material damage and in loss of life. The few surviving faculty would need at least a year, it was said, before they were whole enough to start back on the task of training young minds.

The ladies settled back into the debthouse, and got to work right away. There was plenty of opportunity for all of them throughout the city, as everyone needed to clean up, rebuild, and the city officials needed anyone who was fit to work to help out with feeding, clothing, and tending to the injured. Everyone stayed busy.

In all this time, Corrie saw B'enelkha Hajan only once, when they called her down to the holding cell she was being kept in.

"No one can get these manacles off her," one of the officers said. "They're Druth, so we thought you might know how."

Corrie was worried about taking them off of Hajan, for all she knew, those irons were the only thing keeping Hajan's power in check. Plus, while Pop had thrown her the irons, he hadn't given her a key. She wasn't sure how she would get them off, either.

The latter had proven not to be a problem, though. As soon as she touched them with the intention of unlatching them, they came free without any trouble at all.

"How did you do that?" the officer asked her.

"It's because they're mine," she said, hoping he'd take that for an answer.

Hajan smiled and turned to him. "This heathen defies the word of God, she should suffer his wrath."

He just scowled. "You ask me, miss, you should worry about the wrath you're going to suffer."

"Heed the word of God!" Hajan said. "Heed it!"

He shook his head and walked out of her cell. Corrie followed after him, but turned around to face Hajan one last time.

"I did warn you," Corrie said. "Looks like you found out."

A few days later, the testimonies stopped, and declarations were posted around the city about Hajan and several of her followers—the few true zealots who didn't denounce her when her hold broke—had been found guilty of crimes against the city and the people of Jachaillasa, and sentenced to a prison camp in Moca Esail.

"What is Moca Esail?" Corrie asked Srella that night.

"The region north of the city that's part of the Mocassan state while not quite being 'the Mocassa,' I think," she said. "I honestly don't understand all the distinctions among the different regions and boroughs and what is 'the Mocassa' and what isn't." There had been, Corrie had heard from the other girls, some heated discussion among the locals—especially the rich ones who had successfully fled the island—about officials from the other boroughs enacting emergency powers to impose themselves upon Jachaillasa and the local authority.

At the moment, the city guard from the other boroughs had taken to patrolling and policing the streets, and what Corrie had seen was quite effective and just.

She didn't mind that they often gave her a small nod, saying, "Sergeant," whenever she walked by. Several stopped her to talk about whistle calls, or offered to buy her a coffee and swap stories.

Then Nalaccian came back to the island. Or rather, was brought back. Corrie hadn't been given the full story at first, but he had gotten off the *Queen Mara's Pride* on Hussua, and had been keeping a low profile until his creditors laid down claims which forced the local authorities to round him up and bring him back. When that happened, several officious prats came to the debthouse, nailing up several bright notices of foreclosure and lien, and issuing writs—they had another word, *wu'swi*, but they were writs—to each of the women who Nalaccian held a debt ward on. They were compelled to come to a hearing of the financial courts so the matter of his outstanding assets could be fully examined and appraised.

They were his assets.

"Exactly as he said," Srella said as they all got ready for their appearance. "We would be sold off to other debt wardens."

"After everything we did, this is what we get," Hezinaz said.

"We did right," Corrie said. "Never forget that."

"I won't," Hezinaz said. "But it won't help me sleep if I'm sold to a flesh peddler."

There was something fascinating—and revealing—about how the financial courts, like that first debt auction Corrie had found herself at, were so much more organized than their criminal courts. After all these months in the Mocassa, Corrie was still amazed how little was made of crimes like murder or assault, even now, but collecting money was paramount.

When they all arrived, they were shuttled onto a seating area that was up on a platform, to the side of the main proceedings. The platform was boxed in, so they could see Nalaccian as he sat in a judgment seat, and they could see the assessor panel that presided over the hearing, but they could not see the crowd who had come to observe. But Corrie could hear them, and it was clearly a large crowd.

"So many people come to see a man's assets get appraised?" Corrie asked. "This is what passes for fun in this town?"

"Well, they don't drink and they frown upon music," Eana said.

"If our debts are to be auctioned off, debt wardens could buy our debts at a fraction of their value," Srella said. "And simply put . . ."

"Mine is quite the ripe plum," Maäenda said. "Every warden in all seven boroughs would want it."

"Blazes," Corrie said.

"Peace and silence!" the head assessor called out. "We are to begin the assessment and liquidation of assets. Nalaccian Assema, are the assembled ten women the full assets of your wardenship?"

"They are, sir," Nalaccian said.

"And with your losses at present, what is your shortfall to your current obligations?"

"By the agreed assessment of my records, as certified by the court, it is approximately two hundred forty thousand kessirs."

"And you are not able to demonstrate holdings to that end?"

"Not at this time, no."

"What does that mean, exactly?" Corrie whispered to Srella. "Is he in debt as well?"

"Not like we are. Basically, to have the right to warden our debts, he needs to have cash or property equivalent to our debts. Unless he has the backing to guarantee our debts, he has to sell it off to another warden."

"So, if our debts were lower, he wouldn't be in trouble."

"Ironically, yes."

Rutting madness, Corrie thought.

"To confirm the assessed value of the debt holdings in your wardenship, I will read off each property and—"

"Objection!" Corrie shouted.

The head assessor looked over to Corrie. "I'm sorry, what?"

"Our debts may be assets you can sell or auction, sir," Corrie said. "But we will not be called property."

He looked somewhat embarrassed, and nodded. "So noted. Here is the list of debtors with the assessed value of their wardenship. Henik ab Srella, one hundred eighty-five kessir."

"That little?" Corrie asked.

"I've been paying."

"Corrianna Welling, one thousand, eight hundred thirty-five kessir. Eana Mellick, one thousand three hundred twenty-one kessir."

"You've been paying off mine!" Eana hissed at Corrie.

"Damn right I have," Corrie said back.

The assessor rattled off more: Hanakhla and Pume both had less than a thousand, Saa and Basichara both had about three thousand, most of the rest of the girls in between.

"Finally, *Iketro* Maäenda Sækira of the Oshai Fleet, two hundred seventy three thousand, nine hundred eleven kessir."

There was a lot of murmuring and whispered in the unseen crowd.

"With that assessed, we will begin—"

"Your pardon, Assessor," a voice came from the crowd. "On behalf of the Mocassan Conservatory of Knowledge, we would offer a payment of *zirrba pa'hi* to the debts held by these women, to the order of four hundred kessir each, as gratitude for their service on the day of the eclipse."

"Ah," the lead assessor said. "It is so tabulated, and we are grateful for your act of charity."

"What just happened?" Eana asked.

Basichara answered. "*Zirrba pa'hi* is a payment that anyone can make at this time, out of charity, to lower the debt burden of any of the assets to be auctioned, and thus lower the obligations of the assessed."

"So it helps us and Nally?" Corrie asked.

"It *never* happens, though," Basichara said.

"I would offer a payment of *zirrba pa'hi* to the order of five hundred kessir each," another voice said, this one speaking the Imach in a flat accent. "As gratitude on behalf of King Maradaine XVIII."

"Thank you, Mister Ambassador," the assessor said. "This does place some of the assets in surplus. Mister Assema, would you want the remainder—"

"Spread evenly to the others, yes," Nalaccian said.

"Then if we can—"

"On behalf of the Grand *Teknosom* of the Tsouljan *Rekfonwik*, we offer *zirrba pa'hi* to the order of four hundred kessir each, as gratitude on behalf of the advancement of science."

"Kow," said a voice that Corrie instantly knew was Ang's.

"That is," the original Tsouljan voice said. "Five hundred kessir each on behalf of the Grand *Teknosom—"*

"Doub," Ang said.

"Nut pom sats," he urged.

"Pol sem woban doub."

"What is happening?" the assessor asked.

"My apologies," the Tsouljan voice said. "After . . . conferring with my colleague, we will offer . . . seven hundred kessir each on behalf of the debtors."

"So noted," the assessor said. "Are there any other—"

Voices spoke up, some of them pledging just a handful of kessir, some over a hundred. There was quite a bit of chaos and numbers thrown around, and Corrie couldn't keep track of it all. After a few minutes, the head assessor banged on his table.

"Is that all?" he asked.

The room was silent for once.

"Give us a moment to finalize our tabulations."

Corrie, as all the rest of the ladies in the box, looked to Srella.

"Enough was pledged to pay almost all of our debts," she whispered. "Except for . . ."

"Except for me," Maäenda said. She reached over and took Srella's hand. "It's all right."

"But you should—"

"Thousands of kessir were paid on my debt, love," Maäenda said. "And the rest of you are unburdened. It is glorious."

"Attention," the assessor said. "By our tabulations, the sole remaining asset is *Iketro* Maäenda Sækira of the Oshai Fleet. Her debt now stands at two hundred sixty-nine thousand, five hundred ninety-seven kessir. With no further acts of *zirrba pa'hi,* we will proceed with the auction of this asset, unless someone offers a preemptive at cost." He said this with a sly chuckle, as if he had presented a complete absurdity.

Then his face dropped as a collective gasp rippled through the crowd.

"Are you certain?" he asked. "Your funds can be confirmed?"

"What?" Eana asked.

"Someone just bought Maäenda's debt at full price," Hezinaz said. "Who would even—"

"It is so done," the assessor said. "The full asset is so sold to Tletanaxia of the House of Taa-shej. And with that, these proceedings are completed, thank you for your time."

"Tleta . . ." was all Corrie could say. Did she really pay that kind of money? Did she have that kind of money?

Nalaccian came up to the box, his eyes wet. "My dear ladies, I am . . . I am overwhelmed. You did something remarkable, and God has answered you in kind."

"Are we . . . are we really paid off?" Meija asked.

"You are," he said. "Feel free to have your tattoos marked in blue, or removed, or whatever you wish. However . . ." He produced a small key and came over to Eana, and with a few quick motions, removed the debt bolt from her ear. He went down the line, taking each one out, ending with Corrie.

"Of course, for each of you, your rent is paid for the rest of the *mnu,* and you are welcome to stay there at the same price if you so desire. But I imagine you will make other arrangements. And, as for you, *Iketro,* you must report to your new debt warden. But for now, all of you . . . you are free to go."

CODA:

THE SUNRISE HORIZON

CHAPTER SIXTY-SIX

CORRIE AND EANA FOUND THEMSELVES walking almost in a daze in the warm sunlight. Corrie remembered that summer was coming—she didn't quite understand it, even when it had been explained to her, that she had missed winter completely because winter at home was summer here. Not that it truly mattered. Every day here was just hot or absurdly hot.

"So now what do we do?" Eana asked, as the rest of the ladies scattered off in various directions. Corrie looked around for Tleta, but she didn't see her anywhere. She did see a few officious-looking fellows cart Maäenda off to a pullcab and spirit her away. Srella stood in the courtyard, watching forlornly in that direction long after it went off.

"Let's first check on Srella," Corrie said. "And then, well, we'll see."

They went up to her. "Hey, are you going to be all right?"

Srella turned to them, lifting her chin up high. "Of course I am. I am Henik ab Srella Ariska Miezhta mik Giowen lek Ni— No, wait." Her hand went to her bare ear, caressing the exposed skin. "Lek *Ona* vil Ousnaa sim Jiul. I am unburdened and free. Why would I not be all right?"

"I would bet whatever intentions Tleta has for Maäenda right now, she would let you be a part of those plans."

"Do you? I have to accept your trust in her to believe that, I do not know her."

"I can tell you, I don't know why Tleta bought Maäenda's debt—I am fixing to find the blazes out, mind you—but I can tell you, she has nothing but high regard and respect for her."

"I shall make prayers that you are right. I will see you at the house, if you intend to stay there any further length."

"I don't have anywhere else to sleep tonight," Corrie said. "And we'll figure out tomorrow, tomorrow."

"Then I will see you," Srella said, heading off.

"Should we follow her?" Eana asked.

"She needs space," Corrie said. "We'll give it—Ang!"

Ang Rek-Nouq almost pounced on Corrie, her smile as wide as her face as she grabbed Corrie in a wild embrace.

"Look at you! You're free!"

"Thanks to you," Corrie said.

"In *part* to me," Ang said. "Which was only fair and just."

"How did you convince your people to pay so much toward our debt?" Eana asked.

"I did . . . what is the Druth word for it? Is it darkletter?"

"Do you mean blackmail?" Corrie asked, unable to hold in the laugh.

"That is the word, yes. They were very interested, of course, in all the information I had compiled with my observations, calculations, and long hours of work. They made it very clear to me that they had invested a great deal of resources in me to acquire the fruits of my labor. And that's when I realized that I had leverage. So I gave them all my work. Which I had encoded with a mathematical cypher."

"What?" Corrie asked.

"They were very angry, but I made the succinct and logical argument that I had, in fact, fulfilled my obligation by attending to the work and delivering it to them, and that there were several mathematicians in Tsoulja who had the capacity to crack the cypher if they wished. Or, they could buy the key to the cypher from me, by providing *zirrba pa'hi* to all the women who literally put their lives on the line to protect the information they craved."

"I'm sure the Tsouljan Commission was anxious to get their precious information."

"Oh, rather," Ang said. "I was reminded that men, good men of the Vil, also died for the sake of this information, and it should be treated as sacred."

"Hmm," Corrie said.

"They told me that I had much duty to fulfill, especially in light of these events where knowledge was lost. They reminded me how critical my work is for the greater regime of Tsoulja, and I must submit to the circles above me and follow the orders of my betters."

"I do not like these people . . . I know they're yours, but—"

"It is fine," Ang said. "Because, in that moment I asked myself, what would Corrie Welling do?"

That was interesting. "And?"

"And I had a revelation. Answering that question turned out to be very freeing."

"What did you do?"

"I told them to drink a tall cup of my hot piss," Ang said. "I thought that would give them a suitable sense of my mood."

Corrie couldn't stop laughing. "Oh, that's glorious. I will need to add that to my vocabulary."

"The last thing she needs is more disgusting things to say," Eana said.

"I disagree," Ang said. "I've noticed that, if your vocabulary is any indication, Druth Trade is surprisingly limited in its scope of expletive. An obsession with defecation and copulation, mostly."

"Shows you a lot about the Druth mindset," Corrie said. "No wonder we're kind of a mess of a people."

"I would never say that."

"Thanks," Corrie said. "So what does this mean for you and the Tsouljan Commission?"

"I am at liberty," Ang said. "Which is a polite way of saying I am expelled from the commission. There was a time where I would have been very upset by that, but it is no longer that time. Besides . . ." She reached under her robe and pulled out a bound bundle of papers. "I made a copy of my work for my own purposes."

"As you should."

She put the papers back. "The point is, I successfully extracted from them the funds that helped put you both at liberty. We are quite free, friends."

"What does that mean for you?"

"Most immediately, that I have no place to sleep tonight," Ang said. "Could I impose upon your hospitality?"

"Absolutely," Corrie said.

They went back to the debthouse—just a house now, Corrie thought. Hanakhla was hanging out of her window, and laughter, music, and glorious scents were coming from inside. And standing outside the door-frame: the Death Caller.

"Go on in," Corrie told Eana and Ang. "I'll be right there."

They went on, and Corrie waited until they were up before addressing the Kelliracqui woman.

"I haven't seen you about," Corrie said. "Lost track of you after the library."

"I sort of lost track of myself there," she said. "I . . . I've had these voices with me as long as I can remember, driving me, urging me. I ended up in this city because I was directed by them. I kept coming to you because of them. And now, for the first time, my head is quiet."

"You aren't hearing the dead anymore?"

"Not since the eclipse ended. I don't know if I burned myself out, or if Hajan shredded my power or . . . I don't know. But the dead have been guiding me for so long, I'm not sure what I am without them. Who I am."

Corrie laughed. "I'm sorry," she said, stifling it. "I just realized that after all this, I don't even know your name."

She laughed. "Mayetek du Mosh."

"Mayetek. A blazing good name."

"I agree," she said. "Now I need to figure out who Mayetek even is."

"Listen," Corrie said. "Those irons that my father gave me, that I stopped Hajan with. I still have them, and . . ."

"What are they?" Mayetek asked. "I haven't the slightest. I do know that when the dead give you something, it is yours, and it charges you with great purpose."

"This seems like another trick of Saint Veran," Corrie said. "My prayers were answered, with the price. Is this another price on me?"

Mayetek looked off in the distance. "I think your burdens are all paid, Corrie Welling. But you are a creature of duty, and perhaps that purpose you are charged with is one that accompanies the duty you take on. I . . ." She paused for an uncomfortable period of time, her face in thought.

"What?"

"It is gone, but for a wisp of memory. But I remember your father's spirit, which I think you share in your heart. That spirit that drove him, that is also in you, is one that will always answer one more call. Your burdens are paid, Corrie Welling, except the ones you'll never put down."

Corrie chuckled wryly. "That's some rutting truth."

"I'll leave you to yours," she said.

"Nonsense," Corrie said. "They're celebrating and cooking up a storm up there. We wouldn't be standing here without you, and . . . come have some blazing supper with us, hmm?"

The *ghose'a* was full for the evening. Full of laughter and joy and dance. Full of more food than Corrie had eaten in some time, as Basichara had gone above and beyond her usual cooking. She had, apparently, gone to the market square and bought meat and spices with the wild abandon of a woman with no debts to pay off. Hezinaz danced with jubilation, and Meija and Hanakhla sang. Pume and Saa laughed and chattered and at some point in the evening started kissing in the water room before going upstairs. Only Srella was somewhat subdued, the sad smile on her face, until she retired early to her room.

Even as everyone else stumbled off and fell asleep, Corrie and Eana kept talking long into the night, devising a plan for the coming days to get to the embassy, thank the ambassador for his part in their debts being paid, and arrange transport home. Corrie didn't remember falling asleep, but she woke on the floor of the *ghose'a* to sunlight streaming through the window, Eana curled up next to her. She quietly got on her feet and went to make a pot of coffee.

"Hello, household!"

Tleta was calling from the street below. Corrie stuck her head out the window to see Tleta and Maäenda standing in the street, both of them dressed as richly and finely to fit their noble station, even as Maäenda's arm and ear was still very marked with her debt.

"What are you rutting doing?" Corrie asked.

"We are here to talk to talk to the whole house," Tleta said. "May we come in?"

"Of course you rutting can," Corrie said. "Get in here."

They came in and up to the *ghose'a,* and Corrie woke Eana to fetch everyone else.

"What is going on?" she asked Tleta.

"Allow me some indulgence," Tleta said. She waited patiently while the rest of the ladies staggered down the steps in a sleepy daze. Most of them went straight for the coffee Corrie had made.

"Ladies," Tleta said, "in the wake of the tragedies and troubles, I have found myself in a very strange position. I have inherited by mother's holdings and wealth, but as I am unable to continue my studies at the conservatory, and . . ." She paused for a moment, looking to the ground. "As my mother's home is a source of great sorrow, I have no desire to stay in this city. I imagine many of you feel similarly."

There was a murmur of general agreement among the ladies.

"So I took stock of the wealth I had, and how to best apply it to my desire. Thus I purchased Maäenda's debt, and as her debt warden, have granted her dispensation of free travel in exchange for services only she can render."

"What services?" Srella asked cautiously.

Maäenda spoke up. "That I take my place as captain of the *Chiishwi* and deliver the ladies of this household to whatever port in the world they wish to go to."

Srella's face lit up. "You get . . . you get to go back to the sea? On your ship?"

"On my ship," Maäenda said, her smile lighting up the world. Srella jumped into her arms as kissed her for long enough to make the moment a bit awkward.

"So, anywhere?" Corrie asked.

"Anywhere," Maäenda said. "Obviously, we'd have to chart the best course for all our destinations. But, of course, I've always wanted to sail to Maradaine."

CHAPTER SIXTY-SEVEN

THEY WENT TO THE DOCKS, and on board the *Chiishwi,* with no one barring their way. They had packed up all their posses- sions from the house, loaded them in cases and crates, and brought them on board the ship.

The *Chiishwi* was like no other ship Corrie had ever seen. She had, of course, seen plenty of sailing ships and galleons in the Maradaine River, but the *Chiishwi* was a piece of art, sleek and shining, a bright white knife in the water. Walking on the deck, Corrie could see why Maäenda loved it so, why it was home to her. It was clear how she never could let it go.

"Of course, you're all going to have to learn to sail," Maäenda said as they loaded provisions and supplies. She had a few loyal Keisholmi who had been her skeleton crew, who had kept the ship in port and tended to it all this time, but hardly a full crew. "Can you handle that?"

Saa laughed and said something in her native tongue.

"What was that?"

"She said she thought she had proven she wasn't afraid to work!" Nas'nyom, dressed in his iridescent robes, came over to the gangplank. "Permission to board?"

"Are you looking to come along with us?" Maäenda asked him.

"I have no place to go to school," he said. "And if you have need of a translator, I'd like to earn my keep."

Maäenda looked to Corrie. "He's your friend."

"He is," Corrie said. "If he wants to rutting come, he should."

"Hanakhla won't be happy," Maäenda said.

Hanakhla, who had been taking barrels below deck, sauntered over to Nas'nyom, and despite the scowl on her face, patted Nas'nyom on his shoulder. "Useful," she said.

The ship was loaded and ready by sunset, filled with her passengers from nearly every corner of the eastern world. Basichara, Meija, and Hezinaz from Imach kingdoms. Hanakhla from Ch'omikTaa. Nas'nyom from the Jelidan city of Tekir Sanaa. Pumesticolomikal of the Turjin Empire. Saa Njien of the Lyranan state of Zhai Zrao. Mayetek du Mosh of the Kellirac kingdom of Kuvar. Henik ab Srella Ariska Miezhta mik Giowen lek Ona vil Ousnaa sim Jiul of Fuerga. Ang Rek-Nouq, honored if exiled scientist of the Tsouljan *rekfonwik*.

Tletanaxia, First Daughter to the *quqô tśînôsho* of the *tśîtśesh* of Taa-shej, third in the court of the Tchoja, the Children of the Sky, and the jewel in the eye of all Xonaca, the motherland of all people, whose womb is ever fruitful.

Iketro Maäenda Sækira of the Oshai Fleet of the Oceanbound Keisholmi, captain of the *Chiishwi.*

And two lost rutting girls from Maradaine.

They doubled up in the cabins, Corrie bunking with Eana. As they lay in their hammocks—lined with Turjin silk, as divine a place as Corrie had slept in for months—Eana drowsily said, "You know, you've done enough. We're on our way home. Eventually."

"What do you mean eventually?"

"I talked to Tleta and Maäenda about our route. We're going to go a lot of places, you know."

"I know."

"I told them, and I want to make it clear to you, that we don't have to rush to Maradaine first. We have a lot of places to go, and they should choose the best route for everyone."

Corrie looked at Eana. "Don't you want to get home?"

"Of course I do," Eana said. "But we have to think of the whole family. There's no hurry."

"Right," Corrie said. "But I'm happy to sleep and find out the plan tomorrow."

"Hey, you know what tomorrow is?"

"It's *pe'urr zha rez u Orewes*."

"I meant in *our* calendar."

Corrie couldn't work it out. "I have no idea."

"It's the first of Keenan. New Spring. The new year starts tomorrow."

Corrie laughed. "Then to a joyous new year." Keenan 1st, 1216. She drifted to sleep, wondering what that year would bring to her family. Both the old one and the new one.

She woke with the dawn, coming to the top deck as the crew were just starting to get the ship out of the harbor, raising the sails to work their way around the island of Jachaillasa, and out to the open ocean.

"Morning," Maäenda said as Corrie approached her by the helm.

"Eana said something about the best route for the family?" she asked. "What are you thinking?"

"Well," Maäenda said, "talking to the other ladies, I've got a rough idea. We're going to head east, first to Xonaca."

"Really?"

"Tleta, even if she doesn't like it, should return to Xonaca and settle her family business. Apparently there might still be people after her unless she renounces her claim?"

"There is that," Corrie said. Farther and farther east, away from home. "And then?"

"I was thinking from there, continue to the east, around the northern part of Tyzania, to get to eastern Turjin and Zhao Zheng. And from there . . . I've always wanted to sail the Eenyäf Chĕft."

"The what?"

Maäenda unrolled a chart, another map of the world. "East from Tyzania, the largest span of ocean on the globe, Corrie. We then go past the Poasian continent, the Napolic Islands, and we finally reach the western coast. Druthal."

Corrie found Maradaine on the map, and traced her finger down the coast, around the Ihali Cape, up to the Mocassa in Imachan, and then east past Xonaca, past Turjin, and then brought her hand to the other side of the map, running in over the swath of ocean past the roughly drawn Poasian continent, the Napolics and back to Maradaine. "Around the whole rutting world, huh?"

"That's the plan. You ready?"

Corrie looked up as the ship came out from past Jachaillasa, the passage between the last parts of the Mocassa clear ahead of them, and nothing but the sunrise on the horizon.

"Blazes, yes," she said. "Let's get to work."

RECOMMENDED READING ORDER

It is the author's opinion that the best reading order for the Maradaine Saga is in-world chronological for Phase One, and the release order going into Phase Two. Therefore:

PHASE ONE

Thorn of Dentonhill
Murder of Mages
Holver Alley Crew
Way of the Shield
The Alchemy of Chaos
An Import of Intrigue
Lady Henterman's Wardrobe
Shield of the People
The Imposters of Aventil
A Parliament of Bodies
The Fenmere Job
People of the City

PHASE TWO

An Unintended Voyage
The Assassins of Consequence
The Mystical Murders of Yin Mara
The Quarrygate Gambit
Hultichia
The Withered Boy

That said, there is no "wrong" order. Read the books as you like, as much as you like, and enjoy it your way.

PHASE TWO OF THE MARADAINE SAGA

COMING SOON

AN UNINTENDED VOYAGE

Moving outside the city of Maradaine, the prelude to Phase Two follows Corrie Welling as she navigates a new but just as dangerous city.

THE ASSASSINS OF CONSEQUENCE

The Thorn faces his hardest fight as the second phase of the Maradaine Saga begins.

THE QUARRYGATE GAMBIT

The Rynax family is strongest when they are together. Torn apart by a nefarious plot, they face their hardest trials alone.

AN UNKINDNESS OF UNCIRCLED MAGES

A series of murders and a fugitive mage coincide with mysterious warnings of Minox's missing cousin as tragedies come closer to home for the inspectors.

CITY OF THE TRUTH

A major political trial brings conspiracies and secrets come to light, threatening to tear apart the Tarian Order, and possibly the entire government of Druthal.

ACKNOWLEDGMENTS

Years ago, when I first conceived of the Maradaine Saga, I actually had a solid idea of the shape it was going to take. I knew who my main characters were, I knew their arcs, and where it was going. But the process of writing, especially writing something epic, will always surprise you.

This book had not been a part of the plan at that point. More to the point, Corrie Welling hadn't even been part of the plan at that point.

Corrie didn't even manifest in my head until the second draft of *A Murder of Mages.*

To take a step back, when I first wrote the rough draft of *A Murder of Mages*, I knew I had gotten something wrong with Minox. I couldn't figure it out for quite some time, and then it hit like a thunderclap: I had talked about him coming from a Constabulary family, but in that draft, none of them showed up. His Constabulary family was entirely abstract. So I tore down the draft to the studs, and rebuilt it with the idea that he not only had a family, but a *big* family. Nyla Pyle became his cousin in this draft, and I decided I needed one more family member at his stationhouse, someone who could be *very* different than Minox but also have his back unconditionally.

Corrie Welling came out of that, and she was *so much fun* to write.

Possibly too fun. Especially using her as a point-of-view in *An Import of Intrigue*.

So then while writing *A Parliament of Bodies*, the wild idea hit me: Give Corrie her own book. Take her all the way out of her comfort zone.

And here we are.

This book was written entirely in the unsure, unstable times of 2020, and thankfully I had plenty of support and help in getting things done.

Continuing to write in 2020 required patience and support, and I was very fortunate to have quite a lot of both.

Daniel J. Fawcett, as usual, has been the best sounding board for Big Ideas that someone could ask for, and Miriam Robinson Gould remains the best first reader Both of them were instrumental in so many ways in helping shape The Mocassa into the city that we have in this book.

Also instrumental was the work I've been doing on my podcast *Worldbuilding for Masochists,* and I can't express how much my co-hosts, Rowenna Miller and Cass Morris, not only fueled ideas of how to improve the work and craft in this book, but helped keep my sanity on an even keel this whole time. More support came from patrons and fans, like Nina Mulligan and Ember Randall.

Of course, as usual, I relied heavily on my publishing team, including my agent Mike Kabongo (who was *all in* when I said I had a weird idea with motorcycles and psychic mushrooms), my editor Sheila Gilbert, and everyone at DAW and Penguin Random House: Betsy, Katie, Josh, Leah, Alexis, and Stephanie, plus countless others whose names I don't know.

On top of that, my family remains a source of strength and inspiration. This includes my parents Nancy and Lou, and my mother-in-law Kateri. And, of course, my son Nicholas and wife Deidre, who have continued to put up with me during this incredible journey through Maradaine and now, beyond.

But also: you, with the book in your hand. Hopefully you've been with me throughout all the Maradaine so far, or if not, are inspired to go back and catch up with it all. It's been such a joy sharing this world with you, and I've been blessed to be able to keep writing in this world, and that is very much thanks to you.

As for what's next for Maradaine, all I have to say is: Ride's not over yet. Let's get to work.

Acknowledgments from original edition, October 2021

ABOUT THE AUTHOR

Marshall Ryan Maresca is a fantasy and science-fiction writer, author of the Maradaine Saga: Four braided series set amid the bustling streets and crime-ridden districts of the exotic city called Maradaine, which includes The *Thorn of Dentonhill, A Murder of Mages, The Holver Alley Crew* and *The Way of the Shield*, as well as the dieselpunk fantasy, *The Velocity of Revolution*. He is also the co-host of the Hugo-nominated, Stabby-winning podcast **Worldbuilding for Masochists**, and has been a playwright, an actor, a delivery driver and an amateur chef. He lives in Austin, Texas with his family.